"So you've got a baby to raise, Dr. Tate,"

Zoe said with a smile.

Jonas wished he could embrace the same warm, positive attitude about it. "Yes," he replied.

And with that simple, one-word response, he felt the world drop out from beneath him. Everything he'd been refusing to think about since the baby's arrival exploded in his brain like a time bomb. He was solely responsible for another human being, a little girl he didn't know the first thing about raising.

"Help me, Zoey," he said suddenly. "Please. I can't do this by myself."

She stared at him in disbelief. *Help* him? she thought incredulously. Help *him?* Help Jonas Tate? With a baby? What was he, nuts?

Dear Reader:

Welcome to **Silhouette Desire**! This month we've got something special in store for you—book one of a new Silhouette mini-series, WEDDING BELLES. These linked books by Carole Buck tell the stories of three friends who were bridesmaids together. See how Annie Martin gets to walk up the aisle herself in ANNIE SAYS I DO and don't forget to keep an eye out for the follow-up stories in coming months.

In addition, we have a wonderful MAN OF THE MONTH by award-winning author Jennifer Greene called SINGLE DAD. Josh is a hero you'll never forget.

Don't miss DR. DADDY, book three in Elizabeth Bevarly's series FROM HERE TO MATERNITY. And we have Anne Marie Winston's RANCHER'S WIFE, Jackie Merritt's HESITANT HUSBAND and NOTHING BUT TROUBLE from Beverly Barton to complete what I feel is a perfect month!

Silhouette Desire—you've just got to read them all!

The Editor

Dr. Daddy

ELIZABETH BEVARLY

SILHOUETTE

Desire

DID YOU PURCHASE THIS BOOK WITHOUT A COVER?
If you did, you should be aware it is **stolen property** as it was reported
unsold and destroyed by a retailer. Neither the author nor the publisher
has received any payment for this book.

*All the characters in this book have no existence outside the imagination
of the author, and have no relation whatsoever to anyone bearing the
same name or names. They are not even distantly inspired by any
individual known or unknown to the author, and all the incidents are
pure invention.*

*All rights reserved including the right of reproduction in whole or in part
in any form. This edition is published by arrangement with Harlequin
Enterprises II B.V. The text of this publication or any part thereof may not
be reproduced or transmitted in any form or by any means, electronic or
mechanical, including photocopying, recording, storage in an
information retrieval system, or otherwise, without the written permission
of the publisher.*

*This book is sold subject to the condition that it shall not, by way of trade
or otherwise, be lent, resold, hired out or otherwise circulated without the
prior consent of the publisher in any form of binding or cover other than
that in which it is published and without a similar condition including this
condition being imposed on the subsequent purchaser.*

*First published in Great Britain in 1995
by Silhouette Books, Eton House, 18-24 Paradise Road,
Richmond, Surrey TW9 1SR*

© Elizabeth Bevarly 1995

*Silhouette, Silhouette Desire and Colophon are
Trade Marks of Harlequin Enterprises II B.V.*

ISBN 0 373 05933 7

22-9511

Made and printed in Great Britain

ELIZABETH BEVARLY

is an honours graduate of the University of Louisville and achieved her dream of writing full-time before she even turned thirty! At heart, she is also an avid voyager who once helped navigate a friend's thirty-five-foot sailboat across the Bermuda Triangle. "I really love to travel," says this self-avowed beach bum. "To me, it's the best education a person can give to herself." Her dream is to one day have her own sailboat, a beautifully renovated older-model forty-two-footer, and to enjoy the freedom and tranquility seafaring can bring. Elizabeth likes to think she has a lot in common with the characters she creates, people who know love and life go hand in hand. And she's getting some firsthand experience with maternity as well—she and her husband recently welcomed their first-born baby, a son.

Other Silhouette Books by Elizabeth Bevarly

Silhouette Special Edition

Destinations South
Close Range
Donovan's Chance
Moriah's Mutiny
Up Close
Hired Hand
Return Engagement

Silhouette Desire

An Unsuitable Man for the Job
Jake's Christmas
A Lawless Man
*A Dad Like Daniel
*The Perfect Father

From Here to Maternity

For Veronica Marie Bevarly,
completing the first round nicely.
Happy Birthday, sweetie.

Prologue

———

"It can't be as bad as all that, Zoey."

Zoey Holland glanced up from the baby girl in her arms and nodded her head fiercely at the baby's mother. When she did so, she felt a tug on her hair and realized the infant clutched a generous handful of the straight, fiery red tresses in her tiny fist. She gently tugged her hair free and tossed it over one shoulder.

"Oh, it's definitely as bad as all that, Sylvie," she said adamantly. "The guy's a complete ogre, and he won't be happy until he has my head on a spit and my butt in a sling. Ask Livy."

Sylvie Buchanan turned to her sister for verification, arching a quizzical blond brow in question. Olivia Mc-Guane nodded in agreement with Zoey.

"He really does seem to have it in for Zoey for some reason," she said, trying to dodge her own toddler as she zig-zagged across Sylvie's expansive, ultramodern kitchen. The trio were meeting for their monthly Sunday brunch, at Sylvie's house for the first time since she had brought Genevieve home from the hospital three months ago. "Be careful, Simon," she admonished her twenty-two-month-old as he flew by. "And watch out for the plants. Auntie Sylvie and Uncle Chase aren't nearly as untidy as Mommy and Daddy are. They won't be as understanding if you make a mess."

Sylvie emitted a sound of disbelief. "You mean Uncle Chase isn't as untidy. He still hasn't gotten over how messy everything seems to become once babies arrive—including the babies themselves—and he's still convinced there's some way to keep this house clean every minute of the day. Of course, just because I married the guy doesn't mean I've mended my ways, either. Gennie and I are both driving him crazy." She leaned over Zoey's shoulder and chucked Genevieve under the chin. "Aren't we, sweetheart?"

The baby gurgled and ducked her head in response to the tickle, reminding Zoey of a turtle. "Looks like she's going to have Chase's green eyes and your blond hair," she said of the infant. "Nice combination."

"Yeah, how come Gennie got hair right away and it took Simon more than a year?" Livy demanded.

All three women looked over at the dark-haired little boy who squatted in front of the air vent in that odd, flat-footed way of children, peering intently into it. The air rushing out tousled the thick, dark curls he'd inherited from his mother.

"That's just the way babies are," Sylvie said. "Besides, once his hair started coming in, it took off like a bunch of weeds. You've got no cause to complain."

"Yeah, so much for his future doing late-night bald-guy commercials on TV," Zoey said wistfully. "You could have made a fortune."

"Thanks, but I like him just the way he is," Olivia told her.

"But we digress," Sylvie said, turning to Zoey again. "You were talking about this new doctor at Seton General, Dr. Fate."

Zoey chuckled as she placed Genevieve back in the baby carrier situated at the center of the kitchen table. "That's Dr. *Tate*," she corrected her friend. "Please, don't suggest it was destiny that I be tortured by the guy. That makes it sound like I'll be stuck with him forever.''

Dr. Jonas Tate had shown up on the scene six months ago at Seton General, where Zoey and Olivia both worked as nurses in the maternity ward—Zoey in the nursery and Olivia in obstetrics. He had come to the South Jersey hospital from a prestigious private hospital on the west coast, where he had been the head of cardiology. Everyone at Seton had heard how he'd completed his residency with flying colors at Johns Hopkins twelve years ago, had received his M.D. with highest honors from Harvard before that and had fulfilled his premed undergraduate courses with near-perfect scores at Columbia before that.

He was, as Zoey had heard through the hospital grapevine on many, many occasions, an amazingly gifted physician. Now he was also on the board of Seton General, an administrator of stellar reputation and limitless ability. He was loved and respected by everyone.

Everyone except Zoey Holland.

Oh, she respected his education and his position at the hospital, of course. And she had even liked him well enough when he'd first come aboard, had liked his casual good looks and the pleasant smiles he seemed to have for everyone. But she hadn't had much to do with him then, and somewhere along the line he'd begun to change. Lately, it seemed as if every time she turned around, she was going toe-to-toe with him on something, everything from the hospital's policy on maternity leave to whether or not they were ordering enough sterile swabs. And always, *always,* she was forced to back down. Because no matter what else he might be—a jerk, a creep, a misogynist and a major thorn in her side—he was also unfortunately her boss.

"So what's his problem?" Sylvie asked.

"You got me," Zoey told her, honestly mystified. "All I know is that it seems like every chance he gets, he's breathing down my neck about something."

Olivia grinned. "Then again," she said suggestively, "there are a lot of nurses who would be perfectly happy to find Dr. Tate breathing down their necks. Not to mention their blouses. Preferably in a dark linen closet in the middle of the third shift.''

Zoey expelled a rush of air in an unmistakably rude sound. "Well, not me. The guy's nothing but a jerk. He's arrogant, abrupt, rude, egocentric, bad tempered, sexist, pigheaded—"

"And has the nicest brandy-colored eyes you've ever seen," Olivia completed with a wistful sigh, turning to Sylvie. "Not to mention those dark curls. I just love men with dark curls, don't you?" she added with an affectionate glance at her son. "They're just so adorable."

"I like dark hair," Sylvie agreed with a nod.

Zoey looked at Olivia as if her head had just exploded. "You have *got* to be kidding, Livy. Jonas Tate? Adorable?"

"Hey, it's not my butt he's chewing off at every turn," Olivia said. "He's always been perfectly polite—if a little cool and distant at times—to me."

Zoey couldn't believe what she was hearing. "The man is never polite, cool or distant to me, although as much distance as possible would be welcome. He has a more heated personality than anyone I've ever met. And as for polite . . . Hey, wait a minute," she added when she reconsidered her friend's statement. "Are you trying to imply that it's *my* fault I'm at the top of his hit list?"

Olivia shrugged, obviously thinking hard before voicing her reply. "Not so much your *fault,*" she said slowly. "But I think his bad moods might just possibly be a direct result of your presence."

Now Zoey was really confused. "What's that supposed to mean?"

"Just that some personalities don't jibe with others, you know?"

Sylvie nodded her understanding. "*I* know what you mean. That's exactly how Chase and I were for a while. We had almost nothing in common—except for Gennie, of course—and there were times when he just absolutely drove me nuts. But," she added with a serene smile, "we worked through all that. Now everything's peaches."

"Well, things will never be peaches in my life as long as I have to deal with Dr. Jonas Tate," Zoey said decisively. "There's just something about that man...."

"Don't sweat it," Sylvie told her. "Listen, I'm going to give you the sagest, most profound bit of bartender advice in my ample arsenal, advice that has never failed me or any of my customers before."

Zoey didn't try to hide her skepticism, but asked anyway, "And what's that?"

"Just go with the flow, Zoey."

Zoey glanced from Sylvie to Olivia and back again. "Go with the flow," she repeated blandly, enunciating each word clearly lest she had misunderstood one of them.

Sylvie nodded. "You'd be amazed at how many of us inadvertently create our own problems by battling against the very things we should be accepting. Look at Livy and me and the problems we had with Daniel and Chase. She and I are two prime examples." She looked down at the baby dropping off to sleep in her carrier and smiled. "Just relax and let nature take its course, Zoey. You and Dr. Fate will work things out."

"Dr. *Tate*," Zoey corrected her friend again. Sylvie waved her hand negligently and bent to kiss her daughter's forehead. "Tate, fate," she said quietly. "Whatever."

One

Jonas Tate was not having a good day, and it was all Juliana's fault. She was the most demanding, petulant female he had ever had the misfortune to know, an absolute monster hiding behind big blue eyes, soft blond hair and delicate, cupid's bow lips. As she did virtually every night since she'd invaded his home two months ago, she had woken him in the middle of the night, insisting that he see to her needs—and by God, Juliana's needs could exhaust an army of men—and hadn't allowed him to go back to sleep after he'd satisfied her. Once awake and sated, she had ordered him to further entertain her, commanding stories and music and clever conversation.

She was that most deadly kind of female, he thought, charming and surprisingly alluring one minute, needful and completely dependent the next. There was no doubt in his mind that she would be the death of some unfortunate man someday.

All that, and she was barely three months old.

Jonas pulled open the top right-hand drawer of his desk, pushed aside a sheaf of papers, a banded bundle of pencils and a wayward pacifier until he located a bottle of extra-strength pain reliever. He tossed back three of the capsules without water, grimacing when one got stuck halfway down his throat. When he went to the water cooler in the corner of his office, he caught a quick glimpse of himself in the mirror hanging near it and wished he hadn't.

He looked like hell. His dark curls were ragged looking and badly in need of a cut for which he had absolutely no time to spare. He'd also had no time to spare for a shave that morning, and his three-o'clock shadow—normally heavy on the best days—shaded the lower half of his face like a Mack truck. What had once been faint purple crescents beneath his eyes due to a little overwork were fast becoming indelible black smudges due to an almost total lack of sleep. He looked not like a man who oversaw a hospital wing, but a man who was confined to one—whichever one it was that housed the psychiatric ward.

A quick rap at his office door caused him to turn around abruptly, icy water sloshing over the side of the cup and onto the sleeve of his white dress shirt. His reaction to the cold liquid was to jump, an action that spilled even more water onto the front of his shirt.

"Come in!" he shouted out angrily, holding the wet fabric away from his skin.

The door opened slowly, barely enough for one of the new interns to stick her head inside. "Uh, Dr. Tate?" she asked.

"Yes?" He couldn't remember the young woman's name, but he didn't really care. From what little he'd observed of her, she wasn't long for the program, anyway.

"They, uh, they need you in the maternity ward, sir."

"Why?"

"I, uh, I don't know. They just asked me to bring you."

"Is it an emergency?"

The young woman narrowed her eyes as she considered the question. "I don't think so. They probably would have told me if it was, don't you think?"

"One would think so, yes."

"Or else they would have paged you. I guess."

Jonas studied the woman for a long time before he spoke further. When he did, it was brief and to the point. "What's your name?" he asked the intern.

"Mills, sir. Uh, Dr. Claudia Mills."

"Mills," he repeated, making no effort to hide the displeasure and exasperation he felt. "*Dr.* Mills," he corrected himself, placing a sarcastic emphasis on her title. "How long have you been with us here at Seton General?"

"About two weeks, sir."

"Two weeks. I see. And in that very brief amount of time, you've already managed to forget the most basic principles of your medical education, is that right?"

Her eyes widened in surprise before she dipped her head to avoid meeting his gaze. "No, sir, I—"

Jonas strode forcefully to the door and jerked it open, out of the intern's grasp, causing her to stumble forward past him. He turned again before he left and addressed her one final time. "The next time someone asks you to do something, *Dr.* Mills, do try to get the particulars before you go trundling off on your merry way, won't you?

"And one more thing," he added when he saw tears forming in her eyes. "If you expect to last in this profession, you'd better develop a thick skin. I won't be the last doctor to take you to task for stupid mistakes. Just watch that you make as few of them as possible. Someone might wind up hurt. Or dead. And then where will you be, hmm?"

As the door closed behind him he thought he heard the young woman sniffling, and he frowned. Interns, he thought with a cynical shake of his head. These days none of them seemed to have the backbone for the job.

He was still angry, and his head was still pounding, when he arrived in the maternity ward, finding the unit surprisingly quiet so close to a change of shifts. Only one nurse commanded the main station, and she was bent over a clipboard, making what appeared to be standard notations on a patient's chart.

"What is it?" he asked when he approached her.

"Oh, yes, Dr. Tate," she said, standing. "Dr. Forrest wanted to see you in LDR room C."

Jonas was puzzled. "Did she say why?"

The nurse shook her head and shrugged. "Nope. Sorry. Just that I should send you in as soon as you arrive."

He rubbed vigorously at his forehead, trying to will the throbbing between his temples to go away, since the pain relievers were doing no good whatever. He was still cradling his forehead in his palm when he pushed open the door to LDR room C, so he didn't realize it was packed full of people until they all shouted out, "Surprise!"

Immediately, Jonas looked up to find himself surrounded by doctors, nurses, interns, orderlies and other representatives of every unit housed in the east wing. Intermingled between them were several dozen colorful balloons—some of which, he noted, were actually inflated surgical gloves with smiley faces drawn on them in Magic Marker—and a huge sheet cake ablaze with candles and billowing smoke.

"You didn't think you could hide the big four-oh from us, did you, Jonas?" Lily Forrest, the head of neonatal intensive care asked him.

Lily and her husband, Mike, had been the first friends Jonas had made after his arrival in New Jersey. Actually, he realized reluctantly, they were the *only* friends he'd made since moving. Then again, he thought, he was a man who liked to keep to himself. At least, he had been, before the social worker holding Juliana had arrived at his front door. On top of every other lousy thing that had happened since New Year's Day, Jonas was turning forty. He had no idea how Lily had discovered that today was his birthday. And he'd certainly told no one how old he was going to be. Hell, he didn't even like to think about that himself.

But now, as he stared out at the eager, smiling faces surrounding him, and the cake with enough candles burning atop it to make it appear comical, he felt a genuine smile start to curl itself onto his lips. Until his gaze traveled over the crowd and settled on one woman in particular.

A redheaded nurse stood alone in the corner. Her long, straight ponytail, crisp, blue surgical scrubs and the stethoscope dangling around her neck made her appear a vision of efficiency and calm. Jonas couldn't deny that Zoey Holland was the epitome of efficiency. However, he also knew she was anything but calm. Her ramrod-straight posture, and the perfectly manicured, red fingernails digging into the arms she had crossed over her chest gave her away. That and the scowl she always seemed to reserve for him alone.

Jonas knew Zoey hated him. And, he conceded reluctantly, maybe she had a right. He hadn't been the easiest man to get along with lately. And, dammit, for some reason, she really rubbed him the wrong way. He couldn't put his finger on why, exactly, but the two of them had been butting heads almost since day one.

"Well, aren't you going to say something?" Lily asked him, circling an arm around his shoulder and pulling him close for an affectionate hug.

"Frankly, Lily, I'm not quite sure what to say," he told her honestly. "Who's minding the store? There must be countless women in labor wondering what's happened to the staff."

"They've all been nice enough to time their contractions to convenience our little party. Besides, there's just been a shift change. What you've got here is the first shift on their way out."

"Yet you all made time to wish me a happy birthday," Jonas remarked, honestly flattered by their gesture. "Thank you," he added. "I'm not sure how you knew it *was* my birthday...." His voice trailed off as he offered Lily a look of mock censure. "And it might be best if I don't find out, but..." He didn't know what else to say, so he simply repeated, "Thank you."

"You're welcome," Lily told him. "Now hurry up and blow out your candles before someone calls the fire marshal."

As Jonas approached the cake, he glimpsed Zoey from the corner of his eye trying to make a discreet exit. There was no doubt in his mind that she had been pressed into attending this party against her will, and suddenly feeling inexplicably devilish, he called out after her, "Give me a hand here, will you, Zoey? I'm not sure I can do this by myself."

She paused, her long, fiery ponytail shivering like liquid copper as she clearly tried to control what was at best her pique—and at worst her rage, Jonas was certain—at being singled out from the others.

"Sorry, Dr. Tate, but I'm kind of pressed for time," she said as she spun around quickly. "I'm pulling an extra shift later tonight for Jeannette, and I've really got to get home and catch a little shut-eye before I come back."

Her long hair kept moving even when she stopped, cascading over one shoulder in a ruddy stream. Jonas's fingers twitched at his sides. Normally she wore her hair confined in a tightly woven French braid or wound into a bun. This was the loosest he'd ever seen it, and he was helpless to deny that, at the moment, he wanted nothing more for his birthday than to bury his fingers in the silky tresses. He wondered if her "little shut-eye" after work included a man, and if that was why she was wearing her hair almost loose like that. Her green eyes flashed at him as he formed the thought, as if to demand what business it was of his if she were.

"Oh, come on," he cajoled her. "This will only take a minute."

Zoey Holland glared at Jonas Tate with all her might, willing him to spontaneously combust so that she could go home and soak in a hot bath. It was no secret to anyone in the east wing that she and Jonas Tate did not, to put it politely, get along with each other. Yet here he was, in front of God and everyone, daring her to be nice to him. His challenge didn't sit well with Zoey, and she wondered what he was setting her up for.

On top of that, she'd had a lousy day. The only thing that had made it bearable was that it had looked as if she would see it through to its completion without running into the infuriating Dr. Tate. She had been *this* close to grabbing her coat and leaving the floor when she'd been corralled by Dr. Forrest.

Only because Zoey had such enormous respect and admiration for Lily Forrest had she conceded to the woman's request that she attend this surprise party for Jonas Tate. She didn't have to stay long, only a few minutes, Lily had promised her, knowing as well as everyone that Zoey didn't get along with the good doctor. But maybe, Lily had suggested further, Zoey's appearance would help mend the rift that seemed to be growing wider everyday between the two.

Zoey knew the only thing that would mend the rift between herself and Dr. Tate would be to erect a wall three feet thick between the two of them. But, nonetheless, she had promised Lily she would come. What would a few minutes hurt? she had reasoned. She could hang back in the corner and sneak out when no one was looking. Besides, Lily had said there would be cake. Chocolate cake with white icing, without question the most favorite culinary treat Zoey could name. She'd grab a piece and take it home, and have it with her coffee after dinner.

A few minutes, she repeated to herself now. That was how long Lily had said Zoey would have to stay. Well, a few minutes were up, and she wanted to go home. Still, Jonas Tate's eyes glittered with the light of combat as he awaited her reply, and she had never been one to back down from a challenge. Especially when she'd been challenged by an overblown, egocentric, self-important, male chauvinistic—

"Zoey?" he asked again, his deep, rusty-sounding baritone grating on her nerves. "Better hurry. This cake's going to set off the sprinkler system if we don't put it out soon."

She wasn't sure when or why she decided to play along, but Zoey suddenly found herself moving slowly toward the good doctor. He looked like hell, she noted absently. His hair, normally a little longish, but nonetheless neat, was becoming pretty shaggy, and he clearly hadn't shaved that morning.

She wondered idly if he had overslept at the house of a female companion after spending the night practicing all kinds of sexual gymnastics, and simply hadn't had the time—or the energy—to make himself presentable for work. Come to think of it, he did look pretty exhausted, she thought as she drew nearer. Just what kind of women did he date, anyway?

He smiled at her when she halted beside him, and she wondered why she even cared about the type of woman who would interest Jonas Tate. She already knew the answer to that—someone coy, petite, demure and submissive. Which, of course, left her completely out of the running. At five foot ten, she stood nearly eye-to-eye with him, fewer than two inches shorter than he was. She was big boned, too, her hands strong and capable and not much smaller than his. And as for the coy, demure and submissive part, well . . . Zoey Holland had never been accused of being any of those things. She spoke her mind when it suited her—and often when it did not—and no one, *no one,* ever told her what to do.

Except for Jonas Tate, a little voice in the back of her head taunted. *He can get a rise out of you faster than a thoroughbred through the gate.*

Zoey doubled her fists at her sides when she realized how easily she had fallen into the trap. Just by succumbing to his dare that she do something he knew she otherwise wouldn't, she'd played right into Jonas Tate's hands. Once again, he'd told her what to do.

"On the count of three," he instructed her softly, his voice coming from dangerously near her ear.

She turned to find his face scant inches away from her own and started to back away. But his fingers circled her wrist and held her close, a cryptic smile that curled his lips her only indication that he'd known how she was going to react before she'd even formed the thought in her head. Reluctantly, she stayed put in her position beside him, but she couldn't quite shake the shivery sensations that spiraled up her arm and through her heart to pool in a tightly wound coil in her stomach.

She scarcely heard him count the numbers, but reacted accordingly when he reached three. Zoey and Jonas both inhaled deeply, bent forward at the waist and expelled their breaths in a long gust of wind. The candles sputtered and went out, every last one. The group surrounding them laughed and applauded, and even Zoey felt oddly pleased by their accomplishment.

"Guess this means my birthday wish will come true," Jonas said, his voice low and suggestive and once again closer to Zoey's ear than she found comfortable.

When she turned to face him this time, his eyes were lit with a bold fire, and she got the unnerving feeling that he was trying to tell her something.

"Yeah, well, that's what they say, isn't it?" she replied, her own voice sounding breathless and weak.

His fingers on her wrist tightened, not painfully, but insistently. "Don't you want to know what I wished for, Zoey?"

The light in his eyes took on a new dimension, now becoming undeniably libidinous. She felt his thumb stroking over the pulse in her wrist, felt her own heart racing. Was this some kind of joke? she wondered. What was he trying to do to her?

She shook her head feebly as she replied, "No. I don't think I do."

One corner of his mouth lifted in a wry grin. "Well, since my wish is destined to come true, you'll find out about it soon enough, seeing as how it includes you, too."

She tried to laugh off the odd sexual tension that had suddenly leapt up between them, but her laughter came out sounding hollow and false. Finally, she tugged her wrist out of his grasp, circling it with her free hand as if she'd been burned.

"Oh, I get it," she said with a flip shake of her head, regaining enough of her senses to issue a chuckle that was almost convincing. "I know what you wished for."

The gleam in his pale brown eyes brightened, and he took a step closer to her. "Do you?" he asked.

Zoey nodded and took a step in retreat. "You want me gone. You're either going to demand my resignation, or you're expecting me to foul something up so badly you'll have the perfect excuse to fire me."

This time Jonas Tate was the one to chuckle, a single, solitary sound that lacked all humor. "Is that what you really think?" he asked her.

Zoey nodded harder. "It's what I know."

She took another—giant—step away from him, and the distance seemed to give her more strength, more energy, more conviction that he would not throw her off balance. She glanced quickly around to make sure the others in attendance were occupied elsewhere before she continued, somehow managing to keep her voice low.

"Well, don't hold your breath, Dr. Tate," she continued. "Because I've been at Seton General for too long and like it too well to give up my position just because some doctor finds me an annoyance. And all modesty aside, I'm too good at what I do to ever make a mistake that would end my career here."

She waited to see how he would respond, and wondered if maybe in speaking to him so boldly she had just made precisely the kind of mistake she'd sworn not to. But instead of retorting angrily or threatening to fire her, Jonas Tate just smiled.

"Touché, Zoey," he finally said quietly. "Touché."

And with that he turned to the cake that Lily had finished slicing and was now passing out to everyone present. He didn't look back at Zoey once, didn't even seem to notice she was there. For just the briefest of moments, she felt jealous indignation that the man had the nerve to slight her in such a way. Then she realized how ridiculous a reaction that was. She *wanted* Jonas Tate to ignore her, she reminded herself. And if that meant she had to be dismissed by him, so be it. It was better than being singled out for his full attention.

Wondering why she should suddenly feel cheated that she wasn't the center of his universe when she had been trying for months to steer clear of him, Zoey backed away. Someone pressed a paper plate with a generous slab of cake into her hand, and she looked down at it blindly. Then, making her way to the LDR room door, she quietly slipped outside. Sleep, she repeated to herself as she went. She needed to catch a few z's. That could be the only reason for her odd reaction to Jonas Tate just now. By this evening, she wouldn't even be able to remember what his careless touch had done to her.

Two

Zoey stretched her arms high above her head and watched the clock at the nurses' station, smiling as the minute hand reached toward the twelve and brought her another hour closer to a long weekend. She had forgotten how pleasant the third shift could be sometimes, when it was quiet and slow moving and passed without incident. In a little over an hour, she'd be heading home to enjoy a leisurely Friday, followed by an even more leisurely Saturday and Sunday. Normally she would be rushing around to get ready for work right now. It was nice how occasionally an otherwise inconvenient scheduling change worked out just right.

Nonetheless, she had been quite happy to leave the eleven-to-seven shift for regular daytime hours three years ago, having grown weary of living her life upside down. Back then, she hadn't been able to manage any kind of social life, because she had worked while most people slept and slept while others were out enjoying the day. Of course, back then, she'd also had an excuse for why she seldom dated. Now that she was working more regular hours, she still went out with men infrequently. And now she was hard-pressed to figure out why.

Because most men were jerks, she answered herself immediately. Case in point: Dr. Jonas Tate.

Just who in the hell did he think he was? she asked herself for perhaps the hundredth time since yesterday afternoon. He could have caused a nuclear meltdown with those boiling magma glances he had tossed her way. She felt her temperature rise at the simple recollection, telling herself the heat was a result of her anger and nothing more. She had *not* found his suggestive comments intriguing, she assured herself. Insulting, yes; infuriating, yes; incendiary, okay, maybe. But intriguing? Uh-uh. No way. Absolutely not.

Zoey was still telling herself this when seven o'clock rolled around and Jeannette came in to relieve her. Instead of feeling tired, however, she felt oddly reenergized by her late night's work and looked forward to a day of play. Olivia would be working, but Sylvie's bartender hours left her free during the day. Maybe she and Sylvie and Gennie could have an adventure, Zoey thought with a smile. March was still kind of cold to be out and about, but maybe they could take in a movie or do some shopping.

When she'd gathered her things and shrugged into her parka, she exited the nurse's lounge and punched the button for the down elevator. With a tinny-sounding *ding*, the doors unfolded, and Lily Forrest stood ready to exit in much the same way Zoey was poised to enter. For some inexplicable reason, when she saw the doctor on the elevator, Zoey suddenly felt the urge to run. There was just something about the expression on Lily's face that made her feel a little wary.

"Zoey!" the doctor cried when she saw her. "Are you on your way out?"

She nodded, edging closer to the elevator, stretching her arm across the open door, instinctively preparing herself for a hasty retreat. "Hi, Lily. Yes, I'm leaving. Jeannette and I switched shifts, so she'll be working my hours today. I'm on my way home. Sorry."

"No, don't be sorry," the other woman assured her. "This is perfect. I couldn't have arranged it better if I'd tried."

Zoey gazed at Lily warily. The elevator door banged against her arm insistently, as if to urge her, *Run! Run while there's still time!* "Arranged what?" she asked, feeling somehow that she was going to be sorry for asking the question.

"You live in Haddonfield, don't you?" Lily asked.

Zoey nodded. "Uh, yeah, I do. I rent an apartment there."

"Wonderful," Lily said with a smile. "I really hate to ask, but since you're on your way out and headed in that direction, anyway, I wonder if you might do me a favor?"

"What's that?"

"Would you mind dropping off a patient file for me in Tavistock on your way home?"

Zoey released a breath she hadn't even been aware of holding and smiled in relief. "Sure, no problem."

"It was left here inadvertently yesterday and it's vital to a doctor's presentation at the National Institutes of Health in Maryland later this morning. If he has to drive all the way to the hospital to get it before heading down to Bethesda, he'll never make it on time."

She extended a manila folder toward Zoey, who tucked it under her arm. "Here's the address," she added, jotting it down on a small pad of paper she retrieved from the pocket of her lab coat. "It won't be too far out of your way, will it?"

Zoey shook her head as she glanced at the address. "Don't worry about it, Lily. Tavistock is close enough to my apartment that I take my evening strolls there every night."

And it was a *very* nice neighborhood, she thought as she tucked the scrap of paper into the inside pocket of her parka. Huge homes, many of them lovely Victorians, with perfectly manicured lawns and gardens, and huge trees that stretched to the sky. It was the kind of place she loved— quiet, peaceful, beautiful. After some of the experiences

Zoey had suffered in her life, serenity and beauty were two things she strove to embrace in every waking moment.

"I appreciate it," Lily said as she rushed past Zoey and down the hall toward neonatal, her flat heels clip-clopping merrily on the tile floor. "I owe you one," she called over her shoulder just before she disappeared around a corner.

Zoey waved her off and turned back to the elevator. When she'd taken the address from Lily, she'd released the door, which had closed on a car that was now gone. Oh, well, she thought. She was in too good a mood to let it bother her. She had a three-day weekend before her, with nothing specific she had to do and no one to bother her. Best of all, she thought further with a smile, she was guaranteed seventy-two hours without the specter of Jonas Tate hovering over her. With a satisfied sigh, she punched the button again and settled in to wait.

Jonas Tate stared down at the sleeping baby in the nursery across from his bedroom, thinking about a redheaded nurse and wondering what on earth had made him behave so peculiarly the afternoon before. He had come on to Zoey Holland in a room full of people, had all but undressed her with his eyes while a dozen of his co-workers looked on. No, that wasn't true, actually, he corrected himself. He had indeed undressed her with his eyes. And dammit, he'd liked what he'd seen.

Oh, God, how could he have done that? he asked himself. How could he find such an infuriating woman attractive? Zoey Holland was an overbearing, stubborn, know-it-all loudmouth, a woman more suited to inciting prison riots than caring for infants. There was absolutely no reason why she should turn him on so thoroughly, he told himself. None at all. Yet if that were the case, why had Juliana's cries of an hour ago awakened him from one of the most erotic dreams he'd ever enjoyed, a dream whose focus had been none other than Nurse Zoey?

He just wasn't getting enough sleep, Jonas thought. That was the only explanation he could come up with for behaving so strangely at the hospital yesterday afternoon and for

the unsettling fantasies he'd been indulging in lately about
Zoey. Total exhaustion did strange things to people. And
there was no chance he was going to catch up on his sleep
tonight.

Tonight? he repeated to himself. Hell, it was already
morning again. And once again, he felt more tired upon
waking than he had upon falling into bed the night before.
He was disoriented and dazed and clutching a half-empty
bottle of formula in his hands, but Juliana was sleeping
peacefully for a change and he was terrified of moving away
from the crib lest he disturb her and set her to crying again.

All around him, his house was silent. He couldn't remember the last time he'd experienced such a lack of sound.
When he'd first moved into the rambling old Victorian in
Tavistock, he had loved it—loved its big, airy rooms and
wide windows, the rich jewel-toned colors of the walls and
dark mahogany trim, the huge trees growing outside and
what had seemed a steady, constant quiet. The house, the
neighborhood, everything, had been perfect for the first
several months he was in residence. Then on New Year's
Day, Mrs. Edna Caldecott of International Children's
Services had arrived at his front door with a bundle of bad
news and a baby in her arms.

As if inspired by his memories, the doorbell buzzed loudly
downstairs, and the baby started. For one hopeful moment, Jonas thought Juliana was going to slide calmly back
into sleep again, and he cautiously lifted one foot to step
away from the crib. Then her eyes snapped open, and her
chin began to crumple, an expression he knew meant she
was about to start howling. As if cued by his thoughts, Juliana opened her little mouth and belted out a high-pitched
scream that nearly shattered his eardrums.

Jonas reached into the crib, but hesitated before touching her, still completely uncomfortable holding the baby
even after more than two months of performing the task. Of
course, he tried to avoid touching her unless he absolutely
had to, leaving that aspect of child care to the countless sit-
ters he'd hired to watch Juliana during the day.

He'd been through a half-dozen since January, dismissing most of them because he didn't trust something or other about them. Mrs. Howard had been too stern looking, while Mrs. Cather had seemed too indulgent and likely to spoil. Evan had been nice enough, but he just wasn't sure a nineteen-year-old boy had the knowledge necessary for caring for an infant. And Melissa . . . Well, the moment he'd come home from work to find her waiting for him in his bed wearing little more than a smile, he'd known she wasn't right for the job, either.

He'd been very pleased with Mrs. Garrison, the most recent one, though. At sixty-two, she'd raised four children of her own and had the nicest blue eyes Jonas had ever seen. He'd begun to look forward to a long and healthy relationship with her as Juliana's nanny, but she had informed him yesterday afternoon that she wouldn't be back. She was scheduled to be arraigned on armed robbery charges the following day, and there was a good chance she was going to be occupied elsewhere for the next five to ten years. Although with time off for good behavior, she'd told him, she might be available again before then, if he was still interested.

The doorbell buzzed again and Juliana cried more loudly, jerking her tiny arms and legs in a silent demand to be held.

"All right, all right," Jonas muttered, lifting the baby gingerly from the crib and positioning her awkwardly against his shoulder.

He made his way carefully downstairs, deciding not to worry about the fact that he wore only purple silk pajama bottoms and nothing more. He couldn't imagine who would be ringing his doorbell at seven-thirty in the morning, but he sure as hell wasn't going to make himself presentable for them. Juliana's howling increased about ten decibels with every step he took down the stairs, so by the time he reached the door, she was red faced and screechy and almost out of control.

Which was pretty much how Jonas felt, too, when he saw Zoey Holland standing on his front porch.

"What are *you* doing here?" they chorused as one.

"I live here," Jonas replied.

"Lily Forrest sent me," Zoey said at the same time. Then, before he could say more, she demanded, "What on earth are you doing to that poor baby?"

In spite of the fact that her career consisted of being surrounded by moody infants, Zoey couldn't bear to hear a baby crying in anguish. Instinctively, she reached for the child in Jonas Tate's arms, tamping down all the questions that swirled in her head at his appearance. She noted only that he surrendered the baby willingly, and she pushed past him into the house, nudging the door shut with her foot before the cold morning air could chill the infant. She rocked the baby carefully, murmuring soothing, meaningless sounds. The tiny thing stopped crying almost instantly, focusing intently on Zoey's face, blinking her teary, red-rimmed eyes.

"There's my good girl," Zoey said quietly, knowing immediately that the child was female. She placed a soft kiss on the baby's forehead, inhaling the sweet aroma of powder and soap, and she smiled. "Here," she added to Jonas, jerking the patient file out from under her arm and thrusting it toward him without looking at him. "Dr. Forrest asked me to drop this off on my way home. She said you'd need it today."

When he didn't take the file from her right away, Zoey glanced up. Now she had no choice but to take note of him, and she didn't like what she saw. Well, she *liked* what she saw, she amended reluctantly, taking in the expansive chest covered with dark hair and corded muscle, the broad, steely shoulders and the pajamas dipping low on trim hips beneath a flat abdomen. She just wished the attributes she was appreciating belonged to someone other than Jonas Tate. When her gaze traveled up to meet his, he had arched a dark brow in question, and she realized he knew full well how closely she'd been inspecting his wares. She felt herself blush.

Unwilling to trust her voice just then, she shook the file in her hand to bring his attention to it. When he still did not take it from her, she cleared her throat discreetly and said, "Dr. Forrest seemed to think it was important."

Jonas took the folder from her hands and tossed it onto the sofa without looking at it. Instead, his attention seemed to be focused completely on Zoey and the baby, who still stared solemnly up at her. And because she felt infinitely more capable of dealing with a baby than a nearly naked man, Zoey dropped her gaze back to the infant in her arms.

"What's your name, sweetheart?" she asked in a soft, breathless voice, rubbing her bent knuckle gently against the baby's cheek. "Hmm? What's your name?"

The baby gurgled and smiled, making Zoey laugh in response.

"Juliana," a deep, husky voice said beside her. "Tate. Her name is Juliana Tate."

Zoey feared that if she looked up, she would find Jonas standing much too close to her, and then she would no doubt do something really foolish. Like reach out to touch him, which was what she definitely wanted to do. So she kept her gaze trained tightly on the baby and spoke to her instead. "Well, that's an awfully big name for such a little baby, isn't it, Juliana? Yes, that's an awfully big name for you to grow into."

Juliana cooed and smiled again.

"How did you do that?" Jonas asked.

Zoey glanced away from the baby and up at Jonas and, sure enough, regretted the action completely. Up close this way, she could see that his shoulders were deliciously freckled, and could make out every smooth plane of muscle from his neck to his waist. She swallowed with some difficulty before asking, "Do what?"

"You made her stop crying," he indicated. "Just by holding her, you made her stop. And now she's actually smiling at you. She's never smiled at me."

"I...I don't know," Zoey said honestly. "You can't 'make' babies do anything. They choose whether to smile or to cry or to stop, and usually they have very good reasons for doing all three."

His lips thinned into a tight line, and he settled his hands on his hips, an expression and pose Zoey had seen often enough to know what it meant. It meant she'd made him mad.

"So you're saying *I* made Juliana cry," he said in a deceptively calm voice.

"Not necessarily," she replied quickly. "You're her father, after all. Why would that make her cry?"

Although the realization almost made Zoey want to cry. She'd had no idea Dr. Tate was married with children. She didn't think anyone at the hospital knew. Too many nurses and other doctors were lusting after him, something that wouldn't be quite so prevalent if the women in question knew he was already attached. Until now, Zoey would have sworn she was one of the minority who couldn't care less if the man had a dozen women stowed away. But faced now with the unequivocal evidence of his tie to at least one, she felt a funny little hole open up in her heart.

"I'm not Juliana's father," he said. "I'm her uncle." He sighed wearily and scrubbed his hands over his face as if feeling utterly defeated. "And frankly, you're right," he continued softly as he dropped his hands back to his sides, "*I* make her cry. For some reason, the kid hates me. And I have no idea what I'm supposed to do about it."

Zoey studied Jonas for a long time before responding. He looked like a man who was at the end of his rope, a man who was two steps away from throwing himself off the Ben Franklin Bridge. His eyes were shadowed and exhausted looking, his mouth bracketed by white lines of strain. When he reached up to run a big hand anxiously through his hair, he closed his eyes and sighed deeply again, and she could see that he felt completely hopeless.

"Where are her parents?" Zoey asked quietly, softening at this vulnerable side of Jonas Tate she'd never seen before.

"Dead," he replied bluntly.

Her heart turned over that the child in her arms had suffered such an enormous loss at such an early age. "I'm sorry," she said softly.

Jonas shrugged off her condolences. "I didn't really know them. Her father was my brother, but I hadn't seen or spoken to Alex for more than thirty years."

Which would mean the two men were separated when they were children, Zoey thought, unable to deny her curiosity about how such a separation might have occurred. She wasn't about to pry into the man's personal history by asking him about it, but Jonas must have picked up on her thoughts, because he sighed again.

"It's a long story, Zoey," he said softly, his gaze falling to the baby in her arms. "Why don't you take off your coat while I put on a pot of coffee?"

Actually Jonas did more than put on a pot of coffee. At Zoey's insistence, he readied himself for work while she kept an eye on Juliana. For the first time in months, he took his time in the shower, managed to shave himself without a single nick and not only matched up his clothes—opting for a gray dress shirt, plum patterned tie and charcoal trousers—but ironed them, as well. By the time he exited his bedroom, he was in a better mood than any he could remember for the past two months. And oddly enough, he owed it all to Zoey's appearance at his front door that morning.

He bumped into her—literally—as she was coming out of Juliana's room. He grabbed her shoulders to steady her, and she pressed her palms flat against his chest to regain her balance. For a moment, neither moved from the position, but their gazes remained locked, as if each was awaiting the other's move. Finally they sprang apart at the same time, mumbling excuses and apologies. Jonas swept his arm forward, indicating Zoey should precede him down the stairs, and she pulled the nursery door closed silently behind her before doing so.

Only when they were well away from Juliana's room, safely ensconced in his kitchen with the baby monitor turned on, did Jonas trust himself to speak. Yet he still kept his voice down, certain the slightest disturbance would have the baby screaming again.

"She ate a bit more while you were getting dressed," Zoey said, as if reading his thoughts. "I think she'll sleep for a while."

He nodded, but wasn't completely convinced. "Coffee?" he asked.

"Please."

He brought two generous mugs steaming with the strong brew to the table, then went back for sugar and cream. "Are you hungry?" he asked her. "I could fix you some scrambled eggs and bacon."

She shook her head. "Thanks, but that's all right. I'll have something at home later."

He nodded again, and suddenly had no idea what to say. So he sipped his coffee and stared at Zoey and wondered how she could look so beautiful after coming off the graveyard shift.

"You were going to tell me about Juliana's parents," she said after a sip of her own coffee.

That's right, Jonas remembered. He knew there was another reason for her having remained at his house after completing the duty assigned her. Other than the simple fact that he wanted her there, of course.

"But if you'd rather not," she added.

"No," he quickly assured her. "It's not that."

"Then what?"

He shook his head. "It's nothing. Forgive my frequent bouts of miscommunication. I just haven't been getting much sleep since Juliana's arrival."

"How long ago was that?" Zoey asked.

"New Year's Day," he said, still marveling at the irony of the date. "My brother, Alex, and his wife were killed in a car accident in Portugal on Christmas Eve just a couple of weeks after Juliana was born. They left behind a will that donated everything they owned to charity and indicated that the care of their daughter should fall to me."

"Yet you hadn't seen your brother since you were a child," Zoey said, sipping her coffee again.

She wasn't nearly as unaffected by the story as she was letting on, Jonas thought. He could see in her eyes how deeply moved she was by Juliana's situation.

He shook his head. "No, but we somehow kept up with each other so that we at least knew where the other was and what he was doing. My mother and father split up shortly after my fifth birthday. Alex was about two when it happened, I guess. By my parents' mutual agreement, I went to live with my father in upstate New York, and Alex accompanied my mother back to Europe, where her family lived. My father remarried when I was about ten, and I've always thought of my stepmother as my mother. I can just barely remember the woman who gave birth to me."

Zoey nodded. "I lost both my parents when I was three. I can't remember much about them at all."

For some reason, Jonas wasn't surprised. He had detected something in her demeanor that seemed to sympathize immediately with Juliana. "Who took care of you after their deaths?" he asked.

"Two of my aunts raised me," she said. "They were nice enough ladies, but they weren't very realistic about the needs of a little girl growing up when I did. As a result, I was something of a . . . a difficult child."

Jonas couldn't help smiling. "That doesn't surprise me. You're a difficult adult, too."

Zoey's head snapped up and her eyes were ablaze when her gaze met his.

He chuckled. "Why is it so easy to get a rise out of you?"

She lifted her chin defensively. "Why do you get such a kick out of provoking me?"

He couldn't deny her assertion, but he didn't want to fight with her right now. So he went back to the original topic, picking up where he left off.

"All in all, my parents' divorce was a surprisingly painless experience. Four people who split up and went their separate ways only to find happiness in other arenas. To this day, I can't even form a mental picture of Alex as a two-year-old."

"Then why did he leave his daughter in your care?" Zoey asked.

Jonas shrugged. "I've asked myself that question a hundred times since January. Our parents have both been dead for years. And from what the attorney said, Alex's wife had estranged herself from her own family to the point of not seeing them at all. I suppose I am, in effect, Juliana's closest living relative. And really, what couple in the prime of life draws up a will expecting their wishes to be fulfilled before their child reaches adulthood?"

Neither answered the question, because no response seemed necessary. They sipped their coffee in thoughtful silence for a moment until Zoey ended it with a quietly offered, seemingly benign observation.

"So now you've got a baby to raise, Dr. Tate," she said with a smile.

Jonas wished he could embrace the same warm, positive attitude about it that she so obviously did. "Yes," he replied.

And with that simple, one-word response, his first good mood in more than two months evaporated, and he felt the world drop out from beneath him. Everything he'd been refusing to think about since Juliana's arrival exploded in his brain like a time bomb. He was solely responsible for another human being, a girl child he didn't know the first thing about raising.

"Help me, Zoey," he said suddenly, unable to stop the words that tumbled from his mouth without him even thinking about saying them. "Please. I can't do this by myself."

Three

———

Zoey stared at him in disbelief, her voice failing her completely. *Help* him? she thought incredulously. Help *him*? Help Jonas Tate? With a baby? What was he, nuts?

She continued to gaze at him in silence, and the coffee she had sipped as he'd uttered his request—his plea—sat in her mouth until it tasted like mud. Finally, she remembered to swallow, but when she did, she gagged and began to choke. The hacking that ensued brought Jonas around the table to pat her soundly on the back, an action that just made her cough harder because it was such an unexpectedly inflammatory gesture. Inflammatory because the feel of his palm pressing into her well-covered flesh, in a manner that was in no way seductive, somehow felt just that—seductive.

Alarmed, Zoey jerked away from him and leapt out of her chair, moving blindly toward the sink in an effort to escape. But Jonas followed her, seeming to pen her in where the countertops came together at a ninety-degree angle. Honestly, all he was doing was making sure she was okay, she told herself. But for some reason, he seemed to be much closer than he really needed to be, seemed to be intent on doing much more than helping to alleviate her cough.

Zoey had never liked it when people got too close—emotionally or physically—without her permission. There was a reason for that, she recalled all too readily, and without thinking further, she flattened her palms against his chest and pushed him away. Hard.

Jonas stumbled backward, his eyes reflecting his surprise at her gesture. But apparently undaunted, he approached her again and lifted his own hand slowly toward her. "Are you all right?" he asked as he cupped his palm cautiously over her shoulder.

Zoey flinched a little, but made no move this time to restrict him. Evidently encouraged by the less violent reaction, he dipped his hand lower to rub her back again. She told herself to stay calm and not overreact, forced herself to stand still and let him touch her. Unfortunately, that plan of action didn't work, either. Because his simple caress still felt like the most inviting of gestures and, instinctively, she wanted to pull away before things got out of hand.

"I'm fine," she lied, taking a few deep breaths to steady her heart rate and get her lungs moving normally again. For some reason, though, when she inhaled the musky aroma of him, her heart rate became anything but steady, and her lungs wanted to gulp in the air at a staggering speed. "I'm fine," she repeated, though whether she was trying to convince Jonas or herself of that, she wasn't entirely sure.

His hand continued to make lazy circles on her back, and she found herself standing there, immobile, gazing into pale brown eyes that were fixed on her face. For long moments, the two of them only stared at each other in silence, until Zoey made a halfhearted move to pull away.

But instead of removing his hand from her back to allow her passage—because, clearly, she was okay now, Zoey thought, and there was no need for him to remain so close—Jonas settled his free hand on the counter to prevent her from going anywhere. He cupped the fingers of his other hand lightly over her nape and, exerting just the slightest pressure on her neck, he started to bring her head toward his.

"Don't," she said softly, trying to pull back.

But Jonas seemed not to hear her and continued the gentle coercion of her head toward his. For one wild moment, Zoey forgot about the animosity she felt for him, forgot the reason she was normally so cautious around men. For one wild moment, she allowed herself to be drawn forward. His eyes were so compelling, the shape of his mouth so intriguing. He smelled so good and his touch was ... oh ... so gentle. No man had ever touched her in quite that way before. But when she realized what he was trying to do, understood that he had every intention of kissing her, she panicked, bolting from his arms to race to the other side of the room.

She purposely positioned herself so that the kitchen table was between them, knowing the gesture was silly even as she completed it. As if that meager barrier might actually keep him away from her if he wanted to try to again kiss her again, she thought. As if such a move would prevent her from reaching out to him.

"I'm fine," she insisted for a third time, clutching the back of a chair when she realized how badly she did, indeed, want to reach for him again. Good heavens, what was happening to her?

"You certainly are," Jonas agreed in a quiet, ragged tone of voice unlike any she'd ever heard from him.

He cleared his throat abruptly and returned to his seat at the table, then proceeded to sip his coffee casually, as if the past few moments had never occurred. Zoey eyed him curiously, wondering if maybe she had completely misinterpreted what had just happened between them.

Of course she had, she told herself with a silent sigh of relief, lifting a shaky hand to her forehead. She *must* have. He'd only been trying to stop her coughing. There was no way he had intended to kiss her. She simply must have misread the signs. She'd just pulled a double duty at the hospital, she reminded herself, and had just come off the graveyard shift. She was tired and, as usual, Jonas Tate's presence was making her edgy. Considering their history and the quickness with which the two of them generally went for each other's throats, the last thing the man would want to do was kiss her.

The realization brought with it an odd mixture of reassurance and regret, but she ignored the feeling as she returned to her own seat at the table and pulled the chair away. Before she could sit down, however, Jonas stood, moving quickly toward the other side of the room to stand in precisely the same spot Zoey had just vacated.

Stuffing his hands into his pockets, he stared at the ceiling as he asked, "Would you? Help me out, I mean. With . . . with the baby. With Juliana."

When she said nothing in reply, he dipped his gaze to the floor and rushed on, "You're obviously good with her. She took right to you, the moment you held her in your arms. She likes you, Zoey. That's a hell of a lot more than I can say she feels about me. I don't know what to do. I've had her for more than two months now, and I . . ." He lifted his head to meet her gaze levelly as he concluded, "I just . . . I don't know what to do."

It was costing him plenty to ask for her assistance, she realized. Clearly, he was at his wit's end if he was coming to her for help. The two of them were mortal enemies, completely at odds over just about everything. He didn't like her, and she didn't like him. But he was desperate for help. So desperate, he'd even ask *her* to come to his aid. It was a strange feeling to have Jonas Tate dependent on her.

Zoey knew what it was like to have a newborn suddenly placed in one's care—the shock and panic, the lack of sleep and abundance of exhaustion, the feelings of helplessness and fear that accompanied a baby's arrival. And that was with people who'd had nine months to prepare for the event. Jonas had become a father virtually without warning and was obviously still unequipped for the responsibilities that had been heaped upon him. He did, indeed, need help. And she was perfectly capable of helping him.

If she wanted to.

"Why do you need *my* help?" she asked him. "Don't you have someone looking after her during the day while you're at work?"

"Not anymore. No one has seemed appropriate. I don't know if you realize it, but there's a real child-care crisis going on in this country."

She twisted her lips into a wry grin. "So I've heard. There's also a very good day-care center at the hospital for employees. Olivia McGuane keeps her son, Simon, there during the day while she's at work. So do most of the other nurses who have kids. I'm sure Juliana would thrive and be perfectly happy there."

Jonas shook his head. "Juliana hasn't thrived or been happy since she arrived. I'd worry about her constantly if I didn't think she was getting continuous, one-on-one supervision at this point. At least until she gets over this...this anguish...this *despondency* she seems incapable of ridding herself of."

Zoey shook her head in disapproval. "She's only a baby, Dr. Tate. She's not in charge of her happiness and contentment—you are. You can't expect her to behave and react like an adult."

"I don't, I—" He ran a big hand helplessly through his hair. "Look, Zoey, I know we've had our differences in the past," he continued, moving slowly back toward the table. "And I know we haven't always gotten along very well."

"Very well?" she repeated with a unfelt chuckle. "We haven't gotten along at all."

"I know," he told her as he sat down. "And I apologize for that. I haven't been the easiest person to deal with since Juliana's arrival, and I've been rough on everyone at the hospital."

"Maybe so," she agreed. "But you seem to go out of your way to come after me in particular. Most of the people at Seton like you in spite of your behavior."

Jonas noted well the unspoken statement that Zoey was one of the people who didn't. He wished he could deny her assertion, wished he could laugh off the pronouncement as simple paranoia on her part. Unfortunately, he knew what she said was true. There were times when he did seem to single her out for some reason. And if he were in a crowded room, a room full of people who'd ticked him off for one reason or another, he knew it would always be Zoey he wanted to come down on first.

Nevertheless, he said, "Now you know that's not true. There are plenty of people at Seton who would tell you that *they're* the ones I go after most often. That's how many enemies I've made since I came to work here."

He paused briefly before continuing, "I can't manage Juliana on my own. Not yet. I need help. And you're as likely a candidate as any. You know about babies—you're surrounded by them every day. It's your job to care for them. I realize there's absolutely no reason why you would want to help me, but I'm asking you, anyway. I'd appreciate it, Zoey. It would mean a lot to me. And I'll return the favor somehow, someday. So what do you say?"

She studied him thoughtfully for a moment and opened her mouth to speak, but Juliana's cry rang out from the monitor on the counter. Quickly, she jumped up and headed for the stairs with Jonas right on her heels. She pushed open the nursery door and immediately reached for the crying infant, and he watched with much interest as she cradled the baby's head in one hand and settled Juliana easily against her shoulder.

"Shh," she murmured to the baby, moving her own body back and forth to rock the child. "Shh. You're all right now. Zoey's here. I won't let anything happen to you, sweetie. You're all right."

Immediately, Juliana stopped crying and nuzzled closer to Zoey's neck. Zoey smiled and kissed the baby's temple, then turned to look at Jonas. For one brief moment, he experienced the oddest sensation that the three of them were perfectly situated there in the baby's room. That he and Zoey and Juliana belonged together in a way that was solely restricted to other people—to people who comprised families.

Then he shook the feeling off and tried to put it out of his head, in much the same way he tried to forget how badly he'd wanted to kiss her in his kitchen only moments ago. He *must* be exhausted, he thought now, if he'd actually had the urge to take Zoey Holland into his arms.

"I can give you two weeks," she said suddenly, and he could tell by the tone of her voice that the offer was drawn from her reluctantly. "Jeannette's sister is in town and she wanted me to trade shifts with her for two weeks. Originally, I was only going to switch with her on a few nights because I didn't want to give up that much of my time."

"But now you will?" Jonas asked.

She shrugged negligently. "Now I will. I'll stay with Juliana during the day while you're at work and then spend part of the evening helping the two of you get comfortable together. I'm not sure when *I'll* find the time to sleep," she added after she placed another soft kiss on the infant's head, "but it's only for a couple of weeks."

"You're willing to surrender that much of your life for me?" Jonas asked quietly.

"No, not for you," she told him with an adamant shake of her head. "For Juliana."

He nodded his understanding but said nothing.

Zoey turned to look at the baby again. "I know what it's like to be a burden," she said so softly that Jonas had to strain to hear her. Bending her forehead to Juliana's, she whispered further, "I know what it's like to be thrust on to someone who doesn't want you. Who has no idea about your needs and desires. I know what it's like to be resented."

Jonas wasn't sure what to say, so he remained silent. But as he continued to look at Zoey and the baby, he felt a strange heat wander through his body and settle around his heart. Relief, he told himself. That's all he was feeling. Relief that there would be *someone* to help him get through this ordeal. Oddly enough, however, that relief was accompanied by an inexplicable satisfaction that the someone in question would be none other than the infuriating Nurse Zoey.

* * *

When Jonas pulled into his driveway late that afternoon, he was beat. He was also frankly amazed that he hadn't killed himself or someone else driving home from Bethesda, so exhausted had he been by the end of the trip. Only God and drive-through coffee had prevented such a catastrophe. Now, in addition to being exhausted, he also had way too much caffeine zinging through his system, a combination that resulted in a very strange view of the world.

That could be the only explanation for why, when he stumbled up the stairs and into Juliana's nursery to find Zoey sitting in the rocking chair singing to the baby she cradled in her arms, he wanted to walk across the room and plant a very thorough kiss on the woman's lips.

She had changed her clothes at some point during the day and no longer wore the blue hospital scrubs in which he normally saw her—the scrubs that had only hinted at the lush curves he knew must lurk beneath. Now Zoey was dressed in faded blue jeans and an oversize pink sweater that begged him to reach out and feel how soft it was, when what he really wanted to explore was the softness of the woman beneath it.

And her hair... Jonas curled his hands into fists lest he do something really stupid. Because Zoey had let her hair down. It hung loose and cascaded over one shoulder in a shimmer of copper that seemed to catch fire as it reflected the rays of the setting sun streaming in through the window behind her. Never before had he realized just how long and straight, how silky and rich, her hair was.

And in that moment, Jonas knew he was in serious trouble. Because instead of stirring up the anger and resentment he normally felt when he encountered her, Zoey was stirring up something else entirely. Something he hadn't experienced for a long, long time. Something that felt dangerously like desire. Hot, heavy, urgent desire.

"Hi," she said with a smile when she looked up at him.

Jonas wasn't sure, but he didn't think Zoey had ever smiled at him before. And the knowledge that she was doing so now, that the inviting, welcome-home expression on her face was meant for him and him alone, was staggering to say the least. As if to illustrate, he took a step backward, nearly reeling. Then she looked back down at the baby and, with the distraction of her beauty gone, he was finally able to catch his breath.

"How...how did it go with Juliana today?" he asked, hoping his voice revealed none of the troubling thoughts parading through his brain.

"Great," Zoey told him.

He eyed her suspiciously. "Really?"

She nodded. "Really."

"No fitfulness?"

'No, nothing unusual for a baby this age."

"No crying jags?"

"Only when she was hungry."

"No screaming fits?"

"Not a one."

She continued to look at Juliana, and her next words were expressed in the high-pitched, breathy voice people normally adopted when addressing an infant. "We did very well today, didn't we, sweetie? We ate well, and we played on our quilt, and we watched some birds at the feeder outside, and we read *Curious George,* and we listened to some reggae music, and—"

"Reggae music?" Jonas repeated. "Where did you find reggae music? I don't have any reggae music."

Zoey looked up at him and smiled that mind-numbing smile again. "I brought some tapes in from my car. It's been my experience that babies love reggae music."

"They do?"

She nodded. "Evidently. At least, the limited study group I've used for experimentation has."

"How limited?"

"Three. Well, four now, if you include Jules."

"Jules?"

She nodded again. "I think it fits her much better than 'Juliana'. Don't you think she's more of a Jules?"

Jonas shook his head, feeling more and more bizarre with every passing moment. Zoey Holland was in his home, speaking to him quite civilly, rocking a child in her arms upon whom she had bestowed an affectionate nickname and behaving as if this were the most normal thing in the world.

"I—I don't know," he stammered. "I never really thought about it."

Zoey dipped her head toward the baby, who stared back at her with frank adoration. "Well, I think she's definitely more of a Jules."

As if voicing her agreement, Juliana smiled and cooed with much contentment. Zoey laughed and rose from the chair, lifting the baby to her shoulder.

"I wasn't sure what you planned to do for dinner," she said, "so I took the liberty of fixing some seafood stew and a tossed salad."

Dinner, too? Jonas marveled. On top of everything else, Zoey was actually cooking for him? "Where did you find the ingredients?" he asked. "I always order something in or eat out on my way home. There's never any food in this house."

"Well, there is now. Jules and I went to the grocery store and stocked up for you. You can pay me back before I leave tonight."

"You took Juliana to the grocery store?" he asked incredulously.

"Didn't I just say that I did?"

"You took her *out?* In this weather? To a public place?"

Zoey laughed as she approached him. "It was a beautiful day today, and—"

"It was thirty degrees!"

"—and Jules had a great time. She's three months old, Dr. Tate. She's in excellent health, and she was dressed in perfectly warm clothing. You don't have to keep her hidden away. On the contrary, you should expose her to as many environments as possible. Stimulate her senses a little. She's going to get bored if you keep her at home all the time. Come to think of it, maybe that's why she cries so much."

Zoey had paused scant inches away from him, close enough for him to reach out and touch the errant strand of hair that fell over her forehead, if that was what he wanted to do. And strangely enough, it was. But before he could lift a hand to do so, she extended the baby toward him.

"Now kiss her hello and take her in your arms," she instructed.

The panic that always seized him whenever he had to come into close contact with Juliana gripped him fiercely, and he took another step backward. "I can't," he said.

Zoey took a meaningful step forward. "Of course you can."

He shook his head. "You hold her for a while longer."

"No, *you* hold her."

With much reluctance, Jonas turned his hands palm up and slowly, ever so slowly, extended them forward. Zoey stared at him for a long moment before turning her mouth down in disapproval.

"See? Now that's your problem," she told him.

"What?" he asked. "What's my problem?"

"You're terrified of her."

"Well, of *course* I'm terrified of her. Who wouldn't be?"

"Oh, for Pete's..." Zoey sighed in exasperation. "She's a *baby,* Dr. Tate. Why do I have to keep reminding you of that? She's not some knife-wielding stalker, she's not running for public office and she won't call you on the phone and try to sell you aluminum siding. There's no reason to fear her. She doesn't even have teeth! Now kiss her hello and take her in your arms."

With some hesitation, Jonas leaned forward and placed a kiss on the crown of the baby's head. Much to his surprise, she didn't start howling. In fact, when she turned her head to face him, to see who had just kissed her, she smiled at him. She actually smiled. He couldn't remember anything else in his life bringing him more pleasure, more joy, than that simple gesture from Juliana. She had smiled at him. And in that small moment, he felt ten feet tall.

"Now take her in your arms," Zoey repeated softly.

Not quite as reluctantly as before, Jonas extended his arms. Zoey shifted the baby carefully and placed Juliana capably in his hands. He was astounded that she could have such faith in him, amazed that she would trust him with such a fragile life. Still, he reminded himself needlessly, Juliana had been with him for more than two months now, hadn't she? And he hadn't broken her yet. Even in those early weeks when she had seemed little more than a wisp of life, he had managed to keep her fed and clean and warm and safe, hadn't he? He must be doing something right, even if the baby hadn't come to love him completely. At least he'd managed not to hurt her in any way.

"That's right," Zoey said when Jonas tucked Juliana into one arm and settled her more closely against himself.

He waited for the howl of discomfort in which the baby always erupted when he held her, braced himself for the wildly flailing limbs that seemed intent on beating him to death. But Juliana only mewled a little this time, only fidgeted slightly as he shifted her into a more natural position. Even when she looked up and saw clearly who was holding her, she didn't cry. Instead she only fixed him with an intent blue gaze and studied him with all her might.

"What did you do to her today?" he asked Zoey quietly, staring back at the baby with as much wonder as she seemed to hold for him. "She's so calm, so good. Did you put something in her formula?"

"Of course not," Zoey said with a chuckle. "You're just starting to feel a little more confident with her, that's all, and she's picking up on that. Babies sense our emotions. If you're distraught, then she's going to be distraught. If you're content and confident, then she usually will be, too. You just need to spend more time with her, Dr. Tate, holding her, touching her. You just need to get more comfortable with her. Let her know you care about her."

"Jonas," he said, still looking at Juliana.

"What?"

He met Zoey's gaze levelly over the baby's blond head. "Call me Jonas."

That look was back in his eyes again, Zoey noted with much apprehension. The one that had so unsettled her yesterday afternoon when he'd mentioned that his birthday wish—a wish that included her—was going to come true. It was a heated look, a suggestive look, a look that promised something she wasn't sure he had any business promising her. And, boy, did it make the nursery seem warm.

"Okay," she said softly.

"Go ahead," he instructed her.

"Go ahead and what?"

"Call me Jonas."

Her mouth went dry as she said, "Jonas."

He smiled, and his expression turned into something even more unsettling. Unwilling to consider just what was happening between the two of them, Zoey moved quickly toward the nursery door and stepped through it.

"I'm going to check on dinner," she said. "After we eat, we can go over some real simple child-care and development basics, and then I'll head home, okay?"

Jonas shifted Juliana from one shoulder to the other and smiled more broadly at Zoey, clearly feeling more confident than ever. Unfortunately, that confidence seemed to extend beyond the baby he held in his arms and enveloped her, as well. And confidence was something she decided she didn't want Jonas Tate to feel around her.

His anger, she could handle. His resentment, she could handle. But confidence... He'd never seemed to feel that in her presence before. It was part of why she'd never had any trouble facing up to him when the occasion called. Now, however, she felt the situation changing, felt the earth shifting a little under her feet. What was worst of all was that she was on his turf at the moment, and would be for two weeks to come. The more confidence he came to feel, the more likely she was to lose her own. And confidence was something she most certainly could not afford to lose. It had taken her too many years to find it.

"Dinner will be ready in about fifteen minutes, if you're interested," she said as she took another step backward.

"Oh, I'm definitely interested," Jonas told her.

"Great," she replied with a shaky smile. "Umm, I'll just call you when I'm . . . when *it's* ready, shall I?"

"I'll be waiting. But, Zoey," he called out when she turned to leave.

She turned back reluctantly. "Yes?"

"Don't make me wait too long."

She chuckled, hoping to dispel the undeniably sexual tension that seemed to have sprung up out of nowhere. Unfortunately, the sound she uttered was anything but light and dismissive. No, it was more like the strangled sound a small animal must make when it stumbles into the headlights of an oncoming truck.

And all she could do after that was run.

Four

After dinner, Juliana slept peacefully in her bassinet while Jonas cleaned up in the kitchen and Zoey sat in the living room wondering what on earth she was doing in Dr. Tate's home.

Jonas's home, a little voice at the back of her brain reminded her. *You're supposed to call him Jonas now.*

She sighed in spite of herself. For the most part, Zoey had been using his first name, whether speaking to him directly or simply thinking about him. And as much as she hated to admit it, referring to her sworn enemy by his given name had been surprisingly easy, had actually come to feel as natural as using her own name did.

"This is not good," she murmured to the sleeping baby in the white wicker bassinet, adjusting Juliana's flannel blanket to cover her little feet. "Not good at all."

"What's not good?" Jonas asked as he entered the living room.

Reluctantly, Zoey turned around to face him. He'd changed his clothes before dinner and now wore a baggy, oatmeal-colored sweater over extremely faded Levi's. His sleeves were pushed up to his elbows to reveal some of the sexiest forearms she had ever had the pleasure to observe, and his jeans hugged his trim hips and lean legs in a way she discovered—much to her surprise—made her feel very envious. On his feet were thick, rag-wool socks and no shoes.

No shoes, she marveled for the umpteenth time. This was truly a side of Jonas Tate she'd never encountered before. A rumpled, cozy, sexy side of him she would just as soon have never discovered. Because if she'd thought her relationship with the man was difficult before, now it was almost intolerable. In addition to finding him infuriating, she was also coming to find him more than a little intriguing. And she hated being intrigued by a man. Invariably, it led to trouble.

"Nothing," she replied quickly. "Jules and I were just having a little discussion. Girl talk. That kind of thing."

Jonas nodded and sighed, a tired, almost helpless sound. "I see. So she's awake again, is she?"

Zoey shook her head. "Uh, no, actually, she's not. It was kind of a one-sided conversation."

He moved to stand beside her, gazing down at the sleeping infant with a look she could only liken to defeat. Juliana continued to doze peacefully, her only movement the subtle rise and fall of her torso with every deep breath she took.

"I wish she would sleep this well at night," Jonas muttered.

"She doesn't sleep through the night yet?"

He made a derisive sound. "Not unless you consider waking up every two hours with a screaming demand to be fed 'sleeping through the night.'"

Zoey turned to look at him. "She shouldn't be doing that. By now she needs to be getting into a much longer sleep pattern at night. A lot of formula-fed babies this age sleep seven or eight hours a night. Some even longer. And even if she's got her days and nights confused, she shouldn't be feeding so often."

He looked back at her, narrowing his eyes in obvious concern. "She shouldn't?"

Zoey shook her head. "How much does she eat at a time?"

He shrugged. "A few ounces before losing interest. Then she dozes off for a little while. She's been doing that since she arrived. Isn't that how much she ate for you today?"

Zoey shook her head. "I offered her six, and she drank the bottle dry every time. And it wasn't every two hours, it was about every five. She should be taking more than a few ounces at a feeding and eating a lot less often than every two hours." She studied him in disbelief. "Haven't you talked to her pediatrician about this?"

"Yes, at her two-month checkup. He wasn't too worried."

"Then you need to find another pediatrician," she told him. "He should have talked to you more about your concerns. You've really been getting up every two hours to feed her at night?"

He nodded silently.

"Jeez, no wonder you look like hell."

He grimaced. "Thanks a lot."

"And no wonder you've been such a pain in the butt to deal with."

"Zoey—"

"When was the last time you slept for an entire night?" she interrupted him before he could say more.

Jonas sighed his fatigue and scrubbed a hand tiredly over his face. "I don't know. Not since Juliana came, that's for sure." He gazed back down at the baby. "See, Zoey? This is why I need your help. I don't even know how to feed her. What if I've already done irreparable harm? What if she's going to suffer for the rest of her life because of the mistakes I've made over the past two and a half months?"

Zoey softened at the obviously worried tone of his voice and circled his forearm with gentle fingers to squeeze lightly. "She's not going to suffer permanent damage because of any mistakes you've made. As long as she's been growing and gaining weight at a steady pace, that's all you have to worry about." She smiled at the sleeping infant. "Look at her. She's pudgy and rosy, in tip-top shape. You're feeding her enough. You're just not doing it on the right schedule, that's all. We'll get it worked out. Everything is going to be fine."

Jonas gazed down at the fingers wrapped around his arm, feeling their warmth penetrate to his very soul. There was something incredibly erotic about the red manicured fingernails cushioned against the dark hair that swirled over his skin. Without thinking, he covered Zoey's hand with his. He liked the way she had said, "*We'll* get it worked out," and promised him that everything was going to be fine.

And he liked how softly she had touched him. He liked that a lot. More than he probably should.

He was tempted to tangle his fingers with hers and pull her hand to his lips, but about the time he made the decision to do so, Zoey removed her hand from beneath his and tucked it nervously into the pocket of her jeans. When he looked at her face, he could see that she had been as confused and agitated by the touch as he had been, and he wasn't sure what to say that might alleviate the awkwardness of the situation. She met his gaze for only the briefest of moments, then cleared her throat anxiously and looked away.

"It won't happen overnight, you know," she said quietly.

For one crazy moment, he thought she was referring to the two of them, thought maybe she was suggesting that something substantial was going to happen in the not-too-distant future.

Then he realized he must be insane if he thought Zoey Holland was entertaining the same warm, fuzzy feelings he'd begun to have himself. After all, she'd pulled away from him that morning when, for some absurd reason he still wasn't able to understand, he'd tried to kiss her. And just a moment ago she'd removed her hand from beneath his. It didn't take a fool to see that she wanted no part of him.

"What won't happen overnight?" he asked.

"Jules sleeping through the night. It's going to take time."

He sighed wearily. "No kidding."

Zoey studied him again, still looking anxious and confused. "You really do need to get some sleep," she said. "Sleep deprivation can lead to all kinds of health problems, not to mention making people just plain crazy. There are places in this world where they use it as a torture technique, you know."

"Well, I'm not likely to get much sleep anytime soon, am I?" he asked, suddenly feeling impatient for no good reason he could name.

"It really is unhealthy, the way you've been going. You should have gotten some help sooner."

"I didn't know who to ask."

"You could have—" She abruptly stopped speaking and looked away.

"I could have what?"

She paused for a telling moment before continuing, "You could have asked one of the nurses in neonatal or pediatrics. Or one of the doctors. They would have been glad to help you out."

"Would *you* have been glad to help me out?"

"I'm helping you now, aren't I?"

"But are you glad to do it?"

When she looked at him again, he was amazed to see that she was smiling. "Yeah, as a matter of fact, I am," she said, seeming as surprised by the revelation as he was. "It's been a long time since I—" She stopped abruptly, and before he could ask her to elaborate, she added, "In fact, if you want me to spell you tonight, I'll do it."

"'Spell' me?"

"It doesn't take a physician to see that you're stretched way too thin here. You need to get some sleep before you kill yourself. Good sleep, for a change. If you want, I could stay here tonight and get up with Jules when she cries. That way you can sleep a solid eight or ten hours, whatever you need."

Zoey wasn't sure when or why she'd decided to make her proposal, especially since she hadn't had much sleep in the past twenty-four hours herself. But once uttered, there was nothing she could do to take back the words. And if she were perfectly honest with herself, she'd admit that she didn't want to rescind her offer. She'd had a great time caring for Jules that day, and had found her to be a wonderful little baby. Almost at once, she'd felt a certain kinship with the infant. They'd both lost their parents at an early age. They'd both been foisted off on relatives who didn't want them.

What was truly remarkable, though, was that spending so much time with Juliana had touched off an instinctive reaction in Zoey that she hadn't felt for a very long time. She would have thought the regeneration of that long-buried emotion, the love for a child who was well and truly a part of her past, would make her turn away from the responsibility of caring for another one. Instead, she found herself wanting to see a lot more of Juliana. It was just too bad that would also involve seeing more of Juliana's uncle.

"You want to spend the night here?" Jonas asked. "With me?"

Zoey fought down the anger that bolted up her spine at his tone of voice, one that clearly indicated he understood her offer to be of a more personal—decidedly more sexual—nature. "Not with you," she stated through gritted teeth. "With Jules. I'll sleep in the nursery with her. Look, never mind—just forget I offered," she added quickly, realizing what a terrible mistake she'd made in voicing her plan. "I think it would be better if I just went on home."

It would be just like Jonas Tate to think she was using his niece as an excuse to get into his pants, she thought. The man's ego was legendary, and she had witnessed for herself how he could turn even the most harmless situation into a sexually charged come-on. Without further comment, she gathered up her purse and went to the foyer closet to retrieve her parka. There was no way she was going to offer this jerk her assistance, even if his niece was a kindred spirit. She'd have to think of another way to help Juliana out. Like maybe running down her uncle with a New Jersey Transit bus.

"Zoey, wait," Jonas said as she threw the closet door open. He flattened his hand against the door and slammed it shut again. "I didn't mean that the way it sounded."

"Didn't you?" she asked without looking at him.

He hesitated for a moment before replying. "Okay, maybe I did mean it the way it sounded. But not really. Not the way you think."

She kept her back to him, but felt the fight go out of her at the uncertain timbre of his voice. "I don't understand you," she said softly. "At the hospital, you treat me like I'm some kind of obstacle to be overcome. You berate me for the slightest thing, try to bully me for no reason and just generally make my working atmosphere hell. Now, suddenly, you're...you're..."

"I'm what?" he asked quietly from behind her.

She expelled an exasperated breath and swung quickly around to face him. When she did, she felt a soft tug on her hair and realized belatedly that Jonas had entwined a handful of the tresses between his fingers without her feeling it. Now he stood clutching her hair in his fist, stroking the shaft of burnt copper between his thumb and index finger as if it were a talisman of some kind. Yet he continued to stare at her face, as if he didn't even realize he was performing the action.

She felt that caress in ever fiber of her being. For long moments, she could only watch the play of his fingers on her hair and wonder what his touch would feel like elsewhere on her body. A shudder of heat wound through her, moving from the ends of her hair to the tips of her toes and back again. Before that heat could consume her, she wrapped her own fingers around the length of hair he continued to stroke and pulled it carefully out of his grasp.

"Dammit, you...you're *flirting* with me," she whispered hoarsely, unable to muster any of the indignation she knew she should be feeling. She gathered her hair in both hands at her nape, then pulled the mass of red back over her shoulders and out of his reach. "Worse than that," she went on weakly, "you're propositioning me. Given our history of antagonism, it doesn't make any sense."

Much to her irritation, Jonas seemed not to hear what she had said. He just looked down at his empty hand as if she hadn't removed the length of hair he'd held. Finally, however, he dropped his hand back to his side and lifted his head to gaze at her. Then, ever so slowly, he smiled at her accusation. Then he began to chuckle. And then, he began to laugh. Hard. More than almost anything else in the world, Zoey hated being laughed at. And the realization that it was Jonas who was doing the laughing only compounded her anger.

"What's so funny?" she demanded.

"Propositioning *you?*" he asked through his laughter. "You must be out of your mind. A man would have to have a death wish to proposition you."

She narrowed her eyes at him. "Is that so?"

His laughter subsided some, but he continued to smile at her as he told her, "You bet it's so. Unless he had some desire to lose a body part most men consider extremely important, no man in his right mind would even think of coming on to you."

Zoey clamped her teeth together hard. "Oh, really?"

"Yes, really. Surely that's no surprise to you."

"Why wouldn't I find it surprising that men fear for their manhood where I'm concerned?" she wanted to know. She thought it was a very good question.

He gaped at her, clearly stunned by her appalling lack of knowledge about herself. Zoey began to steam even more.

"Oh, come on. It's common talk in every men's room in the east wing."

"What is?"

"That black belt in karate you have. And about how you took down Jeff Pearson with one swift kick to his... person."

Zoey arched her left brow marginally, something she normally only did just before landing a blow. This time, however, she managed to keep herself in check. "Jeff Pearson completed a few questionable maneuvers of his own," she said softly. "He's lucky I didn't call the cops and have him charged with sexual assault after what he tried to do.

But I don't suppose any of the boys in the men's room ever mention that, do they?''

Jonas stopped smiling immediately. "What did he do to you?"

Zoey decided then that she'd had enough. Typical male reaction, wanting to hear all the lurid details. It was pointless trying to have a reasonable conversation with Jonas Tate. Didn't she already know that? How could she have forgotten so quickly what kind of a man he was? She reminded herself that she hated him. Had hated him for months. He'd made her working environment almost intolerable since the day he'd arrived at Seton General, and now he was fast on his way to making her personal life unbearable, too. Why on earth had she ever agreed to help him out?

"It doesn't matter what he did," she muttered wearily. She turned to the closet again and extracted her coat, thrust her arms into the sleeves of her parka and then began to fidget with the zipper, striving for a quick departure. But naturally, the mechanism didn't want to catch.

"Man, you guys are all alike," she added as she continued to struggle with the scrap of metal, more to prevent Jonas from prying further into her personal experiences than because she agreed with what she was saying. "You think you're doing any woman a favor to exchange a few meaningless words over dinner, then you can't understand why she doesn't want to hop in the sack with you as soon as the sun goes down."

The zipper finally caught, and Zoey tugged it up to her chin. When she looked up, Jonas was watching her levelly, his hands settled on his hips, his eyes stormy.

"Hell, at least Jeff took me out before he tried to nail me," she said. "All you did was clean up the dirty dishes—which, incidentally, were your own, anyway."

Zoey told herself that the only reason she didn't bolt through the front door after that was because Jonas was standing between her and it. But really, she knew she was waiting for him to deny what she had said about all men being alike. She wanted him to assure her he was not like other men, wanted him to say something, anything, that would change her mind about the entire male half of the population. Worse than that, she realized suddenly, she wanted him to reach out to her. Wanted to feel him touch her again. And if that realization didn't make her go racing in fear out of his house, she didn't know what else would.

Until Jonas reached over and opened the front door for her. The cold March wind whipped around them, but it was nothing compared to the chill in his eyes. "If that's the way you feel," he said quietly, "then you're right. It would be better if you went home."

Zoey opened her mouth to object, started to voice her concern about how Juliana would fare without her. Then she reminded herself that Jonas and Juliana had been managing, however questionably, without her for two months now. Neither of them was her responsibility. If he wanted her to leave, then there was absolutely no reason for her to stay.

Except for the fact that it didn't feel right to leave the two of them alone. Something inside her balked at the thought of Jonas and Juliana not needing her. In spite of her assurances to the contrary only moments ago, Zoey wanted very badly to remain there with them. And it wasn't, she realized much to her dismay, just the baby who roused such a desire in her.

But Jonas still stood across from her with the door wide open, a clear indication that he didn't share her feelings. So instead of saying all the things she wanted to say, instead of telling him that she hadn't meant it when she'd lumped him into the same category as that creep, Jeff Pearson, instead of insisting that she wanted to help with Juliana, Zoey turned silently and crossed over the threshold of Jonas Tate's front door.

She listened helplessly as it immediately clicked shut behind her. And for some reason, as she stood there shivering in the icy cold wind, it occurred to Zoey that she'd never heard a more distressing sound.

"Hey, Red, why so glum?"

Zoey looked up from a patient chart she had been studying for five minutes, still unable to recall why she had picked it up in the first place. The melancholy mood that had been dogging her for days, two to be exact—ever since she'd left Jonas's house the Friday night before—lifted somewhat when she saw Cooper Dugan, one of the paramedics who made frequent deliveries to the hospital, leaning over the nurses' station counter.

"Hi, Coop," she greeted him as she laid the chart aside. "I'm not glum, just a little distracted is all. Early Monday morning blahs, I guess. What are you doing here so late? Did you get stuck with third shift, too?"

He nodded, his carelessly long, pale blond hair falling forward over clear green eyes. "Yeah, every now and then I get tagged with the graveyard shift. Just brought in a major coronary arrest. I've got twenty bucks that say the guy's not going to make it till morning, so I thought I'd hang around for a while and see if I invested my money wisely."

"Cooper!" Zoey exclaimed. "Shame on you."

He shrugged off her chiding. "Hey, he looked like a wide-mouthed bass by the time we got there. 'Course, I could be wrong," he added with a negligent swipe of his hand over his cheek. "Wouldn't be the first time. Anyway, I heard you were pulling night duty, too, and I thought maybe we could catch a bite to eat together. What do you say? You coming up for a break anytime soon?"

She sighed and looked at her watch. "Not for another hour or so. Sorry."

Zoey and Cooper had been friends since they were teenagers, having met in an urban shelter adolescents on the run eventually wandered into for a hot meal. Her month-long stint on the streets of Philadelphia after running away from home was a part of her life about which Zoey preferred to forget. And except for her friendship with Cooper, she let most of her experiences from that time remain well buried in the past. She'd run to escape what she had thought at fourteen was a miserable life-style. And she'd learned pretty quickly what truly constituted misery.

"Well, how about breakfast when we get off?" Cooper added. "My treat. I might be twenty bucks richer by then."

Zoey shook her head. "No way. I will not be treated to waffles with your ill-gotten gains. Besides, I have plans for the·day. At least, I think I do."

"Doing what?"

"Baby-sitting."

He curled down his lips in mock disgust. "Ugh. How can you stand it? You're surrounded by screeching infants all day long. I'd think you'd want some time to yourself on occasion."

"I have plenty of time to myself," she told him, squelching the little voice that wanted to say she spent *too* much time alone. "And I love being around babies."

"I notice you don't seem to have any of your own."

Instinctively, her back went up at the comment. "And you know why, too."

He nodded, making a face at her. "I know why you *say* you don't. 'Because the world's a terrible place'," he recited in a bland voice. "Too horrible for you to bring another child into it to suffer. Blah, blah, blah." He leaned farther over the counter and tugged playfully on her braid. "Better be careful, Zoey. One of these days, you might even start to believe that."

"I do believe that."

He eyed her skeptically. "And your lack of children would have nothing to do with the fact that you're just too terrified to let a man get close enough to father one or two for you, right? It has nothing to do with what happened to Eddie."

She felt her cheeks flame and stood to face him, eye to eye. However, unlike most men, he was in no way intimidated by her overbearing posture. Cooper, after all, was the one who had pulled her out of the blackest period of her life. He was the only human being in the world who had known her during a time of despair, a time of weakness, and he wasn't afraid of her in any way, shape or form. And that, she supposed, was one of the many reasons why she liked him so much.

"You have no idea what you're going on about, Cooper," she said. "It has nothing to do with fear. Nothing to do with what happened to...Eddie." God, she thought as she stumbled over the final word of her assurance. How long had it been since she'd spoken his name?

Cooper relaxed his posture, and his voice was softer when he replied. "Hey, Zoey, you forget who you're talking to. I know better than anyone why you don't want to set yourself up for a fall. And after what happened to you, that's perfectly understandable. But—"

"What happened to me," she interrupted him, "is a part of my past. It has nothing to do with who I am now."

He nodded, but she could see that he was in no way agreeing with her. "Right. Whatever you say, kid. Whatever you say."

"Look, shouldn't you be heading over to CCU to find out if your guy made it or not?" she asked pointedly. "I have a lot of stuff here that needs my complete and undivided attention."

"Message received," he told her with a brief salute.

As he spun around to leave, Zoey remembered something she wanted to ask him. "Hey, Coop," she called out after him.

"Yes?" he replied, spinning back around.

"You kill a lot of time in the east wing, don't you?"

He lifted one shoulder in a casual shrug. "Sure. When there are no runs I need to make. All the best-looking nurses work in the east wing," he added with a wink.

She ignored the compliment and said instead, "Meaning you spend a lot of time gossiping, right?"

"Well, now, I wouldn't exactly call it gossiping," he defended himself. "I prefer to think of it as networking."

Zoey nodded blandly. "Right. Networking. At any rate, do you..." She paused for a moment, wondering how best to discreetly ferret out information about herself without having it sound as if she was, well, ferreting out information about herself. Finally, she stammered, "Do you...do you ever hear any...you know...talk...about me?"

Cooper arched his brows, though whether in surprise or to stall for time, Zoey wasn't sure.

"Talk?" he echoed. "About you?"

"Talk," she repeated dryly. "About me."

"Oh..." he hedged. "Gee, it's hard to say. We men talk about so many things, you know. Swimsuit calendars, hockey, liquor, stewardesses, guns...."

"Me?" Zoey asked again. "Do you ever talk about me?"

He eyed her warily. "Why do you ask?"

"I have it on very good authority that I'm known among the men of Seton General as a real, um, as a real threat to the family jewels."

"Oh, *that*," he said with a careless wave of his hand.

She gaped at him. "What do you mean, 'Oh, *that?*' Is it true? Is that what all you guys think about me?"

"Don't worry about it, Zoey. You should consider it a compliment. Nobody likes Jeff Pearson anyway."

"But—"

"We men have nothing but respect for you, kid. You're practically one of us."

Practically one of them? she thought. Good heavens, who'd want to be one of *them?*

"Then it is true," she said dismally.

"Hey, there are worse things you could be considered," he remarked. "There's no shame in being a tough broad." And with that heartening reassurance, Cooper saluted her again and made his way toward the elevators.

A tough broad, Zoey marveled as she watched him leave. Her male co-workers thought of her as a tough broad? Is that what Jonas thought her to be, too? Well, so what if he did? she thought further. She *was* a tough broad. Wasn't she? Hadn't she been going out of her way for years to convince people that she was someone they'd be better off not messing with? Why was she surprised to discover she scared men? At least, this way, they'd leave her alone. Wasn't that what she wanted?

It used to be, she realized. Until a couple of days ago. Until she'd wandered blindly into Jonas Tate's house to find him struggling to raise a baby girl, and had witnessed a side of him that was scared and uncertain and vulnerable. Until she'd realized that maybe men weren't quite the ogres she'd always thought them to be. At least . . . one of them didn't seem to be.

She glanced down at her watch again to find that it was not quite 2:00 a.m. She wondered if Jonas was asleep or awake, wondered if Juliana was blissfully lost in slumber or crying out in distress. And for some reason, she knew she belonged in that big house with them. For some reason, she suddenly felt responsible for them both.

Until the two of them were on more solid footing, anyway, she amended. The least she could do was make sure Juliana was comfortable and happy. Zoey felt she owed it to the little girl to make sure she never felt as out of place in Jonas's life as she herself had felt for so long in her aunts' lives. And, she realized reluctantly, Jules was a baby Zoey could actually help. A baby she wouldn't have to sit by and watch suffer because there was nothing she could do.

Two o'clock, she repeated to herself as she reached once more for the patient file she had abandoned. She imagined Jonas in his purple silk pajama bottoms balancing Juliana in one arm while he tried to heat formula with his free hand. They really did need her, she told herself. And just because he had asked her to leave his house the other night didn't mean she couldn't return this morning.

She could handle Jonas Tate and the confusing feelings he aroused in her, she vowed certainly. She was a tough broad, after all.

Five

It was a bad dream, Jonas decided as he stood in his pajama bottoms and robe, framed by his front door. He frowned at the maddeningly cheerful woman who had arrived on his porch. The sun was just coming up over the house across the street, staining with orange and gold the long hair that streamed from beneath her red knit cap, throwing a circle of light around her head that looked incongruously like a halo. Yet he knew Zoey Holland was anything but an angel. The emotions she stirred in him were devilish, to say the least.

Her parka was open enough that he saw she was wearing a dark burgundy Haddonfield High School sweatshirt over faded jeans, instead of the hospital scrubs she had sported on her arrival a few mornings before. She carried a sack of groceries in one hand and a small canvas weekender bag in the other. Clearly, it wasn't an errand for Lily Forrest she was running this time. Evidently, this time she had every intention of spending some serious time with him.

"I'm baaaaaack," she said with a smile as she nudged past him and into his living room.

Jonas pushed the door closed and pulled his robe more tightly around himself, securing the belt with an extra knot. Why he should do so was a mystery, since Zoey had never expressed the slightest interest in disrobing him before, and really, should she decide she wanted to do so now, he had no desire to stop her. There was just something about her having come to his house with her own free will that unsettled him. That, accompanied by the fact that she seemed to be in such a good mood, had him thoroughly rattled.

"Yes, but what are you doing here?" he asked.

"I'm baby-sitting," she told him. "Remember? I'm going to be watching Jules for the next two weeks and helping you out with her."

"I thought you'd changed your mind about that."

She shrugged, clearly unconcerned. "So I changed it back. Besides, you still owe me for the groceries I bought Friday." She indicated the paper bag in her arms. "I'll just put it on your tab. Now where can I stow my stuff?"

"Your . . . stuff? What stuff?"

"My pajamas and toiletries and stuff."

Jonas was still struggling to comprehend her quick change of heart, and as a result, her intentions didn't quite register. "You're moving in?"

"Only for a couple of days. Until you get some sleep. Then I'll just come over in the mornings and stay until you get home from work. Eventually, I'll have to get some sleep, too, you know."

"I know, but—"

"So where can I put my stuff?"

"Aren't you working nights for Jeannette? How are you going to manage this?"

"I got my shifts covered for tonight and tomorrow night."

He eyed her suspiciously. "You're juggling your schedule an awful lot for me."

"It's not for you," she reminded him.

Jonas nodded, feeling more tired than he'd ever felt in his life. "That's right. How could I forget? You're only doing this for Juliana."

"Right. So where can I stow my stuff?"

He lifted his hand to his forehead, as if by doing so he could keep his thoughts from spilling out of his brain. "Hold on for a minute," he said. "Let me just get my bearings here. You're still willing to give me a hand with Juliana?"

"Sure."

"Even after I propositioned you?"

Zoey arched her brows in mock censure. "Oh, but you didn't proposition me, remember? At least, you said you didn't."

"Okay, even after I *allegedly* propositioned you?"

"I'm sure that was all just a misunderstanding," she said indulgently. "Wasn't it?"

Jonas tamped down the urge to yank her into his arms and kiss her senseless to illustrate just how perfectly she *had* understood his intentions of the other night. Instead he only sighed and nodded. "Yeah," he finally said. "You completely misunderstood."

She smiled, clearly comprehending just what a big lie that was. "I thought so."

"You really don't mind sacrificing two weeks to help out me and Juliana?" he asked softly.

"I really don't mind," she assured him.

"Thanks."

"You're welcome."

Jonas studied Zoey for a long time without speaking, almost as if he were seeing her for the first time. As usual, he marveled at how beautiful she was, noted how her green eyes reminded him of a summer field, and was amazed by how badly he wanted to bury his hands in her mass of red hair and bring it to his lips. But he noticed other things about her, too, when he looked at her this time. He'd always thought of Zoey Holland as little more than a pain in the butt, had considered her to be a mouthy, militant man-eater placed on this planet to do nothing but make his life miserable. He'd always seen her as edges and angles and no softness at all.

But now he could see that he'd been wrong about that. There was, indeed, a softness in Zoey. More than that, there was a definite uncertainty about her. He understood suddenly that it was all an act, this tough-guy attitude she adopted around other people. She wasn't all edges and angles. She had some definite soft spots and curves. And not just of the more obvious physical variety, either. All at once, Jonas was anxious to know more about her. He wondered why she behaved the way she did when, clearly, she wasn't a tough guy at all. And all at once, he felt himself warming toward her even more.

"You can put your stuff in the spare room next to Juliana's nursery," he heard himself say, unable to recall when he'd chosen to speak. "You'll be able to hear her with no problem."

"Sounds good," Zoey replied. She placed the sack of groceries on the coffee table and extended her weekender bag toward the stairs. "I'll follow you," she told him.

He wondered briefly just how far she would follow him, wondered what would happen if he led her into his room instead of the spare room and encouraged her to spend the night there. She'd probably pop him in the eye, he assured himself, only half in jest. And then she'd walk out of his life for good.

"This way," he said, pushing the errant thought away. Visualizing Zoey in his bed, naked and demanding, was just too troubling an activity to continue. "Juliana is sleeping," he added as they ascended the stairs, dropping his voice to a low whisper.

"Did she do any better this weekend?" Zoey asked as they crept past the nursery.

He shook his head. "No. Except for Friday night, while you were here, she's screamed like a maniac every time I've tried to comfort her. Obviously, she still hates me and can't stand to have me come near her."

"I'm sure that's not it."

He uttered a derisive sound as he entered the spare room with Zoey on his heels, but made no further comment.

"You should find another pediatrician," she told him again as she tossed her bag onto the bed. "Maybe it's something organic."

Jonas tried to banish the image of Zoey tossing herself down on the bed beside her bag and throwing her arms open wide to welcome him. "The doctor she's seeing is one of the best we have on staff," he replied gruffly. He cleared his throat before adding, "He assures me there's nothing physically wrong with her. So I can only surmise that it must be something *I'm* doing wrong."

Zoey wanted to disagree with him, wanted to reassure him that whatever was troubling Juliana probably had nothing to do with him at all. Unfortunately, she wasn't sure she'd be telling the truth. After all, Jonas had done nothing but trouble Zoey since the day she'd met him.

"Well, put your mind at ease for a little while," she told him. "I'll see to Jules for now, and you can take a breather. Tonight you can get a good night's sleep, and you'll be amazed at how much better you'll feel in the morning. Things are going to work out fine, Jonas. I know they will."

His eyes fairly lit with fire when she spoke his name, and she got the distinct feeling that he was thinking about something he really shouldn't be thinking about. His spare room suddenly seemed uncomfortably small, not to mention warm, and she squelched the instinct to run like some small quivering prey.

"Umm, why don't you go ahead and get ready for work?" she suggested. "I'll go downstairs and put away the groceries. When Jules wakes up, I'll see to her. You just take the day for yourself."

"Take the day for myself," he repeated quietly. He shook his head slowly. "What a concept. I can't remember the last time I had a day to myself. It seems almost too strange to even consider it."

Zoey's heart picked up pace a little at the note of helplessness in his voice. "Jules has really turned your life upside down, hasn't she?"

Jonas sighed heavily. When his gaze met hers, he suddenly appeared more exhausted than she had ever seen a human being look. "More than you could ever know," he said softly. "Had someone told me a year ago that the arrival of something as small and harmless as a baby could change things so utterly and irretrievably, I never would have believed it. I can't begin to describe to you how much Juliana has disrupted things."

"I think I can imagine," she said softly.

Something in her voice disquieted Jonas, but before he could pursue the matter, she spoke again.

"You resent her a little for it, don't you?" she asked.

He shrugged, but couldn't deny the truth in the charge. "Yes, I suppose I do sometimes. I want things to be the way they were before. Just for one day, I'd like for my life to be my own again. I'd like for things to go back to being normal."

"That's never going to happen," Zoey told him, "so you might as well resign yourself to it."

"I know."

"You can achieve a new kind of normal, though, if you work at it."

"What do you mean?"

"I mean, no matter what, you'll never have your old routine back. But you can get into a new one. Once you and Jules establish a routine, things will start to feel, well, normal. A new kind of normal, like I said, but still..."

Jonas smiled, wanting to kiss her for trying to reassure him. Oh, hell, he thought. Who was he kidding? He wanted to kiss her for significantly other reasons than that.

"Thanks, Zoey," he said instead.

She was clearly taken aback by his words. "For what?"

"For trying to help."

"It will get better, Jonas," she promised him with a soft smile that sent his senses reeling. "You'll see. It won't always be like this. The first six months of a baby's life are always the toughest for parents. But it does get easier eventually."

"You talk as though you're speaking from experience."

A ripple of melancholy threatened to undo her for a moment, but she recovered quickly. "A couple of close friends have become parents recently, that's how I know. Me, I don't want children."

"You sound awfully certain about that."

"It's something I decided a long time ago."

"Why?"

"It's not important. Just a fact."

"But—"

"You're going to be late for work if you don't hustle," she interrupted him before he could inquire further into her personal life. "And if what you say about Juliana is true, she's going to be waking any minute. I need to get organized before she does."

Jonas didn't want to hustle. He wanted to keep talking to Zoey. This was the first conversation they'd ever shared that hadn't led to some kind of verbal assault. He discovered to his surprise that he very much wanted to learn more about her. Wanted to know why she didn't want children when she obviously liked babies enough to work around them every day. More than anything, though, he wanted her to keep looking at him as she had since her arrival on his doorstep that morning—as if she really cared about what happened to him.

He opened his mouth to say something—though what exactly, he wasn't sure—when, as if on cue, Juliana erupted into consciousness in the room next door. Her unrelenting wails sent Zoey scurrying through the door and left him standing alone in the spare room. Only then did Jonas realize something very strange—*someone else was seeing to Juliana's needs*. On the heels of that revelation, he discovered something else—for the first time he could recall, it felt kind of odd not seeing to her needs himself.

He shook the feeling off as he followed Zoey and the baby down to the kitchen, then watched as she expertly juggled infant in one hand and formula in the other. Her movements with Juliana were fluid and graceful, confident and capable. She cooed words of comfort to soothe the child while her breakfast was heating, and Juliana replied by quieting considerably. Zoey was clearly a woman who was more than comfortable caring for a baby, a woman who would obviously be able to handle a few of her own. Yet she had assured him she didn't want any of her own. He couldn't help but wonder why.

"Go on," Zoey told him as she seated herself at the kitchen table to feed Juliana. "Don't give either one of us a second thought. Enjoy your day of freedom."

Enjoy your day of freedom. Zoey's words resounded in his brain as if bouncing off metal walls. Somehow, having the day to himself left him feeling anything but free. Zoey and Juliana would be ominously absent. And he was quite certain he would be giving more than a second thought to each of them.

Jonas nodded mutely and staggered backward from the two females in his kitchen. Never in his wildest dreams had he thought there would come a day when he'd find two females invading his home. Two females, he marveled further, and neither of them caring a whit for him. What was really funny, though, was the quietly dawning realization that he was growing quite fond of them both.

"Lesson number one," Zoey said that evening as she and Jonas bent over the bathtub in the master bathroom. "Bathing the baby."

She looked over to see how he was faring and was helpless to stop her smile. To say he appeared to be uncomfortable was a gross understatement. In fact, he seemed to be terrified.

She had placed Juliana's plastic tub inside the larger bath tub, and now the baby sat inside it, splashing merrily at the warm water with swiftly gyrating hands and feet. Jonas supported her head with one hand and cupped the other over her pudgy little tummy, and the vision of the tiny, helpless baby held so securely by big, capable hands made Zoey's smile broaden. Maybe there was hope for the two of them yet.

"Do I really need to learn how to do this?" Jonas asked. "Juliana is going to have a nanny, after all. Someday," he added with a hopeful sigh. "Eventually. When I find someone suitable. Isn't giving her a bath something a nanny will see to?"

"Usually," Zoey conceded. "But you are, in effect, Juliana's father now. And you should be familiar with the basics—feeding, diapering, bathing. The feeding, we've already started working on. The diapering you seem to have down pretty well—"

"That's another duty I won't mind relinquishing to a nanny," he said with a grimace.

"—so that just leaves bathing," Zoey concluded. "Besides, unless you're planning on having a live-in nanny...?" Her voice rose in question.

He shook his head.

"Then that's another reason you'll need to learn how to bathe her—emergency cleanups. In case you haven't noticed, babies tend to get pretty messy pretty quick. Has Juliana had any of those *Exorcist* vomiting episodes yet?"

Jonas's eyes widened in shock. "*Exorcist* vom..." His voice trailed off as he considered her question. "Babies do that?"

"Some do. Not all of them. And don't worry," she added with a playful grin, "they don't start spinning their heads around afterward. But you're going to need to be prepared just in case."

He nodded, still clearly shaken by the possibility.

All through their conversation, Juliana had sat patiently in the tub, gazing from one to the other as if she were following their dialogue perfectly. When Zoey finally turned her attention to the infant, Juliana smiled at her, then slapped her hands more furiously in the water to send a series of sprays up onto the two adults.

"Wouldn't this be easier downstairs on the kitchen counter?" Jonas asked, shifting his weight from one knee to the other.

"Probably," Zoey told him. "But you need to get used to doing it here. As she gets bigger, baths are going to get a lot messier."

He glanced down at the big wet stain darkening the front of his blue chambray work shirt and frowned. "Messier than this?"

She laughed. "Just be glad Jules isn't a boy. At least you don't have to worry about dodging an upward stream of baby pee-pee."

He laughed with her. "Pee-pee. Now there's a word I can't recall ever using in my adult life. It's incredible how much your vocabulary changes when you have a baby. I mean, here I am, a grown man, using words like *pee-pee* and *poo-poo*. And *onesie*. Now who the hell came up with that? Why can't they just call baby underwear *baby underwear?*"

"You're just getting started," Zoey told him. "Wait until Jules starts talking. You won't believe some of the things you'll hear and repeat back to her."

Evidently impatient to have her bath, Juliana splashed them again, a substantial arc of water that landed soundly in Zoey's face.

"All right, all right," she told the baby. "We'll get on with it."

Zoey walked Jonas through all the steps of bathing an infant, the procedure taking three times longer than it would have if she had performed it alone. Nevertheless, she couldn't help but marvel at how careful and gentle Jonas was with Juliana. He should have been an artist instead of a cardiologist, she thought. He just had such wonderful hands.

"Now what?" he asked after Juliana's final rinse.

"Now you dry her off."

"With what?"

She shook her head at him. "Oh, gee, I don't know. A towel, maybe?" She reached for the hooded towel she had placed close at hand with the other numerous items necessary for keeping a baby clean. "Here, hand her to me."

Jonas did as she requested, settling the baby gingerly into her outstretched arms. As Zoey dried Juliana off, he went about collecting the assortment of baby paraphernalia,

mumbling something about how amazing it was that someone one-tenth his size used ten times his toiletries.

"Yeah, well, *you* don't have to worry about cradle cap
and diaper rash, do you?" Zoey muttered in response.

He looked at her aghast. "I should hope not."

"I love the way babies smell," she said suddenly as she
scrubbed the towel gently over Juliana's downy hair. As if
to illustrate, she held the baby close, bent over her head and
inhaled deeply. "So sweet and soft and clean. They almost
smell new, don't they? So full of potential. Just think about
it, Jonas. Jules is only three months old now. Where will she
be in thirty years? In sixty?"

"I can't think that far ahead. I scarcely know where she
and I will be next week."

Zoey drew the baby's hand from beneath the towel and
curled five tiny fingers over one of her own. "She has long
fingers. Maybe she'll be a pianist. Or a masseuse. Or a pas-
try chef."

"Maybe she'll be a nurse," he said with a smile.

She glanced up at him and smiled back. "Maybe she'll be
a doctor."

"Maybe she will."

"A doctor who gives nurses a lot of grief, just like her old
man."

Jonas frowned. "Now just wait one minute. I told
you—"

"What do you say, Jules?" Zoey interrupted him, pretending not to hear the objection. "You want to be a part of
the wonderful world of modern medicine?"

Juliana cooed and sighed and didn't say for sure.

"A pianist," Zoey finally decided. She went back to drying the baby off and avoided Jonas's gaze. "She's too smart
to get involved with moody doctors."

Jonas watched Zoey tend to Juliana and contemplated the
wild influx of emotions the sight stirred in him. How could
a woman he'd always considered big, forceful and belliger-
ent make him feel so calm and pleasant inside? Zoey Holland was truly an enigma. With him and others at the
hospital, she was a raging bull. With Juliana, she was a

cream puff. Although he knew she worked in the hospital nursery, he'd never considered that she might have a tender, nurturing side. Yet here she was, cuddling a baby with all her heart, clearly content in the softer aspects of her character.

So why couldn't she show some of that softness to him? he wondered. And, dammit, why did he ache so badly to have it?

"Lesson number two," she said as she stood, oblivious to the turmoil tearing him up inside, "dressing the baby."

"Oh, no," he told her. He, too, stood, but he backed away with his hands held high to ward off Zoey and the baby. "This is where those onesie things come in. Juliana absolutely hates to have anything put over her head. She'll scream at me. And I hate it when she screams at me."

"She won't scream at you."

"Yes, she will."

Zoey held the baby out toward him in a silent indication that he should take her. "Then that's all the more reason for you to practice, isn't it?"

In fact, Juliana did scream when Jonas tugged the cotton undershirt over her head. Until Zoey showed him how to hold the neck wide so that it didn't obscure the baby's vision. She also let him in on a few of her diapering-made-easier secrets, gleaned from years of working in the hospital nursery. And finally, as she darkened the room and sat down to rock the baby, she offered him a few tips on how to get Juliana to sleep a little more peacefully at night. And then, as he watched in awe, she began to sing to the baby in a soft, comforting voice he never would have guessed could come out of Zoey Holland.

Jonas stood rapt in the nursery doorway as he watched her easy, comfortable motions with the baby. He knew her confidence came from years of working with newborns, but there was more to it than that. She was a natural at nurturing, he thought. A definite people person—at least where babies were concerned. Why, then, was she so antagonistic around grown-ups?

And then the answer came to him out of nowhere. Zoey was comfortable around babies because babies didn't pose a threat to anyone. Because they couldn't hurt her. He didn't know why the thought should occur to him that way, but suddenly Jonas was as certain of it as he was his own name. All of Zoey's swaggering machismo, the black belt in karate, the incorrigible reputation at the hospital.... All at once, everything made sense. She wasn't tough because she was so fearless. She was tough because she was so frightened.

Frightened of what, he couldn't imagine. But Zoey was scared of something.

The realization made him feel funny inside. Before, it had been so easy to stay angry with Zoey all the time. And staying angry with her had been imperative, because it kept his mind off of more disturbing things—like wanting to get to know her better. A woman was the last thing he needed or wanted in his life, especially some pushy broad who would turn his life upside down. It was bad enough that Juliana had disrupted things so thoroughly and completely scattered his brains. A woman like Zoey could easily deliver the final, fatal blow.

He wouldn't succumb, he assured himself. He would not, ever again, allow himself to be preoccupied by idle, erotic thoughts about Zoey. She was here to help him out with Juliana. Period. He'd just have to remember that the next time he started wondering what she was, or wasn't, wearing under those hospital scrubs of hers.

But as he listened to the quiet timbre of her voice as she sang to the baby in her arms, as he noted the way the dim glow from the Noah's ark night-light danced in her hair like fire, as he inhaled the spicy scent of her mingling with the aroma of baby shampoo...

Jonas squeezed his eyes shut and mentally plugged his ears and nose. Man, he must be going crazy, he thought. For a minute there, he could have sworn he saw tears forming in Zoey's eyes.

A preoccupation with her, he could handle, he thought. But hell, he was becoming obsessed. And an obsession, he decided, was going to be much more difficult to handle. Especially when Zoey would be invading his house for two weeks.

Two weeks had never felt so much like a lifetime.

Six

It was no use, Jonas decided sometime later as he lay wide-awake in his bed. For the first time in months, he had the opportunity to indulge in guilt-free, untroubled sleep for as many hours as he needed—and seeing as how he had been exhausted for those months, he needed it badly—and all he could do was lie there wondering about Zoey. More specifically, wondering about how Zoey looked when she was sleeping. Even more specifically, about what Zoey wore while she slept. Or if she wore anything at all.

He groaned and rolled fitfully to his stomach, burying his face in the pillow he'd scrunched beneath his head. So much for not being preoccupied with idle, erotic thoughts about Zoey.

Sleep, dammit, he ordered himself. But his brain would not process the command. Instead, it replayed for him the sight of her bending over Juliana's crib to tuck in the infant a short while ago. No one could do justice to a pair of jeans the way Zoey Holland did, he'd decided then. His fingers curled into fists as he recalled the way he'd itched to cup his hands over her derriere.

"Stop it," he instructed himself out loud. "This will get you nowhere except more exhausted."

He lifted his head and squinted at the glowing green digits on his alarm clock. It was nearly midnight. He'd been lying in bed for more than an hour and was nowhere closer to sleep now than he had been that afternoon. What the hell was wrong with him? Why couldn't he sleep?

Maybe a glass of brandy, he decided. A nightcap had always helped him unwind before.

He rose from the bed, slipped his paisley robe on over his pajama bottoms, then padded barefoot down the stairs to the den. Without bothering to turn on the light, he made his way to the bar and splashed a small portion of cognac into a snifter. Outside, a light snow had begun to fall, and he stood at the floor-to-ceiling window for a moment to watch. Slowly, gradually, as he observed the softly cascading bits of white make their way to the ground, he felt the tension leaving his body. Snow made everything seem quieter somehow, he thought. It buffed all the raw edges from life.

He abruptly turned away from the peaceful scene when a lamp snapped on behind him. Zoey had come into the room without seeing him and strode toward the television to turn it on. He had wondered what she wore to sleep in, he recalled as he watched her unobserved. He'd seesawed over whether it was something in clingy black lace or chaste white cotton. Now he had his answer. Neither. Zoey slept in flannel. Red plaid flannel. Red plaid flannel pajamas whose sleeves fell to her fingertips and whose pants flowed to her ankles over thick, woolen socks.

Jonas was mystified by why her nighttime attire should so surprise him. It was perfect—practical, comfortable, no-nonsense. Just like Zoey. And instead of being disappointed by his erroneous assumption about her sleepwear, he was somehow reassured by it. Hey, what could he say? She looked good in red.

"Good evening," he greeted her softly.

She whirled around so fast, he was afraid she might go spinning right out of the room. Her hand splayed open over her heart, and she gasped audibly. When she saw that it was him, however, she relaxed some. But only for a moment. Then the wariness that always seemed to overcome her in his presence returned, and he felt like he always did when confronted by her—confused.

"I couldn't sleep," he said before she had a chance to accuse him of anything. "I thought maybe a little cognac might help me to relax."

She nodded. "I'm sorry, I didn't mean to intrude. I just remembered that Keanu Reeves is on 'Letterman' tonight. I thought maybe I still had time to catch him."

"Keanu Reeves?" Jonas asked, taking a few idle steps toward her. "Isn't he a little young for you?"

She lifted one shoulder in what he supposed was meant to be a careless gesture, but somehow careless was the last thing Zoey appeared to be at the moment. For every step he took forward, she took one of her own in retreat.

"What's wrong with an older woman going for a younger man?" she asked him as she came to a halt near the door. He couldn't help but notice that she was perfectly poised for flight. "No one ever comes down on a man who's with a woman considerably younger than he is."

"No, not usually," Jonas agreed, continuing with his approach until he stood nearly toe-to-toe with her. "Not unless the reason he's with a younger woman is because he's afraid of women his own age."

Zoey arched her left brow at him in a way he was beginning to find very alluring. "Are you suggesting I'm afraid of men my own age?" she asked.

He shook his head. "Word around the east wing has it that you're afraid of men of any age."

She stiffened, then strode past him in a wide arc to turn the television off again. "You shouldn't listen to idle chatter, Dr. Tate," she said as she spun around to make her exit again. "Somehow, I thought you were above gossiping."

"Zoey, wait," he said, placing his drink on an end table before intercepting her. He caught up with her in time to block her retreat by positioning himself in front of the door. "I'm sorry. That comment was uncalled for."

Her green eyes flashed fire at him. "I'll say it was. Jeez, I'm trying to help you out here, and you still can't keep yourself from picking on me."

"I'm not picking on you."

"Oh, yes, you are."

"No, I'm not."

"You are, too."

"I am not."

Once again, they stood toe-to-toe and eye-to-eye, hands fisted belligerently on their hips as their argument escalated. Fighting with Zoey was the last thing Jonas wanted to be doing on a quiet, snow-crested night. One of his wildest fantasies of late had virtually come true—he had Zoey in his house in the middle of the night, her hair hung loose about her shoulders, and she was wearing what she would normally wear only in bed. Granted, in his fantasies he had envisioned her dressed in something decidedly less concealing than flannel jammies. But two out of three wasn't bad.

So, without thinking further, Jonas did what his instincts had been commanding him to do since the first day he'd laid eyes on her. He pulled her into his arms and kissed her.

Almost immediately, he realized what a terrible mistake he had made. Almost, because for one brief, wonderful moment, he felt Zoey's warm mouth open beneath his, felt the soft swell of her breasts pressing into his chest as her body relaxed against him, felt her fingers curl possessively into the lapel of his robe.

Then he felt her knee come up faster than he ever could have anticipated, with just enough force to make him reconsider his action.

So he did. Quickly. And he decided right away that he probably should stop kissing her. That he probably shouldn't have kissed her in the first place. Not like that. Not without some kind of warning.

"Jeez, why did you do that?" he gasped as he jerked away from her. Only a herculean effort—that and his determination that she would *not* see him in such a state—prevented him from doubling over to protect himself from what might be a second, more damaging, blow.

"You're lucky you're still standing," Zoey told him, her own breathing decidedly ragged. She lifted the back of her hand to her lips, as if trying to wipe away the sensation of his mouth covering hers. "I could have made sure that you'd never sing baritone again."

"But why did you do it?" he repeated. He threw his shoulders back, regaining his manly composure, then took a step forward.

"Don't," she cautioned him, raising her hands in front of herself in what was an obviously defensive pose. "Don't come near me."

"Why, Zoey?" he demanded again. He ignored her warning and took two more steps toward her. "What's with you and the knee treatment? Why did you do it?"

She hesitated for a moment, watching Jonas as if she were carefully studying him. "Why...why did you?" she finally asked, her voice suddenly sounding as haunted and fearful as her eyes looked. "Why did you...kiss me?"

That was what made Jonas stop dead in his tracks—the look in her eyes. She was scared, he acknowledged. Really, truly scared. Of *him*. The realization hit him square in the gut, as if that's where she had landed her knee instead. Try as he might, he couldn't recall a single time in his life when he had caused a woman to be scared of him. Certainly not by kissing her, he thought. Hell, the way he'd kissed Zoey hadn't even been one of his better efforts.

"Zoey, there's no reason to be frightened," he told her in the most reassuring voice he could muster.

"I'm not frightened."

"The hell you're not."

"I'm not frightened," she repeated adamantly.

"Okay, you're not frightened," he conceded in a dubious voice. "Then why did you just try to turn me into a eunuch?"

She relaxed a little—but only a little, he noted—and sighed. "I'm sorry. You caught me off guard. Now you answer my question. Why did you kiss me?"

He opened his mouth to toss off some casual remark, but all that emerged was the truth. "Because I've wanted to kiss you since the first day I met you."

Well, that certainly seemed to do the trick. Immediately, Zoey's posture changed. She relaxed her body completely, dropped her hands to her sides, inclined her head forward and said, "What?"

Jonas frowned. "You heard me. I said I've wanted to kiss you since the first day I met you."

She gaped at him incredulously. "The first day you met me, you chewed my butt off for clocking in three minutes late because Dr. Michaelson had waylaid me in pediatrics."

"It was a defense mechanism," Jonas said. "I wanted to kiss you, so I chewed your butt off instead."

"Oh, that really makes sense. It's all so clear to me now."

"Don't be so sarcastic."

"Then don't tell me things that aren't true."

"I am telling you the truth." He bunched two fistfuls of hair in his hands and sighed in exasperation. "Dammit, Zoey, the reason I couldn't sleep tonight was because I kept thinking about you. About you sleeping in my spare room. About—" He stopped abruptly, deciding it probably wasn't in his best interest to reveal that he had been wondering what she looked like naked.

Zoey shook her head slowly and tried to pretend she wasn't hearing what she was hearing. Mostly because what Jonas was saying about her mirrored her own thoughts about him. The reason she had forgotten about Keanu Reeves on 'Letterman' was because she had been too preoccupied by visions of Jonas Tate dancing in her head. Much to her horror, she had been drifting off to sleep wondering what it would be like to be nuzzled up to him in his bed instead of trying to warm up her own sheets alone. That was when she had decided she needed a little diversion before hitting the hay. And Keanu Reeves had always been a surefire distraction for her before.

Before she had been thrust into such close quarters with Jonas, anyway. Now even Keanu had taken a back seat.

"Don't say things like that," she told him, her voice sounding quiet and uncertain, even to her own ears.

Much to her dismay, Jonas took two more steps toward her, closing the distance between them. Slowly, as if to give her plenty of time to stop him if she wanted to, he lifted a hand to her face and brushed her cheek softly with the backs of his fingers. Zoey closed her eyes, telling herself she should push him away as she had that morning. But his touch was so gentle, so tentative, so utterly arousing, that all she could do was stand there and enjoy it.

"Don't," she said again, even as she tilted her head toward his caress.

"I want to kiss you, Zoey," she heard Jonas say from what seemed like a million miles away. "If you don't want me to, tell me now, and I won't."

Her brain screamed at her to tell him to stop, to assure him that she wanted no part of him. But her heart squelched the command entirely. Her heart bade her welcome his embrace with everything she had. So instead of shouting at him to leave her alone, all she could do was stand there and let him come closer.

With her eyes closed, the brush of his fingers against her face felt like the glide of satin over her skin. She couldn't believe how gentle he was. Couldn't recall a single time in her life when she'd met with such docility from a man. Granted, she hadn't allowed very many men to get this close to her. Or any men for that matter, she amended reluctantly. Not since her husband had checked out on her so many years ago.

The thought evaporated as Jonas began to stroke his fingertips over her lips. When Zoey opened her eyes, she found that his face was only inches away from her own. She waited for the kiss he had promised her. But he only continued to gaze at her, as if studying her reaction to his touch.

"Who was he?" he finally said, his voice low and level.

She narrowed her eyes in confusion. "Who was who?"

Now he cupped her cheek gently in his palm, threading his fingers into the hair above her ear. An odd electricity shot through her, leaving a trail of tingling heat in its wake. Involuntarily, she flinched and jerked away.

Jonas didn't follow her withdrawal, instead standing motionless with his hand still lifted into the air. His fingers curled into a fist, however, as he asked, "Who was the son of a bitch who made you so wary? Who was the man who hurt you so badly that you shun even the most innocent touch?"

When Zoey shook her head in mute refusal to answer, he turned to retrieve his drink from the end table, then sipped it in thoughtful silence as he continued to stare at her. When still she refused to reply, he cradled the snifter in his palm and swirled the dark amber liquor slowly, watching it as if the swiftly moving contents of the glass were the most fascinating thing he'd ever observed. But she could tell he was nowhere near as nonchalant as he was letting on.

After a moment, he said, "You told Juliana the other day that you know what it's like to be a burden. To be foisted off on someone who doesn't want you. You said you know what it's like to be resented. Does your reluctance to be civil to the entire male population all go back to that?"

She shook her head. "No."

"Then what? Why won't you even let me touch you?"

Zoey sighed wearily, lifting a hand to her forehead to scoop back a fistful of her bangs. He wouldn't rest until he had her figured out, she thought. Which meant he wouldn't be retiring anytime soon tonight. Jonas Tate was the last person on earth she wanted knowing about her past. But she supposed having been kneed in the groin—even though she'd gone easy on him there, and even though he'd asked for it—entitled him to some kind of explanation. Nevertheless, she wasn't sure how much she should tell him about herself.

Then Jonas gave her the opportunity to stall by asking, "This doesn't have anything to do with those elderly aunts who raised you? I can't help but wonder if they were single for a reason."

Zoey smiled. "They weren't man-haters, if that's what you're asking."

"That's what I'm asking."

"No, it wasn't like that," she assured him. "My parents were killed in a boating accident when I was three years old. My father's aunts—one widowed with no children, the other having never married—took me in after that. Neither of them was overjoyed about the prospect of raising a child. And neither of them had a clue about the needs of a growing girl. In spite of the giant steps forward in social progress that came with the sixties, Aunt Celeste and Aunt Millie remained pretty much entrenched in the forties where rules and manners were concerned. As a result, when I hit adolescence, they had no idea what to do with me."

"They thought you should behave like Donna Reed's kids, is that it?"

"Oh, no," Zoey said with a smile. Nowadays, it was much easier to smile about her aunts than it was back then. "Aunt Celeste and Aunt Millie thought the television kids of the fifties were way too mouthy and undisciplined. To them, Ward and June and Ozzie and Harriet were the most permissive parents on earth, and their children were all headed straight to skid row."

"I see."

She chuckled involuntarily. "In spite of everything, I love them like crazy, you know? I mean, they're still caught in that post–World War II America state of mind, but they've accepted the fact that I have to do things a little differently than they did, and I've come to appreciate them precisely because they refuse to give in to contemporary society."

Jonas smiled, and she could tell he was relieved that she was offering up her explanation, even if it wasn't exactly the one he had asked for. He didn't have to know that, did he?

"But the three of you didn't always get along, is that it?" he asked.

She shook her head. "There was always that unspoken resentment on both our parts. I didn't want to be there any more than they wanted me there. I couldn't stand them when I was a kid. And they couldn't stand me. I have to ad-

mit that there were times when I went out of my way to
misbehave just to get a rise out of them. At one point, when
I didn't think I could tolerate their rules and regulations
anymore, I even ran away from home.''

He had lifted his glass to his lips for another sip, but
dropped his hand again to gape at her. "You did what?"

Without asking, Zoey moved to the bar and uncorked the
bottle of brandy that still sat atop it. She filled the bottom
of a tumbler with cognac and swallowed an ample mouthful before continuing. "I ran away from home," she repeated.

"Why?"

"I was very unhappy. My aunts expected a type of behavior from me that I didn't think was realistic. What was
worse, though, was that I knew they really didn't want me
there—that I had upset their life-style without their willingness to have it upset. I felt unloved, unwanted. I turned into
your typical rebellious teenager, and I ran away from
home.''

"But obviously you came back, right?"

"Eventually."

"How long is 'eventually'?"

"I was on the streets for five weeks."

Jonas came to stand beside her. "And just what exactly
does 'on the streets' mean?"

Zoey swallowed more of the brandy without looking at
him. "Just what it sounds like. I slept under bridges and
behind Dumpsters, stood on corners holding out my hand
to strangers for money, waited for people to throw food
away so I could pull it out of the garbage can to eat it.''

"And exactly how old were you when you did all this?"

"Exactly? Fourteen."

"You were sleeping behind Dumpsters and eating from
garbage cans when you were fourteen?" Jonas asked, his
quiet voice thunderous in the otherwise silent room.

She nodded. "Yeah, I was just a kid when I left home.
But I was infinitely older and wiser when I returned.''

He was silent for a moment, digesting the information,
she supposed, and probably wondering if he could poten-

tially drive Juliana to the same type of rebellion. Then he said, "This still doesn't tell me why you hate men so much."

Damn, she thought she had sidetracked him enough that he would have forgotten about that. There was no way she was going to tell him that her brief stint on the streets had taught her nothing compared to the education she'd received later in her teen years. Because there was no way he could understand unless she told him about Eddie. And Eddie was something she didn't talk about anymore. Not to anyone. There was no way she was going to open up her heart to that crippling grief again.

"It's not that I hate men," she said softly. "Everyone seems to think that I do, but that isn't it at all."

"What, then?" he asked.

"It's not men," she insisted. "It's involvement. I don't want to get involved with anyone."

"Why not?"

For a very good reason, she told herself. A reason that was really none of his business. "I had a bad experience once," she said evasively.

She heard Jonas sigh beside her. "We've all had bad experiences with the opposite sex, Zoey. That doesn't mean we give up on everyone else who happens to share the same gender-specific organs."

She smiled in spite of herself. "Maybe not, but..."

"But what?"

Another memory flashed into her brain then, the recollection of a baby lying in a hospital crib—a baby who'd been pasty white and comatose, a baby she had been completely unable to help. And as quickly as the memory surfaced, Zoey tamped it down. That child was part of her past, part of another life. There was no reason to bring him into her present. Especially a present that was so well-organized, so utterly under her control.

"But nothing," she said resolutely as she swallowed the last of her drink. When she finally mustered the nerve, she turned to Jonas and threw him what she hoped was a reassuring smile. "I'm really tired. I'm going to bed. Good night." And with that, she turned to leave, praying that Jonas would let her go without pressing the issue further.

She should have known better.

"Zoey, wait," he called out after her.

Reluctantly, she paused, but didn't turn around. "What?"

"This conversation isn't really over, is it?" From the sound of his voice, she could tell he still stood at the bar.

"Of course it is," she told him. "There's nothing more to discuss."

"There's plenty more to discuss."

Still unwilling—or unable—to turn around and meet his gaze, she laughed. The nervous titter she uttered sounded as forced and hollow as it felt. "Like what?" she asked, certain she didn't want to hear his answer.

She heard him place his glass on the bar, heard the brush of quiet footsteps on the carpet as he came to stand behind her. She felt his hands cup her shoulders and was helpless to stop herself when he urged her to turn around to face him. His eyes were clear and honest and curious. His mouth was set in a tight line. He wasn't trying to invade her privacy, she told herself. He just wanted to understand.

"Like what?" he echoed her question. "Oh, how about, like the fact that I told you I've been wanting to kiss you since the day I met you. You never really did respond to that."

Zoey's mouth went dry at the way he spoke. His voice was low and languid and very, very seductive. His fingers curled ever so slightly, exerting just the tiniest pressure on her shoulders that bade her draw nearer. Without thinking, she took a step forward, until her body and his were separated by scarcely a breath of air. Her lungs filled with the clean, soapy scent of him, and she swore she could taste the smoky flavor of the brandy that clung to his lips. She opened her mouth to speak, then forgot what it was she had meant to say.

"How about it, Zoey?" Jonas asked her.

She closed her eyes lest the sight of him looking so warm and gentle and full of desire make her feel something she had no business feeling. Yet still she was unable to answer him.

So Jonas continued, "What if I told you the reason I wasn't able to sleep tonight is that I couldn't stop thinking about what it would be like to make love to you?"

"Jonas, don't." She groaned softly.

"That all I could do was lie there in bed and wonder what you look like naked."

Something hot and wild exploded in her midsection. She wanted to berate him for his boldness and assure him there was no way on earth he would ever find out. But all she could manage in protest was the whisper of his name.

"Wonder how you'd feel, warm and willing beneath me," he added, pulling her against him as if to illustrate. "How I'd feel beneath you," he added, his voice lowering even more. "How I'd feel beside you. Behind you. Inside you."

"Oh..."

He buried his hands in her hair again, cupping the back of her head. "Wonder what you'd smell like, what you'd taste like."

"Oh, Jonas..."

"Wonder what I'd have to do, where I'd have to touch you, to make you as crazy as you make me."

"Jonas, please..."

"Please what?" he murmured, his voice raspy and low. He had pulled her closer still, had circled his arm around her waist, and his lips hovered only a hairbreadth over her own. "Please describe for you in explicit detail all the things I've already done to you in my mind? Or please just go ahead and do them?"

Zoey's senses were spinning out of control. She was confused and confounded by the emotions he had set reeling inside her. Part of her knew she should push him away and run in terror for her life. But another part of her, a bigger part, was eager to discover more about these new sensations—sensations she'd never felt for Jonas Tate. Sensations she hadn't felt for anyone in a very long time.

Why did it have to be him? she wondered. Why did Jonas Tate have to be the man who would stir her again when she had been so certain she would remain dead inside forever? What was it about him that made her willing for the first time in nearly two decades to put aside her fears and risk everything?

Maybe because he was the first man in two decades who had tried to understand her withdrawal, she thought. Even a knee to the groin hadn't dissuaded him.

Before she realized what she was doing, Zoey lifted her hands to his face, brushing her fingertips gingerly over his cheeks. She couldn't remember the last time she'd touched a man's face, had forgotten how rough and angular they could be. When he did nothing to stop her explorations, she ventured more boldly, stroking her thumbs over his cheekbones and temples and eyebrows. Then she dropped a hand to his lips, skimming over them with the pads of her fingertips.

And that's when Jonas became undone.

It was too much, he thought. Too much like his imaginings about her. The way Zoey was touching him now was precisely the way she touched him in his dreams. And suddenly, he couldn't be satisfied with a fantasy any longer.

His hand joined hers at his lips, slipping her fingers into his mouth for an idle taste. Zoey's eyes fluttered closed, and her own lips parted on a soft gasp. Jonas smiled, skimmed his tongue softly across her fingertips, then opened her hand to brush his lips over her palm. When she sighed, he moved his mouth to her wrist, kissing the rapid-fire pulse once, twice, three times. Then he tucked her hand inside his robe, flattening her palm over his bare chest where she would feel his own heart beating as quickly and frantically as her own.

Her eyes flew open, and when she smiled at him nervously, he knew she understood. He was no less confused and uncertain about what was happening between them than she was.

Zoey dropped her hand to the knot in his sash, fumbling to untie it without much success until he came to her aid. When his robe gaped open, she buried her fingers in the tangle of dark hair scattered across his chest and abdomen, and he was barely able to keep himself in check. Almost automatically, he lifted a hand to the first button on her pajama top and slipped the button through its hole. Then he moved to the second and freed it likewise. Then the third, and the fourth and the fifth.

And then Zoey was as accessible to him as he'd made himself to her. For a long moment, he only gazed at her, at the creamy length of bare flesh revealed by the scarcely open pajama top. He contemplated the perfectly round navel above her dangerously low-riding pajama bottoms. He noted the dusky valley between her breasts, and savored the lower curve of one he itched to explore more fully. Her chest rose and fell with each erratic breath she took, offering him a bit more of her to view with every exhalation.

Unable to tolerate not touching her, Jonas reached for her, dipping his hand just inside her pajama top to push one side away. And when he beheld the exquisite perfection of her breast, he naturally wanted to touch it. Splaying his hand open over her, he fitted the soft flesh perfectly into his palm before closing his fingers more fully over her with a gentle squeeze.

Only then did he detect that something wasn't right.

When he looked at Zoey's face, that look was back in her eyes—the one that told him she was scared of something. He noticed, too late probably, that she wasn't touching him anymore, realized for the first time that at some point in their mutual exploration, she had taken a step away from him. She hadn't fled, however, he tried to reassure himself. And her knee was still exactly where it was supposed to be.

Nevertheless, she was scared again. Scared of him. And for the life of him, Jonas couldn't figure out why.

"What?" he asked. "What is it? What did I do wrong?"

"Nothing," she told him, her voice trembling as much as the rest of her suddenly appeared to be. "It's not you. It's me. It's... I..." She shook her head mutely, clearly unwilling or unable to explain.

"Zoey, tell me," he said, forcing his voice to stay level and calm when inside he was ready to burst. "What is it? What are you so afraid of? Surely you're not scared of me?"

For a moment, he didn't think she was going to answer. Then she pulled her pajama top closed and began to redo the buttons with shaking fingers. She seemed to have her attention utterly focused on the task, but she missed a hole without realizing it until she was at the top. When she discovered her gaffe, she dropped her head into her hands and sighed.

"I haven't done this for a long time," she said without looking up.

"That's okay," he told her. "It's been a while for me, too."

"No, Jonas, you don't understand. I haven't done this for a *long, long time.*"

"Zoey, it's all—"

"Not since I was a teenager," she continued, her face still buried in her hands. "It's been almost twenty years."

Jonas assured himself he must have misunderstood what she said. A single woman in her late thirties, especially one as worldly as Zoey, must have had a string of lovers in her time. Right?

"You're not serious," he said with an anxious laugh. He hadn't meant to laugh. It had just come out. What she was implying was just so incredible. Big, tough Zoey Holland, out of the loop for nearly twenty years? It was just too hard to believe. "You're not honestly trying to tell me you haven't been with a man in that length of time," he clarified. When she didn't reply, but continued to stand with her head in her hands, he asked further, "Are you?"

She dropped her hands to her sides and raised her head to look at him. Jonas was shocked to see that her eyes were wet and red-rimmed. When she sniffled and scrubbed a finger under her nose, two fat tears tumbled down her cheeks, and he felt as if someone had just kicked him hard in the stomach. He'd never seen Zoey cry. She was too strong, too self-assured, too macho. Until now, he would have sworn she was incapable of such a display.

"Sorry, doc, but that's exactly what I'm telling you. I haven't been with a man in so long, I'm not sure I can even remember what goes where. Pretty scary, huh?"

"Pretty incredible is more like it."

Again, he'd spoken without thinking and, too late, acknowledged his mistake. She was serious, he realized. And she was telling him the truth. Somehow he knew that with every cell in his body.

She nodded resolutely and wiped her palms over her cheeks to erase the trail of tears. "Yeah, well, I guess I was right the first time, then, wasn't I?" she said coolly.

It was amazing, Jonas thought, how quickly and completely she could hide what she was really feeling. "Right about what?" he asked.

"About you being like other guys."

He shook his head to deny the charge, but Zoey turned away.

"Excuse me," she said as she began to fumble with her buttons once again. "But it's getting late, and I'm really tired. I'll check on Jules on my way to bed. Don't worry about her. And don't worry about me, either."

Easier said than done, Jonas thought as he watched her leave. Because the more he learned about Zoey, the less he knew her. And suddenly, getting to know Zoey, the real Zoey, the one he'd only glimpsed for a brief moment here and there, became more important than anything else in his life.

Two weeks, he told himself. He had two weeks to figure her out. He assured himself it would be more than enough.

Then he remembered that haunted, fearful look in her eyes, recalled the two solitary tears she had allowed to escape. And somehow, he wondered if even Zoey knew who she really was inside.

Seven

As she pushed Juliana's stroller along King's Highway in Haddonfield, Zoey marveled again at her confession of the night before. Why on earth had she told Jonas about the length of time that had passed since her last sexual encounter? she wondered for perhaps the hundredth time. She'd never revealed that to anyone before—not Cooper, not even Livy and Sylvie.

She supposed all that was about to change, however. The hospital grapevine was an awesome thing—rivaling even fax technology as the fastest way in the world to send information. By the end of the week, everyone at Seton General would know about her condition. And then she'd really become a target. Every jerk male in the east wing would be hitting on her, to see if he could be the first man to get back into Zoey Holland's pants, the one guy who could make her change her mind about abstinence.

Abstinence, nothing, she thought as a flutter of apprehension flickered to life in her midsection. Abstinence suggested a well-thought-out willingness to avoid sex. What she had, she conceded reluctantly, was a bad case of fear. Jonas had been right about that, at least, she had to admit now.

He had avoided her quite capably that morning when she'd come downstairs to pour herself a cup of coffee. Granted, she had timed her arrival in the kitchen so that he would be allowed scarcely a minute to linger lest he be late for work, but he hadn't even dawdled for a minute. Instead, he'd spared one quick glimpse for her wrinkled pajamas and messy hair, had gulped whatever was left in his mug and had brushed by her with a hastily muttered comment about helping herself to coffee. Then he'd grabbed his coat and briefcase and headed out the door as if he were being chased by a man-eating tiger.

Zoey sighed helplessly as she recalled the expression on his face when he'd looked at her—one that indicated he had no idea how to approach her. She was an oddity, she supposed—a mature, modern woman who hadn't a clue about current sexual relations. No doubt Jonas was wondering now if she'd be worth the effort. Frankly, she couldn't blame him. She probably *wasn't* worth the effort.

Hoping a little fresh air and good conversation would ease her mind, she had dressed in jeans and a thick, oversize green sweater, bundled up Juliana and telephoned Livy and Sylvie to invite them to lunch. Then she and the baby had headed out into the surprisingly mild morning. There was no evidence of the previous evening's light snowfall—the temperature had risen well into the fifties, and the bright sun made it feel even warmer. Almost automatically, she had pointed the stroller toward Haddonfield, hoping the brick sidewalks and quaint old shops would distract her from replaying last night's debacle over and over in her brain.

Unfortunately, she supposed she'd never quite forget the way Jonas had laughed at her when she'd told him she hadn't been with a man in almost two decades.

She closed her eyes in an effort to chase away the memory of the tinny-sounding chuckle, but to no avail. When she opened them again, a display in a travel agency caught her attention, and she paused to stare wistfully at an advertisement for a cruise ship. Wouldn't it be nice if she could just sail away? she thought. Pack up her troubles and drift off into the sunset without another care in the world?

Juliana cooed and laughed in the stroller, and Zoey looked down to smile back.

"Don't worry, sweetie, I'd pack you up and take you with me," she said to the baby. "I certainly couldn't leave you behind."

The truth in the statement startled her. In a few short days, she'd become more connected to Juliana than she had thought possible. Why this development had occurred was a mystery. Zoey worked around babies every day, but she'd never become so entranced by one that it broke her heart to think about saying goodbye. That was what she loved about working in the hospital nursery. She could be around babies, but never long enough to get too attached to them. It never hurt when they had to leave her.

Yet she knew when her two weeks with Jules came to an end, the baby's absence would leave a little vacant place inside her that wouldn't easily be filled. She was fast growing to love Juliana. Really, truly love her. It would be more than a little difficult to say goodbye when the time came. The thought alone was enough to trouble her.

Even more difficult, she thought, would be saying goodbye to Jonas. Because he, too, had become entrenched pretty deeply inside of her in a short time. He'd come to occupy a big space in her heart where she would have sworn no man would ever reside. She was still mystified by why he should be the one to rouse her in a way no man had ever been able to before, but she couldn't deny her attraction to him any longer.

She wondered if perhaps that was why she'd resented him since his arrival at Seton General. Because perhaps deep down, she had felt an odd, immediate desire for him that she'd held for no other man before. Maybe all these months of telling herself she hated him had been an unconscious attempt to protect herself from getting hurt. Unfortunately, she hadn't quite been able to convince herself he was as awful as she tried to make him out. And now that she'd been up close and personal with him, it was impossible for her to continue with the charade. She wasn't sure how much longer she could fight her feelings.

"As if it makes any difference," she said to Juliana, setting the stroller into forward motion as she continued with their walk. "Whether I fight my feelings or not, Jonas isn't going to care."

Juliana squealed happily, then smiled at the sound she made. Zoey couldn't help but laugh.

"You're not helping matters, kiddo," she said. "The cuter you are, the tougher this whole thing becomes. It's bad enough that I'm getting tangled up with your uncle. I don't have any business getting tangled up with you, too."

Juliana uttered a coo that sounded suspiciously like, "Oh yeah?" and Zoey chuckled again.

"Lunch," she told the baby meaningfully. "Let's go to Clemente's and have some lunch. Maybe Sylvie and Livy can shed a little light on this matter."

The following Friday night, Jonas worked late. Again. He had worked late every night that week, slumping home at well past the dinner hour with the full knowledge that Zoey would have to rush home herself if she wanted to get any sleep before pulling her shift at the hospital.

And as much as he wished the reason for his diligence at work was simply a profound professional devotion, he couldn't deny that his late nights at the hospital were instead a direct result of trying his damnedest to avoid Zoey. He simply hadn't been able to get Monday night out of his head, hadn't quite come to terms with what she had told him.

Twenty years. Zoey Holland hadn't been with a man for almost twenty years. The revelation amazed him still.

He told himself there must be something wrong with her. What healthy, normal, mentally well-adjusted adult in her thirties would shun sexual activity in this day and age? Zoey was a beautiful, intelligent, assertive woman. There must have been dozens of men in her life who had been more than willing to make love to her. No, if she had been avoiding a sexual relationship, it was because *she* had been the one to make that choice. But why? What was the big deal about sex, anyway? *Everybody* had sex. So what was Zoey's problem?

There had to be something wrong with her, he thought again. Some deep-seated Freudian *something* that kept her from being a healthy, normal, mentally well-adjusted adult. So why was he still so fascinated by her? Even if something more substantial did blossom between them—something of, say, a sexual nature—he told himself the end result would no doubt be a major disappointment. She'd be shy, inhibited and awkward, more than likely having forgotten how to please a man. She wouldn't have a clue how to perform, and he'd wind up having to do all the work himself. It would be an empty, frustrating experience.

Nevertheless, he couldn't quite rid himself of the thrill of excitement that shimmied through him when he thought about being the one who brought her back to the fold.

"It won't happen," he told his reflection in the rearview mirror as he pulled his car into the driveway at half past ten. "It will never, ever happen."

The house was silent when he entered it. He shrugged off his coat and hung it in the foyer closet, tossed his keys onto a table and went in search of Zoey and Jules. Jules, he marveled with a silent shake of his head. Now Zoey even had *him* calling the baby by that ridiculous nickname.

He found the two females in question in the den. Zoey lay stretched out on her back on his sofa, sound asleep. The baby was lying atop her, stomach to stomach, cheek to chest, equally lost in slumber. Jonas smiled in spite of himself. Juliana wore a pink sleeper decorated with cavorting bunnies. Zoey had on her standard blue jeans and a tattered lavender sweatshirt. She had kicked off her boots and wore thick, woolen socks. They were the same kind of socks she had worn with her flannel pajamas Monday night, and the reminder of that evening made his heart pound a little more erratically than it was already.

He was thinking about her breast again. About the way her pajama top had fallen open for one solitary moment to expose that exquisite example of perfect beauty. Long

enough to let him know what he was missing, he realized
with a suppressed sigh of frustration. Long enough to make
him want her for the rest of his life.

As quietly as he could, he approached the dozing duo,
lifting Juliana as carefully as he could from Zoey's embrace. Both of them stirred as he did so, Juliana only mo-
mentarily, Zoey a little longer. Her arms fell reluctantly
away, and she murmured some soft protest in her sleep. But
she didn't quite wake up. Amazingly enough, Juliana, too,
slept on peacefully.

Zoey had worked wonders with the baby in one short
week, he thought as he carried the slumbering infant up to
her nursery to tuck her into her crib. And even though she
still wasn't sleeping through the night, she no longer awoke
screaming in two-hour intervals. She continued to have occasional bouts of fussiness, but the howling, which he had
begun to think would never leave her, had abated. Slowly,
finally, he was growing accustomed to having a baby in his
home. And slowly, finally, his life with Juliana was beginning to slip into some kind of vague routine.

A routine that included Zoey Holland, he realized reluctantly. Any semblance of order he had managed to develop
in his life was there as a result of her efforts. And she would
only be with him and Juliana for another week. What were
they going to do when she was gone? he wondered. What
was *he* going to do?

He returned to the den to find the woman to whom he
owed so much still sleeping soundly. God, she must be exhausted, he thought. He'd been coming home late enough
every evening that there was no way she could have been
getting more than a few hours of sleep a night. Even less
than that on those nights she'd spent at his house taking care
of Juliana. He suddenly felt like a heel for keeping her from
her rest. He above anyone knew how debilitating it was to
go without sleep.

Not having the heart to rouse her, he pulled a heavy cotton throw from the back of a chair and draped it over her.
He was tucking it up under her chin, being careful not to
awaken her, when she did just that. Her eyes fluttered open,

widened when she saw who was tending to her, then narrowed in what Jonas couldn't decide was curiosity or apprehension. Probably a little of both, he finally concluded. Heaven knew he'd done nothing this week that might inspire her to feel anything else for him.

"You're awake," he said softly.

"You're home," she remarked at the same time.

Both of them chuckled, realizing the superfluousness of their statements in light of the obvious.

"I'm sorry I'm late again," he apologized. "But a meeting ran long, then something came up in cardiology, and—"

"Don't worry about it," she interrupted sleepily. She sighed, pulling her hand out from beneath the throw to swipe it slowly over her face. "I don't have to work tonight, remember? I started my weekend when I got off this morning." She glanced at her watch. "But I really should get going. It's late."

Her face was rosy from sleep, and she'd messed up her hair when she ran her hand through her bangs. Her green eyes were dreamy and soft, and she suddenly seemed approachable in a way she'd never been to Jonas before. Far too approachable for his peace of mind.

"Why don't you stay here tonight?" he asked, the words out of his mouth before he realized he'd planned to say them. "It's freezing rain outside," he rushed on, pretending that was the reason for his invitation, "and they're predicting it will be mixed with snow before eleven. You're obviously exhausted, so it could be treacherous trying to get home. I almost didn't make it into the driveway myself."

For a moment, he thought she was going to agree to his suggestion, but she never opened her mouth to do so. Instead, she looked at him kind of funny, almost as if she were grateful to him for something.

"Why didn't you tell anyone at the hospital about me?" she finally asked him.

It took a moment for him to figure out what she meant. When he did, so taken aback was he by the question that he dropped to sit on the sofa beside her. Then, for some reason feeling suddenly and inexplicably devilish, he stretched one arm across her to rest it on the back of the sofa. "How do you know I didn't?" he asked her softly.

She was clearly unshaken by his question. "Because it would have gotten back to me by now if you had."

He studied her acutely, wondering how she could even ask him something like that. "Why would I go out of my way to tell anyone at work about your sex life—or lack thereof?"

"Because most men would."

"Then you obviously don't know me at all. I'm not most men."

She shrugged and looked away, squirming visibly beneath the cover. "Maybe I don't," she conceded.

It was the first time he could ever remember her admitting that she might have been wrong about something. And the fact that her admitted mistake involved her feelings toward him made Jonas feel a little giddy inside. Without thinking, he dropped the hand he had settled on the back of the sofa to Zoey's waist, skimming his fingers lightly over the throw until he had her loosely penned in. He knew he was asking for trouble, knew he might be setting himself up for another swift knee to the groin. But something in her expression made him willing to take the risk.

Slowly, Zoey sat up from her prone position. But she didn't scoot away from him as he had thought she would. Nor did she double up her fist and smash it into his face, as he also might have anticipated. Instead, she just sat there, her face mere inches away from his, and watched him, waiting.

"We could…we could change that, though, you know," he told her, lowering his voice. "If you want. We could get to know each other better."

She shook her head almost imperceptibly. "It's probably not a good idea," she said, her own voice scarcely a whisper. "I don't think—"

Jonas silenced her with a kiss he knew he was mad for stealing. But he couldn't help himself. She was just so beautiful, so warm, so soft and inviting. He waited for her to retaliate, waited for the rush of pain she would surely inflict when she realized what he had done, what he continued to do. But instead of injuring him, Zoey kissed him back. Gingerly, tentatively, as if she were thinking hard about what she was doing. She kissed him, he realized suddenly, as if she really meant it.

"That's it," he murmured against her mouth. "Don't think. Just feel. Feel what it is you do to me. What I can do to you."

And with that, he kissed her again.

Zoey wasn't sure why she let Jonas kiss her. She only knew that when he did, something about his embrace blinded her to everything but him. There was nothing in her past to trouble her, nothing in her future to concern her. All she could register was the tangle of his fingers in her hair, the way he smelled like Ivory soap, the brush of his lips on hers and the way his eyes had held a promise—the promise that nothing he would do would ever cause her pain.

And then even those vague perceptions began to fade away, and she was left with the dizzying sense that she was falling. Jonas roped one arm around her waist to pull her closer, then cupped her nape with his free hand to rub idle circles on her neck. His mouth moved to her cheek, her temple, her jaw, then down to her neck where he tasted her with the tip of his tongue.

"Oh," she murmured softly. "Oh, Jonas."

"I don't want to rush you," she heard him say, his voice a scant whisper beside her ear. "I don't want to make you do anything you don't want to do."

"Why?" she asked breathlessly. "Because you're afraid of getting kneed in the groin again?"

She had meant the comment to be a joke and waited for him to laugh, or chuckle, or even smile. Instead, he pulled away from her, dropped his hands harmlessly to her waist and studied her.

"No," he said evenly, his eyes blazing with something she couldn't quite identify. "Because I don't want to hurt you or scare you the way he did."

Her heart hammered hard in her throat. "The way who did?" she asked.

"Whoever it was that made you so intent on steering clear of men for so long." He lifted a hand to curl his fingers gently over her jaw and cheek, and she nearly melted with the gentleness of the gesture. "Look, Zoey," he went on, "I can't imagine any other reason why a woman like you would so steadfastly avoid a romantic entanglement. You're too...too..."

"Too what?" she demanded, feeling suddenly defensive.

He smiled as he said, "Too incredibly amazing. You're like no woman I've ever met. Any man would bend over backward to make sure he pleased a woman like you."

She uttered a dubious chuckle. "That's what you think. Most men these days don't give a damn how they treat a woman, as long as they get what they want."

"Then you've been running around with the wrong kind of man."

"Nowadays, there's only one kind of man."

"No," he told her with a decisive shake of his head. "That's not true at all. And I think, deep down, you know that. You're just afraid to admit that there might possibly be someone out there you could care for. Someone who could care for you in return. I think you're just afraid of getting hurt, because some jerk guy did a number on you somewhere in your past."

A long, silent moment passed that Zoey spent wondering just how much she should tell Jonas about herself. "Two," she finally said, surprised at the decision she made.

He stared at her blankly. "What?"

"Two guys did a number on me somewhere in my past. But it wasn't what you think. It didn't happen that way at all."

His expression went from blank to wary, but she had no idea what he was thinking. "Do you want to talk about it?" he asked her.

Not really, she thought. She'd told no one about what had happened to her all those years ago. The only reason Cooper knew about it was because he had been the one to pick her up and shake some spirit back into her again after her husband had left her. But there was something about Jonas that made her want to open up and tell him about that time. Zoey wasn't sure what it was or why he should be different from other people in her life, but for some reason, sharing her past experience with him felt like the most natural thing in the world.

"I was sixteen when I got pregnant," she began, feeling as if she were speaking from somewhere very far away.

"Pregnant?" Jonas repeated.

She could hear his astonishment in that one-word question, but she didn't comment on it. If he thought he was astonished now, she wondered, how he would react when she concluded her story?

"Yes, pregnant," she continued. "I was very much in love with my baby's father, and he was in love with me. We were just a couple of kids whose adolescent passion got out of hand, but that's where the cliché ends." She sighed as she recalled the memories she had forbidden herself for so many years. "I had the baby shortly after we graduated from high school, but it wasn't your typical teens-in-trouble scenario. Jack had a pretty good job working as a mechanic, and we'd been planning to get married after we graduated, anyway. The baby just moved the timing up a little, that's all."

She smiled as she remembered what happened next. "We left Pittsburgh and found a little apartment in South Philly, downstairs from Jack's grandmother. She helped me out a lot with the baby when he arrived. Jack and I named him Eddie, after Jack's late father. The first few months were pretty rough on both of us, but once we got used to parenting, we really got into it. And we were really good at it," she added enthusiastically. "We may have just been a couple of kids, but it was like Jack and I were made for being a dad and mom. The three of us had so much fun together. Jack and I made all kinds of plans for Eddie's childhood."

There was a long, silent pause, presumably because Jonas was waiting for her to continue. But the rest of the story came to Zoey reluctantly, and for a long time she simply couldn't speak.

Finally he asked, "So what happened?"

She sighed again and stared down at her hands. Without realizing it, she had tangled them up in the throw's thick fringe while she was speaking. Now she released the heavy fabric and began to smooth out the wrinkles, but she didn't really pay much attention to what she was doing. "What happened was that Eddie never quite made it into childhood," she said quietly. "When he was eighteen months old, he came down with bacterial meningitis. Before a week was out, he was gone."

"Oh, Zoey." She felt Jonas's hand cover hers and reflexively curled her fingers with his. "Zoey, I am so sorry."

She felt her chin begin to crumple and bit her bottom lip to stop the action. "Yeah, me, too," she finally said, her voice sounding weak and distant. "He was such a sweetheart, you know? And so incredibly bright. By the time he got sick, he was walking and talking better than most two-year-olds. Big gray eyes, curly blond hair. Eyelashes that would have been every woman's downfall," she added with a forced chuckle. "That little guy could charm the birds right out of the trees. I can only imagine what he'd be like now. He would have turned twenty this summer."

The realization stunned her. She hadn't, until that moment, allowed herself to think about how old Eddie would be now. "It's just as well," she said softly, still staring at her hands. "He probably would have caused me all kinds of grief, been in trouble all the time. He would have had to fight off the girls with a big stick. Who knows? He probably would have wound up in the same kind of trouble as Jack and me. I might even be a grandmother by now."

Something wet and warm fell onto Zoey's hand, and only then did she realize she had started to cry. It felt strange crying for Eddie. So many years had passed since she had. What had happened to her when she was a teenager seemed almost as if it had occurred in another person's life. She didn't allow herself to think about her son these days. Sometimes, if she tried very hard, she could almost make herself believe the whole experience had been a dream.

"Zoey..." Jonas began again. But his voice trailed off after he uttered her name, as if he simply couldn't think of anything adequate enough to say.

"Jack and I tried to make it alone after Eddie's death," she began again. "We really did try. We even talked about having another baby. But we were both so devastated that we just couldn't do what was..."

This time it was Zoey's voice that faded away for a moment. She rubbed at her eyes before she spoke again. "I guess I never have forgiven him for not being there for me when I needed him. Then again, I wasn't there for him, either. We were so young, and our emotions were still kind of immature. We finally split up about six months after Eddie's...six months later. The divorce became final on my twentieth birthday. The next day, I enrolled in nursing school."

"Because of your son's illness," Jonas said. His comment was a statement, not a question, as if there were no way of denying its truth.

She nodded. "I'd never considered a career in nursing before Eddie. But the nurses at the hospital were always so helpful, so comforting. I don't know what Jack and I would have done without them. I guess, somewhere along the line, I decided it was the kind of job I wanted."

Jonas paused for a moment before venturing, "No, I meant, maybe you went into nursing for another reason that had to do with your son." His next words were offered slowly, as if he were being cautious about Zoey's reaction. "Maybe because you felt helpless to prevent Eddie's death, but by becoming a nurse, you could help other children."

Zoey shook her head. "Oh, no. I'm sure it's not that at all."

Jonas didn't contradict her, but she had the feeling he wanted to. Before she could address the matter, though, he asked, "Did you see much of your ex-husband after...after that?"

"Only once," she told him. "About five years ago at Terminal Market. I was waiting in line to buy some halibut, and I saw Jack standing in line at the next stall to buy produce. He'd gained a lot of weight and lost a lot of hair, but I recognized him immediately. He didn't see me, though, so I didn't say anything to him.''

What Zoey didn't tell Jonas was that one reason she had said nothing to her ex-husband was because she had noticed the gold band on his left ring finger. The other reason was that a little girl who looked to be about six years old had run up to him with a demand to be held by her daddy. Jack had laughed—the way he used to laugh, Zoey recalled, before Eddie had died—and scooped up the child into his arms, and the little girl had hugged him back with all her might.

Jack had gotten on with his life, Zoey thought now. So why couldn't she get on with hers?

"Zoey, I had no idea—'' Jonas began.

"No, of course not,'' she interrupted with a sniffle, swiping at her eyes. "How could you? I haven't told anyone about it. Cooper is the only one at Seton who knows, and that's only because he and I have been good friends since way back. Not even Livy and Sylvie know about Eddie. And I'd appreciate it, Jonas, if you wouldn't repeat any of this to anyone. It's not something I can share easily. And it's certainly not something I want to relive again.''

But she had shared it with him, Jonas thought. And she had relived it for him. Why had she told him about her baby when she hadn't revealed it to even her closest friends? And now that he was one of the few people who had knowledge of her past, how was that going to change things between the two of them?

"I haven't been romantically involved with anyone since Jack,'' Zoey continued. "I don't know why, really. For years after my marriage dissolved, I just wasn't interested in starting a relationship. Then when I finally did start dating again, no one seemed to be worth the trouble somehow. All the guys I've known have wanted to move things along so quickly. And nurturing a new relationship takes so much time. Eventually I just lose patience or get exhausted. Does that make sense?''

He wanted to tell her that she was being unrealistic or that her expectations were too high, that relationships were there to be had for anyone looking hard enough. He wanted to say that shutting herself off from the possibility of falling in love again was just a way of hiding from life. But for some reason, what she said did, indeed, make sense. Hadn't he felt that way himself for the most part? That he simply didn't have the energy or time to spend on developing a lasting relationship? Now that he thought about it, maybe he was the one who was being unrealistic, the one who was hiding from life. At least Zoey had a legitimate reason for her hesitation to get involved. What was the explanation for his?

"I should go," she said softly when he offered no response to her question.

She struggled to liberate herself from the tangles of the throw, but unless Jonas rose from the couch, there was little chance she would free herself. So he remained where he was, his hands still settled loosely on her hips, waiting until she realized he wasn't going anywhere.

"Jonas?" she asked when he made no move to facilitate her movements. "Would you mind shifting over a little so I can get out?"

He nodded. "Yes. I'd mind very much."

She looked at him then, the first time her gaze had connected with his since she had begun her story about the loss of her child so many years ago. But she said nothing in response to his statement, only stared at him as if seeing him for the first time.

"I don't want you to leave, Zoey," he told her softly. He lifted his hand to her shoulder, pushing back a long shaft of hair. Then he cupped her cheek in his palm and touched his forehead to hers. "In fact, I think it would be a terrible mistake if you left. For both of us. I think you should stay here with me tonight. All night. I think we should be together."

Something inside Zoey sputtered to life at his quietly voiced desire, something vaguely familiar but virtually forgotten. He made her feel warm in a way she hadn't felt for a very long time. He made her feel good. Telling Jonas about her son had changed things between the two of them. And it had changed something in her, too. She felt freer somehow, less burdened. Before tonight, she would have sworn she had left her pain well buried in the past, that what had happened to Eddie in no way colored the way she lived her life today. Now she saw how wrong she had been. Eddie's death weighed heavily on her still. But somehow, in recounting the experience to Jonas, she had let a little bit of her grief go.

She had also moved herself closer to him than she had moved to anyone else in her life. By sharing with him something she had shared with no one else, she had invited him into a part of her heart that had been empty for years. And suddenly, she had no desire for him to leave there. Like Jonas, she wanted them to be together. She only wished she knew what would happen once they were.

"Don't go, Zoey," she heard him say.

And feeling as if she were speaking from a part of herself she didn't even recognize, she heard herself reply, "I won't."

Eight

It was uncanny, the way Jonas's softly uttered plea made Zoey forget about everything. Gone was the newly roused grief for her long-dead son. Gone were the memories of a young husband who had been unable to help her out of the darkest time in her life. Gone was the guilt that she had been likewise incapable of coming to his aid, and helpless to keep her son alive. All were buried deep inside her once again. But for how long they would remain so well concealed, Zoey could only guess.

Forever, she tried to tell herself. She wouldn't think of such things ever again. At least, not until tomorrow. And right now, tomorrow felt as though it were a lifetime away.

She wasn't sure how she wound up in Jonas's bedroom. She only knew that one moment the two of them had been in the den talking, and the next she was standing beside him in his room, a thin silver shaft of moonlight that fell across the bed the only illumination to guide them. It was so quiet, she marveled. The murmur of their breaths commingling in the darkness was the only sound she registered.

And then Jonas kissed her, and even that sound faded away. His lips on hers were warm and tender—more loving than passionate, more persuasive than demanding. He kissed her mouth, her jaw, her cheek, her temple, then he bent and pressed his forehead to hers.

"I don't want to rush you," he told her again. "You're the one who should set the pace here. You tell me what to do."

In the dim light from the full moon outside, all Zoey could make of his eyes was a soft glimmer of earnestness. "Hold me," she said quietly. "For now, just hold on to me, as if you'll never let me go."

Jonas enfolded her in his arms and held her close, bunching her hair in one hand, stroking her back with the other. For a long time they only stood locked in their embrace, then something inside of Zoey began to stir. What started as a warm sensation uncoiling in her stomach gradually grew to a flame of heat that licked at her heart. She curled her fists into the soft fabric of his shirt, digging her fingers into the warm flesh beneath, and pulled him closer to her still.

He smelled wonderful, she thought, tilting her head to nestle her face in the warm skin between his shoulder and jaw. So clean and musky and masculine. He had unbuttoned the top two buttons on his shirt, and his tie hung askew where he had loosened it. She lifted a hand to trace her finger along the strong line of his throat, loving the rough feel of the skin she encountered. Dipping her hand lower, she ventured inside his collar, curving her hand around his nape before kissing the side of his neck.

Salty. His skin was warm and salty. She licked her lips to savor him again, and the knowledge of his taste on her mouth sent a shiver of delight shimmying through her. She wondered if he tasted that good all over. She dropped her hand gingerly to the front of his shirt, slowly unfastening the rest of his buttons in an effort to find out.

Jonas stood perfectly still as she undressed him, save the occasional brush of his knuckles along her arm or the touch of his fingers on her face. Zoey couldn't look at him as she performed the task, so unfamiliar was she with it. Little by little, she revealed more of him for her inspection, studying each part of him as she went along, renewing so much she had forgotten. His arms were strong, roped with sinew and corded with veins. His chest and torso were a symphony of muscle and dark hair. His legs were the legs of an athlete, brawny, vibrant and powerful looking.

He could crush her with those legs if he had a mind to, she thought. Or he could imprison her in the sweetest kind of vise. The realization made her feel a little giddy.

When he stood before her naked, Zoey could only stare at him. Stare at him and be thankful that the light wasn't better than it was. Even in the scant ray of moonlight, Jonas was magnificent. Her gaze traveled the length of him from head to toe, lingering just long enough at his midsection to gauge the full potential of his masculinity.

"Oh, my," she whispered with a reverent smile before lifting her gaze to meet his.

Jonas smiled back at her. "Not yet. But I will be yours. Anytime you're ready."

Zoey's smile grew broader. "I'm ready now."

It was a lie, but she couldn't tolerate the distance between them any longer. She wanted to touch him, all of him, and wanted him to touch her in return. But something inside her still quailed at the threat of closeness. It had been so long since she'd opened herself up to another human being. So long since she had felt any kind of deep emotional response to anyone. The last time she had done so, she'd ended up cold and numb inside. For the first time in almost twenty years, she was beginning to warm up again. She wasn't sure she would make it if she lost that warmth again.

Jonas approached her slowly, as if giving her ample time to change her mind. He cupped his palm over one cheek as he bent to press his lips softly against the other. Zoey closed her eyes when he dropped his hands to the hem of her sweatshirt, then lifted her arms obediently when he tugged it up over her head. When her hair fell in a fiery cascade over her face, his fingers joined hers in brushing it back over her shoulders. Then his hands were on her shoulders, his thumbs hooked deftly beneath the straps of her brassiere to drag them down over her arms.

Instinctively, she crossed her arms over her chest in a gesture of self-preservation. Jonas curled his fingers to brush the backs of his knuckles over the tops of her breasts, skimming them back and forth, lower and lower, until he gently urged her hands away. Zoey reached behind herself to unhook her bra, forcing herself to stand still when the wisp of white lace fell away. For one silent moment, Jonas only stared at her, then he cupped his hands over her breasts and bent to taste one.

The sensation was exquisite. Zoey squeezed her eyes shut and let the ripple of heat wind through her. His mouth opened more fully over her, and he drew the dusky peak of her breast deep inside to suckle hungrily at her. She buried her fingers in his hair to pull him closer, then gasped when he nipped her playfully with his teeth. Immediately he laved the place he had violated, then tugged her deep into his mouth again. For long moments, he so favored first one breast, then the other, until he dropped his hands to the waistband of her jeans.

Button by button, he unfastened the folds of denim, dipping his hand inside the heavy fabric to explore her more explicitly. Zoey gasped at the intimate touch, the heat that had been simmering inside her suddenly exploding into a white-hot incandescence. Jonas moved his hands to her waist, then scooped them inside her jeans to cradle her derriere before shucking the garment away with her panties.

Then, Zoey, too, stood naked, and Jonas was the one to admire. A wicked smile curled his lips, and his eyes glittered hotly in the pale light.

"Oh, my," he said, mimicking her remark of some time ago.

She smiled back at him. "Anytime you're ready," she whispered.

"I've been ready for months," he told her as he reached for her.

And although she didn't say so, Zoey wondered if maybe she hadn't been waiting for him for even longer.

The feel of his body against hers was like something from a sleep-scattered dream. She had forgotten what it was like to be this close physically to another human being, had forgotten what such nearness could stir inside her. She had forgotten how a man could make her feel inside—safe and secure, beautiful and loved. How long had it been since she'd felt any of those things?

When they tumbled backward onto the bed, he was hot and hard and heavy atop her, and Zoey was nearly overcome by a need she would have sworn she was no longer capable of feeling. A need for him. For Jonas. No one else would do.

He rolled to his back and pulled her on top of him, wrapping his arms fiercely around her waist as if he feared she would try to leave him. "You set the pace," he told her again. "Tell me what you want me to do. Where you want me to be. How fast I should go."

It was a dizzying assignment, a heady obligation to have. A powerful surge of desire rocked her as she considered the task ahead. And then, with great care and much thought, she carried out his instructions.

"I want..." she began slowly, "I want you, Jonas. All of you. However you'll come to me. Wherever you want to be. Let's just let it happen. Let's both set the pace."

"You're sure?"

"I'm sure."

"Well, if you say so..."

He kissed her again, turning so that their bodies were side by side. He grazed his hand over her bare back to settle it securely on her bottom, then looped a long leg over her thigh. Effectively penned, Zoey tangled her fingers in the coarse hair scattered across his chest, raking her nails down along his abdomen until she encountered the part of him that had so intrigued her. Cradling him intently in her hand, she let her fingers explore him.

Jonas growled for mercy, but uttered the words into Zoey's hair, therefore making them unintelligible. As she continued with her cautious ministrations, though, he decided maybe the misunderstanding wasn't such a bad thing, after all. He'd never in his life experienced the overpowering response to a woman's touch that Zoey commanded with her tentative caresses. Inspired by her tender manipulation, he rolled until she sat atop him, straddling his waist. Then, fixing his hands firmly on her hips, he urged her body forward.

She moved willingly with his silent command and, evidently understanding his intent, arched her back to give him fuller access to the prize he sought. When Jonas tasted her the first time, she sucked in her breath as if fearful of drowning. When he tasted her the second time, she exhaled in a rush of delight. When he tasted her the third time, she groaned and leaned over him, her long hair flowing down to envelop them like a ruddy curtain that kept the rest of the world at bay.

Only when she could no longer tolerate the wonderful torture of his mouth pressed so intimately against her did Zoey move away. She scooted back down the length of his body until she again encountered his solid presence, curled her fingers firmly around it and guided him toward the heated center he had so inflamed.

Before she could join herself with him, however, Jonas rolled again, shifting their positions so that she felt the warm sheet against her back and smelled the lingering remnants of him on the pillow beneath her head. His face hovered only inches above her own, his breath like a warm summer breeze against her neck.

"I want to be close to you when I'm inside you," he told her, his voice a rough, ragged whisper. "I want to be touching every part of you I can reach. I don't want to know where my body ends and yours begins. I want us to be one."

She smiled as she lifted a hand to brush back a damp lock of his hair. "I thought this was about what *I* want," she said softly.

"It's about what *we* want," he reminded her. "You said you want me however I'll come to you. And this is it. I'll come to you with every inch of my body, every fiber of my soul, every ounce of my emotions, every—"

She pressed her fingers against his lips to halt the flow of promises. "Don't," she whispered. "Don't give me that much."

He gazed at her, and even in the moonlight she could see that he was puzzled. "Why not?" he asked.

"Because it's too much."

"But—"

"Just give me tonight," she told him. "That's the only promise I want from you. I can't think any further ahead than that."

And before he could deny her, she circled her fingers around him and brought him inside her. Then, arching her back, she urged him further still, so that Jonas could only close his eyes and forget what he had been about to say. He pulled out of her, only to thrust himself even more deeply inside, and Zoey, too, became lost in the erotic dance.

Further and further he drove her to delirium, deeper and deeper she descended. A kaleidoscopic burst of light played before her eyes at the same time a similar explosion of sensation rocked her body. For what seemed like hours she hovered on the brink of a tumultuous euphoria, until she finally allowed herself to free-fall with the waves of delight that shook her. For the first time she could ever remember, Zoey felt liberated. She let herself go wherever Jonas wanted to take her. And he took her to places she never could have imagined.

Eventually, however, she was forced to return. All too soon she was back in his bed, her damp cheek pressed against his, her arms coiled over his slick, hot back. Her hair was tangled in his hands, and her legs were entwined with his. He had gotten what he wanted, she realized vaguely. The two of them felt as one.

Sleep claimed her quickly after that. Never had she felt so exhausted and emptied. Her last thought before unconsciousness claimed her was that empty shouldn't be how she felt. After what she and Jonas had shared together, a person was supposed to feel replete and satisfied, wasn't she? Yet satisfaction eluded Zoey. In its place, she felt confusion and dismay. Thankfully, the feelings didn't last because she drifted into a welcomed slumber that chased away her fears. Thankfully, she wouldn't have to think about them until tomorrow.

It was amazing, Zoey thought early the following morning, how two people could do what she and Jonas had done the night before and be expected to behave normally the next day. The sun had yet to rise into the sky, but there was just enough light present in the room for her to watch him sleep. As she lay naked beside him, wrapped in the striped sheet, she replayed again their performance of a few hours before and felt herself blush from head to toe. Had she really done all that? she wondered yet again. Funny, how quickly a person could lose her inhibitions. It was as if no time at all had passed since the last time she and Jack had made love.

And making love with Jonas had been nothing like making love with her ex-husband. She and Jack had been kids, eager and avid, but in no way expert. Jonas was clearly a very experienced lover. He had been inventive and arousing and more than thorough in seeing to her needs. He'd obviously had a lot more practice than she had.

The realization troubled Zoey. Just what had last night meant to Jonas? Was she simply one more in a string of women he invited to bed with little more than a promise of a very satisfying experience? Would he even want to find her in his bed this morning? Or would she be expected to have risen and returned to her own home with a breezy little lipstick-stained goodbye note?

Better yet, just what had last night meant to *her?* Zoey wondered further. To be honest, she still wasn't sure. Had she actually told Jonas about Eddie? Or had that just been a distant, distressing dream? How could she have revealed the most painful experience of her life to someone she had, until recently, considered an enemy? What had Jonas done to make her open up so easily, so quickly?

She tried not to think about her son these days, tried to classify the entire episode as something that had happened to a young girl she scarcely knew. Sometimes that worked. There were periods when she could go days, even weeks,

without a single thought for Eddie. But ever since she had
taken it upon herself to help Jonas and Juliana, thoughts of
the child she had lost so long ago were creeping more and
more insistently to the forefront of her brain.

And Zoey didn't like that at all. It had taken her so long
to erase the specter of Eddie from her life and move forward. At least, she had thought she had erased him. She had
thought she was moving forward. Now she was beginning to
wonder.

Jonas stirred beside her, and she was helpless not to reach
out to him. She touched her index finger gingerly to his
mouth, tracing the strong line of his lips with much affection. Then she dropped her hand to his chin, drew it along
his rough jaw and down along his neck. Yet he did not rouse
again.

He was so handsome, she thought. He would father
beautiful children. Why, the two of them together could—

She halted the thought as abruptly as it had developed
and jerked her hand away. As quietly as she could, she
pushed herself away from him, taking care not to awaken
him as she climbed out of bed.

The two of them together might have already made a
child, she realized fearfully as she gathered her scattered
clothing. They'd taken no precautions last night, had done
nothing to prevent such an occurrence. A shudder of horror wound through her when she considered the possibility.
She couldn't be pregnant, she told herself as tears stung her
eyes. She couldn't have another child. There was no way she
would survive something like that again.

She hurried from the bedroom and scurried across the hall
to dress in Juliana's room. The baby awoke at the noise of
Zoey's clumsy movements and, relieved, Zoey scooped her
up to take her downstairs for her morning bottle. With any
luck at all, Jonas would sleep late and, after feeding Juliana, she could, indeed, creep out of his house without the
awkwardness of a morning-after goodbye. She'd figure out
the rest of it later.

As quickly as she could, she changed Juliana's diaper and
crept down the stairs, praying silently that the baby's fret-

ful whining for food wouldn't wake up Jonas. So far, so good, she thought as she took a seat at the kitchen table and offered the warmed bottle to Juliana. No sign of the man in question.

Until Juliana drained the bottle dry. Just as Zoey lifted her to her shoulder for a final burp, Jonas stumbled into the kitchen wearing a smile and rumpled pajama bottoms, his robe gaping open to reveal that intriguing expanse of chest she had so reveled in exploring the night before. His hair was wonderfully mussed from the way she had repeatedly wound her fingers through it, and his eyes were lit with laughter and affection.

Affection, she marveled. Was that really what he was feeling?

"Good morning," he greeted her softly.

Zoey opened her mouth to reply, but no words emerged. So she only smiled, hoping the gesture looked more genuine than it felt.

"I didn't even hear Juliana," he said as he shuffled toward her. "Thanks for getting up with her."

"That's okay," Zoey finally managed. "She didn't make much noise. And you were sleeping pretty soundly."

He smiled that toe-curling smile again, and something warm and watery splashed through her midsection. "Gee, I can't imagine why," he murmured lasciviously.

Zoey closed her eyes to the picture of sexy coziness he presented lest she do something really stupid—like put the baby back down in her crib for a long snooze so that she herself could fall face first into Jonas's bed for a quick tumble. Fortunately, Juliana burped—long and loud—and Zoey found an excuse to laugh off the tension bubbling up inside her.

"One thing about Jules," she said when her chuckles subsided. "She really knows how to let go when the time comes."

She continued to pat the baby's back gently as she met Jonas's gaze. He looked unhappy suddenly, and she was pretty sure she knew why.

"Meaning what?" he asked quietly.

Zoey maneuvered Juliana into her arms and stood. "Meaning it's time for me to leave," she said as she approached him.

She extended the satisfied infant toward him, and he automatically lifted his arms to receive her. He was getting better about that, she noted. Gone was the hesitation and reluctance he used to show at the prospect of holding Juliana. He felt more natural with her now, had gained a good deal of confidence where dealing with the baby was concerned. There was really no reason for Zoey to keep coming around, she thought. From here on out, Jonas and the baby were going to be fine together. Nevertheless, a deal was a deal. She still owed him another week. And another week she would give him.

But no more than that.

"You're coming back, right?" Jonas asked, as if reading her thoughts.

"Of course I'll be back. On Monday. To take care of Jules. How's the search for a nanny going, by the way? Do you have any prospects?"

Jonas frowned at her. "I was hoping you meant you were just going home to change your clothes," he said, ignoring her questions. "That you'd be back in a couple of hours. I kind of thought we'd spend the day together—the three of us. After last night—"

"Yeah, last night," Zoey interrupted him. "I hope you aren't going to play more into it than there actually was."

His frown became a glare. "And what *actually* was there?"

She glanced down at her hands, feigning great interest in her recent manicure. "Don't get me wrong, Jonas. It was wonderful. But..."

"But what?"

Finally, she gathered the nerve to meet his gaze. His eyes were stormy and troubled, no longer affectionate.

"But it wasn't...it wasn't..."

"It wasn't what?" he demanded, his voice growing more insistent.

She sighed, rubbing a hand over her forehead in exasperation. "It wasn't something that's going to be repeated," she finally said.

"Why not?"

"Because it shouldn't have happened in the first place."

"Why not?"

Something inside Zoey snapped at the sound of propriety in his voice, and she lost her patience. "Because it was a mistake, that's why," she blurted out.

"It sure as hell didn't feel like a mistake last night. *You* didn't seem to think it was a mistake last night."

"I wasn't thinking last night, period," she said softly. "If I had been, I never would have wound up in your bed. And I certainly never would have told you about—" She bit her lip to keep herself from saying Eddie's name out loud again.

"About your son," Jonas finished the statement for her.

Until he mentioned it, Zoey had been hoping that she did, indeed, dream her revelation of the night before. But clearly Jonas had knowledge of Eddie. And that alone was enough to make her want to steer clear of him forever. The last thing she needed was another reminder of her painful past.

"That's what this is really all about, isn't it?" he asked, his voice softening somewhat. "You shared something with me last night that was a lot more significant than sex and a lot more difficult for you to offer than your body. You told me about your son, something you've told no one else. And now you're scared that you're connected to me in some way you don't want to be connected."

"That's not it at all," she denied, dropping her gaze to her hands once again.

Jonas shifted Juliana to his shoulder and watched Zoey make every effort to keep from falling to pieces before his very eyes. She was lousy at trying to hide her feelings, he thought. He wondered how he could have been fooled by her for so long. Had there really been a time when he'd thought she was hard as nails and tough as leather? Had he actually been convinced that there wasn't a soft spot to be found inside her? That she was incapable of feeling even the remotest kind of warmth?

What an idiot he'd been. Any fool could see that Zoey Holland was a walking mass of emotion held together by little more than an invisible thread of fear. That tough exterior she'd tried to keep hardened had only served to illustrate exactly how fragile she was.

"You don't have to run from me, Zoey," he said softly. "Just because I know something about you that's painful for you to remember, that doesn't mean you have to avoid me."

She shook her head and continued to avoid his gaze. "You don't understand," she said.

"What? What don't I understand?"

"This has nothing to do with...with Eddie," she insisted, her stumble over her son's name telling Jonas just about everything he needed to know. "Last night, we didn't..."

He couldn't prevent the smile that curled his lips. "Didn't what? I thought we pretty much covered the gamut of sexual encounters last night. I did have to draw the line at dressing up like the cowboy and the schoolmarm. But only because by the time you asked me to do it, I didn't have the strength to manage it." His smile broadened. "That and the fact that I really want to invest in a good lariat first. Maybe next time."

"I was only kidding about that," Zoey said with a soft smile.

"Were you?"

She nodded. "For the most part."

His voice softened as he said, "Then I still don't understand what it is you say I don't understand."

She sighed and tried again. "Last night, we didn't...use anything. Any contraceptives."

Jonas's eyes widened in shock at the realization. Good God, they hadn't taken precautions, had they? The thought of doing so hadn't even occurred to him. He was accustomed to going out with women who'd already taken it upon themselves to prevent the possibility of pregnancy. But seeing as how Zoey had been out of commission for so long—and seeing as how what happened last night had come as a pretty big surprise to both of them—there was no reason for her to have taken such an initiative, was there? She could get pregnant, he thought. Hell, she could already *be* pregnant. With his child. The concept numbed him from head to toe.

"Not a pretty thought, is it?" she asked.

As much as he hated to admit it, she had gauged his reaction accurately. The idea of taking responsibility for another baby when he hadn't yet managed to come to terms with the one in his arms was more than a little troubling. Still, once he gave the possibility more consideration, he decided maybe it wasn't such a horrible thing to imagine, after all.

"Don't worry," Zoey went on when he didn't respond. "I'm pretty sure the timing is all wrong for something like that to happen. And anyway, even if it did, it wouldn't be any of your concern."

That remark brought him up short. "Excuse me?" he asked petulantly. "Wouldn't be any of my concern? I think you might be a trifle mistaken about that."

She covered her face with her hands so that he had no idea what her reaction to his assertion might be. She only shook her head and said quietly, "Look, Jonas, I'm not going to argue with you about something that might not even be a reality." She dropped her hands back down to her sides and met his gaze levelly. "For now, just suffice it to say that last night was a mistake. And not just because we didn't take any precautions. It shouldn't have happened in the first place. And it won't happen again."

For a long moment he said nothing, just continued to rock Juliana gently against his shoulder. Finally, he asked, "Are you so certain about that?"

She nodded vehemently. "Absolutely certain."

"You don't want to be around me any more than you have to, is that it?"

"Jonas . . ." She left unsaid whatever it was she intended to tell him, and somehow he had the feeling that it was just as well. He probably didn't want to know what else she had to say.

"So I guess the three of us spending the day together is out of the question," he muttered wearily.

She crossed her arms over her chest as if she were trying to keep them from straying elsewhere. Her expression was bland, however, and could have been indicative of any number of things. "I'm afraid so," she told him. She strode quickly past him and through the kitchen door, calling a quick, "See you Monday," over her shoulder as she went.

The kitchen was annoyingly quiet after she left. Juliana nodded off blissfully on his shoulder and, without thinking, Jonas lifted a hand to splay it open across her back. As he marveled again at how small and fragile she seemed to be, the baby snuggled closer to him and sighed with much contentment. She was his brother's daughter, he reminded himself. Why then, lately, did she feel like his own?

And why, dammit, was he starting to feel as if Zoey would be the perfect mother for her?

He'd never entertained a single thought about having a child of his own. Hell, he'd never even wanted children. With one single tragedy, Jonas had become a father to Juliana. And with one simple gaffe, he may have opened up the possibility of having another child brought into his life.

A father, he thought. Until that moment, he hadn't much felt like one. But as Juliana nuzzled even more comfortably against him, Jonas felt a warmth and satisfaction seep through him. It was unlike anything he'd ever known. No, not a father, he decided, a daddy. He wanted to be a daddy. They were so much more fun than fathers.

He rubbed his chin over the downy hair on Juliana's head and smiled. There was just the question now of finding a mommy to join him. Fortunately for him, Jonas knew exactly where to look.

"Jules," he said softly to the infant dozing on his shoulder. "We have a lot of work to do if we're going to bring Zoey around to our way of thinking. Lucky for us, I have a plan. But I'm going to need your help to execute it."

Nine

"**H**ow did you guys know when you were in love with your husbands?"

Olivia and Sylvie glanced up at each other, exchanged wary looks, then turned to Zoey again.

"Say what?" Sylvie asked.

"Excuse me?" Olivia said at the same time.

Zoey's gaze traveled from one woman to the other, then down to Juliana, whom she cradled in her arms. The baby stared back at her intently, her lower lip thrust to the side. Zoey smiled before looking at her companions again. The three friends had met for lunch at Olivia's house, and each had brought her baby along.

No, Jules is *not* my baby, Zoey reminded herself. Her baby was dead and buried. Jules belonged to Jonas. Zoey wouldn't be having another child, ever again. There was no way she could handle the emotional demands and upheaval that went along with motherhood. Losing Eddie had numbed her to life for years, had wrecked her marriage and damn near eradicated her soul. She knew she couldn't open herself up to the possibility of something like that happening again. It would kill her to lose another family. She simply couldn't take such a risk.

Nevertheless, she continued to wonder if making love with Jonas three nights before had generated a life within her. It was still too early for her to know for sure, but in a matter of days she would have her answer. She told herself she wasn't pregnant, and knew that was for the best. But a part of her simply couldn't be satisfied with that. A part of her wished with all her heart that the two of them had, indeed, created a baby. And that longing inside her was what she feared most. Even more than the possibility that she had fallen in love with Jonas.

Loving Jonas was something she could deal with. Probably. Eventually. In one way or another. The desire to have a child, however, was something else entirely. Something she just wasn't sure she could face.

"I, umm," she began again, "I was just wondering how you two knew for sure when you fell in love with your husbands."

"Why?" the two sisters chorused.

Zoey shrugged. "Just curious is all."

Olivia and Sylvie exchanged suspicious looks again, then eyed their companion with much speculation.

"Is there something you want to tell us, Zoey?" Sylvie finally asked.

"Yeah, we haven't seen too much of you since you took over Jeannette's shift at the hospital," Olivia agreed. "Just what have you been doing with your time these past couple of weeks, anyway? Besides baby-sitting for Jonas Tate's niece?"

"Which in itself has been weird enough," Sylvie remarked. "All this time you've been going on about what a pain in the posterior Dr. Fate is, yet you've gone out of your way to lend him a hand where the baby is concerned."

"And I told you why, too," Zoey reminded them. "Because Jules is a kindred spirit. I don't want her to wind up as some scared kid on the streets like I did because I felt out of place at home. I want her and Jonas to feel comfortable together, that's all.''

"You know, at first, that did seem like a likely enough explanation for your actions,'' Olivia said with a sage nod, "but now that this has been going on for more than a week, I can't help but wonder if your intentions might have changed just a tad.''

"My intentions?'' Zoey echoed, feeling her back go up defensively. "Just what the hell is that supposed to mean?''

"Nothing,'' Olivia said breezily. "Except that maybe you started this little project with Juliana's needs at heart, but that at some point along the way, your intentions, and your interests, went off in a different direction.''

Zoey narrowed her eyes warily. "Oh, really? And just what the hell is *that* supposed to mean?''

Olivia looked over at her sister. "You did finally meet Dr. Tate, didn't you, Sylvie?''

"Yeah, you introduced him to me at the hospital that day Gennie and I stopped by, remember?''

Olivia nodded. "That's right. And what did you think of him?''

Sylvie smiled, wiggling her blond eyebrows suggestively. "I thought he was pretty dreamy. A real slab, if you know what I mean.''

Zoey bit her lip to keep from describing for her friends in vivid, erotic detail exactly what a slab Jonas was when exposed to the elements. Instead, she remained silent and wondered about her sanity in bringing up the subject of love in the first place.

"That's what I think, too,'' Olivia agreed. "How about you, Zoey? Word around the hospital has it that you and he aren't quite the antagonists you used to be. Cooper Dugan, for example, has even gone so far as to call the two of you friends.''

"Cooper has no idea what he's talking about,'' Zoey told them. "As usual.''

"Really?'' Olivia asked. "Then that story about you spending two nights at Jonas's house is completely false?''

Zoey felt the blood rush to her face and dropped her gaze once again to the baby in her lap lest her friends see how badly she was blushing. Dammit, why had she mentioned to Cooper that her baby-sitting activities for Jonas had included a couple of nights' sleepover? Never mind that *those* two nights had been perfectly innocent—well, at least to an extent. She should have known the paramedic wouldn't be able to keep the news to himself.

"You didn't!" Sylvie exclaimed. "Zoey, how could you do something like that? How could you spend the night with that man—*two* nights with that man—a virtual stranger, and not give your two best friends all the gory details afterward?"

"Because there weren't any gory details," Zoey told them. No, she thought further to herself. The details had been more of a torrid nature. But there was no reason Sylvie and Livy had to know that, right? "And Jonas was hardly a stranger," she added. "I'd been working with him for months."

"And hating him for months," Sylvie reminded her. "At least, that's what you always *said.*"

"Because it was true," Zoey told her.

"*Was* true," Olivia repeated. "We must take note of the use of the past tense here. I think it might be significant. Especially since the past in question involved hate, and I distinctly remember this conversation starting out with the subject of love." She turned to look at her sister. "Sylvie, I do believe this is going to be interesting."

Sylvie nodded in return. "Livy, I do believe you're right."

In unison, the two sisters turned silently to Zoey for clarification.

"Okay, okay," she relented. "I did spend the night with him. More than once. But those two nights Cooper told you about weren't what you think." There, she thought, that was suitably evasive enough without being untrue, wasn't it?

"You didn't sleep with him?" Sylvie asked pointedly.

Zoey felt herself blushing again and tried to stall. She and Jonas hadn't actually done much sleeping that one night, had they? she tried to tell herself. So denying Sylvie's charge wouldn't exactly be a lie, would it? Still, her friend's implication was unmistakable. Then again, it was really none of Sylvie's business.

"Oh, come on, Zoey," Sylvie cajoled. "Fair's fair. Livy told us about doing the wild thing with Daniel that one night. And I told you guys all about it when I slept with Chase that first time."

"I only told you two about Daniel because you guys bullied it out of me," Olivia reminded her sister. "And you only told us about sleeping with Chase that first time because you got pregnant as a result. You had no choice but to tell us about it. I think we would have suspected something of the kind after you started ballooning out like a blowfish."

"Yeah, but you wouldn't have known Chase's identity if I hadn't told you," Sylvie said petulantly.

"Oh, and when did you tell us his identity, hmm?" her sister asked. "Not until you were about four centimeters dilated, if memory serves."

"That's beside the point, Livy. We have as much right to know about Zoey as she—"

"All right, yes, I slept with him," Zoey interrupted. Only after the words had left her mouth did she realize what she had done. Too late, she slapped a hand over her lips, as if in doing so she could take back her momentous confession. Unfortunately, when she saw two stunned faces staring back at her, she realized there was no way she was going to escape this one.

"You didn't," Olivia said with a satisfied smile.

"You did?" Sylvie asked at the same time.

Zoey nodded. "I did. Friday night. But that was the only time. I honestly didn't plan on it happening. It just sort of... happened. I don't know how. I really can't explain it. I just..."

"Hey, you don't have to tell me," Olivia said. "That's pretty much how it was with Daniel that first time. But everything worked out great, didn't it? We've got a perfectly good happily-ever-after going."

"Me, too," Sylvie volunteered.

"Yeah, but your first time with Chase was no accident," her sister reminded her. "The only reason he showed up was because he was contractually obligated."

"That wasn't the *only* reason," Sylvie said with an indignant sniff. "And besides, he and I have a perfectly good happily-ever-after going, too."

Zoey studied each of the women carefully. "But you two got married to the men in question," she said, as if marriage and happily-ever-afters were mutually exclusive conditions. After all, they were, weren't they? Her marriage hadn't exactly ended up happily. Quite the contrary.

"Of course we married the men in question," Olivia said. "That's what you do when you fall in love."

"Not necessarily," Zoey objected. "Not always."

"Well, no, not if you're stupid," Sylvie conceded. "Not if you want to let something incredibly wonderful slip away."

Zoey opened her mouth to protest, then closed it again, mostly because she couldn't think of an effective protest to utter. What Sylvie said made sense, she thought. When two people fell in love, they did naturally want to spend the rest of their lives together. Therefore, what she felt for Jonas must not be love. Because she had no desire to be with him forever.

What the two of them had now, although hazy by definition, wasn't a forever-after kind of thing. Friday night, she had experienced with Jonas a pleasure unlike anything she could have imagined. And of course, there was Jules, for whom she cared a very great deal. Zoey did enjoy being with Jonas and Juliana on a day-to-day basis. Her life had grown richer over the past two weeks because of their presence in it. But surely that wasn't enough to constitute love, was it?

"So how did you know when you were in love with your husbands?" she asked her friends again.

Olivia thought for a moment before replying. "I think the exact moment was when he took me to that horrible biker bar and threatened to have his way with me on the pool table," she finally said.

Sylvie nodded as if she understood perfectly. "With Chase, I think it was when he forced me to eat brussels sprouts."

Zoey shook her head at the two women. "Some help you are."

Olivia and Sylvie patted her on the back simultaneously.

"Any time we can be of service, Zoey," Olivia said.

"You just let us know," Sylvie concluded.

Zoey was emptying the dishwasher of clean baby bottles on Tuesday when Jonas came home from work early. He was accompanied by a woman Zoey had never seen before, a woman who was older than he by a good twenty years and who reminded Zoey a lot of her Aunt Celeste in the early days. Both women had ample torsos, lovely white hair tinged with pink, the sheen of support hose covering their legs and an obvious affinity for solid, no-nonsense shoes. He introduced the woman as Mrs. Standard, a name Zoey somehow found extremely appropriate for her, and said she was to be Juliana's new nanny.

Just like that.

Zoey stood dumbfounded for a moment, looking at the two of them in silence, then forced herself to smile. "You found someone," she managed to say. "That's wonderful." She made herself move forward to shake the other woman's hand, her frozen smile beginning to feel frigid. "It's so nice to meet you. I'm a friend of Dr. Tate's, Zoey Holland. Jonas, can I speak to you for a minute?" she added without missing a beat.

"Sure, Zoey," he replied, not moving from Mrs. Standard's side.

"Alone?" Zoey clarified, hoping the nod of reassurance she offered to the other woman at least *looked* genuine.

"Oh. Sure. Mrs. Standard?"

"I'll just wait in the living room," the older woman said with a smile that was, in fact, quite warm and friendly. Her voice was lightly accented with a Southern flavor, and Zoey could tell she was just dripping with pleasantness and decency. Damn her.

"Thanks," Jonas said with a smile that was equally sunny.

God, all this smiling was going to make her sick to her stomach, Zoey thought. Nevertheless, all the smiles told her a lot. Mrs. Standard's told her that the other woman was happy to have the job of nanny and felt perfectly capable of performing it. Jonas's told her he trusted the other woman implicitly with his niece's care, illustrated beyond question that he found Mrs. Standard to be a person of unimpeachable character. It told Zoey he had no doubt that he had found the perfect care giver for the little baby she had considered her responsibility for the past week and a half.

And it told her she wouldn't be needed around here anymore.

In spite of the fact that Mrs. Standard was well out of earshot, Zoey kept her voice low as she asked, "Are you sure she's right for the job?"

Jonas looked puzzled. "Of course she's right for the job. Look at her. She's perfect. She raised five kids of her own and has twelve grandchildren."

"And they don't keep her busy enough?"

"She and her husband moved up here from Tennessee, which is where the rest of her family still lives.'

Zoey nodded knowingly. "Oh, so in other words, she could be moving back there anytime, abandoning Juliana without a backward glance, thereby wreaking potentially irrevocable damage on her developmental growth."

He narrowed his eyes somewhat at her charge, but shook his head slowly. "No, that won't happen. Her husband is from South Jersey originally, and they're retiring to his family home in Cherry Hill.''

She nodded again, more vigorously this time. "Oh, so in other words, they have plenty of money, and she doesn't need to work and will quit as soon as the novelty wears off or she realizes how demanding a full-time job is, without a care for what her callous change of mind could do to Jules's fragile self-esteem."

"No," he told her, rubbing his chin thoughtfully, "she went to work full-time as a nanny once all of her children were in school. That was more than twenty years ago. And because her husband was self-employed, he doesn't have a pension for them to rely on. She really needs this job."

Zoey bit her lip while she tried to think of another objection. "Does she have references?"

Jonas nodded. "Of course. And only of the most glowing variety. The only reason her former employers let her go is because all of their children grew up."

Zoey tapped her foot uneasily and tried to think of something else that might impede Mrs. Standard's employment, all the while assuring herself it was only because she was concerned for Juliana's welfare. "How about her health?" she finally asked. "Let's face it, she's no spring chicken. She could drop dead of a major coronary anytime." Her eyes widened as she thought of something else. "Oh, jeez. What if Jules was the one to stumble onto her body? And what if she'd been dead for a while and was blue and smelly? If Jules has to face the ghastly specter of death too early in her life, she could be—"

"Mrs. Standard is only fifty-eight," Jonas interrupted. She could tell he was losing his temper. "And she's never been sick a day in her life."

"How do you know? She could have any number of communicable diseases—hepatitis, cholera, Legionnaires', and did you read that typhus is on the rise again? Typhus is something you definitely don't want to mess around wi—"

"I'm a doctor, Zoey. It's my job to know when someone is sick. Mrs. Standard isn't." His mouth tightened into an impatient line. "What the hell is the problem? I thought you were anxious for me to find someone appropriate to care for Juliana."

"Yes, someone *appropriate*," she agreed. "How do you know this Mrs. Standard is appropriate? She might be a smoker, for all you know. And secondhand smoke can cause all kinds of problems for an infant. I'm sure you read that article last month about—"

"She's not a smoker," Jonas said tightly. "And even if she were, as long as she confined her smoking to outside the house, I wouldn't object to it."

Zoey paused only a moment before asking further, "Is she now, or has she ever been, a member of the Communist Party?"

"Zoey!"

"Look, I'm just concerned about Jules is all."

"Well, you don't have to be. Not anymore."

Meaning Jonas wanted her out of Juliana's life, Zoey reasoned. And likewise wanted her out of his. Pronto. She should have expected it. Jonas had gotten all he wanted from her Friday night, and now he wanted her gone. After all, he hadn't even mentioned that night once he'd seen her again Monday morning, had he? No, he'd acted as if nothing at all had changed between them. Of course, Zoey had acted the same way, and had told herself she was grateful for his sudden memory loss, but that was beside the point.

The point was that Jonas didn't need her anymore. And that, she realized, hurt a lot more than she had thought it would.

What was wrong with her? She should be pleased that Jonas had found someone kind and capable to look after Juliana. She should be relieved that she wouldn't have to subject herself day after day to a wonderful little baby that had only brought her painful reminders of the son she had lost so long ago. She should be asking how soon Mrs. Standard could start, should be eyeing the front door in anticipation of her own escape. And she should be jumping for joy that she'd no longer be obligated to a man she had always considered her enemy.

And that was another problem, she thought. Jonas wasn't her enemy anymore. Whether she liked it or not, he had become her lover. Even if for just one night. And that, Zoey decided, was what really troubled her most.

She could probably surrender Juliana into Mrs. Standard's care without worrying about the little girl's welfare *too* much, and without missing her to the point of feeling lost. After all, it wasn't as if the baby was going to be taken from her forever. She could still visit with Jules whenever she wanted. She couldn't see Jonas keeping her from that. If she wanted to, Zoey could probably even still play an active part in Juliana's upbringing as she grew older—taking her out to the zoo or for strolls in the park or on shopping sprees in the city. There was no reason for her to think that Jules couldn't still be a part of her life.

But that would mean tying herself to Jonas, too, even if somewhat tenuously.

And in spite of the confusion winding her up tight inside, confusion over whether or not she wanted to be involved with him, and to what extent that involvement would go, Zoey was pretty certain Jonas had just taken the decision out of her hands. She wasn't necessary to him anymore. He didn't need her around. Not for Juliana, and not for himself.

Which was just as well, she told herself. Regardless of whether or not she wanted to be involved with Jonas, the last thing she needed or wanted was to set herself up for another fall.

"Are you home for the day?" she asked him.

She could see that her question surprised him, but he nodded his response.

"Yes. I thought I'd introduce Mrs. Standard to Juliana and let the two of them get a little used to each other. Then I'll show her around the house, let her know where everything is. She's going to start work on Monday morning, just in time for you to get back to your regular shift at work, not to mention your regular life. Not that I don't appreciate what you've done, Zoey," he added, and she couldn't shake the feeling that it was almost as an afterthought. "You've been a lifesaver. I couldn't have managed—"

She held up her hand to stop the flow of thanks she didn't want to hear. She didn't want gratitude from Jonas Tate. She wasn't sure exactly what she *did* want, but it certainly wasn't that.

"Then if you're home for the day, I'll just head home early myself if it's all the same to you," she said. "If nothing else, I can catch up on my sleep."

"But I thought—"

"Jules has been napping for nearly an hour now," she interrupted him, "so look for her to wake up anytime. I've made enough formula for you to get through to tomorrow morning, and there's a load of her laundry in the dryer that should be done in about twenty minutes."

"Zoey, I—"

"She's starting to get a little rash on her face, around her eyebrows, but I think it's probably just seborrheic dermatitis, a by-product of her cradle cap. Still, you might want her pediatrician to check it out."

"Zoey—"

"I do hope you've gotten a new pediatrician for her, Jonas. That other guy you've been taking her to sounds like a real quack. Julie Kenner over at the medical center is wonderful, and—"

"Zoey!"

He had raised his voice to a decibel that commanded her attention, so she had no choice but to cease the monologue she had hoped would keep him at bay. "What?" she asked him quietly.

"We have to talk."

"About what?"

"About Juliana. About us."

"What about Juliana?"

Jonas duly noted Zoey's focus on the baby and her obvious reluctance to discuss the two of them. Well, tough, he thought. She was going to face a few facts whether she liked it or not.

He took an experimental step toward her as he said, "I realize you've been Juliana's primary care giver for more than a week now, and that you've developed a wonderful rapport with her as a result."

"She's a great baby, Jonas. How could I not develop a rapport with her?"

A second step brought him a bit closer, and he took heart in the fact that she didn't seem inclined to retreat from him. "Actually, it's more than a rapport. Jules clearly adores you, and there are times when you're the only one who can comfort her. I don't think it would be a good idea if she lost you completely."

Jonas took a third, larger step toward Zoey, bringing him within touching distance of her, then cursed himself for pressing his luck. Now she began to look as if she was ready to bolt, as if she didn't want to hear whatever else he might have to say.

That's why he was surprised when she asked, "What do you mean?"

He started to reach out to her, but stopped himself lest even a harmless touch make her skittish. Instead, he curled his fingers into fists and shoved them deep into his trouser pockets. "I mean," he said quietly, "that I'd like for you to still play an active role in Juliana's life, if that's all right with you. I thought maybe you might still want to see her from time to time. Come by the house now and then. Take her places."

When she said nothing in reply, Jonas surrendered to temptation and pulled a hand from his pocket to brush back a length of her hair. Her eyelids fluttered closed, and she inhaled a deep, ragged breath. He took it to be a very good sign.

"I'd also like," he began again, dropping his voice lower, "for you to play an active role in my life, too."

Zoey's eyelids snapped back up at that, and she gazed at him with wary, troubled eyes. "Why?" she asked him.

That was a good question, Jonas thought, and one that deserved a good answer. But he was afraid that if he told her the truth, Zoey would run screaming in terror in the other direction, never to darken his door again. He was quite certain that the last thing she wanted to hear was that he was in love with her.

He shrugged, hoping the gesture came off as careless, when that was the last thing he felt. "Because...because I think there's something going on between the two of us that needs further investigation."

She chewed her lower lip thoughtfully for a moment, then took a step away from him. "If you're talking about Friday night," she said, "I thought we'd already settled that."

Jonas sighed. "Hardly. If anything, your assurance that it was a mistake, never to happen again, has only agitated me more than I was already."

He could see that he'd made her angry with his statement. But instead of regretting having made it, he was glad to finally see some kind of an emotional response from her, even if it was a negative one. After all, this whole thing between them had risen up out of antagonism, hadn't it? Maybe a little good old-fashioned animosity would kick some life back into her. He was tired of seeing her looking so exhausted and defeated. And hurt. Dammit, she looked hurt all the time lately, too.

"Oh, really?" she snapped. "Well, I'm real sorry if you can't control your...your...your agitation, but that's not my problem."

"Oh, yes, it is," he countered. "Because I'm not letting you off the hook until you face up to a few facts."

"Oh? Like what?"

"Like the fact that you and I made love Friday night, and the incredibly satisfied feeling I experienced afterward wasn't just a result of simple sexual gratification. Like the fact that I care about you, Zoey, and I know you care about me. Like the fact that—"

"Whoa, whoa, whoa," she interjected. "Hold it right there. Don't you dare presume to know how I feel about anything. Any caring I may have done about you—"

"*May?*" he demanded. "*Have* done?"

"—has just been because I want to make sure you're not going to shortchange Juliana," she concluded, ignoring his burst of outrage. "It has nothing to do with us...with me."

"Oh, really?" he asked, not even bothering to hide his doubt. "Then that was what Friday night was all about, was it? For two decades—*two decades,* Zoey—you abstained from having sex with anyone, but you made love with me because you were worried about Juliana's welfare? You risked becoming pregnant again because you were concerned that I might not raise her properly?"

A muscle in Zoey's cheek twitched almost imperceptibly, and she clenched her teeth together, hard. But she said nothing in response.

So he continued, dropping his voice to a near whisper. "You could be carrying a baby right now, Zoey. A baby that would be partly mine. If you think I'm going to leave something like that up in the air, then—as I've said on so many occasions—you've misjudged me terribly."

When she continued to remain silent and only arched her left eyebrow at him, Jonas was reminded of the first night she had spent at his house. She looked as if she was ready to belt him again, and he wanted instinctively to cup his hands over that tender part of himself she'd assaulted before. Instead, he curled his fingers over her shoulders and pulled her toward him, pressing his mouth to hers.

Immediately, she melted against him. All the tension, all the anxiety, all the fight, fled from them both, and they fell into the embrace as if it would be their last. Zoey kissed him back with a fervor that put his own to shame, knotting her fingers in his hair, tasting him as if he were a delicacy like none she'd ever savored before.

And then she pushed him away.

Without a backward glance, without a word of farewell, she fled from the kitchen as if in fear of her life. Jonas watched her go, standing in place because he hadn't the energy to move, panting for breath because he'd forgotten to breathe while he was kissing her. His fingers were curled before him as if he still clung to bits of fiery hair, and his lips still burned from her touch. He could still feel the way she had leaned into him, could almost swear the soft globes of her breasts were still pressing against him.

Somehow, Zoey Holland had become a part of him. And there was every possibility that he had become a part of her—physically if not emotionally. She couldn't change that simply by leaving his house. He was damned if he would let her get away that easily.

He dropped his hands to his sides and suddenly remembered that he had a nanny orientation to perform. What was her name again? he wondered for a moment. Standard. Right. Mrs. Standard. Juliana's new nanny.

But just having a nanny wasn't good enough for Jules. Jules deserved a mother, too. Once again, Jonas's thoughts turned to Zoey, and how perfectly suited she was to the part. And once again, he began to hatch a plan. It wasn't perfect, but it wasn't bad. He only hoped Zoey would give him a chance.

Friday would be his last opportunity. Come Friday, one way or another, he'd make Zoey see what was already so clear to him. That she couldn't live without Juliana and him. And they sure as hell couldn't live without her.

Ten

———

Friday morning couldn't have arrived soon enough for Jonas. Not only was it the first opportunity he'd had in months to take a day off, but he'd made very big plans he was anxious to carry out. As he waited for Zoey's knock at his front door, he checked for the third time to make sure he had everything they'd need for the romantic encounter he had spent the past two days planning.

It had been damned difficult yesterday to act as if there wasn't a thing in the world wrong between them, but he'd taken Zoey's lead in the matter. She had come into his house in the morning acting as if she hadn't a care in the world, so he had, too. Today, however, *he* was going to set the tone.

"Picnic basket, check," he noted. "Fresh flowers, check. Candles and matches, check. Lightly chilled chardonnay, check. Clean diapers, check. Favorite rattle, check. Formula, check."

He turned to look at the baby sitting in her bouncer seat at the center of the kitchen table. Juliana gazed back at him with wide blue eyes.

"I think we have everything, don't you, Jules?" he asked her.

She kicked her legs fiercely and set the chair to rocking, then smiled and gurgled at her success.

"You're absolutely right. We *do* need to pack some tunes. How about a little Edith Piaf, hmm? And maybe some Tony Bennett? Oh, okay, and we'll throw in Alvin and the Chipmunks for you."

Juliana cooed her thanks.

"Don't mention it."

The doorbell rang at seven-thirty on the dot, and Jonas freed Juliana from her seat so that the two of them could answer the door together. They opened it to find a shivering, exhausted-looking Zoey on their doorstep, her hands shoved deep inside the pockets of her parka, her nose and eyes red from the cold. Which was odd, Jonas thought, because the temperature was well into the sixties.

"Good morning," he said, hoping the greeting sounded easy and casual and completely free of expectations. He didn't want her to be the slightest bit suspicious of his intentions.

"Borning," she replied, pushing past him. "Sorry I'b lade. Der was a wreck on rude dirdy-aid dat backed up draffic from Cherry Hill all da way do Haddafeel."

It *sounded* as if she was speaking English, he thought. Sort of. At any rate, he was pretty sure she was apologizing for an accident and the rush-hour traffic making her run late.

"That's okay," he told her. "Uh, are you all right?"

"I hab a bad code." To punctuate the announcement, she sneezed. Loudly. Four times.

"Bless you," Jonas said automatically.

"Danks."

"You're welcome."

"I probably shuddin baby-sid wid Jules dooday. Bud if you're pressed, I could wade undil you call someone else. Like Bizzus Standard or sombding."

"Actually, I'm taking the day off today."

Zoey exhaled a deep sigh of relief. "Grade. Dad's grade. Den I'll go hobe and go do bed."

Jonas nodded. "Good idea. Just let Jules and me get our coats, and we'll go with you."

She held up her hand, palm out. "Nod necessary. I don wan do infec' you guys. I'll be okay."

"Forget it," he told her. "You look and sound awful. You shouldn't be by yourself. Jules and I will take good care of you. You'll see."

She opened her mouth to object, but he halted her with a hastily uttered, "I'll drive. You can get your car later."

Before she could insist otherwise, Jonas spun around and returned to the kitchen to retrieve the props he had planned to use that day to bring Zoey around to his way of thinking. She couldn't have timed her illness better, he thought. Naturally he didn't like to see her with a bad cold, but he certainly wasn't going to miss such a prime opportunity. She needed looking after while she was sick, and he was just the person to do it. He was, after all, a doctor. Better than that, he was a doctor in love.

Once and for all, he'd teach Zoey Holland a few lessons that she desperately needed to learn. He'd show her that he wasn't the kind of man she insisted on thinking him. He'd show her that it was possible to go on living after suffering a tragedy like the one she'd suffered so many years ago. And most important of all, he'd show her that the two of them were perfectly suited to each other. Together, he'd prove to her, they could create a miracle. For all he knew, they already had.

"I don wan do expose Jules do my code," she insisted when he returned to the living room.

"As long as you don't pick her up, she'll be fine," he told her. "As you yourself pointed out to me not long ago, she's perfectly healthy. And as members of the medical profession, you and I know that colds are spread through contact. Just don't contact Jules. She'll be fine."

The baby in his arms smiled and cooed her agreement.

"See there?" Jonas said. "She wouldn't think of letting you go home alone."

"Danks, Jules," Zoey muttered dryly. "Bud I hobe you know wad you're gedding yourself indo." Then she noted the picnic basket in Jonas's free hand and the diaper bag that dangled from his shoulder. "Wad's all dat?"

"A sure cure," he told her. "For a lot of things."

"Bud—"

"Now let's go, before you faint from exhaustion."

"I'b nod exhausded, I'b—"

"See there? You're so sick, you're starting to blather incoherently."

"I'b nod bladdering. I'b—"

He cupped his free hand over her forehead. "You feel like you have a slight fever, too," he finished for her. "The sooner we get you to bed, the better."

Zoey eyed him warily and decided not to pursue the obvious double entendre. Maybe Jonas had intended his statement to be suggestive, maybe not. There was no way she could tell, because he was looking at her so blandly—as if nothing in the world had changed about their relationship. As if there wasn't a mountain of muddled emotions messing up everything between them. As if they hadn't spent last Friday night doing all sorts of incredibly arousing things together and had risked the possibility of her becoming pregnant.

As if he had no idea she was fast falling in love with him.

She pushed the thought away. It wasn't love she was feeling for Jonas. It was just some mixed-up, misguided, mistaken sense of yearning, compounded by the bad cold with which she had awakened the night before. Some sappy desire she knew better than to feel, a longing for something she'd had ages ago but would never experience again—the longing for a family.

Spending time with Jonas and Juliana had stirred things in Zoey she hadn't felt since she was a teenager. She should have seen it coming, she told herself now, should have anticipated from the beginning that devoting her time to Jonas and his niece would arouse feelings in her she had thought long dead. How could she have opened herself up to something like this? she asked herself. How could she have let herself become so involved with the two of them?

That had always been the beauty of her job, she reminded herself, the ability to not get so involved. Working as a nurse in the hospital nursery had always been perfect. She'd been able to spend time with infants, but not so much time that she ever grew attached to them. Babies came and went in a matter of days in the maternity ward. They were cute and cuddly, and they needed her up to a point, and she could give them whatever they commanded.

It had always managed to give her some small degree of comfort, knowing she could care for those little ones without losing them. Maybe Jonas had been right about that, she thought now. There had been nothing she could do for her son except sit by and watch him succumb to the illness that gradually overtook him. But there was plenty she could do for the babies at Seton General.

She just never had time to fall in love with them.

Even Livy's and Sylvie's babies hadn't roused the deep-seated anxiety she had feared her friends' children would stir in her. And Zoey had ultimately concluded that was because she wasn't the one taking care of them. Simon and Gennie were great kids, and she enjoyed being around them. But they weren't hers. She didn't take care of them. She wasn't responsible for them. Her affection for them didn't extend beyond anything she felt for a number of other people in her life.

That wasn't the case with Juliana. Zoey had gotten to know the little baby too well over the past week and a half and loved her too much as a result. Even though Jules belonged to Jonas, Zoey had come to feel a real love, a real sense of responsibility, for the infant. Something warm and painful tore at her heart at the realization that she had succumbed so easily to the baby. And now, looking at the man who cradled her in his arms, Zoey knew she had also succumbed to him. Just as easily. Just as painfully. And she had no idea what she was going to do.

"Well?" Jonas asked as he moved toward her.

Juliana smiled when Zoey came into her line of vision, reaching her chubby little hands out toward her. The baby was wearing a pink sweater and white knit cap that set off her clear blue eyes beautifully, and her gummy, toothless smile was almost Zoey's undoing. She, too, extended a hand toward Juliana, then dropped it when she realized she shouldn't touch the baby lest she give her a cold. She didn't want to make Juliana sick. So she dropped her hand back to her side and felt the hole in her heart open a little wider.

"I . . ." she began. But her voice trailed off, and she forgot what she was going to say.

"You need to be in bed," Jonas finished for her. "You need for someone to take care of you."

Zoey said nothing in reply, but, at his silent gesture that she should precede him, she exited through his front door with Jonas and Juliana bringing up the rear.

"I'll dribe," she said softly. "I don wan do leabe my car."

"Fine," Jonas relented, obviously exasperated.

Someone to take care of her, she repeated to herself. That was what he thought she needed. She wanted to tell him that couldn't be further from the truth, wanted to assure him she had been getting along just fine on her own for more than fifteen years. But somehow, that argument suddenly seemed ridiculous. She wasn't getting along just fine these days. Not if she spent them thinking about a life she could never have again.

It should all be over now, she told herself. She owed Jonas and the baby nothing beyond today. After today, with the constant reminder of Juliana gone, she could go back to storing memories of Eddie in that quiet part of her brain that normally lay locked up and forgotten. After today, with the constant lure of Jonas gone, she could put silly thoughts of having a family again well and truly behind her.

And after today, it *would* all be over, she told herself, and she *would* go back to getting along just fine. She only hoped "just fine" would be enough to see her through the next forty or fifty years.

* * *

Spending time with Jonas and Juliana at their house was one thing, Zoey decided sometime later. But having the two of them invading her own abode was something else entirely. Something more troubling, more confusing, more anxiety provoking and more threatening. As she stood at the doorway of her tiny kitchen, watching Jonas in his stocking feet, heating up a can of chicken-noodle soup for her, Zoey tamped down a tingle of delight.

Just because he looked truly scrumptious in his off-duty uniform of blue jeans and rumpled gray sweater, and just because he and Jules were caught up in a cooing match of unprecedented proportions, and just because the three of them together at her place among her things made Zoey feel all warm and gooey inside, and just because everything about the scene just felt too, too right...

It didn't mean she was allowed to enjoy it, she concluded with a wistful sigh. This was only a temporary situation, she reminded herself. When the day drew to a close, Jonas and Juliana would return to their own home together, and Zoey would retreat to hers alone. She told herself she should take comfort in the knowledge. Instead, she found herself feeling almost bereft.

"Almost ready," Jonas said over his shoulder as he rattled a spoon in the pan one final time.

Before Zoey could utter her thanks, Juliana expelled a long, low sputter of vowels mixed with saliva, and the two adults laughed.

"No," Jonas replied to the baby as if shocked by her statement. "You don't say."

The baby's little mouth rounded to an O, and she exhaled on another lengthy coo.

"No, I don't believe a word of it," he continued, still adopting that breathy voice of surprise that Juliana seemed to love. "It's just too incredible."

"Ooohhh," Juliana assured him.

"She actually said that to you?" Jonas countered. "And what did you say in return?"

"Heeeeee," the baby replied.

"Well, I don't blame you. I would have said the same thing."

"Nnnnnng."

"I can imagine."

"Skxxxx."

"Well, I would have, too."

It was then that Zoey knew she'd been lying to herself every time she'd told herself she wasn't in love with Jonas Tate. She wasn't sure how or when it had happened, but she couldn't deny the fact any longer. She was in love with the man who, until recently, she had sworn was her most dire enemy. And if she thought back over the past several months, she had to concede that it had probably started a long time before he'd asked for her help with Juliana.

That was probably why she'd always felt uncomfortable around him, probably explained why her back had always gone up whenever he came within twenty-five feet of her. Because some part of her deep down had known how fast she was falling for him. And that part of her had been trying to make her beat a hasty retreat.

That part of her was pretty smart, Zoey acknowledged now. Because falling in love with Jonas was going to bring her nothing but trouble.

"Did you really tell Jules that you find me irresistible?" Jonas demanded, snapping her out of her reverie.

She glanced up to find him smiling at her, and Juliana bouncing in her baby seat with much vigor. She, too, was grinning, and Zoey could almost swear the two of them were sharing some private little secret.

"What?" she asked, still a bit too mystified by her newly discovered emotions to have heard him clearly. Or maybe it was just the antihistamines she'd taken upon her arrival home, she tried to reassure herself. Her stuffy nose was much cleared, but her brain was still a little fuzzy.

"I asked if you really told Jules that you find me irresistible," he repeated. "She claims that you've spent the past two weeks just going on and on about how crazy you are about me, and how you find it incredibly difficult to keep your hands to yourself whenever I'm around."

Zoey smiled, too. "Jules said that, did she?"

Jonas nodded. "She did."

"Well, then, Jules has been telling you tales. I don't recall a single incident where I even mentioned your name. Except for maybe that one day when I did curse you for not having any Tastykake snack cakes in the house."

"That's not what Jules said."

"What does Jules know? She's never tasted Tastykakes."

"And if I have any say in it, she never will."

Zoey made a rude sound of disbelief. "Good luck. You obviously still have a lot to learn about parenting."

Jonas turned fully around to face her. "Then you can't abandon us now, just because the two weeks you promised us are over."

A funny little something turned a somersault somewhere in her midsection at his tone of voice. He sounded uncertain and solicitous and very, very tempting. He sounded as if he needed her.

"You and Juliana have come a long way in the past couple of weeks," she said softly. "You'll be just fine without me. Both of you will be."

He shook his head. "Don't count on it, Zoey. Don't count on it."

Then he turned to the stove again, and all she could see was his back. She wished things could be different between them. If only she could erase everything that had happened to her when she was a teenager . . .

No, she didn't want to do that, she decided. Changing her past would mean she could never have known Eddie. And in spite of the turmoil the loss of her son had caused her, at least she'd had him for a short time. She'd known the joy and wonder that comes with the birth of a child, had seen how different the world could be by the simple addition of a tiny human being into one's life. She'd experienced a love unlike anything else she had ever felt before. A love that had been eclipsed by nothing, not even the pain that had come after it. For a little while, Zoey had been a mother. And she wouldn't trade that for anything.

Nor would she ever undertake such an occupation again. She was just too empty inside to ever manage it.

She looked at Juliana, at the clear, beautiful blue eyes and the gummy smile that twisted in her heart like a dull knife. A part of her had already lost itself to the little baby, and Zoey could feel that part of herself beginning to shrivel up and die. If things kept up at this rate, there wouldn't be anything of her left. She'd go back to being that fragile shell of a human being that was left after Eddie died. Zoey simply couldn't let this go on any longer than it had already.

After today, her obligation to Jonas and Juliana was over, she told herself again. And she couldn't let anything change that. Just because she had fallen in love didn't mean everything was going to be all right. On the contrary, loving Jonas and Juliana might just do her in completely. She had to be strong, had to stand her ground. She was a tough broad, Zoey reminded herself. Everybody thought so. And tough broads could handle anything. Even living alone.

She only wished tough broads could also believe it when they told themselves such lies.

Eleven

Jonas stared at the soup in the pan blindly, thinking about how Zoey had appeared when she'd assured him that he and Juliana would be fine without her. She'd looked sad and distant, and very, very lonely. He wished he knew what to say to make her feel differently, because she couldn't be more wrong about the situation. Zoey had brought things to his life he'd managed to lose somewhere along the way. Pleasure. Comfort. Peace. He couldn't remember the last time he'd genuinely felt any of those things before she had come more fully into his life. And he didn't want to risk losing them because she abandoned him.

And as for Juliana, Zoey had somehow turned the baby into a new person. Gone was the inconsolable, unresponsive, shrieking bundle of flesh that had arrived on his doorstep so many weeks ago. Now Jules was a laughing, cooing, affectionate baby who seemingly couldn't be happier. And Jonas knew full well that Zoey alone was responsible for that. Left to his own devices, who knew how badly he would have raised the little girl? She may have ended up on the streets of Philadelphia when she was fourteen, too.

His obligation to his brother's daughter was enormous, and Jonas knew that the years ahead would hold a number of challenges he just wasn't sure he could face alone. But it wasn't just because of Juliana that Jonas wanted to keep Zoey in his life. No, his desire in that respect was purely selfish and driven by, well, desire.

No, more than desire, he amended immediately. He'd *wanted* plenty of women during his lifetime. But he'd never loved any. Not until now. Not until Zoey Holland had come along with her tough machismo, beautiful hands and flannel pajamas and turned his life upside down. He liked the way she'd jolted things around. He didn't want to go back to the orderly, sterile, solitary existence he'd thought suited him before.

"Soup's ready," he said quietly, wanting to say so much more. "And you should be in bed."

"I don't want to go to bed," she told him.

"Too bad. Doctor's orders."

Zoey opened her mouth to object, but Jonas cupped his hands over her shoulders, spun her around and gave her a gentle push, silently commanding her to march right back to her bedroom and into bed. He shook his head hopelessly as he watched her retreat. She had refused his efforts to get her into her pajamas and wore an exhausted gray sweatsuit instead, but even that shapeless bag and a bad cold had done nothing to quell his desire for her. He supposed there would never be a time in his life when he didn't want Zoey Holland. The problem was, she just didn't seem to want him.

No, that wasn't true, either, Jonas thought as he turned back to the counter to fix up a tray for her. More than once, he'd caught her looking at him with an undeniable expression of longing. She did want him. She just didn't *want* to want him.

"Pretty stupid, huh, Jules?" he asked the baby beside him. "Your old man is crazy in love with a woman who would rather drink hemlock than admit she's even a trifle attracted to him. Now what are we going to do about it, hmm?''

Juliana gurgled and cooed and said she didn't know.

"Well, that's okay," Jonas assured her. "I have one or two tricks left up my sleeve.''

He freed her from her seat and hefted her onto his shoulder, then balanced the tray of food in his other hand. Slowly, carefully, he made his way down the hall toward Zoey's bedroom. He liked her apartment, liked the casual furnishings and scattered clutter, and the appalling lack of housekeeping skill for which she had made no apology. He liked how she had stuck postcards and yellowing comic strips to her refrigerator door, liked the unframed, curling photos of loved ones taped to the bathroom mirror.

This was clearly a place designed to make Zoey feel comfortable. She had surrounded herself with a variety of things that brought her pleasure, without concern for whether or not they all matched, without worrying about whether or not someone else might approve of her decorating choices. It was her home, and she had done a wonderful job of making it feel like one.

As much as Jonas loved his house, and as clean as his housekeeper kept it, and as well as his furnishings complemented one another, he couldn't quite claim it was a home. Not the way Zoey's apartment was. Although lovely, the house he inhabited lacked the warmth and charm of a place where a lot of living and loving went on. Probably because he did so little of that himself. At least, he had until recently.

"Soup's on," he said as he entered Zoey's bedroom. "Along with saltines, tuna-fish salad and ginger ale. Together, these things provide the only known cure for the common cold. But the tuna-fish salad has to be fixed just right. Too much cumin, and you've shot any chance you have for recovery. Lucky for you, I just happen to know exactly—''

He halted his monologue abruptly when he noticed that Zoey wasn't offering much response, and only lay in her bed, curled into a ball, with her back toward him. He was about to praise her for *finally* doing what he'd asked when he noticed that something was wrong. She hadn't acknowledged in any way his arrival, but she wasn't lying quite still enough for her to be asleep. Her shoulders shook almost imperceptibly, and at once, Jonas knew she was crying.

Quickly, he maneuvered the tray onto her dresser, spilling a little of the soup and toppling a tower of saltines. Ignoring the mess, however, he lay Juliana at the foot of the bed and rounded it to look at Zoey. She swiped at her eyes when she saw him coming, but they were still red and damp. As he drew nearer, she pushed herself up off the mattress and settled herself against the bed's headrest, squeezing a pillow in front of her as if she had to hold on to something, but didn't want to reach out to him.

"Thanks," she muttered. "You can just leave it there on the dresser. I'm not very hungry, so I'll just eat later. I'm sure you and Jules have to get going. It's getting kind of late."

"It's not even two o'clock," Jonas countered. "Jules and I don't have to be anywhere but here. What's the matter?"

"Nothing. Nothing's the matter."

"Something's the matter," he insisted. "You've been crying."

"No, I haven't."

"Your eyes are all red and watery."

She sniffled, then lifted one shoulder in a halfhearted shrug. "That's just from the cold."

He shook his head at her, not even bothering to try to hide his disbelief. "I see. Then I stand corrected."

"No problem."

Jonas looked at Zoey, then down at the baby at the foot of the bed. Juliana stared with much fascination at the huge wreath of dried flowers hanging on the wall above Zoey's bed, then doubled up both fists and tried to cram them into her mouth. He decided then that if he lived to be a hundred, he'd never understand the female mind.

"Scoot over and I'll set your tray here on the bed beside you," he told Zoey as he went back to her dresser to retrieve the lunch he had prepared for her.

"But I told you I'm not hungry," she insisted.

"You need to eat," he said. "Now scoot over before I get in bed with you and move you myself."

Immediately, Zoey pushed herself over to the other side of the mattress before Jonas could make good on his threat. The last thing she needed was to have him climbing into bed with her. Look what had happened the last time. A wild little surge of anguish twisted through her at the recollection, and at the announcement she had to make for Jonas.

"Oh, by the way," she said as he slid the tray of food toward her. She reached for a saltine before she continued, hoping she looked and sounded a lot breezier and more nonchalant than she felt. "I'm not pregnant."

Jonas had been straightening as she began to speak, but she noticed he flinched a little when she offered him the information.

"You're not?" he asked when he stood fully erect again.

She wasn't sure, but she thought he sounded almost disappointed at the news. "No, I'm not. I just found out a few minutes ago when I went to the bathroom. Everything's okay."

"Okay," he repeated. But somehow, he didn't seem okay. Then abruptly, his expression changed, as if a light had gone on somewhere in the dark recesses of his brain. He studied Zoey hard, holding her gaze steady with his. "That's why you were crying, wasn't it?" he asked quietly.

A fireball exploded in her stomach, and she felt as if she was going to be sick. "No, of course not," she told him, her voice sounding tinny and weak, even to her own ears. "I mean, I wasn't crying to begin with. It's just the bad cold."

"You *were* crying," he said. "And you were doing it because you found out you're not pregnant. You were hoping you were, weren't you?"

"No, of course not, I—"

But Jonas cut off her objection by jerking the tray of food away and sitting on the bed beside her. Juliana let out a cry at the sudden motion, and he picked her up and lay her between the two of them. As she stared down at the baby, Zoey couldn't quite shake the feeling that he hadn't performed the maneuver so much to quiet Juliana as he had to taunt *her*.

"You want to have another baby, don't you?" he asked her.

"No," she snapped, struggling to regain some of her composure.

What he was suggesting was ridiculous. Getting pregnant again would destroy her. She'd only been crying because she'd started her period. She always cried when she got her period. What woman wouldn't? It had nothing to do with wanting another baby. She continued to gaze at Juliana, who kicked her feet into the air and tugged at her playsuit. When the baby caught Zoey looking at her, she broke into a wide smile. Zoey felt tears sting her eyes again.

"I don't want to have another baby," she insisted softly. "My God, that's the last thing I want." She forced herself to look away from Juliana, but gazing at Jonas was no easier. He looked almost betrayed for some reason. "And since you weren't any crazier about the idea of my possibly getting pregnant than I was," she continued, "I thought you'd be happy to know that I—"

"Oh, but you're wrong about that," he interrupted her.

His contradiction was surprising, to say the least. "What?" she asked.

"Maybe the idea of having my child repulses you, but ever since you reminded me about our little indiscretion in not using any contraceptives last week, I've been able to think of little other than the two of us having a baby. And frankly, Zoey, I can't think of anything I'd like more."

"*What?*" she repeated, certain she must have misunderstood. Surely the cold pills were playing havoc with her mental facilities.

"You heard me."

"I never said having your child would repulse me," she began, knowing her focus on the first part of his statement was simply an effort to avoid acknowledging the second part.

"I hear a 'but' coming," he said.

She licked her lips and swallowed hard, but her mouth remained as dry as a desert. "But nothing. Just..."

"Just what?"

She rose from the bed and stood staring at him, wondering when things between them had become so complicated, wishing she could make him understand.

"Just...just..." She ran shaking fingers through her hair and began to pace restlessly across the hooked rug that covered a patch of bare floor between her bed and the bedroom door. "Just that I can't have another child, Jonas," she said without looking at him. "I won't."

"Why not?"

Her jerky motions calmed somewhat, but she continued her back-and-forth motions along the side of the bed. "What happened to...to...Eddie...it nearly killed me. For months after his death, I was just a shell of a human being. I stayed in bed almost all the time. A lot of days, I never got up. Not even to take a shower or fix breakfast. There just didn't seem to be any point."

She finally stopped pacing and turned to meet his gaze fully. "All I could do was lie there, wishing I had died with him," she said. "Instead of him. I didn't want to live. Who knows? If I'd had the energy to do it, I might have actually taken my own life. It wasn't until years and a number of counseling sessions later that I finally began to cope with what had happened. Even now, there are occasional days when I still just have a tenuous grasp on my peace of mind. I couldn't deal with it if I lost another child. I just couldn't."

"Zoey, just because you have another child doesn't mean you're going to lose it."

"How do *you* know?"

Jonas stared at her, amazed. She honestly believed there was a good possibility that if she had another baby that child would die as her son had. Even though the disease that had taken her son wasn't a common one for children to experience, even though most children who contracted it didn't die. There was absolutely no good reason for Zoey to expect that she would suffer another terrible loss like the one that had nearly destroyed her so many years ago. No *good* reason. But he supposed the pain she had experienced was rooted deeply in her soul. And fear was a powerful persuader.

"Zoey, the chances of something like that happening again—"

"Jonas, the chances of something like that happening in the first place were pretty low," she interrupted. "But it happened, didn't it? My son died in spite of the odds."

"But—"

"It's no use," she told him, her voice softening. "It's just not going to happen for us. I'm never going to be able to..."

"To what?" he asked quietly.

She shook her head slowly. "Just let it go, Jonas."

"No, I won't let it go," he told her evenly. "Don't you see, Zoey? It's already happened for us. Even if I wanted to, I couldn't let it go." He paused for only a moment before telling her, "I love you. And you love me. I know you do. I can feel it."

When she didn't contradict him, but only stared down at the floor, he, too, scooted off the bed and stood to face her. And when still she did nothing to acknowledge his declaration of love, he pulled her into his arms. She didn't struggle; didn't try to push him away. But she didn't return his embrace, either. It was as if she were feeling nothing at all, as if she had withdrawn into herself, had retreated to some secret part of her soul that she would expose to no one.

And it scared Jonas to see her that way. She'd always reacted to him in the past, no matter what the situation. Granted, her reactions hadn't necessarily been favorable most of the time, but at least she had responded in some way. Right now he'd welcome one of those angry outbursts of hers that had always driven him crazy before. If she shoved him frantically away from herself, or if she shouted out that she hated his guts, at least he'd know she was feeling *something,* that he still had a chance to make her see reason.

But for her to simply stand limp and quiet in his arms, for her to look pale and weak and utterly defeated... It was as if she'd given up completely on any future she might have with him and Juliana without even offering it a chance. Worse than that, it was as if she'd given up on herself. He'd never seen Zoey like this before. And he didn't like it at all.

"Zoey?" he asked, pushing her at arm's length to look at her.

But still she gazed down at the floor, still she said nothing, still she seemed not to realize that he was even there.

So Jonas tried again. "Zoey, I told you I love you. Doesn't that mean anything to you?"

Silence was his only answer.

"Aren't you going to tell me you love me, too?"

Still no response.

"Come on, say something. Tell me what you're feeling."

He curled his finger under her chin and tilted her head back in an effort to force her to look at him. But her eyelids remained lowered, her lips pressed together in a tight line, and she steadfastly refused to acknowledge him.

So he tried a different tack. "You know, the least you could do is knee me in the groin again. At least then I'd know where I stand."

He thought he detected a slight smile, and jumped on it. "On second thought, though, I probably wouldn't be standing at all. But at least you'd make a point. Among other things."

"Jonas, don't do this."

Her voice sounded as hollow as she looked, but he tried to pretend he didn't notice. "Don't do what?" he asked.

"Don't try to cheer me up. It's not going to work."

When she finally lifted her face to look at him, he didn't like what he saw. Her eyes were wet again, red-rimmed and puffy, and he could tell she was fighting back the tears hard.

"I don't love you," she said softly, nearly choking on the assurance. "I don't. You're just wasting your time with me. It's over, Jonas. I promised you—I promised *Juliana*—two weeks, and now I've fulfilled my obligation. From here on out, you're on your own."

"But what about . . . ?"

His voice trailed off before he could complete the question. There was still so much he wanted to tell Zoey, and still so much he needed to know about her. If only he knew what to say to her, if only he could convince her that she was so very wrong about so many things. About herself and the two of them. About her past and their future.

And there was Juliana. How could she possibly turn her back on the baby?

"What about Juliana?" he asked, knowing the question was a completely calculated, and probably vain, last-ditch effort to sway her thinking on the matter. "What's she going to do without you?"

Zoey's expression became absolutely pained at his roughly uttered inquiry. "Jules will be just fine without me," she said quietly. "In fact, she'll probably be better off. I'm a scared, unhappy, confused woman who can't even deal with something that happened to her half a lifetime ago. All in all, not exactly a great role model you'd want to expose her to."

"But don't you see, Zoey?" he asked, squeezing her shoulders hard. "It doesn't have to be that way."

She shook her head slowly. "That's the way it is. That's the way it's been for a long, long time. That's the way it's always going to be."

"But—"

She lifted a hand to his mouth, stanching the objection before he could utter it. "Just because you want things to be different doesn't make them so. I know you doctors have egos the size of Montana sometimes, but there are some wounds even a doctor of your talent and skill can't heal."

He lifted her hand away from his lips, studied the beautifully manicured fingers carefully, then kissed her fingertips one by one. Zoey's eyelids fluttered down again, and her own lips parted on an almost imperceptible sigh. He saw the pulse in her throat jump erratically, watched as two bright spots of color darkened her cheeks. There was no way she would ever make Jonas believe she didn't care for him. Not in a million years.

"Maybe not," he finally whispered. "Not completely, anyway. But I could do a hell of a lot more than just put a little Band-Aid on it, like you have. If you'll just let me try."

She shook her head, but didn't open her eyes. "It's no use," she told him.

He dipped his head to kiss her, the only way he could think to respond, but before his mouth could connect with hers, Juliana cried out from her prone position on the bed. It wasn't a demanding cry, but it was enough to make Zoey pull away.

"Juliana needs you," she told Jonas, stepping backward until the bedroom wall prevented her from retreating any farther.

He turned to look at the baby, then back to Zoey. "She also needs you," he said softly. "And I need you, too."

Zoey lifted one shoulder in a shrug that tore at Jonas's heart, because it was so obviously unfelt. "You'll be fine without me. You both will."

He moved to the side of the bed and picked up the baby, settling her easily against one shoulder. He patted her back and cradled her tiny head in his hand, and found some small degree of satisfaction in the fact that he was at least able to comfort *one* of the two most important females in his life.

"You keep telling me that, Zoey," he said as he turned to face her. "But you couldn't be more wrong. We won't be fine without you. Neither one of us will be. And no matter what you say or think, you won't be fine without us. Yet you won't even give us a chance."

She bit her lip as she studied the two of them, and Jonas couldn't shake the feeling that she was about to reconsider her decision. Then she shook her head and lifted a hand to her mouth as if trying to keep the words she really wanted to utter in check.

"There was never a chance to begin with," she said through her fingers. "I've only been kidding myself if I ever thought there was."

"Zoey, please . . ."

"Go home, Jonas," she said resolutely. "You and Juliana go home."

"Come home with us."

"I am home."

He offered her one more long, speculative look, then passed through the door without comment. He made it halfway down the hall before turning back around. "Are you so sure about that?" he asked softly.

She narrowed her eyes at him curiously. "What do you mean?"

"There's more to a home than comfortable surroundings," he told her. "When I first came into your apartment, it really did seem like a home because it was so casual and such a clear reflection of you. I even went so far as to think it was more of a home than my place was. But now I'm beginning to wonder. Because there's something missing here, after all."

"What's that?"

"Love," he said simply. "It had been missing from my home until you and Juliana arrived, but that's no longer the case. But here... I can't find it anywhere here."

"Well, like you said, Jonas, my apartment is a reflection of myself."

He emitted a soft sound of disbelief. "Yeah, right. I guess it's important that one of us believes that."

And with that, he turned again and made his way back to the kitchen to collect the things he had brought with him. The things he'd been so certain would make Zoey see the light and bring her around to his way of thinking.

What a laugh, he thought. Somewhere along the line he'd forgotten what a pain in the neck Zoey Holland could be. She never did anything the way she was supposed to.

Twelve

—

Zoey had been sleeping soundly and dreaming about an elementary-school-age boy racing to meet the ice-cream truck when a ringing telephone abruptly intruded into her dream. She fought fitfully against consciousness for some moments without acknowledging the relentless sound and continued to chase after her son, because she wanted desperately for him to turn around—just once, so that she could see what he looked like at that age. In spite of her struggles, however, she did finally awaken. Then she lay in the darkness staring at the ceiling for a moment before reaching for the telephone.

"Hello," she said automatically into the receiver.

"Zoey, it's Jeannette down at Seton."

Zoey sighed and ran a hand through her bangs and was surprised to find them wringing wet. Her pajamas, too, clung to her in sticky patches, and she kicked the covers into a heap at the foot of the bed.

"No, Jeannette, I will not come in and cover your shift for you again," she said. "For Pete's sake, your sister can't be back in town already. It's only been a few weeks since we switched our shifts back.''

"No, I'm not calling about anything like that," her co-worker muttered dryly. "Do you think I'd call you at 2:00 a.m. about a schedule change?''

Oh, yeah, Zoey thought, her brain still a little muddled. It was the middle of the night, wasn't it? "So what's the problem?" she asked.

Jeannette hesitated a minute, then spoke softly into the phone, as if she were fearful of being overheard. "I'm really sorry to wake you up, but I thought you'd think this was important. Dr. Tate didn't want me to call you when I offered to, but I was sure you'd want to know.''

"Know what?"

"I was down in ER about an hour ago talking to Cooper when he came in with his little girl.''

Zoey shook her head, certain she must be hearing things. "Cooper has a little girl? Since when?''

"No, not Cooper. Dr. Tate. He brought his little girl into emergency about an hour ago.''

Zoey jackknifed up in bed and swung her feet over the side. "Juliana?" she asked. "What's wrong? Has she been hurt?''

"I'm not sure what the whole story is, but apparently she was having convulsions due to a high fever. She was unconscious when they got here.''

"What?"

"I told Dr. Tate I'd call you and let you know, but he told me not to. What's up with you two, anyway? For a while there, you guys were getting along great. But for the past few weeks, the tension has been deep enough to wade through. Just like old times, huh?''

Zoey's head was spinning, and she scarcely heard what Jeannette said. "What's Juliana's status now?" she demanded.

"I don't know. Like I said, I just happened to be down in ER when they came in, and things have been so hectic up here since then—full moon tonight, you know—I haven't had a chance to find out. I just now had a moment where I could call you."

"Thanks, Jeannette, I'll be right in."

She was just about to drop the phone receiver back into its cradle when she heard Jeannette's voice cry out from the other line, "Hey, Zoey."

She pressed the phone back against her ear. "Yeah?"

"You didn't find out about this from me. I don't want Tate coming down on me the way he does you."

A twinge of something Zoey didn't want to identify twisted through her. She had thought Jonas would avoid her after the way they had parted three weeks ago. Instead, he'd seemed to go out of his way to find her and give her a hard time, on everything from a coffee stain on her scrubs to whether the floors in the nursery were sterile enough.

"No problem," she told Jeannette, shaking her head at the irony of the assurance. Problems were all she seemed to have lately where Jonas was concerned.

Zoey was fully dressed almost as soon as the phone receiver had settled back into place. Without even bothering to check her sleep-scattered braid, she snatched her car keys from their place by the door, stuffed her wallet into her blue jeans pocket and thrust a red hooded sweatshirt over her white T-shirt. She scarcely recalled the drive to the hospital. She only knew that what seemed like a few moments after Jeannette's call, she was rushing through the emergency-room doors, searching frantically for some sign of Jonas.

One of the new residents whose name she didn't know directed her back to an examining room. There she found Jonas sitting slumped over in a chair, his head cradled in his hands, his fingers clenched in his hair as if he'd been trying to pull it out by the roots. An empty polystyrene cup, nibbled down to nearly nothing, sat among its snowlike remnants on the chair beside him. His khaki trousers were wrinkled, and the tail of his white oxford shirt spilled half out of the waistband. He wore no socks, and she noted vaguely that not only did his shoes not match, but that they were both intended for the left foot.

He looked like a father who was scared to death for the safety of his child. He looked like she must have looked herself when she'd haunted the pediatric wing of another hospital so many years ago.

"Jonas," she called out quietly.

His head snapped up immediately, his face white and tight with anxiety, his eyes red-rimmed.

"Zoey," he said, whispering her name as if he couldn't believe she was there.

"I came as soon as I heard."

"And just how did you hear?"

"Hey, you know Seton General," she told him with a soft smile. "You can't keep a secret here."

He nodded, but said nothing.

She moved slowly across the room, brushed the tattered bits of coffee cup from the chair beside him into her palm, deposited them into a wastebin and sat down beside him. Without even thinking about what she was doing, she took his hand in hers and threaded their fingers together.

"How's Juliana?" she asked.

He looked down at the hands she had clasped together and squeezed her fingers hard. "I don't know. They're running some tests now. They think it's an infection, but they're not sure. Until they find out, they've put her in isolation, just in case. They won't let me see her, Zoey. It's driving me crazy. I mean, who do they think they are? For God's sake, I *am* a doctor, after all."

She cupped her other hand over the one she held. "You're also her father," she said softly.

He expelled a long breath, leaned back in his chair and stared at the ceiling. After a moment, he said, "Yeah, I suppose I am."

Zoey leaned back, too, rested her head against the cinder-block wall and stared at the ceiling with Jonas. It would probably be a while before they heard anything. There was nothing either of them could do but wait. For a long time, neither spoke or moved, they both just continued to hold hands and count the pinholes in the plasterboard overhead.

Finally, Jonas stirred, lifting Zoey's hand to his mouth as if it were the most natural thing in the world for him to do.

"Thank you for coming," he said, turning to look at her. "It suddenly doesn't seem quite so scary as it did before."

She nodded, but said nothing, not sure she could trust her voice. She wished she could say the same thing. But the fact of the matter was, Zoey was terrified. Ever since passing through the doors to the ER, she'd been nearly overcome with memories. She recalled all too vividly her fear and anxiety about her son's illness, remembered all too well how it had felt to cradle Eddie's limp, lifeless body in her arms when she'd carried him into another emergency ward, another lifetime ago. As worried as she was for Juliana, Zoey couldn't help but feel relieved that she hadn't seen the little baby convulsive and unconscious. She wasn't sure she would have been able to handle it.

"It must be costing you a lot," Jonas said, as if he'd been able to read her mind, "sitting here like this. Waiting to hear the verdict on a sick child."

Zoey nodded silently again.

"It's the feeling of helplessness that's worst of all, isn't it?" he asked, his voice lowered now, almost as if he were talking to himself. "The realization that your child—a completely helpless human being—is in terrible, terrible danger, and there's absolutely nothing you can do to save her. Nothing."

He turned to look at her, but his expression indicated he was seeing something else entirely. "You like to think that you're the only one who can take care of her properly, then you have to turn her over to strangers, and hope and pray that they know what they're doing. I just feel so…helpless. I want to make sure she stays safe and happy for the rest of her life, and that nothing ever holds her back. And it's just now occurring to me how little control I have over her future. Being Juliana's father is going to drive me nuts, I just know it is."

"Now you know what it feels like to be a parent," Zoey told him with a soft smile.

He shook his head slowly, seemingly overwhelmed by all that awaited him in the years to come. Then he refocused his gaze and studied Zoey levelly. "I'm sorry to put you through something like this again," he told her. "I can only think you're doing it because you care about Juliana. And maybe...maybe because you care about me."

She stared straight ahead, trying to focus her mind on one matter at a time. "Let's just get through this, Jonas, okay? Let's just worry about Juliana for now."

He tilted his head back to stare at the ceiling again and sighed. "Yeah," he agreed. "When this is over, when we know for sure that Juliana is going to be just fine, then we can talk about us."

"I hope we get to have that conversation," she said quietly. "God, I hope you're right about Juliana being just fine."

"I am," he said with absolute certainty. "She will be. She has to be." He tilted his head so that it was settled securely against Zoey's and squeezed her hand hard again. "She just has to."

It was nearly dawn before Juliana's doctor came in to speak to them. Zoey's heart nearly stopped beating when she noted the expression on his face. Dr. Haggarty, the hospital's leading pediatrician, wasn't smiling. She tried to remind herself that he was a dull, humorless man who never smiled, anyway, but the realization did little to alleviate her worry.

She and Jonas had spent hours in the examining room, just holding hands in silence and dozing off occasionally, only to awaken from dreams to a real-life nightmare. Now, as one, they stood to greet the doctor, and Zoey couldn't quite quell the anxiety that something was terribly, terribly wrong. Jonas reached over to take her hand again, clutching her fingers almost convulsively as if he, too, was expecting the news to be bad. What must have only been seconds seemed like hours while they waited for Dr. Haggarty to speak.

"That's one sick little baby you have there, Jonas," the other man said.

All the air left Zoey's lungs in a harsh *whoosh*.

"But she's going to be fine."

Her legs buckled beneath her, and she fell back in an untidy slump into her chair. She dropped her head into her hands, thanked all the gods she could name and was finally able to breathe again.

She only heard half of what Dr. Haggarty and Jonas said after that. Something about a virus that was going around, a new strain of something or other to which infants and the elderly were especially susceptible, a bug that caused symptoms that were more scary than serious. They'd put Juliana on antibiotics and now had her fever under control, but they wanted to keep her another twenty-four hours for observation, just to be sure. In the meantime, Dr. Haggarty suggested, why didn't Jonas go home and try to get some sleep? Zoey, too, for that matter.

"God, who could sleep after a night like this?" Jonas muttered when the other man had left.

Instead, he and Zoey went to pediatric intensive care and watched Juliana sleep. She lay on her stomach with her head to the side, her bow-shaped lips slighted partly, her back rising and falling almost imperceptibly as she breathed. She looked like a perfectly healthy, perfectly contented little baby. And suddenly, for some reason, Zoey felt happier than she ever had in her life.

For a long time, the two of them just stood by Juliana's crib, feeling thankful and hopeful and very, very relieved. Then Jonas yawned, a big, long, from-the-soul yawn, and Zoey laughed softly.

"You really should go home and get some sleep," she told him.

"I can't sleep. I'm too exhausted."

She smiled. "Then at least have a shower and a cup of decent coffee. And change your clothes. Those shoes can't be comfortable."

Jonas looked down and was surprised to see that he was wearing one sneaker and one loafer, and that only the left one seemed to be on the right foot. In more ways than one. Upon further inspection, he realized that not only was the left shoe on the right foot, but it was also on the *right* foot, and that was part of the problem. And somehow, in his fatigue-flustered mind, that all made perfect sense.

"Let me drive you home," Zoey told him. "You're in no shape to manage the trip yourself."

He nodded, but he was reluctant to leave Juliana's side and made no move to depart.

"She'll be okay, Jonas," Zoey told him. "Dr. Haggarty said she can come home tomorrow morning."

"I know."

"She can manage just fine without you for a couple of hours." She smiled as she added, "The nurses at this hospital are wonderful. Especially the ones who take care of the babies. Trust me."

He finally tore his gaze away from Juliana and met Zoey's levelly. "I know," he agreed quietly.

"Now come on," she said.

She flushed most becomingly, and Jonas couldn't help but wonder if maybe, just maybe, he was the one responsible for putting the color back into Zoey's cheeks.

She stopped by the nurses' station in the maternity ward long enough to ask her friend, Jeannette, if she could work a little late, just long enough for her to chauffeur Jonas home and shower and change. Jeannette waved her off with the assurance that she should take her time, that she owed Zoey a big favor, anyway, and the couple finally left.

Jonas dozed nearly all the way home. Zoey pulled into his driveway and let the car idle for a moment, waiting for him to wake up, say goodbye, thank her for the ride home and get out. But when he did none of those things, only sighed in his sleep and snuggled deeper in the bucket seat, she sighed, too, switched off the ignition and unfastened her safety belt.

"Jonas," she said, poking his upper arm.

"Mmm" was his sleepy reply.

"Wake up."

"Mmm."

Realizing she had little choice but to physically help him into the house and into bed, Zoey reached across him to unlock the passenger side door. When she did, she thought she felt him brush his hand against her breast, and she straightened with a quick gasp. But Jonas still seemed to be fast asleep in his seat, so she only narrowed her eyes at him suspiciously.

She got out of the car, rounded to the passenger side, pulled the door open and unsnapped his safety belt.

"Jonas," she repeated, this time a little more forcefully.

"Mmm."

"Wake up."

"Mmm."

She rolled her eyes heavenward, hauled him out of his seat without even trying to be gentle and slung his arm around her neck while circling her own around his waist. This was crazy, she thought. Nobody slept this soundly, not even exhausted fathers.

She kicked the car door closed and stumbled with her burden to the front door, where she encountered another problem. The front door was locked. Eyeing Jonas's pants pockets, Zoey frowned. She was going to have to go in there. She leaned him heavily against her, tightened her hold on his waist and dug into his front pocket.

She thought she heard him giggle, thought he twitched a little *too* much for someone who was fast asleep. And when she brushed her fingers along something that most certainly was *not* his key ring, she thought she heard him groan. But by the time she finally closed her hand over his keys and extracted them from his pocket, she decided she must have imagined the small sound. Surely it had just been the wind.

Once inside the house, she decided it would be foolish to even try to get Jonas up the stairs to his room. So she dragged him back to his den, dropped both their bodies to the sofa and tried not to remember that this was exactly where their one sexual encounter had begun more than a month before. She turned loose of him, trying to get him into a horizontal position, but the more she struggled to make him release her, the tighter his hold on her seemed to become.

"Jonas," she said again.

"Mmm."

"You've got to let go of me."

"Mmm...mmmake me."

He opened one eye and smiled at her, and she knew he'd been awake all along. But instead of feeling angry, she wanted to smile back at him. Fortunately, she was able to control the action, and instead pretended to be put out as she pushed him down on the sofa.

"So you *were* copping a feel out in the car, weren't you?" she said as she stood up, crossing her arms over her chest.

"Why not?" he rejoined. "You were copping a feel at the front door."

Zoey opened her mouth to deny the charge, realized there was some validity to it, then decided it might be best to remain silent, after all.

Jonas smiled up at her from the sofa, wishing she were lying there with him instead of standing so very, very far away. Without even thinking about what he was doing, he reached out his hand and joined it with hers, then tugged her back down to sit beside him. She squirmed a little, but made no effort to move away. Even when he snaked one arm around her waist and twined the fingers of his free hand with hers, she didn't try to escape.

"Thanks," he said simply.

"For what?"

"For bringing me home. For coming to the hospital. For staying with me all night long. For worrying about Juliana."

Zoey shrugged, but he could see the gesture was in no way careless.

"I...it was impossible not to," she told him. "When Jeannette called and told me what had happened, it never occurred to me *not* to come to the hospital to be with you. I just felt like I belonged there, too." She dropped her gaze to the floor as she added, "I don't know why."

"I do."

She lifted her gaze to meet his, but Jonas didn't elaborate. Instead he said, "Juliana has no idea what she put us through tonight, does she?"

Zoey shook her head. "Kids never do. But I'm sure you'll tell her all about it one day. That first night she goes out with a boy you don't approve of and stays out past curfew."

Jonas grinned, but turned his hand to study how perfectly Zoey's fitted inside it. "Yeah, I'll lay on the guilt trip, regaling her with stories about how her mother and I—"

He stopped speaking abruptly when he realized what he'd said, but knew it was too late when Zoey tried to free her fingers from his and move away. He kept his arm wound tightly around her, however, and refused to let go of her hand. He wouldn't let her escape from him this time as easily as he had before. She'd become far too important to him, and he knew without question that he and Juliana were important to her. They needed each other, the three of them did. He only wished he knew what to do to make Zoey understand that.

"Zoey," he began. Then he realized he had no idea what he had intended to say.

"I'm not her mother, Jonas," she told him, her voice measured, quiet and razor sharp.

"Maybe not. But you should be."

He couldn't help but speak the words, so strongly did he feel they were the truth. And when Zoey only dropped her gaze to the floor in silence, neither agreeing with nor contradicting his remark, he pulled her down to him and kissed her.

At first she halfheartedly balled her fists against his chest and refused to kiss him back. Then suddenly, like a wild animal gone too long without food, she returned his kiss with a fervor that threatened to consume him. She moved her body over his, tangled her fingers in his hair, slanted her open mouth across his and tasted him so deeply he could feel her reaching into his very soul.

Jonas didn't question the fever that seemed to overtake her. He only welcomed it. Welcomed it and returned it with a fire to rival its heat. He threaded his fingers through her hair, and when he realized the long tresses were still wound into a loose braid, fumbled down its length until he found and freed the bit of elastic that bound the plait together. Then he moved his fingers to her waist, pulled her sweatshirt up over her torso and head and tossed the garment into a heap of red on the floor. Her T-shirt came next, and he groaned out loud when he realized she wasn't wearing a brassiere.

Half-naked, Zoey straddled him, and only then seemed to realize what was happening. Her hair cascaded over her shoulders to effectively hide her nudity, but her chest rose and fell as she tried to calm her ragged breathing, offering him brief glimpses of her tender flesh. He waited for her to jump up and flee from him, expected her to gather her clothes and run from his house as if her life were in danger. But she only looked at him for a moment, then touched her finger to his throat, then to his chin, and finally to his mouth.

"We need to talk," she said softly. "But we can do it later."

And with that, she lowered her hand to the buttons of his shirt and unfastened them one by one. When she reached the last, she spread the soft cotton fabric open and twined her fingers in the dark hair on his chest. She found a flat, coppery nipple and rubbed her thumb across it, then lowered herself to lave the area with her tongue. Jonas sucked in a long, uneven breath and settled his hands on her waist. For a long time, he could only try to keep his breathing under control while she suckled him. But when she skimmed her fingernails along his abdomen to dip them inside the waistband of his trousers, he began to have some difficulty maintaining that control.

Within seconds, she had freed him and cradled him in her hand. She teased the heated length of him with her fingers, playing havoc with his senses. Jonas tried to lie still and not go crazy, because he knew the slightest movement from him would only intensify her ministrations. Carefully, he cupped his palms over her fanny, then glided his hands between her denim-clad thighs to explore her as intimately as she explored him. Even through the heavy fabric, he could feel her becoming damp and warm as a result of his touch, and he rejoiced to discover she was as aroused as he. When she sat up straight to facilitate his investigation, he splayed his open hand over her bare back and pulled her down to him again.

Her breast hovered near his mouth, so he lifted his head to taste her, moving the heavy globe closer with one hand while he continued to drive her nether regions mad with the other. Zoey lengthened her body until she lay fully atop him, holding herself over him on her elbows, content to wait until he finished with what he was doing.

But Jonas didn't seem to want to finish. He took his time curling his tongue over first one breast and then the other, working his hands casually in between their warm bodies to unfasten her jeans. Zoey shifted her position long enough to tug them down and off with her panties, and was back with Jonas before the discarded clothing hit the floor.

After that, Jonas did seem to be in a hurry. Without even removing his clothing, he sat up with Zoey in his lap facing him, matching her touch for touch and gasp for gasp. And then, suddenly, he was inside her. Gloriously, heatedly inside her, filling her in places she hadn't realized were empty until that moment. She wrapped her legs around his waist to pull him even more deeply inside, and they groaned their need as one, both having gone too long without that most basic of human necessities—love.

Zoey lifted herself from Jonas only slightly, then lowered herself onto him again, sighing with the sense of repletion the action brought with it. Over and over, she rose and fell, driving him more deeply, more resolutely, more irrevocably, into herself. Just when she thought she was as full as she would ever be, Jonas levered their bodies until they had switched positions, and he was the one who controlled the pace.

Had she truly thought she could bring him no closer? she wondered faintly as he pushed himself still farther inside her. It was as if the two of them became one with his next thrust, as if they would never be able to separate one from the other again. And that was when it finally occurred to Zoey just how true that was. The two of them were one. Had become one the first time they'd made love, and would stay one forever.

As soon as she recognized the fact, Jonas carried her away, off to a place like none she'd ever visited before. As he exploded inside her like lightning striking dry wood, and as she shuddered around him with the ferocity of a storm-tossed ocean crashing against the welcoming shore, Zoey lost all recognition of her physical surroundings. As the two of them slowly descended from their tempestuous union, all she could do was feel.

And it struck her that she was feeling something she hadn't felt for a very long time, something she almost didn't recognize, something she had nearly forgotten. Good. Zoey felt good. For the first time in nearly twenty years, she could find none of the hollowness that had always been present inside her. That cold, vacant emptiness in her heart, in her soul, was gone. Somehow, Jonas had filled all the dark, scary places. Filled them with his love for her.

And with her love for him.

"I love you."

Zoey didn't realize that she was the one who spoke the words until Jonas answered her.

"I love you, too," he said softly, tightening his arms around her. "It's about time you came around and admitted it."

She smiled at him. "It's about time I did a lot of things."

He kissed her temple and wound a length of her hair around his finger. "Like what?"

There was so much, she thought, too much for her to ever begin explaining to him, so she only said, "Like put the past behind me and get on with my life."

Jonas studied a freckle over Zoey's right breast that he could swear tasted like strawberries and sighed. Now was the time to ask her, he thought. While she was mellow and rosy and presumably feeling as contented as he.

"I don't suppose you might have room in that life for more than one?" he asked experimentally. He lifted his gaze to meet hers. "Would you?"

Zoey squeezed him hard as she replied, "Well, maybe. If there are only two of you and one of you weighs less than fifteen pounds."

He smiled. "You know, there could be more than two of us. You and I sort of forgot something again."

She smiled back. "Maybe you did. But I didn't."

"Then you were planning on this happening and took precautions?" he asked, unable to keep the disappointment from clouding his voice.

Her smile broadened. "No, I had no idea this was going to happen. I only meant I remembered, but I didn't do anything about it. On purpose."

Jonas was afraid to believe what he was hearing. "Then you *do* want to have another child."

The sound she uttered was at once sad and hopeful and happy. "I guess I've wanted another child since shortly after Eddie was born. I've just been afraid...of so many things."

"And you're not afraid anymore?"

She cupped her palm gently over one of his cheeks while she pressed her mouth softly against the other. When she pulled back, she felt a single warm tear trace its way down her temple and into her hair. "Yeah, I'm still afraid," she told him. "I don't know that there will ever be a time when I'm not. But now I don't have to face my fears alone, do I?"

Jonas stroked his hand over her hair and bent his head to kiss away the damp trail of her tear. "No," he told her. "You'll never have to face anything alone again. Jules and I will always be here for you, no matter what happens."

"Always?"

"Always."

Maybe Zoey believed that, and maybe she didn't. But for now, she had happiness. Complete, wonderful, honest happiness. Even if it wound up being only short-lived, it was far better than the false life she'd been leading for so long.

"It will be forever, Zoey," Jonas told her, as if she'd uttered her thoughts aloud. "I promise."

And somehow, Zoey decided, that was all she needed to hear.

Epilogue

———

The maternity ward was busy the morning Zoey delivered her twins, Leo and Lucy. Jonas had paced and worried throughout the night like the typical expectant father, and three-year-old Juliana had asked all kinds of questions about what her new baby brother and sister would be like. Olivia had made frequent visits to Zoey's delivery room during her shift, and afterward had stood vigil in the waiting room with Daniel and Simon and two-year-old Samantha, and Sylvie and Chase and Genevieve. What, only a few years ago, had been a trio of friends had become an extended family of twelve.

At the end of the day, when the men took their children down to the snack bar to ply them with hot dogs and soft drinks, the three women stood outside the nursery, looking through the glass at the multitude of babies, each recalling her own with a proud and loving heart. But they spoke of the newest additions to the circle, the tiny baby boy and girl who lay squirming in side-by-side bassinets labeled "Tate," their red faces screwed up into matching squalls, their hands and feet moving slowly about, as if they couldn't get used to the big, wide world outside the womb.

"Boy, are they in for a surprise," Sylvie said as she flattened her palms against the glass.

"What do you mean?" Zoey asked.

"Just think about everything that's going to happen to them," she clarified. "They're just twelve hours old. Their lives have literally just begun. In thirty-something years, they'll be where we are. And think of all the weird stuff that comes in between."

Olivia nodded. "It's going to go by fast, too. I can't believe Simon's five years old and Sam is already two. It just doesn't seem like that much time has gone by since Daniel and I got married."

"And Gennie's three," Sylvie added. "It almost seems impossible." She paused for only a moment before adding, "And you know what else seems impossible, but is true nonetheless?"

"What?" the other women chorused.

Sylvie's eyes fairly sparkled with laughter as she announced, "Chase and I are expecting again. I'm fourteen weeks along."

Her sister and friend cried out their delight.

"That's wonderful!" Zoey exclaimed.

Olivia hugged her sister hard in congratulations. "But I thought you were having problems. I mean, after all, that's what got you and Chase together to begin with. According to your doctor, the batteries in your biological clock were about to run down."

"Yeah, well, I guess doctors don't know everything, do they?" Sylvie asked.

Zoey and Olivia expelled identical sounds of heartfelt agreement.

"You got that right," Zoey said.

"Amen," Olivia conceded. A quiet moment passed before she added, "I wasn't going to say anything yet, but now that Sylvie's set the stage, I might as well. Daniel and I are pregnant again, too. Due in eight months."

"No way!" Sylvie cried.

"Way!" Olivia mimicked.

"Oh, boy, this is gonna be great," Sylvie said with a smile. "Babies busting out all over. Who would have thought ten years ago that the three of us would be responsible for so many new lives in the world?"

"Yeah, the World Health Organization is going to start sending us nasty letters if we don't stop overpopulating the planet," Zoey added with a laugh.

"Oh, let 'em," Olivia said with a negligent wave of her hand. "Our kids are so smart, they're going to solve all the problems of the world when they grow up."

"Speak for yourself," Sylvie interjected. "Mine are going to be rabble-rousers. I've already decided."

"Rabble-rousers and saxophone players," Chase added as he came up behind his wife. He held Genevieve in his arms, but the little girl reached for her mother, and Sylvie took her with a smile. "Look at those fingers," he added, touching the tiny hand to his own. "Definitely the hands of a musician."

"A piano player," Sylvie told him.

Chase shook his head. "Tenor sax. Mark my words."

"Simon's going to be a carpenter, like his old man," Daniel added as he joined them. Simon held fast to his right hand, little Samantha toddling along, gripping his left. "And Sam... Well, I'm not sure. She's the Bohemian one. She'll probably be a poet."

"She can write the lyrics to Gennie's songs," Chase decided.

"What about Jules and Lucy and Leo?" Zoey asked Jonas as he and Juliana joined the others. "The other fathers seem to have charted their children's futures. Have you made any plans for ours?"

Jonas looked at the little girl who hugged him tight, then through the glass at the newest additions to his family. "They can all be whatever they want," he said softly. "I never imagined I'd wind up with such a beautiful, wonderful family. At this point, I'm open to whatever comes along."

Zoey nodded her approval. "Well said."

"But it might be nice to have another doctor in the family. Or a lawyer. Or a plumber. God knows you never can tell when you'll need one of those."

Zoey shook her head at him, but smiled. "As long as none of them is a Republican."

Jonas moved forward to stand beside her, marveling again at the two new lives they had created together. If he lived to be one hundred years old, he didn't think he'd ever experience another moment like the one he had shared with his wife after their twins had been born. Never. And the knowledge that a part of both of them had worked together to create such a miracle stunned him still. He looked at Juliana, who had tilted her head to the side to study her new brother and sister with a critical eye. He looked at Lucy and Leo. Then he looked at Zoey. No one, *no one,* could be as fortunate and blessed as he.

"You did good," he whispered into Zoey's ear as he tangled his fingers with hers.

"*We* did good," she corrected him with a soft smile. She kissed his cheek and leaned against him, feeling exhausted and euphoric and utterly amazed.

"Oh, Zoey," Olivia said as she pressed her face to the glass to eye the twins again, "you can't imagine how much those little babies are going to change your life. I mean, Jules was three and a half months old when you met her. Unless you've experienced it for yourself, you just can't imagine the trials and wonders and delights that await you when a newborn comes into the house."

Zoey smiled, recalling another newborn she had known so many years ago, contemplating the two new ones on the other side of the glass. She felt at once sad, wistful and joyous. "I think I can imagine, Livy," she said softly. "And I think we're going to be just fine." She squeezed Jonas's hand hard before adding, "All of us. We're all going to be just fine."

* * * * *

Jingle Bells, Wedding Bells

The joy of Christmas and the magic of marriage
await you in this special collection of four
heart-warming love stories.

All I Want for Christmas
Nora Roberts

Jack's Ornament
Myrna Temte

*A Very Merry-Step
Christmas*
Barbara Boswell

The Forever Gift
Elizabeth August

Published: November 1995   **Price: £4.99**

 **SILHOUETTE**

*Available from WH Smith, John Menzies, Volume One, Forbuoys, Martins,
Tesco, Asda, Safeway and other paperback stockists.*

▼SILHOUETTE

Desire

COMING NEXT MONTH

THE DISOBEDIENT BRIDE Joan Johnston

Man of the Month

Zach Whitelaw wanted a bride to give him children. Rebecca
Littlewolf wanted Zach and children, his children, would be a bonus—
what could go wrong?

A CHRISTMAS COWBOY Suzannah Davis

Mac Mahoney was in trouble; he'd got snowed in with his ex-
girlfriend and her five-year-old. The child was convinced that Mac was
the daddy that Santa was bringing him...

OPERATION MUMMY Caroline Cross

Alex Morrison's three little sons had picked out the mother they
wanted and they were determined to get Shay Spencer and their dad
together. Alex couldn't fault their taste but he wasn't getting married
again—ever!

CAT'S CRADLE Christine Rimmer

Dillon McKenna wanted a family and he knew just the right woman
for the task. However, Cat Beaudine had already raised one family and
thought once was enough. But once with Dillon wasn't anywhere near
enough!

THE REBEL AND THE HERO Helen R. Myers

Strong, sexy Logan Powers was the kind of man that rebel Merri
Brown could never understand. So she unwisely married someone
else. But now she was back and the man she didn't marry still wanted
her...

DARK INTENTIONS Carole Buck

Royce Williams had once saved her life, so Julia Kendricks was
determined to help him when a tragic car accident left him blind. He
couldn't recognise her so he need never know who she had been.

▼ SILHOUETTE
Intrigue

Romantic suspense...just what the doctor ordered!

Silhouette Intrigue are pleased to bring you
a brand new trilogy of medical thrillers by
popular author Carly Bishop.

Starting in November '95, don't miss her
first title **Hot Blooded**

And keep your pulse racing with her
next two books:

Breathless in December '95
Heart Throb in January '96.

*Available from WH Smith, John Menzies, Volume One, Forbuoys, Martins,
Tesco, Asda, Safeway and other paperback stockists.*

▼ SILHOUETTE

Sensation

COMING NEXT MONTH

OUT OF THE DARK Justine Davis

Victoria Flynn didn't want to trust the dark and dangerous Texan who was too darn handsome for her peace of mind. But she was in big trouble and he owed her family.

Cole Bannister was prepared to help Tory find out who was out to ruin her reputation and her business, but he made it a rule never to get involved with his clients. *Rules are made to be broken...*

SIMPLE GIFTS Kathleen Korbel

He Who Dares

Rock O'Connor was a cop in Chicago and he'd seen things that had made him lose faith in people, whereas Lee Kendall was an eternal optimist who lived every second of her life to the full, thought people were fascinating and really believed in true love. But it was Lee that someone wanted to kill! Suddenly it had become vitally important to Rock that he solve this puzzle—before Lee got hurt. She might be about to break his heart, but at least she'd be alive!

MIDNIGHT STRANGER Diana Whitney

Ruth Ridenour was on the run, determined to keep her baby son safe. She met Garrett Kincade when he was wounded and fleeing from the corrupt but long arm of the local law. They were two fugitives, guarding secrets too dangerous to expose. No one knew where they were for the moment, but could true love really grow in such tense circumstances?

NO MORE SECRETS Linda Randall Wisdom

Security specialist Nikki Price had returned to Scott Carter's house because she felt she might have unwittingly betrayed him and his young daughter when she'd uncovered a traitor there five years ago. Now she needed answers. Their lives depended on them. But she'd broken the cardinal rule: NEVER FALL IN LOVE...

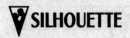

▼ SILHOUETTE

❯ SPECIAL EDITION ❮

COMING NEXT MONTH

A MATCH FOR CELIA Gina Ferris Wilkins

That Special Woman! & The Family Way

This holiday was supposed to be exciting, but Celia Carson had no idea just how much adventure, romance and passion she was in for!

MOTHER AT HEART Robin Elliott

Man, Woman & Child

Tessa's late sister's baby was now her son and his happiness was at risk thanks to Tessa's desire for an arrogant, impossible man—a man who would never acknowledge this child as his…

FATHER IN TRAINING Susan Mallery

Hometown Heartbreakers

Sandy Walker needed a provider for her children, not an adventurer… She just wasn't prepared to talk a walk on the wild side with notorious bachelor Kyle Haynes.

COWBOY'S KISS Victoria Pade

A Ranching Family

Jackson Heller couldn't believe that his father had left this pretty city woman half his ranch! What had he been thinking of? What was Jackson going to do with her?

ONLY ST. NICK KNEW Nikki Benjamin

Taking a job in New Mexico Alison Kent had intended avoiding Christmas, but Frank Bradford and his motherless twins couldn't allow that. They wanted to give her a family for Christmas—them!

ABIGAIL AND MISTLETOE Karen Rose Smith

Could anyone understand and live with Abigail's secret? Was she brave enough to risk revealing her true self to Brady Crawford?

♥ SILHOUETTE

Intrigue

COMING NEXT MONTH

HOPSCOTCH Rebecca York

A 43 Light Street novel

Who was Jason Zacharias? That riddle was the key to Noel Emery's frightening predicament—being pursued by assassins! Her guardian angel was a seasoned veteran of murder...and he claimed to be her husband.

I'LL BE HOME FOR CHRISTMAS
Dawn Stewardson

Ali's 'dead' husband was alive, her son was missing and her mind was reeling. She turned to the one man she could almost trust—the single dad next door, crime writer Logan Reed.

BEARING GIFTS Aimée Thurlo

Just days before Christmas, little Amy Hawken's nightmare began—her mother was attacked and then framed. Bachelor J.D. Hawken would do anything for his special niece, and he was equally drawn to Mari Sanchez, Amy's godmother, now his cohort in both child care and crime solving...

BREATHLESS Carly Bishop

Second in the Pulse trilogy

It had been three long years since Zoe Mastrangelo lost her husband and child in a freak accident. Now her surviving daughter was in desperate need of a donor from her father's side. Zoe set off for Rafe's hometown, unaware she was in for a surprise...

KT-548-003

Catherine Cookson was born in Tyne Dock, the illegitimate daughter of a poverty-stricken woman, Kate, whom she believed to be her older sister. She began work in service but eventually moved south to Hastings, where she met and married Tom Cookson, a local grammar-school master. At the age of forty she began writing about the lives of the working-class people with whom she had grown up, using the place of her birth as the background to many of her novels.

Although originally acclaimed as a regional writer – her novel *The Round Tower* won the Winifred Holtby award for the best regional novel of 1968 – her readership soon began to spread throughout the world. Her novels have been translated into more than a dozen languages and more than 50,000,000 copies of her books have been sold in Corgi alone. Fifteen of her novels have been made into successful television dramas, and more are planned.

Catherine Cookson's many bestselling novels established her as one of the most popular of contemporary women novelists. After receiving an OBE in 1985, Catherine Cookson was created a Dame of the British Empire in 1993. She was appointed an Honorary Fellow of St Hilda's College, Oxford in 1997. For many years she lived near Newcastle-upon-Tyne. She died shortly before her ninety-second birthday in June 1998.

'Catherine Cookson's novels are about hardship, the intractability of life and of individuals, the struggle first to survive and next to make sense of one's survival. Humour, toughness, resolution and generosity are Cookson virtues, in a world which she often depicts as cold and violent. Her novels are weighted and driven by her own early experiences of illegitimacy and poverty. This is what gives them power. In the specialised world of women's popular fiction, Cookson has created her own territory'
Helen Dunmore, *The Times*

BOOKS BY CATHERINE COOKSON

NOVELS

Kate Hannigan
The Fifteen Streets
Colour Blind
Maggie Rowan
Rooney
The Menagerie
Slinky Jane
Fanny McBride
Fenwick Houses
Heritage of Folly
The Garment
The Fen Tiger
The Blind Miller
House of Men
Hannah Massey
The Long Corridor
The Unbaited Trap
Katie Mulholland
The Round Tower
The Nice Bloke
The Glass Virgin
The Invitation
The Dwelling Place
Feathers in the Fire
Pure as the Lily
The Mallen Streak
The Mallen Girl
The Mallen Litter
The Invisible Cord
The Gambling Man
The Tide of Life
The Slow Awakening
The Iron Façade
The Girl
The Cinder Path
Miss Martha Mary Crawford
The Man Who Cried
Tilly Trotter
Tilly Trotter Wed

Tilly Trotter Widowed
The Whip
Hamilton
The Black Velvet Gown
Goodbye Hamilton
A Dinner of Herbs
Harold
The Moth
Bill Bailey
The Parson's Daughter
Bill Bailey's Lot
The Cultured Handmaiden
Bill Bailey's Daughter
The Harrogate Secret
The Black Candle
The Wingless Bird
The Gillyvors
My Beloved Son
The Rag Nymph
The House of Women
The Maltese Angel
The Year of the Virgins
The Golden Straw
Justice is a Woman
The Tinker's Girl
A Ruthless Need
The Obsession
The Upstart
The Branded Man
The Bonny Dawn
The Bondage of Love
The Desert Crop
The Lady on My Left
The Solace of Sin
Riley
The Blind Years
The Thursday Friend
A House Divided

THE MARY ANN STORIES

A Grand Man
The Lord and Mary Ann
The Devil and Mary Ann
Love and Mary Ann

Life and Mary Ann
Marriage and Mary Ann
Mary Ann's Angels
Mary Ann and Bill

FOR CHILDREN

Matty Doolin
Joe and the Gladiator
The Nipper
Rory's Fortune
Our John Willie

Mrs Flannagan's Trumpet
Go Tell It To Mrs Golightly
Lanky Jones
Nancy Nuttall and the Mongrel
Bill and the Mary Ann Shaughnessy

AUTOBIOGRAPHY

Our Kate
Catherine Cookson Country

Let Me Make Myself Plain
Plainer Still

Catherine Cookson

The Invitation

CORGI BOOKS

THE INVITATION
A CORGI BOOK : 0 552 14833 4

Originally published in Great Britain
by Macdonald & Co (Publishers) Ltd

PRINTING HISTORY
Macdonald edition published 1970
Macdonald edition reprinted 1971
Corgi edition published 1972
Corgi edition reprinted 1973
Corgi edition reprinted 1975
Corgi edition reprinted 1976
Corgi edition reprinted 1977
Corgi edition reprinted 1978 (twice)
Corgi edition reissued 1979
Corgi edition reprinted 1980
Corgi edition reprinted 1981
Corgi edition reprinted 1983
Corgi edition reprinted 1984
Corgi edition reprinted 1986 (twice)
Corgi edition reprinted 1987
Corgi edition reprinted 1988
Corgi edition reissued 1993 (reset)
Corgi edition reprinted 1995
Corgi edition reprinted 1996 (twice)

Copyright © Catherine Cookson, 1970

Condition of Sale
This book is sold subject to the condition that it shall not,
by way of trade or otherwise, be lent, re-sold, hired out or
otherwise circulated without the publisher's prior consent
in any form of binding or cover other than that in which
it is published and without a similar condition including
this condition being imposed on the subsequent purchaser.

Set in 10pt Linotype Plantin by
Chippendale Type Ltd, Otley, West Yorkshire.

Corgi Books are published by Transworld Publishers,
61–63 Uxbridge Road, London W5 5SA,
a division of The Random House Group Ltd,
in Australia by Random House Australia (Pty) Ltd,
20 Alfred Street, Milsons Point, Sydney, NSW 2061, Australia,
in New Zealand by Random House New Zealand Ltd,
18 Poland Road, Glenfield, Auckland 10, New Zealand
and in South Africa by Random House (Pty) Ltd,
Endulini, 5a Jubilee Road, Parktown 2193, South Africa.

Printed and bound in Great Britain by
Cox & Wyman Ltd, Reading, Berkshire.

Contents

Part One

Part One

Part One

CHAPTER ONE

SAM

Maggie Gallacher stared wide-eyed at the card in her hand. It had a deckle edge, rimmed with gold. In the right hand corner of the card there was a contortion of initials which she couldn't make out, but she could make out the writing, for the words shone from the page as if they had been printed in pure gold dust, and she saw each one as an obstacle on the mountain that her Rodney had started climbing the day she married him, twenty-seven years ago. The card itself, this piece of cardboard, was the mountain peak, and they were on top of it now and not out of breath, by God no, sitting pretty as it were, in Savile House, in the best end of Felburn, which was not Brampton Hill any more but further out in the district known generally as The Rise. Sitting pretty within twelve rooms and two acres, with a stream at the bottom, the house furnished, as she put it to herself, like nobody's business. And that was not all; the name of Gallacher was ringing through the town like the church bell. Hadn't Gallacher and Sons built the new college and the Rollingdon and Morley Estates? And wasn't her family all set? At least five of them were. And this one sitting at her side now; well, there was going to be glory for her.

She put out her hand and gripped her youngest daughter's wrist, and Elizabeth, her grey eyes wide, her teeth pressed gently into her lower lip, shook her head; then nudging her mother with her elbow they fell together laughing, and they laughed as only the Gallachers could laugh, with a body-shaking, mouth-stretching infectious sound. As Maggie was wont to say, all the Gallachers did things as they should be done, they laughed from their bellies; except – she always made an exception in her mind of Paul. But then Paul, her youngest son, was like nobody but himself. Still, she liked what he was; she loved what he was.

'Shall I ring them?' With the end of her finger, Elizabeth wiped a laughter-tear from her long, black lashes, and Maggie slanted her eyes at her, the glint in them saying, 'What else?' And on this Elizabeth jumped up from the couch, ran across the room to where the telephone stood on a marble-topped reproduction Louis XV commode and she down on the gilt chair before it. But she paused as she was about to pick up the phone and, looking round at her mother, said, 'Sam and Arlette first?'

Maggie moved her head once, then said, 'Of course.'

Sam was her eldest son and so it was perhaps natural that he should be the first to hear the news, but she wasn't so much concerned with Sam's reaction to what he was going to hear as she was with his wife's. Women were supposed to be jealous of their sons' wives, particularly the wife of their first-born, but she had never been jealous of Arlette. She had always considered it strange, her feeling for Sam's wife, because between her and Arlette there was a wide gulf in upbringing, thought and attitude to life, yet in some strange way she felt close to her; she felt she understood her, while the rest of her family had varying opinions about their sister-in-law, some calling her reserve either snobbishness or condescension. But Elizabeth, with her young enthusiasm, dubbed Arlette 'It and a bit', which summed up her daughter-in-law for Maggie too.

She had never said it aloud, not even to Rod, but she had always thought that their Sam was damned lucky to get someone like Arlette. He might be big and good looking and have it up top with regards to business, but he was brash, aye, that was the word, brash. And there was something else, a something else that she had never been able to lay her finger on with regard to her eldest son . . . But Liz was speaking to him now.

'Hello. Is that you, Sam?'

'Who did you expect? Of course it's me. What's up? You sound as if you've been running.'

'You'll never believe what I'm going to tell you . . . it's about Mam and Dad.'

'Don't tell me they're going to be married.'

'Oh you, our Sam! I'll tell her, mind.'

'You do. Well, what's happened? . . . Aw no! She's not going to have another bairn.'

'OUR SAM!'

'Well, go on . . . I know. I know, she's going to take up French to please Arlette.'

'Samuel Gallacher, stop being sarcastic; she could an' all.'

'I know she could, she could do anything she wants, could our fat old mum.'

'You're in one of those moods, are you? Listen. Pin your ears back. They've had an invitation, to a sort of musical evening. Guess who from?'

'The Queen, of course.'

'No; but you're getting warm.'

There was a pause before Sam spoke again. 'You don't say! Go on, put me out of me agony.'

'Well, I am now holding in my hand a beautiful card which bears an invitation from . . . THE DUKE OF MOORSHIRE . . . Are you there? . . . Are you there, Sam?'

'Yes. Aye, I'm here. That's a fact what you're saying, the Duke of Moorshire?'

'Yes; I'm telling you.' The line seemed to go dead again. Then Sam's voice came over, flat sounding now as he said, 'Well, I'll be damned! We are going up, aren't we?'

Elizabeth glanced at her mother again. She wanted to say to Sam, 'You don't sound very excited,' but what she said was, 'Is Arlette there?'

'She's having a bath.'

'Do you think you can come round later? I'm phoning them all.'

'Yes, yes. We'll be round and have a knees-up and a Gallachers' laugh-in.'

'Oh, our Sam . . . Ta-rah then.'

'Ta-rah.'

Sam Gallacher put the phone down and stared at it; then he slewed his lower jaw to the side and gnawed at the corner of his lip, after which his head swung up and backwards and he let out a loud 'huh!'

He walked across the hall, through the long L-shaped lounge and dining-square, and into a smaller hall from which led the doors of the bathroom, lavatory, laundry and kitchen. There was the sound of the bath water running out, and slowly he put out his long arm and very gently turned the handle of the bathroom door. It was locked, as he knew it would be. He now took up a position opposite it between the kitchen and the laundry doors, and he waited, listening the while to the movements in the bathroom. He pictured her now standing before the mirror, her face cool, expressionless, until she realised he was in the house. She would have her dressing-gown on. Oh yes; she never remained naked long, not even in the bathroom. He had suggested one day she should get into the bath in her knickers; he had also suggested that she should live in there, even sleep in there as she liked bathing so much; that was the day he had stirred her to retaliation and she had told him why she bathed so much, and he had punched her in the mouth. Her aunt had been taken seriously ill that same night and she'd had to go straight down to Devonshire. She was almost as anxious to cover up as he was, and he knew the reason, and the reason made him more flaming mad. And the reason had now been invited to meet the Duke. God Almighty! Her, meeting a Duke!

The bathroom door opened and he watched his wife start. He watched the movement of her long hand pulling the dressing-gown closer about her.

'I didn't know you were in.' She went past him into the dining-space and through one of the two doors opposite. He didn't speak but followed her into the bedroom, and he watched her sit down at the dressing-table and start brushing her hair. He knew she wouldn't attempt to put her clothes on while he was there. He went and stood behind her and looked at her face in the mirror; even without make-up and her skin shiny from the bath, and her hair drawn back now tight from her forehead with the hard strokes of the brush, she was beautiful; in an unsmiling, stiff, lifeless way she was beautiful.

When he put his hand on her shoulder and felt her flesh shrink beneath his fingers, the muscles of his stomach knotted, and he warned himself, 'Careful, careful'; and so, looking into her eyes through the mirror, he said with a smile, 'I've got news for you.'

Her eyes waited, unblinking.

'You'll never guess in a thousand years the latest from the house. Didn't you hear the phone ring?'

Still she waited.

'. . . They've had an invitation from the Duke of Moorshire to a musical soirée. Can you believe it? Rod . . . and Maggie.'

He saw her eyes widen slightly and a suspicion of a smile come on her lips, and her voice now held a touch of animation as she said, 'That is nice, wonderful really, I'm so glad for them.'

He reached swiftly out, pulled up a chair, placed it with its back to the dressing-table and close to her stool, and when he sat on it and leant sideways blotting out the mirror he was almost facing her, and his head moved in small nods as he said, 'Yes, you are, aren't you? Well, I can understand him getting the invitation and also being able to carry it off, but Mam . . . her passing herself with the Duke, can you see it?'

Her face only inches from his, her eyes did not waver from his look as she answered firmly now, 'Yes, yes I can. You can't see her doing anything right because of your . . . ' She gulped in her throat, drew her chin in, closed her eyes tightly now and made to rise from the stool. But his hand gripping the top of her thigh held her still, and he said quietly, 'It's funny, isn't it? I bet it doesn't happen once in ten million times the son against his mother and the daughter-in-law for her. And what a daughter-in-law, eh? And what a mother. Look! Look.' He moved his grip on her thigh. 'Tell me . . . tell me the truth. Why do you like her?'

She was swallowing rapidly now and, shaking her head from side to side as if pushing off a bad dream, she murmured, 'Stop it. Stop it. We've been through it all before. I've told you.'

'Tell me again; only don't tell me it was because your mother died when you were six and Mam welcomed you with open arms the first time she saw you, because as I've said afore there would be the same similarity between my mother and yours as there is between Kitty Malone in the office and Princess Margaret – chalk and cheese. No. The truth is, you like to condescend, and you can condescend with Mam can't you, because she's something to condescend to; you can't do it with the rest because they

14

wouldn't stomach it, not even Nancy, and she hasn't the brains she was born with. But Mam laps it up because she's stupid.'

'She's not! Your mother is not stupid.'

Now he had stirred her; she tore at the hand on her thigh while she pushed him so violently with the other that the chair almost overturned. And her surprising action changed his own mood, and he steadied himself and got to his feet.

His face now was transformed, his full-lipped mouth was wide, his dark brown eyes held deep glimpses of amusement, and he coughed as he looked at her where she was standing near the door; her voice almost loud as she cried at him, 'Why do you hate her? Why? And don't you tell me it's because you consider her a slob, because I don't believe it. When I know why you hate her I'll have the answer to everything, everything. None of the others feel like this towards her, only you. You're . . .' She checked herself again, and as she watched him coming slowly towards her every muscle in her body stiffened.

When he stood in front of her his tone was soft, contrite. 'I'm sorry,' he said; 'it's my fault, I know it. It's always my fault that we row. Yet things could be different, fine, if you'd only be a little understanding.' He put his hands on her shoulders and when his lower lip trembled she said swiftly, 'No! No!'

One big hand moved firmly under her shoulder blades, the other slid down on to her buttocks and as he brought her to him he muttered thickly, 'Just natural, that's all, just natural, none of the other, I promise . . .'

'No! NO! I tell you. No. I can't stand it. You can't, we've tried . . . No . . . o . . . o!'

As she had surprised him when she sprang up from the dressing-table, now she surprised him again, for her

15

body, exploding with fear, thrust itself up out of his arms, and her two hands, like claws on his face, pressed his head away from her; then as he renewed his grip on her, without uttering a word she struggled and tore at him until finally they fell to the floor.

CHAPTER TWO

WILLIE

Nancy Gallacher looked over her shoulder and shouted almost before she had put the phone down, 'Is that you, Willie?' and her husband, thrusting his head through the swing door between the kitchen and the hall, grinned at her as he replied, 'Who you expecting? The milk round finishes at twelve; the postman's last round was at four; the butcher doesn't call until the morrow . . .'

Nancy pushed him back into the kitchen with the flat of her hand, saying with a laugh, 'One of these days you'll start me on; there's a fellow on the dust cart that could give you head and shoulders . . .'

'Oh aye?'

'Listen, I've got news for you. That was Liz on the phone.'

'Don't tell me they're making her Mother Superior already. She's mad. I shouldn't say it but she's . . .'

'It's nothing to do with Liz; it's your Mam and Dad.'

'They've split up, I knew it.' He threw out his arm in a dramatic gesture, then ended seriously, 'But Dad doesn't know, I only left him half-an-hour since.'

'You're in one of your funny moods are you? Well, all right. Have your tea, have your wash, put them to bed, and then if you're interested I'll tell you the news.'

'I've had me wash, me tea, and they're in bed, come on.' He pulled her small plump figure towards him and she laughed into his round dark eyes, almost on a level with her own, and said in an undertone, 'You'll never guess,

17

not in a month of Sundays. They've had an invitation.'

'Aye. Well, go on. They've had an invitation?'

'From the Duke of Moorshire.' Her grin widened when his hold slackened on her and his shoulders and head swayed back from her as if to get her into focus. 'Me Mam and Dad's had an invitation from the . . . ?'

'That's shaken you, hasn't it, Mr Gallacher? . . . Your Mam and Dad's going to Lea Hall.'

'Mother of God!' He moved back from her and sat down on a kitchen stool. 'This is because of the college.'

'Yes, I suppose it is. And yet I don't know; there was the opening reception to cover that, they both got an invitation. But remember Mam had the flu and couldn't go.'

'What sort of a do is it going to be, do they know?'

'Sort of musical, Liz said. The card gives the names of a well-known pianist, a violinist and a singer, all bit pots. We'll know more when we go round – they're all going round the night – that's if I can get Mrs Price to come and sit-in with them.'

'You know something?' Willie Gallacher stabbed his finger at his wife. 'I know why they've got that invitation. It's through the de Ferriers. Dad's had a lot to do with him of late. He was in on the college project right from the beginning, an' it was through his influence that Dad got it . . . I'm sure of it.'

'I thought he got it because his was the lowest tender.'

'Aye, that an' all. Oh aye, that an' all.' Willie, getting to his feet now, went and stood near the stove and began to lift the kettle lid up and down, forming the steam into smoke signals. It was a habit of his when thinking and worrying, and Nancy watched him as he now said bitterly, 'It's a wonder that damned college didn't break our back. If it hadn't been for the Morley Estate we'd have been sunk. I kept telling him, but you know Dad, reach for the sky.'

She came and stood close to him as she asked, 'Is anything wrong now?'

He turned his head and looked at her solemnly. 'Aw, nothing much, if it stays there. But there's complaints from the Morley houses that two walls have cracked; it might just be due to a small subsidence. Let's hope to God it is, because if it carries on from those two it will run straight down the belt between Longside Drive and Waterford Way, and there are eighty houses all told in that section. Aw, to hell!' He swung round. 'Let's go and see the bairns, I'm sick of talking. I told him. I told him when he started there, six years ago, that there was a doubt about that area. I'd been talking to old hands from the Beular Mine, but when I put it to him, what did he say? The Beular Mine was eight miles away and the galleries didn't run in this direction and he'd had the best advice on it. The best advice! Bill Teddington. Anyway, he was a surveyor, so what was my say against his, a lad of nineteen then? But as I said, to hell!' He grinned and pulled her to him; then pointing towards his coat that was lying over a chair, he ended, 'There's something for you in me case under there, tights . . . a dozen pairs, and your size this time.' He dug her in the chest.

'A dozen pairs?' She made a long laughing face, then asked, 'Billy Stoddard or Frank Atkins?'

'Frank. They fell off a lorry.' He again pushed her, his lips now tight in a suppressed grin, and she chuckled as she said, 'Eeh! our Willie. Fell off a lorry!'

She picked up the packet of tights, examined them, raised her eyebrows and said, 'Very nice, thank you. Ta.' She leaned over and kissed him, adding, 'I'll give Mam a couple of pairs, perhaps the Duke will notice them.' And to this he replied, 'You needn't bother; I've got a bundle for her.'

As they made their way once more towards the door

he stopped, and putting his head on one side, asked as if of himself, 'I wonder if she'll be able to carry it through though.'

Nancy pursed her lips. 'I don't see why not; she'll be dressed up to the eyes . . . she'll have to get dressed up for this, she's been letting herself go lately. When I first met her she seemed smart-like to me.'

'It isn't how she looks—' Willie smiled wryly at her – 'it's how she sounds when she gets going. A couple of drinks and her laugh would check Newcastle United in full swing.'

'She'll just likely have wine; they serve wine at those dos I think, like the cheese and wine parties.'

'You can get blotto on wine. But still it's not like the hard stuff, and that's her drink.'

He moved forward, opened the door, and as they went through the hall he said, musingly, 'I wonder what Dad will have to say to it.' To this Nancy made no reply because she didn't really know what her husband expected her to say.

Before they entered the sitting-room she touched his arm and said, 'By the way, Sister Martha phoned the day about Moira; she's been playing them up again. She thinks she's a bit too advanced, that's the trouble, and she finds the infants boring. Anyway, she's going to move her up next term. And she also said she's old enough to start taking instructions for her first confession. And while I'm on about that, Father Armstrong called in to ask would you give a hand with the Children of Mary's Dance. Get the lads rounded up; he said some of them are making their way into Newcastle on a Saturday night and taking the girls with them. He's got Liz helping with the refreshments. He's hoping it's going to be a big do and he's wanting everybody to pig in. He hasn't got half the amount of money he needs for the new window.'

'Aw.' Willie shook his head impatiently. 'They're always on the cadge, the three of them.'

'Not Father Armstrong.'

'Aye, Father Armstrong an' all; they're all alike. By the way.' His grin appeared again and he leant his face close to hers as he said, 'I tell you how he could get his window right away . . . Frank Atkins.' At this they fell upon each other, shaking with suppressed laughter.

CHAPTER THREE

PAUL

Paul Gallacher heard the phone ring as he inserted the key into the door of the house, and in his haste some notebooks slipped from his bulging case and fell to the hall floor, and he muttered, 'Damn!' and leaving them there, he dropped the case on to the chair and picked up the phone.

'Hello, Paul.'

'Hello, dear.'

'I've been ringing for ages, where have you been?'

'At school, of course. I suppose no-one else is in.'

'But it's near six.'

'Well, I'm a conscientious bloke. You know me, I don't leave on the bell. But I had a little business to do that held me up. You all right?'

'Yes, yes. I've got some news for you. Can you come round tonight?'

'Oh, that's going to be difficult, I planned to . . . '

'You must, Paul, they're all coming, at least I hope so. You'll never guess what's happened.'

'Not a catastrophe by the sound of you. Come on, spill it out, I'm dying for a cup of tea.'

'Well, hold on to your seat belt . . . What do you think? Mam and Dad's had an invitation to go to a party at the Duke of Moorshire's house.'

'Really!'

'Ah-ha.'

'Well, I never! That's great news. The Duke of Moorshire. Well! We're coming up in the world, aren't we? May they take any of their relations?'

Elizabeth's high laugh came over the wires; then, her voice dropping low, she said, 'Mam's tickled to death.'

'I bet she is. Where is she? Put her on.'

'Oh, she's just gone into the kitchen. She's going to get some bits and pieces ready for you all coming, you know her. And she'll have to do it single-handed tonight I fear, except for your humble servant here.'

'What's the matter? Another fracas with Annie?'

'You've said it.' Her voice dropped lower. 'Annie's threatened to quit unless Mam tells Mrs Slocombe to go. It's all to do with the wage Mrs Slocombe gets. And it is a bit thick when you think of it, because Annie's on all hours of the day and night for her six pounds. I think I would feel like her too.'

'Annie will never go.'

'I know that, and Mam knows that, and Annie knows that, but it still goes on.'

When her deep sigh came to him he said, softly, 'You'll miss it next year. Have you thought well about it, Liz, because there'll be times when you'll wish you were listening to them going at it hell for leather'; and she replied, 'Yes, I often think that too, but at the same time I'm dying to get away and make a start . . . Eeh! I'd better not let her hear me say that. I must talk with you, Paul, sometime.'

'Do that. The address is Flat 4, Marsh House, Talford Road.' They both laughed and she said, 'You'll come round later then?'

'Yes, yes, I'll manage; in fact I wouldn't miss it for all the tea in China. See you.'

'See you, Paul. Bye-bye.'

'Bye-bye.'

He put down the phone, gathered up the books and climbed the stairs to his flat. When he had closed the door behind him he stood leaning against it for a moment, staring across the room. An invitation to the Duke of Moorshire's place. Well, well. They were certainly going up in the world. Would she enjoy it? He moved from the door and threw the books on top of his case, then stopped again. Yes, she'd enjoy it. It was about time she got out and about and had some pleasure from their prosperity instead of being stuck in the house and thinking and worrying about the lot of them. She had been pushed into the background; while his Dad had gone striding away, up and up, and she had taken the procedure as a matter of course, she had seemed to accept being left behind, which was strange when you took her nature into account, fiery, bombastic, warm and lovable. They had all left her, one after the other; except Liz; and now she too was striving to get away, and not into the world, but out of it. One after the other they had sucked her dry emotionally. He himself was not without guilt in this way; in fact he had been the worst offender.

He went into the kitchen, put the kettle on the gas ring, and set a flower-printed tea tray with the tea things. He then cut three slices of bread and butter, put a jar of jam and an eccles cake on the tray, mashed the tea, and took the lot back into the room.

When he had poured out the tea he leant forward to switch on the television, then stopped and, sitting back in the chair again, he sipped at the tea while his gaze slowly covered the room.

It was barely furnished holding only a divan, which was his bed at night, a chest of drawers, a wardrobe, one easy chair, two straight-backed chairs, the round table at which he was eating, and a roll-top desk. The floor was covered with a grey mottled linoleum and there was one small rug in front of the electric fire.

There was not one attractive item in the room; it was devoid of all comfort. But that's how he wanted it. They'd all tried to get their foot inside the door and do something with it but he had remained firm, except about the curtains. He knew that they thought his austere way of living was but a sop to his guilty conscience: the brother, the son, who had walked out on his vocation, who should now be an ordained priest reflecting glory on the whole family, was but a teacher of English at a Secondary Modern School in Bog's End, and you couldn't get much lower, in any walk of life, than Bog's End.

He leant back in the chair; the tea went cold in his cup; he felt very tired. He'd be twenty-five next Wednesday. Funny, but it was near each birthday that his mind forced him back to the beginning. Was it really six years ago since he had decided against it, not six months, six days, yesterday? The hell of it had been so intense that at times it seemed like yesterday. He knew now there was no hell as the Church would have you believe, as Fathers Stillwell and Monaghan still pumped home; not Armstrong, he was too level-headed for that. Hell was the torture of the mind in the night, a deep deep well of despair in which you struggled and fought in darkness, where you vomited out your guilt and watched it rising again like a slimy, stinking bog to choke you. Hell in the day was the kindliness of pastor and priest, that kindliness that shed a veil over their condemnation; the kindliness of brothers in God who looked at you with pity that but veiled their envy, the envy of your will that had the power to turn you back on the path towards God. God, who was but a mirage in thought, a hope with which to inject despair, an imagery in your mind sucked from other minds, those minds which seemed so sure yet still chanted, 'I believe. Help thou my unbelief.'

Hell was the look in the eyes of his mother, the look that asked silently, 'Is it a girl?' And if she had put the question to him what would he have said? He would have said, 'No, it's not a girl, it is a woman,' for even then, with only a year between them, he had seen her as a woman, mature, different.

If he had never seen her, never met her, never spoken to her, would he have turned back down that road? Yes; yes, sometime or other he would have. His youth rising before him in relief, he saw each innocent step of his as keys opening channels in his parents' minds, the altar boy, the server, his love for the Church itself were all misinterpreted. But how could they know and he not know at that early age that the fascination of the ceremonial had him bewitched? The chanting of the Latin at the Mass – he rebelled violently against the mysteries being revealed in English – the apparent camaraderie of the priests, their ever-ready joking, their humanism as they tipped the bottle, drew him with the power of a first love; but most of all it was his mother's almost open adoration of him, her offspring, her son, who was to bring glory on the family by entering the Church, that had pressed his steps forward.

He was seventeen when he finally succumbed, and on that day she had kissed him and held him close and, the tears streaming down her face, she had whispered, 'You're like a penance for all me sins, for I've been a wooden Catholic all me life.' She didn't know it, and no explanation at the time could have made her understand, that she was offering him as a sacrifice.

He was nineteen on the day he told her he was leaving the seminary. Every day and every night for six months he had tried to make himself see sense, but it was no use. From when he had first set eyes on the girl – or the woman – he was lost. And it wasn't that love had come to him for the first time, for since he was fourteen, and before, he'd

26

had his little flings. In the cemetery after benediction on a Sunday night, when it was dark that was, he'd done what his brothers referred to as his homework. Never the whole hog, but enough to satisfy him. He was conceited enough at that time to think he had just to raise an eyebrow and they'd come running; and it was true. So when he first saw her she didn't appear to him one of a species about whose anatomy he knew nothing.

The first sight of her did not only touch his body, or heart, he could have conquered that, but she took possession of his mind. For weeks on end he had talked to his confessor about it. Then they had brought Father Armstrong to him. Father Armstrong had christened him; he had christened them all; he had married his mother and father; he was like one of the family. Father Armstrong probed deeper than his confessor at the seminary, and after it was all over he had put his hands on his shoulders and said, 'Well, there is one thing the Catholic Church can do without, Paul, and that is a bemused and bewildered priest.' He had even smiled at him; Father Armstrong was the only one who didn't seem to be saying one thing while thinking another, and he was the only one who knew the name of the woman who had bewitched him.

He leant forward and picked up the cup and made a face when his lips touched the cold tea. The teapot too was cold, and so, rising, he went into the kitchen and made himself a fresh brew.

CHAPTER FOUR

FRANCES

'Is that you, Frances?'

'Yes. Yes, Liz. Just a minute while I close the door, they're going mad . . . Did you hear them? Their Gran-Walton is here; she's bathing them. I don't know who enjoys it most or makes the most noise. Well, I'm sitting comfortably; now we'll begin.' She laughed. 'Fire ahead.'

'I've got some news that'll surprise you, Frances.'

'You have? Well, I'd like a surprise. I've forgotten what it feels like to be surprised, not counting the time Pauline put the cat in the washing machine.'

'Stop kidding, our Frances, you're all kidding the night. Listen. You'll never guess where Mam and Dad are going.'

'Oh, I can; at least I know what Dad's aiming for, the peerage. I saw him talking to Mrs de Ferrier yesterday, standing chatting to her opposite the club. She must have been there to lunch, in Ransome's you know. Only distinguished ladies are invited to Ransome's. Ha! ha!'

'Well, you're not far out.'

'What!'

Elizabeth's voice dropped to a sacred whisper. 'They've been invited to meet the Duke of Moorshire at Lea Hall.'

'Mam and Dad?'

'Mam and Dad.'

'You're joking.'

'No joking, Frances; I've got the card in my hand. The

Duke of Moorshire requests the pleasure of Mr and Mrs Gallacher at . . .'

'Mam and Dad to meet the Duke?'

'It's 1970, things are happening today.'

'My! I'll say they are.'

'But isn't it wonderful?'

'I suppose so.' There was a strong suspicion of doubt in Frances's tone: then she asked, 'Is Mam going?'

'Is she going? Of course, she's going!'

'When is it?'

'Four weeks today. It'll give her time to get clothes and things.'

'She wants to get her figure down before she thinks of clothes; she must have put on a couple of stone lately.'

'No, she hasn't, not all that; she's not fat.'

'Not fat!' Frances looked scathingly into the phone as if she could see Elizabeth, then she asked, 'Are they all going over the night?' and Elizabeth answered, 'Yes. I haven't phoned Helen yet, but she nearly always pops in on a Friday night anyway. You and Dave will come, won't you?'

'Well, it's our night for the club, but I suppose we could look in. Yes, we'll look in around eightish.'

'All right, Frances. Bye-bye.'

'Bye-bye.'

Frances Walton put the phone down and stood looking at it for a moment before she turned slowly round and walked into the sitting-room, where her husband was sprawled on the couch before the fire, his short legs thrust out, his feet resting on the edge of a chair. She went around the couch and faced him before she said, 'You know the latest?'

'What?'

'Mam and Dad's been invited to a do by the Duke of Moorshire.'

29

'Eh!' Dave Walton's feet came off the chair in a swing that brought his body upright on the couch. 'Say that again.'

'You heard. Me Mam and Dad's been invited to a do at the Duke of Moorshire's house, Lea Hall. You know, the place on the river about six miles out . . .'

'I know, I know.' He waved his hand at her. 'They've been invited there by him?'

'Yes, that's what Liz says. Well!' She drew in a long breath, then let it slowly out before dropping on to the couch beside him saying, 'Dad's flying high.'

'Yes; yes, he is.' Dave Walton reached out and picked up a cigarette from the ash tray on the side table, then as he lit it he said, thoughtfully, 'It'll all be good for business; it's contacts like that that count.'

'Will it affect you?'

'Can't help but, can it? I supply the materials . . . well, some of them.'

Frances pushed her fair hair back from her shoulders with an impatient movement, and her head jerked upwards as she said, 'I think it's too bad of Dad to split the order with Smith's, and I feel like telling him . . .'

'You mind your own business.' He tapped the ash from his cigarette, then wagged it at her before putting it into his mouth again. 'If there's any telling to do in that line I'm quite able to look after myself and my interests; and I think I know why he gave Smith the order.'

'You do? Why then?'

'Well, I must say at this stage I'm guessing, but Smith is full cousin to Redfern, Councillor Redfern. Do you get it?'

'No.'

'Well, if the Council pass it, that's if the ratepayers stand for it, they'll build the marina. Now up river there's a four mile stretch before you come to the shale, and since they're not loading any more in the east dock there's another six miles down river right to the sea. It could be a pleasure-cruise stretch.'

'Past all those factories?'

'Aye, past all those factories. But we're getting away from the point. Building the College will be like building with meccano compared to making that boat haven; cafés, sun lounge and dance hall and the motel thrown in. Your dad's throwing little hooks to Smith in order to land Redfern's vote. Redfern's the big fish on the Council.' His voice now took on a sarcastic note as he ended, 'I hope he doesn't get tangled up in his own lines, that's all.'

Frances looked at her husband. In the natural course of things she should have defended her father's tactics, for they had him alone to thank for their present prosperity, even though this prosperity, gauged in relation to her mother's as represented by Savile House, was still not very evident. She was ambitious, was Frances, both for herself and her small, dark and crafty husband.

'Well—' she rose from the couch – 'I suppose we'd better go and get ready to join the rejoicing.' As she went to pass him he put out his hand and caught her arm and, looking up at her, said with a half laugh, 'Well, look pleased about it, jealousy will get you nowhere.'

'Oh, you!' She flapped her hand at him and went down the room, across the narrow hall and up the steep stairs. At the top she paused and looked down. She didn't like this house, it was cramped and stifling. She hadn't realised how much she had liked her home until she had come here on her wedding day three and a half years ago. She'd never be satisfied until she had a house like the one in which she had been brought up since she was fourteen. She felt she was made for a place like Savile House; she would know how to run it, know how to entertain.

31

As it was now, the place was wasted: her father hardly ever in, Elizabeth leaving it next year for the convent, when it would be occupied almost solely by her mother, except on their occasional get-togethers. She knew her mother would be happier, more at home, in a house like this. Things were very unfair.

CHAPTER FIVE

HELEN

'Trevor! Look, turn that thing down.' Helen Gillespie rushed into the room, dived to the television and not only turned it down but switched it off. Then, bounding back from it, she fell into her chair with such a plop that she almost upset the small modern table on which reposed the evening meal of eggs on toast and, proclaiming the sign of the times, a bottle of seven and six Sauterne from the cut price shop in the market.

'Hel – en. Hel – en.' Her husband always split her name like that when he was slightly annoyed or put out. 'You nearly had the plate over me, on my suit.' He pushed his chair back and examined his trousers, then dusted them with a large orange coloured paper napkin.

'Well, I'm excited. What do you think Liz has just told me?'

'I don't know.' Stiffly and with a look on his face that said nor did he care, he picked up his knife and fork again and continued his meal, his manner of eating matching his pedantic speech and in keeping with his small thin, clean-shaven face and peevish look.

Helen's hands thrusting out across the table, went to grip his arm but stopped just in time. If she messed up his suit that would put a gloom on the evening. Her face now tight with her irritation, she said, 'Aw bust! For heaven's sake what does a spot on your suit matter; you could get it sponged in the shop ten times a day. Suits, suits, suits, that's all you think about.'

'That's what we live by.' He paused with a piece of egg wobbling on the point of his fork.

'Oh we do, we we? What about me, my share doesn't count? Look you here!' She poked her head across the table at him. 'I've been wanting to say this to you for some time. I was working before I married you, I'm still working. My wage is only three pounds a week less than yours. I've had two rises in two years; you haven't had one since we married and that's three years ago; so in future I'll thank you to pick your words.'

As his wife flounced out and into the tiny kitchen of the flat Trevor Gillespie put his knife and fork slowly down on to his plate and stared across the narrow space of the room towards the eucalyptus plant that was beginning to dwarf the frame that divided the dinette from the rest of the room, and that sickening humiliating feeling attacked him yet again, the feeling that made him want to bow his head on to his arms and cry, sob, wail out his frustration, his inadequacy – not inadequacy with regards to Helen; no, it was just in the shop he was a failure. But why was he a failure there? Simply because Pattenden didn't like him, not because of his work. Pattenden had never liked him, and he showed this by promoting others over his head . . . And what had he done about it? What could he do about it? Nothing, for he couldn't stand up to Pattenden; Pattenden who was tall and broad and overpowering, and right, always right. But he wouldn't stand it much longer, no he wouldn't, he would go to the head office . . . He wasn't aware that Helen had come back to the table and was standing near him until she put her arm around his shoulders and, bending down to him, whispered, 'I'm sorry.'

He smiled at her now and, stretching his face up to hers, he kissed her and taking her hand he pulled her down on the chair and said gently, 'What had you to tell me?'

34

Without enthusiasm now she said, 'Mam and Dad have been invited to meet the Duke of Moorshire at Lea Hall.'

She watched his mouth fall into a gape, his eyes widen and his eyebrows form black peaks above them, and she laughed at his expression.

'Really!'

'Ah-ha.'

'How marvellous . . . The Duke of Moorshire.' His mind lifted him into tomorrow, and he could hear Pattenden say, 'Gillespie, here a moment . . . take this gentleman's measurements.'

'Yes, Mr Pattenden. Yes, Mr Pattenden.'

'What's the matter with you, Mr Gillespie, dreaming as usual?'

'No, Mr Pattenden. It's just that I didn't have much sleep last night. We were kept late at our in-laws; they were discussing the invitation to a reception at the Duke of Moorshire's, and were considering what kind of a return they should make, a small dinner party or some such. You know what it is if you're asked out, you must return the hospitality . . . '

'Liz wants us to go round.'

'Yes, yes.' He blinked and smiled broadly at her. 'Of course. I bet your mam's excited.'

She looked at him, her head on one side, slightly puzzled. He very rarely called her mother Mam, it was nearly always your mother, sometimes only she. She had thought of late that he looked down his nose at her mother and she didn't like it because after all he didn't come from much himself; they were respectable but that's all that could be said for his people, for they had pinched and scraped all their lives.

She rose from the chair and began clearing the table, saying, 'She'll have to do something about her figure; she's let herself go lately and she's not all that old, only forty-four.' She stopped with the plates in her hand and

35

said, 'Wait till the morrow when I can tell the doctors. Won't my status go up, especially with Doctor Blake for he's a snob of the first water? And his wife's a length ahead of him, swimming hard.'

Trevor laughed as he picked up the table mats and put them in their rack. He, too, wished it were tomorrow. Yes, how he wished it were tomorrow.

'Yes, Mr Pattenden; yes, Mr Pattenden; yes, Mr Pattenden. NO, MR PATTENDEN!'

CHAPTER SIX

THE BIG FELLOW

It was said that Collingwood Road was more of a boundary between upper and lower Felburn than the river itself, for behind one side of the road Bog's End started, while behind the other lay the market, the municipal buildings, old High Street, new High Street, both giving way to the park, and the park leading to Brampton Hill and, of course, to the now new quarter of the élite, The Rise.

Collingwood Road was lined mainly with warehouses and offices, and placed half on the road frontage and half in Collingwood Mews were the offices of Gallacher and Sons, Builders and Contractors.

The outer office faced the street. Rodney Gallacher's private office was behind this with a window and a door looking into the mews. The mews yard could hold two lorries and two cars, and when the business first started it had to hold them because they couldn't afford to garage them. Now it only held cars, three at the most. Rodney Gallacher's, Sam Gallacher's and the car belonging to the tenant of the mews flat.

The flat was the property of Rodney Gallacher and it was let furnished to a Mrs Morland at eight pounds a week. At least that's what it said on the books, and Mrs Morland's cheque came in every month to prove this. Mrs Morland left her flat every Friday night and was away all week-end, but this fact wasn't known to anyone except Rodney Gallacher and Mrs Morland's very close friend, Rosamund de Ferrier.

Mary Whitaker, Rodney Gallacher's secretary, and his typist, Kitty Malone, occasionally saw Mrs de Ferrier get out of her car and go into the mews flat to visit Mrs Morland, and they always remarked on her dress, so plain but superior like. 'If you saw her clothes hanging in a shop you wouldn't give tuppence for them. It's the way she carries them that makes her out,' Mary Whitaker stated, and Kitty Malone said, 'Aye, you're born with it or without it and all the money in Barclay's Bank—' which was the firm's bank – 'wouldn't help you if you haven't got it, if you know what I mean.'

They knew that their boss knew Mr de Ferrier for he sometimes came into the office, and neither of them cared much for him, uppish, la-di-da as he was, with a face, Kitty Malone said, like a powdered arse and though Miss Whitaker had chastised her for her language she had spluttered while doing so. His wife was quite a bit younger than him they thought. Their ages were discussed and compared. He was over fifty, while she, well, what could she be? She looked about thirty-three or thirty-five, but then she must be more than that having a nineteen year old son kicking around, unless she had started at sixteen, and her type usually didn't. Nineteen or twenty they would say, when she married; that would leave her about forty. Well, that being the case, they had to hand it to her.

One day last week when she had got out of her car the boss happened to be in the office and he watched her cross the pavement, and they watched him and they wondered what he thought of her, or if he thought about her at all, because they both agreed later he could look at a woman and never see her. The only things he saw were bricks, cement, window-frames, floor boards and the like. But now, if it had been Mr Sam, aw, with Mr Sam they would have had a laugh about her; but with his father, never. As Mary Whitaker said, and she should know because she had been with the firm since it had started, the boss was utterly, utterly wrapped up in the business, and what was more he was out and about so much seeing to this and that, she wondered his wife put up with it. But then he was lucky, because Mrs Gallacher, what she had seen of her, looked easy-going. Fat people always were.

The bedroom was decorated in French grey and dull pink. The curtains on the windows that looked on to the main yard were pink and padded and herringboned with grey thread, with a heavy bedcover made to match.

The bedcover was now rolled up towards the foot of the bed and Rodney Gallacher pushed his bare feet into it, stretched his long legs, pulled in his thickening waist and expanded his chest with a long deep breath as he flexed his arms sidewards.

When there was a slight rustle to the side of him he turned his head in the direction of the bedroom door and looked at the woman who had mesmerised him and dominated his life for the past eighteen months. He knew that if he ever lost her nothing in life would be worth its salt.

He turned on his elbow and watched her walking towards him. She was wearing a flimsy negligée that made her body more alluring than it had been when bare. When she reached the bed he fell on to his back again and, putting up his hands, pulled her down sharply beside him, so that her face hung above his, long and pale, her green eyes mocking as always.

Had Maggie looked at him like this he would have said she was sneering at him or bursting for a fight. At times he did wonder what state of mind he had reached that he should take from this woman such things. Had Maggie dared to utter them even in one of her lightning tempers, he would have busted her mouth for her.

All his life he'd had a sneaking respect for class. Behind his bombast and his left wing talk he had admired the tone of class, the look of class, the arrogance of class; if you had class you could get away with things, from insults to love on the side. If you had class you possessed a magic tongue, a magic eye, a magic manner. His feeling for class went back a long way. It must have been this feeling that stirred him when, at nineteen, he used to follow the Armitage girl from the convent right to the top of Brampton Hill, until, day of days, he got to carrying her bag. And that went on for a month until her father espied him, and he not only nearly laid him out but arranged it so that he got the sack from Stevenson's Brickyard.

Funny how things turn out. Papa Armitage, had he but known it, did him a good turn, for he had gone out and got a job on the buildings and had known immediately that this was his line.

It was about this time that Maggie had asked him to her birthday party. She was young, plump and fetching and he had eased himself on her. That is all it had been, but, begod, before he knew where he was he had been standing before Father Armstrong saying, 'I will.'

But he must be fair; it had worked out, it had worked out for years. She was a good cook and housekeeper; she'd given him bairns, she'd satisfied his needs, and his needs in those days were pretty demanding. Any hour any time, to give her her due, she had never said no.

And then he had started up on his own, and Maggie became but a shelter to return to from the blast of the business, for it was a blast. From the time that he built the first house, when he had to run here and there, hell for leather, begging for credit, it was a blast; but it blasted him upwards, and outwards, bigger and better each year. It blasted him into the company of men who previously had just been names, names that were said with hushed breath in the town. Names like Redfern, Pearce . . . and de Ferrier. Names that were in the gilt-edged book of Ransome's.

It was eight years ago that he had first met de Ferrier. He had been on the committee of the proposed new college. He knew about de Ferrier; he had done his homework on all that committee. De Ferrier was connected with all types of businesses, not only in the town and in Newcastle, but over the county. He had been very civil to Mr de Ferrier. If he looked too far back he despised himself, for then he saw his civility as fawning. Anyway, it had paid off and he had got the contract to build the college.

But it seemed strange now that he had never met de Ferrier's wife until two years ago. Perhaps it was as well, for from the moment he had touched her hand in greeting he was ensnared – and so was she, although it took her some time to admit it. If she held a fascination for him he also possessed something that she needed. She had told him frankly it was the size of him, the roughness of him, his almost elemental way of making love. He should have been upset at this, cast down, because if ever he wanted to play the gentleman to anyone it was to her. He wanted to match her tone, her air, but instinctively he knew that, were he capable of this, he would no longer attract her. Strange, when he came to work it out, that it should be his way of making love to Maggie that held this woman. His very coarseness was the magnet that drew her to him.

He looked downwards to where her hand, rather small for her size but soft and white, was pressing the black hairs on his chest away from their natural growth. When her hand moved swiftly downwards over his stomach and she stabbed his navel with her forefinger his body arched on the bed and he made a grunting, chuckling sound in his throat, then went to pull her to him, but she resisted him

41

with a playful flap of her hand, saying, 'Enough! Enough! Listen, I have something to tell you.'

'Well, fire away.' He relaxed on the bed. Whatever she had to tell him it wouldn't be that she was going to leave him. If he was sure of anything in his life he was sure of that.

'You are to meet the Duke . . . '

His deep-set brown eyes narrowed, his thick eyebrows hooded them still further, his puggish nose wrinkled and drew apart his thick, well-moulded lips until his whole face took on the shape of his chin and looked entirely square. 'What did you say?'

With her middle finger she stroked her hair back behind her ear and, her head on one side, she said, 'If you're not galloping into senility then you would have heard what I said, you are to meet the Duke.'

He was sitting up straight now, his arms pushed back into the pillows to support himself. 'The Duke of Moorshire? You mean our Duke?'

Her laugh was thin and merry. 'Our Duke, yes, the Duke of Moorshire. The invitation should be waiting for you when you get back.'

He slid back on to his elbows until he was leaning against the bed head, and after staring at her for some time he nodded slowly, saying, 'You've managed this, haven't you?'

She raised her eyebrows and smiled as she said, 'Well I won't disclaim all credit. I did suggest, when certain names of prominent citizens were being put forth, that Mr Gallacher had done a great deal for the town. Apart from the college there was the Morley and the Rollingdon Estates; moreover, for a man who was likely to – no I'd better not say likely to – I'd better say who *might* stand a chance of getting the contract for the Marina, a little appreciation should be shown him. What did they think? They thought as I did.'

'Oh, Mundy!' He was rolling with her back and forward over the bed, and when they came to rest he looked down into her face and said softly, 'God! If only I was an emperor, I would put you on a throne. You know, the older I get the more I can understand the Duke of Windsor business.'

'Ah! Ah!' She was tapping his lips with her finger. 'She lost him his throne don't forget, she lost him his throne.'

'Well, he had her and that's all that counts. Ah, Rosamund I worship you.' He was speaking through gritted teeth now. 'Do you know that? I wor-ship you?'

'Thank you, Mr Gallacher. I'm so pleased to hear it. By the way.' Her eyes stretched a little wider. 'You'll have to see that your lady is suitably attired for the occasion as it is a musical soirée.'

Slowly he lifted his body from hers. 'What! What do you mean . . . my lady? Maggie, you mean?'

'Who else?'

He was kneeling up now, to the side of her. 'You mean Maggie's been invited an' all?'

'Oh, Mr Gallacher.' She, too, was sitting up. 'The Duke is not holding a stag party, he is giving an evening's entertainment to which he is inviting his friends and a few prominent citizens of the town . . . and he could hardly invite them without inviting their wives.'

He got off the bed, pulled a bathroom robe from the back of the chair and put it on, and he kept his face averted from her as he said, 'It won't do; I'll have to refuse.'

'Don't be a fool, Rodney. Moreover, don't annoy me.' She, too, was off the bed now. 'I have worked to wangle this for you. Besides the Mayor and his wife and you, the only other two local business couples invited are the Redferns and the Pearces; but there'll be lots of county folk present, and you could make contacts, the right contacts.'

He had his head bowed as he walked past her into the bathroom and when he disappeared from her view and failed to make a reply to her statement she reached out, took a cigarette from a box, lit it and drew the smoke well down into her lungs before she said, 'The word snob doesn't fit you; you're an upstart, Rodney. You know that, don't you?' She was now at the bathroom door, and she stood watching him getting into his trousers. Again she waited for a retort, but it wasn't forthcoming. As he pulled his shirt roughly over his head, she said, 'What are you afraid of? She needn't open her mouth. If you are worried on that score, prime her. See that she's dressed suitably; that's all that will be required.'

He paused as he tucked his shirt into his trousers and cast a sidelong glance at her. She could insult him as much as she liked and her insults he took as compliments, but strangely he couldn't take it when she threw them at Maggie. Although a lightning warning told him to watch his step he was snapping at her, 'What do you think she is, a performing pig? She can pass herself if she wants to.'

Her eyes widened slightly; she made a move with her lips. 'I'm glad to hear it,' she said; 'but you must understand that I've based my opinion of her from your own description.'

'I've hardly mentioned her name to you.'

'True, but your silences have been very telling.'

When her lids drooped and she turned sharply from him he hurried after her into the room and, pulling her round by the shoulder, he stared into her face and swallowed deeply before he muttered, 'Don't you understand? I just don't want you two to meet, because . . . well . . . ' He jerked his head. 'You're everything she isn't, and I don't want you to . . . ' He stopped himself from saying, 'look down your nose at her'. Nor could he say, 'be sorry for her', so he substituted, 'I don't want you to be sorry for me.'

She laughed outright now. 'Sorry for you? Oh, Rodney! you are funny. Do you know I could never be sorry for you, not if you were in the direst trouble. Odd that, isn't it? I've thought about it, and I know you could never evoke my pity no matter what happened to you. You're too big, bouncy, bustling.' She pressed her lips together, then ended, 'Boisterous and bumptious and—' she pushed the tip of her nose against his – 'you're also a bugger into the bargain.'

He was laughing now, his head back. That was another thing she could do, make him laugh. He always laughed when she swore, for her swearing was like no-one else's swearing. When she said bloody, bugger or sod, it was as if she were embroidering her speech with humour. When Maggie said bloody or bugger it was with bitterness, or venom; she never used the word sod, she considered it a dirty word equivalent to the four letter ones. Strange the difference in people. Some people's language grated on you, roused you to bitterness, even brawls, as Maggie's did; yet this one here, this fashionable piece, this lady, and she was all that by God, could come out with things that back in the house they would consider coarse, but which, coming from her lips, could be termed wit.

His thoughts touching on the house, he told himself that he must get home and squash any rising hopes Maggie had of them going to meet the Duke, for besides him not wanting Rosamund and her to meet, there was the dread of what she might get up to once she had a few glasses of wine down her gullet. She couldn't carry drink of any sort; it either made her right daft or put her in a fighting mood. He must get home.

He now pulled Rosamund into his arms and kissed her long and hard before saying, 'Thanks anyway for making the effort on my behalf. Although it can't be done, I won't forget it.'

She looked at him blankly. Then, her lips smiling at him but not her eyes, she said, 'As you wish, Milord, as you wish.'

CHAPTER SEVEN

MAGGIE

They were all around her, Sam and Arlette, Willie and Nancy, Frances and Dave, Helen and Trevor, Paul and Lizzie, and you couldn't hear yourself speak. It was a night like they hadn't had for years; not even on New Year's Eve had they been all together and laughed like this. She had laughed more the night than she had laughed for weeks, for months; aye, she had laughed more the night than she had laughed for the past two years. And why had she not laughed? Oh, forget it. Come on, she told herself; there might never be another night like this again, all in harmony, all jolly, all for once thinking of her, all for once talking of her and seeing her as somebody, not just as mam, or the old girl, or fat arse, a term of endearment from Sam, but as somebody . . . a somebody, somebody fit to have an invitation from a duke. By! She never thought she'd live to see this day. For that matter, she never thought there'd be a day in her life when a thing like this would happen to her.

She moved among them, a plate of meat sandwiches in each hand. Annie had brought in tea, and coffee for them who wanted it, looking all the while like the parson's sister, her nose trying to get away from her face. She'd have it out with her the morrow, see if she didn't. That one was getting too big for her boots, that one wanted taking down a peg . . . 'What were you saying, Trevor?'

'I was saying—' Trevor strained his face up to hers as he shouted – 'that you'll have to have a crest on your paper after this.'

Her laugh rang out and she nodded down to him as she cried, 'Aye, an' I'll have the lav rolls stamped with it an' all.'

Trevor gave a thin smile at this but Helen spluttered into her tea as she cried, 'Oh, Mam! Oh, Mam!' then turning to Frances and Nancy, she said, 'Mam's going to have the lav rolls stamped with a crest.'

'What's that? What's that?'

All around the room they were asking the reason for the hilarious laughter in the corner near the fireplace, and like the game of 'passing on the saying', they passed on Maggie's words and when a slightly distorted version reached Sam, he garbled, 'What! She's going to have her crest stamped on her chest?' and the laughter became painful, Helen and Elizabeth hanging on each other's necks in apparent agony.

'Look! look!' Sam was holding the floor again, and the laughter subsided into splutters as they all gave him their attention, for Sam was in great form the night, and when Sam was in form he could make a cat laugh.

'Now, this is what you'll do, Mam.' Sam had his arm extended towards his mother, his finger wagging at her. 'When the butler announces—' he assumed a stance and from deep in his throat cried, 'Mr and Mrs Gallacher—' then went on, 'You'll glide in like this.' He now gave an imitation of his mother gliding, rolling his hips from side to side and bringing fresh outbursts of laughter. 'And when he offers you his hand you take it like so.' He caught at his sister-in-law's hand and, bowing slightly towards her, he said, 'Good evening.' Then turning sharply around and addressing his mother again, he cried, 'Whatever you do, don't say, "Hello, lad, how's the missus?" ' There was laughter again, but not so much this time, and it was strained. Willie hadn't laughed at the last joke; Paul's face was straight, he hadn't laughed at all.

The only other member of the party who hadn't been amused by Sam's antics or any of the fun was his wife. She was suffering from a headache.

And Maggie hadn't laughed at her eldest son's comical advice because she didn't think it was comical, he was going too far. She knew how to pass herself when it was necessary. Sometimes their Sam didn't know when to stop. She picked up the empty plates from the table and went into the kitchen, and looking from the long table to the Welsh dresser, she said to Annie, 'Have all the sandwiches gone?'

'Well, you should know; you've taken them in, an' I haven't eaten them.'

Maggie banged the plates down on the table and looked across the kitchen to where Annie was standing, her hand on the kettle waiting for it to boil, and said, 'Annie Fawcett, if it wasn't that they're all here I'd give you the length of me tongue, but it can wait until the morning.'

'I mightn't be here in the morning.'

'Well, that will suit me nicely.' She glared at the narrow shoulders, the thin head, the hair cut across the back of it as if it had been trimmed under a pudding basin. There hadn't been a day in her remembered life when she hadn't known Annie Fawcett. She had played with her before she had gone to school; they had gone hand in hand to school together; they had left school together; they had gone into the plastics factory together; and after Willie was born in '45 Annie had come to stay with her because she had been shaken by the time bomb that fell near their house in Bog's End, and her visit had lasted twenty-five years; not that she hadn't been glad of her company, and her help, she had, and she hadn't been mean in showing it, but this last three years, since she had started the early change, there was no living with her. Aw, but it wasn't only the change that was the matter with her,

49

it was Ralphy Holland. If her Rod had turned out like Ralphy she would have felt bitter an' all. You had to make allowances. Yes, you had to make allowances.

When she went back into the room the laughter had stopped and they were all in a heated discussion that was apparently bordering on argument; but that's how it went in this house. The evening could range from belly-bursting laughter to two of the brothers or sisters walking out declaring that they were never going to speak to each other again . . . until the next time. She was so used to it, it had no effect on her now; well, perhaps just a little, but not the effect it once had when she would bawl them all down, her·lungs swelling to issue the bellow that would bring them to silence. Anyway she had them all about her; it was as it used to be, except that Rod wasn't here. A feeling that she wouldn't admit to a sadness crept into her chest but she bludgeoned it away as she bent down to Willie and asked, 'What is it this time? Parliament? Ireland?' She almost added, 'The pill?' but that would be bordering on religion and they all kept off religion in their arguments, solely because of Paul. Before Paul had shied away from his duty religion had had its share in the racket like everything else because Arlette Trevor and Nancy were Protestants, and the family was out to make them turn. So, instead of the pill, she said, 'Or what?'

Willie looked up to her, his face straight, dark with an anger that he seldom showed.

'It's that bloody fellow in the *Messenger*, that poor poet. He'd better stick to his love jingles if he knows what's good for him, else . . . he'll fall off a lorry.'

'Fall off a lorry?' She screwed her eyes up at him.

'Aye. Look, Frances; let me Mam see the paper.'

As Frances leant from the couch and handed her mother the paper, Willie said, 'He's a stirrer, that's what he is.'

'Because he's speaking the truth?'

It was the first time Paul had spoken to anybody except his mother since he came into the room, and there was a short heavy silence before Willie turned on him, crying, 'What do you mean by truth? Everybody's at it; things don't fall off lorries only on the roads. You can't tell me that there's a shop or a business in the town where somebody isn't helping himself. And you, can you say that you haven't brought paper from school and used it for yourself? Helped yourself to pencils and . . . aye, books? When you go back to the flat the night have a look round and see how many of the books you call yours have the school stamp on them.'

'It would take a lot of paper, pencils and books to total a hundred and twenty thousand pounds, and that's just a rough account of the stuff that fell off lorries in this town alone last year.'

Another heavy silence followed; then Willie again spoke, his mouth now tight as he said, 'You're for him, aren't you?'

'Yes, I could say I was for him.'

Sam, standing near the mantelpiece, his elbow resting on it, asked quietly, 'Do you know him then, Paul, this chap that writes the poetry?'

'Sort of.'

'Is his name really Lacker?'

'Well—' Paul jerked his head – 'I shouldn't think so.'

'I thought you said you knew him.'

'Well, I know of him.'

'Look, I haven't read it, what does it say?' Helen now looked at her mother, and Maggie, who had just finished reading the piece in question, said, 'Well, I think it's funny, although it doesn't rhyme much.'

'None of his stuff does; he's got the nerve to call it poetry.'

'Why are you so wild about it?' Paul's voice sounded

calm, aggravatingly calm, and once more there was a silence. before it could bring another outburst from Willie, Maggie laughed and thrust the paper sideways to where Arlette was sitting and said, 'Here, you read it. Meself, I think it's funny. Go on, read it out. You're a good reader, read it out.'

Arlette took the paper in her hand. She scanned the page, then raising her head she looked round the half circle of eyes fixed upon her, and her gaze came to rest on Paul. She took in the fact that there was a white line round his mouth, that his eyes had darkened to a deep brown that hid his thoughts and made his expression blank. She looked at the page again and began:

> They fell off a lorry
> Going jiggedy jag:
> Three dozen nylons,
> A bottle of scotch
> And a ham went wham!
>
> It's honest to God,
> I'm not lying,
> Why damn!
> It's the roads, love,
> They tilt on the cam.
>
> It fell off a lorry
> This hair spray, and say,
> Pass these to the priest
> On his visiting day.
> They're on the level,
> Straight, I'm making no mock,
> They fell off a lorry
> The whole box of socks.

Almost before Arlette had finished Willie was on his feet. 'You know something?' He looked from one to the other. 'That bloke could be writing about this very house.'

'Don't be silly.' The protest came from all quarters, and he shouted them down. 'How often have bits and pieces been passed on to Father Armstrong and Father Monaghan, half hams and slabs of butter, bottles of whisky at Christmas?' He was looking at his mother now, and her voice rising, she cried back at him, 'Hold your hand a minute. Hold your hand. It was very often out of the fridge, stuff you and Sam had nothing to do with.'

'Aye, but on the other hand very often it wasn't.'

'Now, look, Master Willie Gallacher; don't you bawl at me, lad . . . '

'I'm, I'm sorry, Mam.' He jerked his head and his voice dropped. 'But . . . well—' His words were cut off by Frances saying in her cold disinterested way, 'It could be about this house at that, and at this very minute.' She was leaning towards Arlette, her eyes on the paper, and she moved her finger on to a part of it and said, 'He's got another one here. Listen. Go on, read that one, Arlette.'

'No.' Arlette went to close the paper but Frances, pulling it from her and sitting up straight, said, 'Listen to this. It's called "Ties". Now just listen:

Blood is thicker than water,
Inanely is relationship explained.
Then does water flow in the veins
Of the mate from where
Sprang the seed,
Or of she who carried the nest
In which to breed?

53

> Love leaps the space to the stranger
> And, entwined, they grow to age
> And see their offspring hate and rage
> One to the other, brother to brother.
> The implication that love flows
> Where blood is a tie
> Is a lie.'

You couldn't call the absence of speech a silence, it was more akin to unconsciousness brought about by shock. It was Elizabeth who brought them to the surface again when she began to cry, for Elizabeth laughed easily and she cried easily. One after the other their voices rose to accuse Frances in varying ways. 'Now look what you've done! You're a starter, our Frances, if ever there was one.' To which were added such comments as, 'It's all right, Liz, it's all right. You should be used to it by now, you know us.'

Maggie went and stood by the side of her youngest daughter; she was sitting on a pouffe, her elbows on her knees and her face buried in her palms. Maggie put her hand on her head and said softly, 'There now, there now, there's nothing to frash yourself about.' But even as she said it she knew there was a lot to frash herself about.

While Liz could give vent to the pain those lines had caused, for Liz was a highly sensitive creature, she herself wasn't supposed to feel things or show her pain. She hadn't grasped the whole gist of the thing, she'd have to read it once or twice over, but that last line – well, a blind man on a galloping horse could have read what that meant. 'The implication that love flows where blood is a tie is a lie.' There was bitterness there. Aye, but truth. Oh yes, yes, truth.

She looked around her family. They were all talking now, except Willie. Willie for the moment was in disgrace; he had started all this. But Frances was taking nothing on herself, she was unconcerned. It was the usual pattern. You knew where you were with Willie; he blurted out what he thought, but he didn't intend to hurt. Not so with others in her family, and she wasn't only thinking of Frances.

At this moment Annie came to the sitting-room door and beckoned her with a lift of her head. There was no anger on her face now. She looked as she used to be, at one with her, all for her. When she reached her, Annie put out her hand and drew her into the hall; then closing the door behind her, she whispered, 'Ralphy's here, and he's mortallious.'

'Oh, my God!' Maggie exclaimed. 'He would come the night, wouldn't he? And he's drunk you say?'

'As ten lords.'

'Where've you put him?'

'He's in the kitchen. I've tried to get rid of him but he won't go, he wants to see you; something he's got to tell you he says.'

'I know what that'll be,' said Maggie as she went towards the kitchen. 'He's broke.'

'No, he's not.' Annie's voice was a whisper, a hissed whisper. 'He's got a pocketful of notes. He says he's been working down the river on that dredging concern and he got good money 'cos they can't keep men there. It's finished now.'

When Maggie entered the kitchen she looked at the man sitting by the side of the table, his legs sprawled out. His head lolling on his shoulders, his long face with more hair on it than was on his head, she thought, as she had done many times before, that it was hard to believe he was the same age as Rod. As she and Annie had been pals all their young lives so had Ralphy and Rod, inseparable they were, and as Rod went up he had taken Ralphy with him. That is until the drink got hold of him; after that he had to sack him three times, and the third time was final. Night watchman's job he had then at the warehouse and had set fire to the whole place. Two-thirds of the window frames went up that night, thousands of pounds worth of timber. That was the finish of Rod and Ralphy; but every now and again when he was on his uppers he would come round to cadge. She didn't mind that, she always gave him a square meal and something in his pocket. But she got him out of the house before Rod came in, for Rod couldn't forgive him the business of the warehouse. He'd had the place over-stacked and the insurance on it hadn't covered his losses. He would have murdered Ralphy if he'd got his hands on him after that night, but he never gave him away to the police as being the instigator of the fire. Still there was one person glad to see him, although she would have denied it with her dying breath.

'Hello, Maggie me love.'

'Hello, Ralphy. You've been a bad lad again I see.'

'I'm always a bad . . . bad lad, Maggie. In some ways that is. To meself I'm a bad lad, Maggie, but I would never be a bad lad to you. If I'd got you, Maggie, I would never 've been a bad lad, not like some . . . Here. Here, Maggie.' He grabbed her hand and as he pulled her towards him he almost fell off the chair and she had to steady him. 'I've . . . I've got somethin' to tell you, somethin' you should know. 'Sprivate. 'Sprivate. Get yourself out, Annie; it's private.'

'Get out yourself, you drunken lout.'

'Aw! misery. Your face's like a dose of jollop. She always was a misery, wasn't she, Maggie? Send her packin', Maggie, send her packin'. I've got somethin' to tell you, Maggie. It's . . . private, 'sprivate like, just for the family. You should know, Maggie, I'm not goin' to stand by and see you made a bloody monkey of, Maggie . . . not me, not Ralphy Holland. By God, no!'

At this moment the door opened and Sam came into the kitchen. He was about to speak, but when he saw the visitor he stood still and, raising his eyebrows and pursing his lips, nodded towards him as he said slowly, 'Hello, Ralphy. You just dropped in?'

'Aye, Sam, just dropped in. Have some news, news for your ma.'

Sam looked at his mother and, jerking his head backwards, said, 'The big exodus is getting under way; you'd better go in.' He jerked his head again and muttered, 'I'll see to him.'

Maggie tugged her hand from Ralphy's and said, 'Annie'll give you a cup of coffee, strong and black.' She smiled. 'I've got to go; I've got all the family in. You understand, Ralphy? Come the morrow an' you can tell me all about it.'

'Aw, it won't take a minute, Maggie. I had to push meself, fight with meself. Wait. Wait. I had to push meself to come I tell you; won't come again. Look, come outside, just a minute. I'm . . . I'm not after anythin'; honest to God I'm not after anythin'.'

He stumbled to his feet and Maggie said placatingly, 'I know you're not, Ralphy; but it's the family you see. Slip down again some time. Bye-bye, Ralphy. Take care of yourself.' She backed a few steps away from him, signalled to Annie to leave him too, then hurried out of the kitchen. Poor Ralphy; there was no hope for him. He always wanted to tell her something, some great scheme he had got for making a comeback and showing up Rod. Poor Ralphy.

Back in the kitchen, Ralphy, his face dark, his jaws moving from side to side, turned about and shambled to the door, and pulling it open, staggered outside. There he turned and looked at Sam who had followed him and, wagging a dirty finger at him, said, 'You know somethin'? Your faather's a nowt, a bloody nowt, and I'm not goin' to stand by and see Maggie being made a monkey of.'

Taking Ralphy by the arm, Sam led him down the long path towards the back gate, saying, 'How do you make out Mam's being made a monkey of, Ralphy? You can tell me.'

'I know what I know.'

'Well, if anybody's making a monkey out of Mam I should know an' all, shouldn't I? I'm the eldest.'

'Aye, you are that.' Ralphy stopped and, placing his hands on Sam's shoulders, supported his swaying body for a moment before he repeated, 'Aye, you are. You are the eldest, aye, and you should know an' all. Well then, here's something for your ears. Well now, you listen to me an' every word I say's true, gospel truth, so help me God. It's your dad, he's running another woman, a swell, been at it for months . . . months and months. Love nest behind the office. Friday night's their night; sometimes Saturday but always Friday. An' I know who she is an' all. Aye, I know who she is. He's picked high. Oh, he was always a bloody upstart, your dad. De Ferrier . . . de Ferrier's wife. You know—' he now pushed Sam in the chest three times '—the big de Ferrier, his lady wife. True as I'm standin' here.'

Ralphy now straightened himself and began to walk on again with Sam at his side. When they reached the gate he said, 'Well, I couldn't keep it, but had to get bloody well plastered afore I could spill it. Still, nobody's goin' to make a monkey out of Maggie. I'd never 've made a monkey out of Maggie if I'd got her. By God no . . . Night, night Sam.' He had staggered through the gate and was some way down the road before Sam answered, 'Night' in reply, but so softly that it couldn't have reached his hearing.

He stood near the gate for some time staring over the evergreen hedge into the sky. His emotions were too mixed to sort out; he couldn't say which he was experiencing more, hate, or that peculiar soothing feeling of joy that power gives a man.

As he made his way up to the back door again he looked over the circle of ornamental shrubbery and saw someone on the point of leaving. He went into the kitchen. It was empty, and he stood with his back to the stove still looking upwards, still thinking, still savouring his emotions.

When finally he crossed the hall towards the drawing-room he saw Arlette and his mother mounting the stairs; only Paul and Elizabeth were in the drawing-room and they were talking quietly, or at least Lizzie was, about that fellow Lacker and his poetry. She was even quoting it. She was saying, 'The week before last he wrote a beautiful one about frost. It began, "The morning is bright, frost glinting on glass, trees silent of rustle, and stiff the grass." I can't recall the rest but it ended something like, "If one wish could be granted when I pass, there will go with me a morning as now, frost glinting on glass, trees silent of rustle, and stiff the grass." '

Poetry! Poetry! That was another thing he'd sort out, who this fellow Lacker was, because their Willie was right, that bit about things falling off lorries and being passed to the priest could be hitting at them, Willie and him in particular. And if it was someone in the know, someone who came to the house, well, when you were forewarned you were forearmed.

Upstairs Maggie held Arlette's coat for her as she said, 'It's been a funny night, hasn't it, starting on a high note and going flat.' She laughed now. 'You know, towards the end nobody remembered why they had come; the Duke wasn't mentioned.' Her laugh became louder then ceased abruptly as she stood before Arlette, her hands joined in front of her stomach, her blue eyes soft, her face sad as she said, 'But seriously, Arlette, I'm really scared to death now that I think about it for I won't know how to go on, what to do, or what to wear.'

'Oh, Mam.' Arlette impulsively caught hold of the plump hands and, squeezing them, said, 'There's nothing to worry about, nothing at all. I tell you what, we'll get together and have a talk about it, have a rehearsal. Not that you need one.'

'Ah, will you now? You know, it's funny.' She shook her head. 'I wouldn't let our Frances, or Nellie, or even Lizzie tell me anything, yet I'd let you.'

'Thank you, Mam.' Arlette fell against her for a moment and when Maggie put her arms about her and squeezed her tightly she gave a slight moan and her body jerked.

'What is it?' Maggie looked at her.

'Nothing; it's . . . it's only a touch of fibrositis, I get it in the shoulder.'

'Have you had it rubbed?'

'No, no it just comes and goes.'

'You want to get Sam to rub it.'

Arlette turned away now, saying, 'Yes, yes, I'll do that.'

Maggie stood still for a moment watching her daughter-in-law walk out on to the landing. There was something she would like to ask her, only she didn't want to pry, but she had the feeling that things weren't as they should be between her and Sam. Yet Sam seemed the same. Sam was always the same, merry and bright. But with Sam you could never tell what the brightness was hiding; Sam was close. She didn't know who he took after; not herself 'cos she was as open as the day, too open for her own good; and Rod, Rod wasn't close, a bit tight lipped about things at times, like when the business wasn't going too well, but you couldn't say he was close. No, wherever Sam had got his secretive traits from, it wasn't from either his dad or her.

A few minutes later, when she had closed the door on him and Arlette she paused a moment, and a strange idea came into her head. 'Now wouldn't you think,' she said to herself, 'he knew what was in me mind about him, the way he looked at me when I came into the room. And to go off like that without saying anything, just nodding his head at me, then laughing. There was something funny in the way he did it.' Aw, she tossed her head. What was the matter with her, she was full of fancies. Where was Liz?

She found Elizabeth in the sitting-room, tidying up, putting the cushions straight, each with a corner upwards. She was always tidying, but she generally did it with a gaiety, often singing. Now her face was straight, her eyes still red from crying.

Maggie went up to her, put her arms around her and said softly, 'What's the matter with your face, has it slipped? Aw, come now, don't take things so hard, it's part of life.'

Elizabeth turned and looked at her mother. She loved her mother, she loved her best in the whole world, and therefore she worried about her most. She nipped at her lower lip before looking downwards and saying, 'Mam, when I go in – you know – well, will you promise me something?'

'Aye, lass; if I can keep it I'll promise you anything you ask.' Maggie's voice was soft and serious now.

'Well, from that day will you—' she swallowed '—will you promise not to take anything more from Willie or Sam? You know what I mean.' She was looking pleadingly into her mother's eyes now, and Maggie said, 'An' all this because that daft fellow wrote that poem in the paper?'

'No, no; it wasn't only that, Mam. It just brought it to a head and gave me the courage to ask. It . . . it worries me; it always has worried me, this stealing . . . '

'Aw, Liz, it isn't stealing.' Maggie's voice held a strong note of protest.

'Well, what would you call it, Mam? Willie brought you a packet of nylons tonight, didn't he? And he hadn't bought them.'

'He had. Well, what I mean is, he could have; they sell them all round the place at half-price.'

'Yes; at half the price, they didn't pay for them at the beginning; our Willie and Sam rarely pay anything for the stuff they get . . . Oh, I know, I know, Mam.' She closed her eyes tightly and wagged her hand towards Maggie. 'Don't try to whitewash them. They give stuff in return, stuff that . . . that's fallen off a lorry, another lorry. It's a racket, and it's wrong.'

'But what can one body do that can make any difference, lass?'

'One body and one body and one body make three people, Mam, and if people said, "No, I don't want them, they're stolen," there would soon be no market, and then the things would stop falling off lorries.'

Maggie walked away towards the fireplace and drew her hand over her mouth and up to her brow as she said, 'Aw, lass. I've always said it, you're too good for this world.' She swung round now, her expression contrite, and added quickly, 'I'm not being sarky or anything, I mean that. The world is a tough place, lass; most people would skin a louse for its hide. Ninety-nine out of every hundred are out for what they can get. If you raise your voice against them and go your own way you're sunk, you're dubbed a mug.'

'Then Jesus was a mug.'

'Aw, Liz.'

'Will you do as I ask, Mam?'

There was a considerable pause before Maggie said, 'Yes, lass; the day you go in that'll be the end of it, I promise. There, I'll cross meself on it.' At this she made the sign of the cross, and Liz, her eyes blinking, her mouth trembling, came slowly forward and kissed her gently on the cheek, then said, 'I'll go up, Mam.'

'Good night, hinny.'

'Good night, Mam.'

Left alone, Maggie sat down close to the fire and a shudder passed over her body, although she didn't feel

62

cold. It was odd the mixture you reared; Sam and Willie, and at the opposite pole, Paul and Lizzie, and hovering somewhere in between, Frances and Helen. Willie would kick up a stink when she told him she was taking nothing more, because let's face it, he was making quite a bit on the side out of her. She never took anything for nothing.

It had been a funny evening, an odd evening. It had started so hilariously, them all coming in laughing and joking and exclaiming in wonder at the Duke's invitation. Then they had gone on to the argument; and Ralphy had come, and after that the evening had somehow petered out.

She wished Rod was in. She wished he had come in when they were all here and she could have watched the pride ooze out of him, although, being Rod, he would have acted offhandedly about the whole affair.

She looked at the clock. Half-past ten. He was usually late on a Friday night; after his business in Newcastle in the afternoon he nearly always ended up at Ransome's. She still couldn't get used to the idea of her man being a member of Ransome's. She never went for him when he came in late. She sometimes chipped him by saying things like, 'Why didn't you phone me and I'd have sent your bed along?' because a man in his position had to get around and meet people, it was part of his business. As he used to say, the day he was elected to Ransome's, the names on that club book would be rungs on his ladder. Yet there were times when she longed for a night out like they had years ago at their club, The Working Men's Club. They were grand nights; good turns, plenty to laugh at, a drink, then home to bed . . . and loving.

At eleven o'clock she went upstairs and she was in bed when she heard him come in, but it was a full fifteen minutes later when he entered the bedroom.

She gave him a twisted smile as she said, 'Oh, hello. I

didn't expect you; I thought you were staying for bed and breakfast.'

He stopped in the middle of the room and stared over the foot of the bed at her. She was wearing a pink nightdress with a lace-type yoke; the hair at each side of her temples was in two long rollers, her round, unlined face was free of night cream. His eyes moved down to her breasts. They were rising like full moons out of the top of her nightdress, and at one time this sight alone would have excited him, causing him almost to jump out of his clothes and into bed with her. But now the sight of her flesh slightly sickened him, and while this reaction filled him with a sensation of guilt he told himself he was only doing what ninety-nine men out of a hundred did; and besides, in his case, no-one was being hurt – ignorance was bliss, at least for her.

'What's the matter?'

She was bending over the counterpane towards him.

'Matter? What should be the matter? I'm tired, that's all.' He turned his back on her and walked into the dressing-room. This was a fad of his of late that she couldn't understand, him undressing in there. He was funny in some ways her Rod. She explained this latest fad to herself with slight amusement, he was aping the gentlemen; they always did the necessary in the dressing-room. Aw, he would get places would her Rod; there was no stopping him. And good luck to him. But what about her? Oh, come off it, she warned herself; Rod would always see to her. What more did she want anyway, she had everything?

'I've got a surprise for you.' She raised her voice.

'Oh? Aye.'

'You'll never guess.'

'Well, you'd better tell me, hadn't you?' His voice was flat, showing no interest.

She pressed her lips together, clamping down on a laugh,

and she let a short silence elapse before she said, 'You've had an invitation.'

'Yes?'

She drew the breath deep into her chest as she imagined the result of her next words, for he would come scooting out of that room as if he'd had a dose of salts.

'Pin your ears back and wait for it . . . We've had an invitation . . . from the Duke of Moorshire.'

Her eyes were fast on the open doorway, but he did not come scooting out. It was almost thirty seconds before he appeared. He was in his shirt sleeves, pulling the bands down from them. 'What did you say, an invitation from the Duke of Moorshire?'

'Yes, yes, that's what I said. Flabbergasted you?'

He wrinkled his nose. 'No, not really. What's the date?'

'The twenty-fourth of June.'

He went slowly back into the dressing-room and when he appeared at the door again he had a diary in his hands, and after flicking the pages he said, 'It's no go; I've got an important business meeting in Doncaster that day.'

She stared at him across the room. Then in two movements she had flung the clothes back and swung her legs on to the floor and was standing facing him. 'Look, Rod!' She thrust her arm out and picked up the invitation card from the side table and held it out towards him. 'You don't seem to have taken in what I said. This is an invitation from the Duke of Moorshire. The Duke mind, the Duke!'

'I heard what you said and you heard what I said, we won't be able to go.' He went back into the dressing-room again and she walked slowly towards the open door, saying, 'Now look you here. I've never asked you for much in me life, you've gone your own way, but this is one time you're going to do this for me. We're accepting this invitation.'

His heavy body swung towards her now, his face was

dark with an unwarranted anger. 'I said we are not going and that's that!'

She stared at him unbelieving. His ferocity meant that he had dug his heels in, but by God, this was one time when she was going to pull them out.

'What's come over you? I thought you would have been over the moon about such an invitation; the top rung of the ladder you would have said. I would have sworn that the only thing which would have stopped you from accepting this—' she flapped the card in his face '—would have been if the Queen herself had asked you up. Half the town will know now that we're going, so what you going to do about it?'

'Half the town?' His face puckered.

'Aye, that's what I said, half the town. They've all been here the night, everyone of them; they left about ten and I'd like to bet their phones have been ringing ever since. There were six people alone that our Frances was going to tell, her very, very dear friends, the ones she thinks look down their noses at her.'

His shoulders slumped, his eyes closed, and his head drooped. He hadn't thought about her telling the lot of them, but it was the first thing he should have thought of – the family must know, the family must know every damned thing. Well, that settled it. But it didn't settle the anger in him. His head jerking up, he yelled at her, 'You, and your bloody big mouth!'

For a moment she was silent under his attack; then, as of old, she let him have it. 'Bloody big mouth is it? Well, I might have at that, but I haven't got a bloody big head; nor am I getting so big for me boots that I can turn me nose up at an invitation like this. The big fella. Big Gallacher picking and choosing now. A few years back you'd have been on your knees grovelling to him for recognising you were alive. And another thing when I'm on, you've never taken me anywhere for years, not since we've come into this house . . . ' Her mouth was open on a word when it became transfixed and gaping as a strange thought intruded into her tirade. Her lids blinked and narrowed as she asked in a quieter, but more deadly tone now, 'Could it be, Rodney Gallacher, that you've got so high up that you think I can't follow you, that you're ashamed to be seen with me?'

If he had bawled at her, 'It could be just that. You've put your finger on it, you've just said it,' she would have known there wasn't a word of truth in it. It would have been like the old days when they cut each other to pieces with their tongues, and the more lacerations they caused the more joy there was in the healing afterwards. But now he didn't turn on her. He turned away and, sweeping up his coat and tie and his pyjamas, he thrust himself past her, stamped across the room and out, and not even when she heard the door bang across the landing and knew he had gone into Willie's old room did she move.

They'd had dos in the past that could have come under the heading of tiffs, quarrels, and battles, but never before had he left the bedroom. At one time they had lain side by side for a week and never touched or spoken to one another, but they had lain there, in their bed.

She felt sick as she had done often when as a child her mother had threatened to wallop her. It wasn't the actual walloping that had made her feel sick but the waiting. Her mother would shove her into the dark cupboard under the stairs and keep her there, sometimes as long as three hours. She used to long for the walloping for then the fear of the dark and the loneliness would be past. She had thoughts and feelings in her that she could never tell anyone, not even Rod, because they were difficult to describe. If she had told Rod that she often felt a great sense of loneliness or aloneness he would have laughed at her and said she had been reading one of those articles in the women's magazines, they were full of psychology these days. But nothing in the articles had explained this feeling that had been with her since her earliest days. She was always one for a joke and a laugh; fat people were supposed to be merry, but she hadn't always been fat. She was only nine stone when she married and that was about right for her height of five foot six, but now she tipped the scales at thirteen stone.

But fat or thin, laughing or singing in the midst of her family, there had always been with her that strange feeling of aloneness. It flooded her now and tears sprang from her eyes, but she made no sound. Her hand tightly across her mouth, she walked to the bed and sat on its edge. She was back in the cupboard under the stairs and she wouldn't get her whacking until tomorrow morning when she looked at his face ... downstairs, for she wouldn't go into the room where he was. No. No. His walking out of their room had stripped her of everything but a shred of pride, and she must hang on to that; at all costs she must hang on to that.

She didn't see him the following morning, for he left the house very early. But he came back into the bedroom that night; then after banging about for a while he turned on her and cried, 'Well, have it your own way then. But see you get dressed properly for it.' Then he got into bed but didn't touch her; nor did she turn to him.

See that you get dressed properly for it. It was like an insult. If it wasn't for the fact that the phone had been ringing all day she would have yelled at him, 'To hell with you! And the invitation an' all.' But she was committed; the family had committed her.

Part Two

CHAPTER ONE

GOD VERSUS A WOMAN

Sam got up early on the Saturday morning and went straight out. This was unusual, for his routine on a Saturday morning was to lie late, clean the car, have his lunch, then go to the football match. But this morning he had left the house by nine o'clock and he did not say where he was going; and Arlette did not ask him, but she allowed ten minutes to elapse before locking up and taking her car from the garage. Three minutes' drive from the house she stopped opposite a telephone kiosk; then having gone in, she rang a number, and when a voice answered she said, 'Hello, John; it's me.'

'Oh, hello, Arlette. How's things?'

'There's been a hitch. I want you to hold everything for a month, till the end of June.'

'Do you think that's wise?'

'Well, I can't tell them now, something's happened. It's . . . it's his mother.'

'What's she got to do with it?'

'She's had an invitation to meet the Duke of Moorshire.'

'But you're not going to let that . . . ?'

'You don't understand, John. I've told you how sweet she is, a real dear person. As . . . as I said, I would have finished the whole thing long before this if it hadn't been for upsetting her, breaking with her; I've told you I'm very fond of her.'

'Yes, you may be, but it's your life; and I mean that literally. How's he been?'

'Pretty much the same. There was a new phase last night. He had been to his mother's – all celebrating the invitation you know – and when we came back he acted like a lunatic. He was still laughing at three o'clock this morning. You know something, John; I've suspected this for a long time, but he hates her. I don't know why, or how anyone could, but he's got something against her.'

'A man like that has always got something against someone.'

'But this is particular, a special kind of hate.'

'Have you been to the doctor recently?'

'I . . . I am going this afternoon.'

'More evidence?'

She remained silent and gnawed at her lip and the voice came to her, saying, 'It's damnable. If I had my way he'd go along the line. He might even yet.'

She said now, 'How is Moira?' and he answered, 'Oh, she's got hay fever, as usual. Time of year. Where you phoning from?'

'A call box.'

'Arlette.'

'Yes, John?'

'You must do as I advised before. Don't tell him in person, just leave a letter and clear out. Moira would love you to come here, but for my part I don't think it would be safe. You must get right away, go to London, or down to the West Coast.'

'It's a pity, isn't it, we haven't any relatives to fly to in times of trouble? Still I've always had you, and I'm so thankful for it.'

'And I'm so glad I'm here for you to fly to. I may as well tell you I'm more than a little worried about the position you're in. And I repeat that I think you've been mad to put up with it for so long. Anyway, when we do start proceedings there'll be no hitch, I'll see to that. I had a word with Whicken the other day. He's the barrister I was telling you about, very clever fellow, and when I told him the facts he said it would be one of those that went straight through. But I hate to think of you lasting out another month; and sweet mother or no sweet mother, I think you should make the break now.'

'There's the pips, John, and I haven't any more change, I must go. I'll pop in one day next week.'

'Very well. Goodbye, Arlette.'

'Goodbye, John.'

She put the receiver down and stood looking in the small dirty mirror on her eye level. 'Make the break,' he had said, 'as soon as possible.' And he was right. It couldn't be too soon, not a split second too soon. Yet in making the break from Sam she was making the break with the only family she had ever known and from the woman who had welcomed her with a warmth that couldn't have been exceeded had that woman been her real mother.

She didn't remember her own mother. She had died when she was three, and her mother's sister, John's mother, had died when John was eight, and strangely both their fathers had died in Korea. More strangely still, their fathers had been only children and their mothers had no other children. Both of them had been brought up mainly in boarding schools. John who had gone in for law was now a junior partner in a firm of solicitors in the town and was doing very well. It was odd but it was at John's wedding to Moira that she had met Sam. He had been a friend, or perhaps it was truer to say a fellow rugby player with Moira's brother.

She sat in the car, her hands on the wheel, staring ahead of her. There was something else she must do this morning but it was going to be difficult, delicate in fact, but she must do it because if Sam started probing in this particular direction, and she was sure that he meant to, there would be trouble, grave trouble in the house.

She started the car and drove by side roads and streets until she came to Talford Road. She did not drive the car down to Marsh House but left it on a piece of spare ground adjoining the main road, then walked down the street of nondescript high terraced houses, pushed upon the iron gate of number seventeen, looked at the four names in their little sockets, and then rang the bell for Mr Paul Gallacher.

She reached the second landing as Paul opened the door. He was in his pyjamas and dressing-gown and he gaped at her as if she was an apparition.

She smiled tentatively at him, saying, 'I'm sorry if I got you up, I know it's early and Saturday, but . . . but I wanted to see you for a moment.'

He stepped back into the room and held the door wide for her, and she passed him and glanced quickly about her. He had evidently just jumped out of bed, but she hadn't woken him because on the top of the divan were spread papers and books, and two pillows rested lengthwise against the bed head. There were the remains of a meal on the table, a parcel of unopened laundry was on a chair and two drip-dry shirts on wire hangers were suspended from a line above the sink at the far end of the room. The place looked so muddled, so cold, so devoid of any comfort that it pained her; she compared it with all the things that Sam demanded for his comfort, things that, up to two years ago, his own money would not have run to, though he had never had any compunction about enjoying the fruits of her private income. The fact of her money being tied up until she was thirty had irked her when she was first married, but now she blessed her father's foresight.

Paul hadn't opened his mouth, not even to say hello. He was backing from her towards the bathroom, and now she

74

was forced to say, 'I'm . . . I'm sorry, Paul; perhaps I can call later.'

'No! No!' His voice cracked on the second no, like that of a young treble singer. 'I won't be a minute. Sit . . . sit down. Please sit down.'

She sat down on the only empty seat, which was opposite his desk. There was silence for a while; then she heard the sound of a splintered bang coming from the bathroom and she guessed he had broken a glass, perhaps dropped it into the bath. She moved her head slowly. She shouldn't have come, not . . . not so early in the morning, she had embarrassed him. She looked down at the desk. It was covered with sheets of paper, lined paper like they used at school. She put her elbow on the desk next to a page covered with italic script, the writing black and bold, each word standing out, and the title at the top of the page read, 'My love is beautiful'. Her eyes, like quicksilver, scanned the lines:

> My love is beautiful;
> She hangs over me
> Like grapes on the vine,
> But her bloom will not fade
> Or be crushed
> By this hand of mine;
> My love is beautiful.

> My love is beautiful;
> Her voice plays on my heart,
> But the theme is mine;
> I make her whisper,
> We shall never part.
> Hold me fast, I am thine.
> My love is beautiful.

My love is beautiful;
And so will remain;
I will not besmirch
Her body or her brain
With fumbling hands
Or senseless chatter.
Oh, but that I could;
I would, if she were mine,
My love is beautiful.

Her eyes lifted to the title again. 'My love is beautiful.' Oh, Paul. Poor Paul. There was a woman. He was in love with a woman. Mam had been right; she had said she thought there was a woman who had put an end to him going in for the priesthood. Yet the years since he had left seemed to have proved her wrong because he had never been known to associate with any woman other than those in the family. But these words were the words of a man who loved.

She gave a loud gasp and bowed her head as his hand came across her shoulder and, picking up the sheet of paper, turned it face downwards. She remained seated, her head low. She couldn't bear to look at him as she muttered, 'I'm . . . I'm sorry, Paul; I . . . I had no intention of prying, but—' slowly now she raised her eyes to his '—it's about this I came.'

'What!'

She watched his eyes widen, his thin lips part; she followed his hand as it slowly went up and the fingers spread out as they combed his coarse tousled red hair back from his brow.

She stood up facing him now, saying, 'Please, Paul, don't mind. I . . . I would never tell anyone, but it's Sam. After last night, and that piece that hit directly home—' she smiled wryly '—It fell off a lorry. I know

76

that Sam's going to probe, and when he starts, well you know Sam, he's just got to get an inkling and like a bull terrier he holds on.'

'Oh.' His chin fell on to his chest and he laughed shakily as his body slumped. When finally he lifted his eyes to hers they had a merry glint in them, and his change of attitude puzzled her for it expressed relief. He was now giving the impression that he didn't care two hoots who knew that he was Lacker of the *Messenger*. Then, the smile sliding from his face, he asked, 'How did you twig, and not the others?'

'It was when Liz and I came to put your curtains up. There was a piece of torn paper lying by the side of the desk—' she pointed '—near the wall, and I picked it up.' She smiled. 'I'm like Liz. I'm always tidying; it's a finicky habit of mine. There were some words written on the paper. They were unusual but I recognised them; I had read them the previous week: "Applauded and lauded, name breathed in awe; a poet, a poet, as never before." '

'Oh, that.' His chin jerked. 'I was showing my spleen in that one. I had just read a fulsome review of a so-called modern poet. I don't mind praise where it's due, but that was a bit too much. It may have read like sour grapes, but it wasn't, for I don't consider myself a poet. I'm just a rhymer, but nevertheless I get over what I mean, and you don't have to have a committee to dissect it before you get the gist of it.'

She stared at him. There was a bitterness in him that she had never detected before and she thought, he may not be a good poet but he takes this seriously. He's like a pamphleteer of old, putting his ideas, but mostly his objections, before the public. She remembered she had been startled by the last lines of the poem: 'It's very obscure as is all that is great, so let us with whores and urine debate.' She hadn't been able to connect this way

77

of thinking and expression with Paul. With Sam yes, oh yes, or Willie . . .

He broke into her thoughts with his characteristic short laugh and shook his head as he said, 'I prided myself on burning all the evidence that time when I knew you and Liz were coming . . . Sit down.' He turned the seat round, then swept the laundry from the other chair on to the corner of the desk. When he was seated opposite to her he looked into her eyes for a moment before saying, 'So Sam is going to probe?'

'Yes. I . . . I've got a feeling he's gone down to the offices of the *Messenger*; he went out early.'

'Did he now?' He tapped his teeth with his fingernail. 'You know, but for one thing I don't really give a damn if Sam finds out or not, or Willie either, because I was hitting at them both. It was an underhand way I suppose, but their fiddling has got on my nerves for years. I'm . . . I'm sorry to say this about Sam . . . '

'You needn't be; it's got on my nerves too, especially when, in his case, there was not the least necessity for it. It has just become a habit.'

'Yes.' He nodded at her. 'A habit.'

He rose to his feet now and stood looking down at the desk and, slowly putting out his hand, began to move the papers around, saying as if to himself, 'If he succeeds in his probing I'll lose the source of my inspiration, because all this—' he scattered the papers with his hand '—comes from the family. Each week I milk them.' He was gnawing on his lip, and he looked at her sideways as he said, 'I would say, "Aw! to the devil. Let him find out," but it's Mam; she'll be upset about this, won't she?'

'I'm afraid so.'

He bobbed his head down at her, took three quick strides towards the door, then turned to her, saying, 'I won't be a minute. There's a phone downstairs; I can check his gallop.' He now cast his eyes quickly between the desk and the bed and gave her a twisted grin as he ended, 'I needn't ask you not to read further.' Then before she could answer he exclaimed on a high note, 'But why not? Why not? Here!' He hurried towards the bed, sorted among the loose sheets, then picked out one and handed it to her, saying, 'That's my conscience speaking; you would have read it next week. I won't be a minute.'

She did not look at the sheet in her hand until he had closed the door behind him; then she read the title 'Retaliation', and she noted that both the metre and the length were the same as always. His work, as he had said, was not that of a poet but a rhymer, yet she knew that his rhyming would reach the hearts of more people than if his words had been so clever as to be obscure to the majority of ordinary folk. She read:

> Do not tempt me to slay;
> In thought, in dreams
> Keep my mind at bay.
> Do not tempt me to slay
> With my tongue, or my eye,
> For by such weapons
> I too shall die.
>
> Let them say what they say,
> My neighbour and my friend.
> Day runs into day,
> My world will sometime end;
> The hurts and the pains
> Forever cannot stay.
> Do not tempt me to slay.

Do not tempt me to slay
My loved ones with a laugh,
Listening to their fancies,
Their foibles, their chaff.
The point of laughter
Is a deadly ray;
Do not tempt me to slay.

Yet he did slay. Every week he had slain, and his own. As he said, he got his inspiration from the family. She put the sheet of paper down on the desk beside the one he had turned over, 'My love is beautiful'. Would he publish that? She liked Paul, she'd always liked him, but . . . but she was a little afraid of him, perhaps because she saw him as not quite an ordinary man. Any man who had harboured thoughts of the priesthood seemed slightly extraordinary to her. Indeed it was this very fact which had prevented her from talking to him as much as she would have liked for she had the feeling that they could be in agreement on so many things. There was a lot of his mother in Paul, yet of all of them he looked least like her, he was the only one in the family with reddish hair. She had read somewhere that red-headed men rarely became priests because their glands were too active. Perhaps there was some truth in it.

He came back into the room, his face straight, his mouth tight. 'You were right,' he said, 'he's been . . . Arthur Dalton, he's the sub-editor, recognised him and was just going to ring me.'

'Did he tell him?'

'No; he said he wasn't at liberty to give names. He asked him why he wanted to know the name of the author, and you know what Sam said?'

She shook her head.

'He was interested in poetry.' He laughed derisively. 'Sam interested in poetry! Sam! Huh!' Again his head went down and, his voice contrite now, he said, 'I'm sorry. You must guess now, if you haven't before, that let alone not loving my neighbour as myself I don't even love my brother.'

'. . . I don't either!'

His head jerked upwards, and they were staring at each other. What, she asked herself in some panic, had made her say that? But she had said it, and to the only one in the family to whom she could say it. It was strange but she realised now that she had wanted to tell Paul this for a long time, but having said it she saw that her words had come as a shock to him. The colour had seeped from his face; all that was left of his fresh complexion were two spots high on his cheekbones. His eyes, curtains always to his thoughts, seemed to have disappeared into the back of his head and were shadowed still further by his drooped lids. But his reaction did not deter her from spilling out her trouble to him.

'I'm going to get a divorce.'

His eyelids rose again, his gaze, tight and deep, fixed on her face. She saw now tiny beads of sweat on the faint line of stubble on his upper lip. She wished he would say something. His Adam's apple jerked up under his chin and fell again, and then he said softly, 'Does he know?'

She shook her head.

'He'll never let you go, never. Not on any grounds, but mostly he'll say on religious.'

'That doesn't affect me, religion. As you know, I'm not a Catholic.'

She had been married in a Catholic church but she hadn't turned. She knew that, before they were married, Sam had promised Father Stillwell to work on her. He had laughingly told her this; but he himself was no true Catholic. Last year he had attended his Easter duties, and Midnight Mass. That was the sum total of him practising his religion. He called his Easter duties keeping up his Union dues. 'As long as your card's stamped,' he had once told her laughingly, 'you're all right.' And she knew he believed this; the stamping of his card at Easter with confession and Holy Communion was a passport to a happy death and the pleasures thereafter. Sometimes her mind grappled with the problem of this man whom she knew to be almost inhuman in his bodily desires but who could yet be so naïve in his religious beliefs.

'On what grounds will you get it?'

She swallowed deeply before she said, 'Cruelty.'

'Cruelty! Mental?'

'Pa . . . partly, but mostly—' she swallowed again and her voice sank to a murmur as she ended, '—physical.'

His eyes were lost again, his face screwed up pulling his lips from his teeth. 'Sam,' he said slowly. 'Sam. But he's mad about you.'

'Yes,' she closed her eyes as she nodded her head, 'that is the correct word, mad, about me.'

'But . . . but how?' He still wasn't believing.

She turned from him now. 'I can't tell you Paul; you'll . . . you'll know soon enough.' She put her hand to her head.

'Does he know, I mean, what you intend?'

'No, not yet. It . . . it was to begin this week, but after last night—' she turned slowly towards him '—it . . . it would spoil things for Mam and the invitation, so I put it off until the function's over.'

'He'll . . . he'll not let you do it, not Sam. Sam is . . . ' He couldn't say to her 'dangerous', but he'd always known Sam was dangerous. There were so many instances he could recall that had proved him dangerous. The first time he became aware of what lay behind his brother's laughing face happened when he was ten and Sam twelve. Sam had been badly beaten in the school yard by Peter

Morrell, and later Father Armstrong had made them shake hands. Later still, when they were outside, Peter, in his magnanimous way had punched Sam in the chest while he grinned at him, and Sam had punched him back, while he too grinned widely. That week-end Peter Morrell's bike had been stolen. They found it broken up on the waste land, but the bell of the bike and the saddle bag they found in Ronnie Dale's shed. Ronnie Dale was one of the lads who had cheered Peter Morrell on; Sam had never liked Ronnie Dale. Ronnie Dale was taken to court; it was his third offence and he was sent to a remand home. He himself always felt guilty when he thought of Ronnie Dale because he knew he had not been guilty. It had been late on the Friday night when he had seen their Sam creeping out of the Dales' backyard. Ronnie Dale's mother and father went to the club every Friday night and Father Monaghan held his boxing class. He had just come from the boxing class himself and left Ronnie Dale there. He should have split on their Sam there and then, but he was afraid of him. He slept in the same room as him and he knew what he could do, such as sticking his knuckles into a nerve in your arm until you nearly fainted.

But that Sam should be cruel to Arlette seemed impossible, because he loved her. As he said, he was mad about her. When first he knew her and was chasing her hard and she didn't show much interest Sam had said to him, 'I'll get her, and God help anybody who tries to stop me.' Yes, God help anybody who tried to stop him. Besides being six foot two and heavy with it, his brother was cunningly intelligent. And there was something else he knew about his brother and had been aware of for quite a while now: in spite of his cunning and his strength their Sam had nothing; there was a great emptiness in him, a great want. There was something wrong with their

Sam. What it was he didn't know, only that there was something radically wrong inside him.

And now Arlette was saying she was going to break with him, finish with him, divorce him. He was pulling himself round from the shock of her words; he still couldn't believe them. But she had said them and she meant to carry them out, and again he thought, He'll never let her, never, never, never. He'll do something to her first.

He took a step towards her, his hands wavering in front of him as if he were about to grasp hers; then dropping them to his sides he said thickly, 'You . . . you mustn't tell Sam; I mean you should let it be done legally by—' He tossed his head. 'What I mean is . . . '

'I know what you mean, Paul. I'm not going to tell him. When the time comes I'm going away. My cousin, you know, John, well, he's seeing to everything for me.'

'You're going away?'

'Yes.'

'Where?'

She shook her head. 'I don't know yet.' Quite suddenly she walked back to the chair and sat down again, and when she looked up at him her eyes were blurred and, her voice breaking, she said, 'That's been the trouble, that's what's made me put up with it and kept me from doing anything about it, the family. All of you, but especially Mam. It's . . . it's this business of having been brought up alone, adrift. When . . . when I came into the family, at first it was wonderful. You . . . you could never understand because you were brought up with a family, and the thought of breaking all ties with them and being thrust out and on my own again was more unbearable than, well, living with Sam; until . . . until recently.'

'Aw, Arlette.' He wasn't really aware that he had dropped on to his knees and that he was holding her hands tightly to his breast, that his face was bowed over them and that his lips were on them, but the awareness returned to him in seconds and he was on his feet again, one hand running through his hair, the other rubbing the front of his shirt. And now he was muttering almost incoherently, 'I'm sorry. It . . . it was your feelings for the family; I . . . I . . . we all feel like that about you too.'

She was gazing up at his averted face now. There was a light creeping into her mind. It seemed to be coming from the far end of a long tunnel, but becoming brighter every moment, until it shone full in her eyes and dazzled her. She blinked and got hastily to her feet, and then her thoughts dimmed it; it was just as he said, the family all liked her, except perhaps Frances.

'I must be going now, Paul.'

He turned to her. His face, the whiteness of lint, accentuated the darkness of his eyes and the redness of his hair. Even his lips looked bloodless; and as she stared at him she recalled an instance before he went to college when she surprised him looking at her. She had thought then he was weighing her up, wondering if she would be a good enough wife for his brother. Even though he was a year younger than herself, she had seen him as someone much older, for she then had the idea that priests, even young ones, were men out of the ordinary, men who had been given an insight into something closed to ordinary human beings, men of high intellect, men enveloped in spirit. She had learned differently since. The three priests at the church had been an education to her. The Rector, Father Stillwell, she knew to be a narrow-minded, ignorant man, while Father Monaghan she saw as a big, brainwashed Irish bumpkin. Only Father Armstrong held her respect, and then he had his flaws, for he was the priest to whom Paul had referred in 'It Fell Off A Lorry'. She had recognised him instantly.

She did not now glance towards his desk but in her

mind's eyes she was seeing the heading 'My love is beautiful' on the turned down sheet, and linking it to his actions of a moment ago. She thought, It's too awful. And yet, what was awful about it? She liked him, she had always liked him, in fact she had at times . . . She must get away because this was really dreadful; she didn't want any more complications, couldn't stand any more complications.

'Goodbye, Paul.'

'Goodbye, Arlette.' He didn't move, not even to open the door for her, only his eyes followed her.

She stood in the dim lobby and drew in several deep breaths, then opened the door and walked into the street and down the road. As she turned the corner she saw her car, and next to it, bumper to bumper, Sam's car.

She halted in her stride, her mind racing. Why was he here? Had he followed her? What excuse could she give him for going to Paul's?

He must have watched her coming towards him in his mirror because just as she was abreast of him he flung open the door and she had to jump back to save herself from being knocked down.

'Sorry. Sorry.' He was standing facing her now. 'I was going to pop along to Paul's. Came to park, and found yours.' He thumbed towards her car. 'You've been along there?'

'Yes.' She looked him straight in the face.

'Early aren't you?' He brought his wrist round and looked at his watch. 'Just gone ten, and Saturday; he'd hardly be up. Likes his bed, does Paul. What you go for?'

'I . . . I wanted to ask him something.'

'Ask him something? Why couldn't you ask him last night? You saw plenty of him last night.'

'I couldn't with everybody there.'

He raised his eyebrows at her and grinned a one-sided grin. 'Oh, really! So very important?'

'No, not all that important, except to me.'

'Well, spill it; I'd like to know, as well as Paul that is.'

'I'm . . . I'm going to take a university course, external, in languages. I . . . I wanted to ask him how to go about it.'

He brought his head towards her but didn't speak for a moment; then he said, 'My! My! A university course in languages. First I've heard of it.'

'I've been thinking about it for some time.' And this was true, she had; but she would have no need to go to Paul about it, she could have gone and had a talk with the Principal of the new college, or she could have obtained her information through correspondence.

'Want to fill your time up, do you? Haven't got enough to occupy you? You should let Mrs Bell go; a bit of extra housework wouldn't do you any harm. Mam will tell you that. It's a wonder she hasn't. Does she know about the new idea?'

'Of course not.' She started to move away from him. 'I told you, I just put it to Paul.'

'Oh, you just put it to Paul. Well, I'm sure Paul will feel honoured.' The smile went from his face leaving his eyes as they had been all the while, greeny blue, like a cold sea, and his voice came from deep down in his broad chest as he muttered, 'And Paul now will have more cause to look down his bloody nose at me.'

She turned now and looked at him, less fearfully than she had done for a long time, and her voice had a chill sound as she said, 'That's your trouble, isn't it, the fear of people looking down their noses at you?' She paused before adding, 'And it says in the Bible that the things they feared came upon them.'

She felt him close behind her as she went to her car door. She wouldn't have been surprised if his hands had come on her neck. Yet she would have; Sam did nothing in public that would cause anyone to point a finger at him. But his voice came at her in a low growl now, saying, 'I'll Bible you one of these days. My God, see if I don't.'

She got into the car and drove straight back home. Hurrying to the hall, she picked up the phone. There was a window to the side of her that looked on to the drive. If he was following her she'd be able to see him coming. She phoned Felburn 1212. It was strange but she hadn't known the number of the telephone in Paul's house; it was as she had paused for those few moments in his hall that her eye had been taken by the number, 1212. It was the old Whitehall number so often heard on the wireless: phone Whitehall 1212.

A woman's voice said, 'Hello,' and she answered. 'Do you think I could speak to Mr Paul Gallacher, he's in Flat 4?'

'Oh aye. Wait a minute, I'll get him.'

She kept her eyes on the window while she waited. It seemed a long time; then Paul's voice came to her. 'Hello?'

'This is Arlette. Is Sam with you?'

'Yes.'

'Has he asked you why I came?'

'No, not yet; he's toying with it, playing cat and mouse.'

'Listen, Paul. He was round the corner waiting. He wanted to know why I had been to see you. I . . . I told him I wanted advice on a university course. Do you hear?'

'Yes, yes, I hear.'

'I said I was thinking about taking it up, in languages. I thought . . . I thought I'd better tell you.'

'Yes, thanks.' His words were terse. Then he added in a whisper, 'Don't worry. Don't worry, Arlette,' and when he spoke her name it was as if there was a link between them, a secret.

She put the phone down; then slowly she took off

88

her things and went into the kitchen and made herself some coffee, and as she sipped at it she tried to recall the look on his face as he knelt before her, her hands gripped tightly in his, his lips pressed to her knuckles. But she couldn't get his features to materialise; they were all running into a white blur, only his eyes were distinct. She felt she was going to faint. She put down her cup and leant back in the chair. A few minutes later, the full significance of the situation came to her and she murmured, 'Oh, Paul. Oh, Paul.' Then another name was added to her murmuring; and this name brought her sitting up straight. If Mam ever got wind of this it would shatter the precious thing that was between them, because her son Paul, while being the apple of her eye, had also been the greatest disappointment in her life.

It was up to her; she should leave now; it would hurt Mam less in the long run.

CHAPTER TWO

THE PREPARATION

'Aw, I wish it had never happened; I wish I'd never seen
the bloody invitation. Do you know, Arlette, I've walked
more miles in this town with our Frances this week than
I've done since I was born. And what have I got? Nothing;
only a frayed temper and half an inch lost off me tongue.
I left it with her this morning. You see—' Maggie bent
towards Arlette where she sat in the button-studded pink
velvet bedroom chair. '—Our Frances thinks she's got
taste, but, Arlette lass, she doesn't know the first thing
about it. She was all for me getting a three-quarter cocktail
affair in taffeta, grey taffeta. Why! I would have looked
like Nanny-cum-canny in it. I walked out of the shop,
and that finished her. She exploded in the street. Well,
not really in the street. She waited until we got into the car,
'cos you know Frances, all for the proper thing.' Maggie
smiled. 'But I exploded an' all. I said to hell with her
and her ideas and the proper thing. Etcetera. Etcetera.'
She put her hand over her face now and laughed. 'She
nearly threw me out on to the drive when we got back.'
She nodded towards the window; then flopping down on
the side of the bed she ended, 'Aw, she means well. But
Frances could always rattle me, she's so damned prim.
Eeh!' She flapped her hand at Arlette. 'I'm a nasty piece
of work, Arlette; I'm always criticising me bairns. But you
know—' again she poked her head forward '—it's a funny
thing but I only do it to you, nobody else, I never talk

about one to the other. No,' she moved her head from side to side, 'I've never done that. I've hardly spoken against them to Rod, even when they were little devils, especially the lads, but to you . . . ' She dropped her hands into her lap and her whole body relaxed. And looking at the slim form of Arlette she said, 'I don't know why but you do me good, lass, you always have. Funny, isn't it? And I keep on tellin' you. I must bore the pants off you.'

Arlette was smiling. 'You could never bore me, Mam. I feel the same way; I could tell you anything. Well . . . ' The smile slid from her face. That was a lie, for she was the last person in the world she could tell everything to because she was the one person in the world she wouldn't want to hurt. She, too, had thought often and often of the strange affinity between this fat middle-aged woman and herself. They had come from different strata of society, they talked differently, their intelligences were on different levels, yet beneath the skin in a realm that could not be explained or defined, they were akin, closer than mother and daughter. There was a love between them that had no sex, that was so ethereal in its substance as to vaporise when brushed by thought.

Maggie was now saying, 'Why didn't I take a pull at meself long before this? I've lost three pounds this week because I haven't eaten any tatties, and no cakes, and hardly any bread. But what's three pounds? If only the rest of me was like me legs.' She thrust them out towards Arlette. 'Isn't it funny? They've never got fat. They're not bad are they?'

'They're wonderful legs, very smart.' Arlette brought herself to the edge of the chair, then asked tentatively, 'Would you let me see to you, Mam; I mean get you dressed?'

'Would I!' Maggie gazed at her daughter-in-law; then

exclaimed with a high laugh, 'Why, lass, I'll be putty in your hands . . . I won't say fat.' Her mouth was wide, her head back.

'It'll cost something.'

'Well, what does that matter; Rod'll come round to it. How much?'

Arlette considered for a moment. 'About a hundred and fifty I should say.'

'WH-AT! A hundred and fifty pounds to rig me out! . . . Aw, lass.'

'I'm afraid so.' Arlette was smiling broadly now. 'You see you'd have to have a good foundation; that's the main thing. There's a rather exclusive shop in Newcastle, Madam Hevell's. You know it?'

'Never heard of it.'

'It's very small. It's in a side street, but she's very exclusive and very pricey. She starts with the foundation and works outwards. She'll fit you out for an occasion right down to the shoes; she's expert at this.'

'But a hundred and fifty pounds, lass.'

'It might be more; it could go to two hundred. This—' she pointed to the French-grey suit with the narrow pink stripe running through it that she was wearing '—This was forty-eight guineas.'

'Never! Never, lass.'

'Yes, it was.'

'But I thought you got most of your things at the big stores, like . . .'

'I do; but now and again I treat myself, about once a year. I've had this three years. They last for ever and never lose their shape. The dress I wore at Christmas, that was from Madam Hevell's; it was sixty guineas.'

'Arlette, you're mad. That little thing, it was almost a mini, and nothing to it, as plain as a pikestaff.'

'It's that what you pay for; it was a model, and if the

fashions don't go out too much somebody will be wearing that same dress twenty years from now.'

'Aye, lass.' Maggie considered for a moment. 'It sounds marvellous but—' she let her body flop on to the bed '—I doubt if Rod will stand for anything near two hundred pounds to rig me out. A new car, furniture, the house decorated, yes; but lass, I've never had a coat over twenty pounds in me life. Nineteen guineas I paid for my brown one.' She nodded towards the wardrobe. 'And this is the third winter I've had that. You see, I don't go out a lot so it seems a waste; and it's still as good as new . . . Two hundred pounds! I'd never have the face to ask him.'

'Well, let me buy it for you?'

'What! You buy me outfit? Not on your life.' Indignant now, Maggie rose from the bed. 'And me man rolling in money? What you thinking of? But,' her face spread into its usual smile and putting out her hand she patted Arlette's shoulder, 'it's nice of you; it's like what you would do.' Then she straightened her back and wagged her head as she said, 'He'll buy it. What time is it?' She looked at the antique gilt travelling clock on the mantelpiece and said, 'Quarter to four. Now if I'm lucky I might catch him at the office. I'll strike while the iron's hot, eh?' She hurried to the side-table, her step like a young girl's, because for all her weight she was light on her feet, and as she dialled the number Arlette said, 'Tell him it's Madam Hevell's you want to go to; tell him Mrs de Ferrier gets her clothes there, that should impress him.'

Maggie pulled a face towards Arlette. 'By! Aye, that should impress him, an' all. Does she get everything there?'

'I should think so. About everything.'

'Hello. Is . . . is Mr Gallacher in? Tell him it's Mrs Gallacher . . .

'Hello there, Rod.'

93

'Hello.'

'Hello.'

'I know it's you. What's the matter, what do you want?'

'Two hundred pounds.' She slanted her eyes and twisted her nose towards Arlette.

'What!'

'You heard. Two hundred pounds. I want to get rigged out.'

'Two hundred pounds! It won't take two hundred pounds to rig you out.'

'That's all you know. I've travelled the town all this week with our Frances looking for something to wear. We parted on fighting terms. But Arlette's here and she's promised to have me done properly . . . done I said.' She was laughing now. 'She said it will take two hundred pounds.'

'Nonsense!'

'Well, that's what she says and she should know.'

'There's shops in Newcastle that'll fix you up for a quarter of that.'

'So you think. But I've tried some of them. There's a lot of me to fix up; perhaps you haven't noticed.' Again she pulled a face at Arlette. 'Anyway, this shop is very classy and I don't see why I shouldn't go and get fixed up there, Mrs de Ferrier gets all her things there . . . Hello. Are you there? . . . Rod . . . Rod, are you there?'

Maggie now turned a blank face towards Arlette. 'He's rung off, or been cut off.' She put the phone down. 'I'll try again in a minute or so, but I'm sure it'll be all right; he stopped bawling me out when I mentioned your name.' She sat on the edge of the bed again and, joining her plump hands on her lap, she said, 'I feel excited, like a young lass, Arlette. Do you think she'll take inches off me?'

'More than inches. But stick to your diet; if you could lose another eight or nine pounds in the next three weeks it would be marvellous.'

'I will, lass, I will. But what about me face?' She jumped up from the bed and leant over the dressing table and looked into the mirror. 'I haven't any lines, have I, and no grey in me hair? It's a funny thing—' she half turned towards Arlette '—that Mrs Burrows-Thompson, you know, who lives in the second house down towards the end of the road, must be sixty if she's a day because she's got a daughter over forty, and her face is a mass of lines. But, you know, I always envy her because in a way she looks younger than me; it's her figure I suppose and the way she dresses. Well!' She stood up straight and gave her stomach a resounding blow with the flat of her hand and laughed as she said, 'Get ye gone Satan and leave Maggie Gallacher slim and alluring.' Then, the laughter dropping from her like a cloak and leaving her face straight, her voice flat and serious, she looked down at Arlette and said, 'I want to do Rod credit. That's all I want to do, ever want to do, do him credit.'

CHAPTER THREE

THE TAXI DRIVER

The dance was at its height. The Felburn Corkers were blasting out the latest pop hit. Elizabeth was in the café at the coffee end of the long table, and her arms were aching and her head was buzzing. Where did they put it all? She must have poured out thousands of cups of coffee. And she said so to Father Armstrong as he bent over the counter towards her and asked, 'How's it going, Nippy?'

'Aw, Father—' she closed her eyes and wiped the sweat, which wasn't imaginary, from her brow with the back of her hand '—where do they put it? I've taken nearly five pounds in coffee alone.'

'Good. Good. It'll be ten before the night's out, at least I hope so, so don't let your pins give way yet awhile.' He nodded his grizzled head at her, then went on, 'Ah, but you want a break; I'll get Mary to come. Mary!' He bellowed across the room to where two girls were standing near the dance room door, and as the shorter of the two turned towards him he said in an aside to Elizabeth, 'It's a kindness putting her out of her misery anyway; she'll never get a partner with those feet.'

'Oh, Father!'

'Well, it's the truth. Poor girl, she was born with two left ones.' His voice trailed away and he turned abruptly and said, 'Ah, there you are, Mary. Now here's Elizabeth done a two-hour stint, what about giving her a break, fifteen minutes or so? And it's a slack time. Go on now, get behind that counter.' He pushed the far from willing girl, saying, 'It's kind of you,' and when she turned to him, about to speak, he said, 'I know, I know; you did your stint last time and at the Children of Mary's on Thursday night. I know, I know all about it. But go on, be a good child. Just fifteen minutes; that's all you want isn't it, Elizabeth?' He didn't wait for her answer; pulling her around the table, he led her across the room, out into the corridor and through another door into a games room that was empty now and, looking about him, said, 'Ah, this is nice. I could do with a breather meself. Let's sit down and have a crack.'

Elizabeth flopped down into a plastic-covered easy chair and stretched out her legs, letting her arms dangle limply over the sides. Anything less like a prospective nun would be hard to imagine. Her dress wasn't a mini but it rose above her knees. Her legs were long and thin, her body equally long and thin; she was tall for her age, but her breasts hardly made shadows in her dress; her face was happy, relaxed and guileless. And so thought Father Armstrong as he looked at her. She looked to him like something that had been dropped from another world and unaware that she was a stranger in this one. He was afraid for her, he had been afraid for her for some time now. Perhaps it was because he remembered Paul. Paul had been like this, unaware, walking in realms of ideas and ideals, out to please, to make people happy, and unconscious of self and the needs of self. Paul had thought of the priesthood not as the further glorification of God and his work on earth, but of the glorification of his family, of his mother in particular; yes, his mother in particular. Maggie had been to blame with regards to Paul, from the very beginning. If the boy hadn't been awakened when he was he'd have likely gone down to his grave never realising that he had become a priest solely because of his parents. Or perhaps he would have, only then it would have been too late. But as with many others, some better, before him, this very awakening could have brought him nearer to Christ than ever a vocation in the first place would have done, because in such a situation a man had great need of Christ, need of his understanding and compassion.

He turned to Elizabeth and said to her gently, 'Do you think you'll miss all this next year, I mean the dancing and the frivolity?'

'No, Father; of course not.'

'Don't you like dancing?'

'Yes, of course; but I've always been able to take it or leave it.'

'Elizabeth.'

'Yes, Father?' She pulled herself up in the chair and turned to him, her grey eyes laughing at him.

'You're sure of yourself and your intentions?'

The eyes widened, her mouth remained open for a moment as if in surprise, then she declared firmly, 'Of course, of course. Yes. I've told you. I feel I've got the vocation.'

He stared at her. He had christened her – he had christened all Maggie's and Rod's children – he had married them and they had turned out a decent enough family, except that they were lapsing here and there. But there were only really two of them he had taken to, Paul and this one here, and he hoped to God, indeed he did, that she knew what she was about. He said to her now, 'Stay where you are and rest your feet a minute, I'm going to look in on the madhouse; you never know, they might start throwing bottles.' He said the latter as if that was the most improbable thing that could happen. But when he reached the door he turned. 'There's a Bog's End element here the night but so far they're behaving like Christians. I hope their good intentions last till twelve.' He put his head back, then ended, 'They've swelled the coffers anyway; we've nearly reached five hundred.'

'Really, Father?'

He smiled at her. 'Nearly five hundred.'

'Good for us,' she said.

'Yes, good for us,' he repeated; 'we'll have that window before the year's out.'

When he had gone she sat thinking about the window. She had never been able to see why he wanted a new window in the Lady Chapel. There was a nice one there already showing the Holy Family, but apparently he had always wanted a great, long window to light up the corner, and now it had become a sort of thing with him, a thing that he wanted to accomplish before he retired in two years' time. Oh well, he had done so much for the parish he deserved his window. Dear Father Armstrong. Retired or no, he had promised to say Mass the day she took her vows.

She rubbed her hands together. She felt hot and sticky and the distant beat of the band was making her head ache slightly; she'd go out and get a breath of air. But she'd better keep away from the car park though for they'd be necking round there like mad. She smiled to herself tolerantly . . . no regret, no desire, no jealousy in her thoughts.

As she passed through the dusty lobby which was the front section of the middle of three Nissen huts she glanced to the right of her to the wide opening that led into the dance section. A tall youth in the latest style of flared trousers and a cord velvet jacket of equal modernity stopped and glanced at her, then moved out into the lobby and watched her as she went through the door on to the narrow flagged terrace fronting the asphalt drive.

Elizabeth was half across the drive walking slowly in the direction of the gates when the youth caught up with her. 'Taking the air?' he asked.

She turned her head quickly towards him and smiled. 'Yes.' She didn't know him, she had never seen him before. He was, she surmised, one of the Bog's End crowd to whom Father Armstrong had referred. She was inwardly amused at the cut of his clothes, and her glancing over them didn't escape him.

He flicked the lapel of the jacket and strutted in almost peacock fashion as he said, 'They're new. I'm in the latest; there's not another rig in Felburn like this.'

She hoped not; she kept her face quite straight as she said, 'Oh.'

He matched his step with hers and walked closer to her. 'You one of Father Armstrong's babies?'

Her face was stiff now and her voice matched it as she said, 'I don't know about Father Armstrong's babies, I'm in his parish.'

'Well, that's what I meant. Not much to choose from in there.' He jerked his head back towards the Nissen huts.

'Then why did you come? And why are you staying?'

'Two questions at once. First, 'cos I thought I might get some kicks; and second, I'm not staying. I'm on me way out. Give you the gripes that lot. And the band, where did they dig it up?'

She didn't answer, and when she reached the gate she turned immediately and began to walk back the way she had come, but he turned with her and said, 'I didn't see you on the floor.'

'You weren't likely to, I wasn't dancing.'

'Don't you dance?'

'No.'

'You mean you don't dance? You can't? Where've you been? Come on.' He took her hand. 'I'll show you.'

She pressed her heels to the ground and tried to tug her hand from his, saying, 'I don't want to dance. Leave go. Do you hear, leave go!'

'What's up with you?' He still held her hand. 'You frigid or something?'

'Leave go of me.'

'I will when I'm ready.'

'I'll call, mind.'

'Go on, call. I can deal with any pasty-faced pup that comes out of there. You're a big girl not to dance.' His other hand moved up her bare arm, and now she beat at him with her fists and cried, 'Stop it! Do you hear? Stop it! Let go of me.'

But his arms went about her and when one hand slid on to her buttocks she kicked at his shin and yelled, 'Father! Father!' When her voice was checked by his mouth covering hers she became like a wild thing tearing at him. Then suddenly, as if lightning had come between them and thrown him from her, she saw him going head over heels on to his back, where he lay perfectly still for a moment with the man who had put him there standing over him. She didn't know what age the man was for he had his back to her, but one thing she took in was that he was smallish, a head less than the boy he had thrown. She became aware of a car standing on the drive where there had been no car before, and as she saw Father Armstrong running down the steps, two of the boys with him, she gave a great shudder and the tears burst from her.

'What is it? What is it, my child? What's happened?' Father Armstrong had his arm round her shoulder while he looked to where a young fellow was turning on to his hands and knees and pulling himself up from the ground. When he reached his feet he staggered, and the man standing in front of him, said, 'Do you want some more?'

'What is it?' Father Armstrong asked again, and the stranger turned to him and said, 'This bloke, he was getting fresh with her and she didn't want any of it. She was screaming.'

Father Armstrong looked from the short young man to the tall one and he wondered to himself how the little one had managed to get the other on the ground for he had never seen anyone lying flatter. The tall fellow was from the dance – he had noticed him – but he wasn't of his parish. As he watched him turn to go back into the hall, he cried at him, 'Not that way! Don't you go in there again. Get going now, while your luck holds. Get going.'

His face twisted in a sneer, the youth dusted down his fancy jacket and his trousers, and making a movement with his shoulders as if hitching on his coat he walked slowly away. Then he turned and, looking at his assailant, shouted, 'You could have broken my back.'

'Aye I could, couldn't I?' the small man called back to him. He then turned towards the priest who was saying, 'There now, there now, give over.' Father Armstrong patted Elizabeth's back and she drew in a shuddering breath, then blew her nose. And now she looked into the eyes of the man who had rescued her. They were on a level with her own but he was shorter than her; he had fair hair, a long face, and his shoulders were very broad and his body stocky. He was a man, she thought, about the age of their Sam, twenty-six or seven. She said softly, 'Thank you. Thank you very much.'

He nodded at her and smiled. 'That's all right. Glad I was in time.'

'Were you coming to the dance?' asked Father Armstrong, and the man laughed, and it had a deep humorous sound.

'No, I was bringing a couple. Picked them up near the park. I run a taxi service, Portman's in Fowler Street.'

'Oh yes, yes.' The priest nodded. 'Portman's. I know it. And you are Mr Portman?'

'Yes, I'm Peter Portman.'

'Well, thank you very much Mr Portman; you came in at an opportune time, you did that.' He looked at Elizabeth and pressed her gently to him, then said, 'How are you feeling?'

'All right, Father.'

'Well, I wouldn't say you were all right. I think you've had enough for one night. What time are they coming for you?'

'I . . . I told Dad not to come until half-past eleven.'

'Oh.' Father Armstrong shook his head. 'That's some way off; would you like to go home now? Would you like Mr Portman to run you back?'

She looked from the priest to the taxi driver, then said, 'Yes; yes, I think so, Father.'

'Go along then and get your things . . . Will that be all right with you, Mr Portman?'

'Yes, sir; that'll be all right with me.'

The use of 'sir' told the priest the young fellow was not of the faith, but he appeared a decent man for all that. He said to him, 'Tell me what happened exactly.' And Peter Portman said, 'Well, when I drove in the gate there I picked them up in me lights. He was holding her and she was struggling, and then he started to kiss her. But I didn't think it was anything serious – you see it all the time in this business – so I turned round, got my fare from the couple, and they got out and ran towards the car park that way.' He nodded in the direction of the dark area at the end of the Nissen huts. 'When I turned to the wheel again she was still struggling, and then she yelled, and that was enough for me.'

'May I ask how you managed to knock him down, flat out like that? He was a big fellow.'

His thin chin moved from side to side before he replied, 'I practise judo. I'm a blue belt.'

'Well, glory be; you are?' The priest's head and shoulders pushed backwards as if to get the small young fellow into better focus. There was deep admiration in his tone as he went on, 'A blue belt indeed! Well, well now. Aw, I wish I'd seen it; I bet that lout didn't know what had hit him.' He chuckled deeply. 'Oh, wait till I tell Father Monaghan about this. He's our curate, young and very keen on the boxing; but I could swear he knows nothing about judo . . . What's your church?'

'Church? Oh.' Peter Portman gave a self-conscious laugh now. 'I'm afraid I haven't one. I'm . . . I'm a heathen. Respectable one you know, but nevertheless a heathen. I'm afraid I've got views about denominations.'

'You have?'

'Yes; yes, sir.'

They both laughed together now.

'I'd like to hear them sometime. I don't suppose with your views you'd like to show some of our boys how to knock big fellows on their backs, now would you?'

'Aw.' Peter Portman laughed again and shook his head. 'Most of me time is taken up with me business; I'm running four cars and have to do the night work. Nobody likes to be on call at night, and my slogan is "Peter Portman will get you there night or day, ring Felburn 60328. Trust Portman, he's never late." '

The priest's head went back again and his laugh rang out. Then he turned and said, 'Ah, here's Elizabeth.' As she came up to them he went on, 'There you are then. I've been trying to do business with Mr Portman here, trying to inveigle him into coming to show the lads how to knock big fellows on to their backs, but he's not having any. You may have better luck; you tell him just how good for the soul self-denial and charitable works are. By the way—' his voice dropped '—how you feeling now?'

'I'm all right, Father, really.' She smiled at him.

'That's it. I'll call round tomorrow, tell your mam. And thanks for your help.'

'I haven't been much of a help, Father.' She bowed her head.

'Go on with you.' He pushed her towards the car where

Peter Portman was standing now with the door open, and when they came up to him he said, 'Do you prefer the back or the front?'

She looked into his eyes again for a fleeting second, and then said, 'I'll sit in the front.'

'Goodbye now,' said Father Armstrong, bending down to the window. Then looking across Elizabeth, he said, 'And drive carefully, mind.'

'Safety is me second name. I've got a slogan about that an' all.' Again they laughed, and then he was backing the car and driving out of the gate.

They drove for some minutes along the main road in silence before Peter Portman said on a deep chuckle, 'I don't know where I'm going; where do you live?'

'Oh, silly of me. We live on The Rise.'

'The Rise!'

'I hope I'm not taking you out of your way . . . '

He said now, 'That's what I'm for, to be taken out of me way. The more I'm taken out of me way the better the business . . . Have you always lived in Felburn?'

'Yes, I was born here, but—' she looked towards him '—not on The Rise. We used to live in Weir Street, just off the Market.'

He glanced swiftly at her before turning his attention back to the road. She was a nice kid, no side. She hadn't had any need to tell him that she had once lived in Weir Street; Weir Street was no cop.

She was asking him now if he belonged to Felburn and he replied, 'No, I hail from Shields, but . . . but my wife was a Felburn lass.'

He had a wife. She had felt at ease with him, but more so now he had a wife. Yet he had said was, not is.

'Have you a family?' she asked.

'No.' He turned a corner, then another, before he ended, 'She died.'

'Oh, I'm sorry.' She glanced at him again. He was a man, but still to her he looked too young to have had a wife who had died.

'Your priest seems a decent old fellow,' he said.

'Oh, Father Armstrong. Yes, he's a decent . . . old fellow.' She laughed. 'But more than that, he's a wonderful man.'

'Aye, there are good and bad in all walks of life.'

She was puzzled by this reply but didn't take it further. He was likely one of those people who held animosity against all Catholics. Yet not all, because he seemed to like Father Armstrong. But there, who wouldn't like Father Armstrong?

As they were going up Brampton Hill and about to turn into the road that led to The Rise she said, 'It's the third turning on the left.' Then when he had turned into this road she added, 'The second gate along.'

The second gate was some distance along the road. He drove slowly through it, then skirted the lawn and drew the car to a stop behind another car, out of which a man was stepping. Before he had time to get out and open the door for her she was on the drive and running towards the man. A minute later they came towards him and she said, 'This is my father. This is Mr Portman, Dad.'

Rodney held out his hand. His face was grim. 'I understand you've been of great assistance to my daughter; I'm grateful, very grateful.'

'Oh, that's all right. I just happened to be there.' He smiled, and Rodney said, 'I wish to God I could get my hands on that lout.'

Elizabeth now put in with a shaky laugh, 'I don't think, Dad, you'd be able to do what Mr Portman did.'

'No?' Rodney looked from her to Peter Portman again, and when he didn't speak Elizabeth said, 'He treated him to some judo; Mr Portman's an expert.'

Rodney stared at the young man before him. Five foot five he would say at the most. He couldn't imagine him throwing another fellow on to his back, yet he knew it could be done, he'd seen it on television. He said now to Elizabeth, 'Have you settled up?'

'Oh no, no. I'm sorry. How much is it?'

'Eleven and six.'

Rodney took out his wallet and, extracting a pound note, handed it to Peter Portman, saying, 'That'll cover it.'

'Oh thanks. Thank you, sir. Well—' he took a step alongside the bonnet '—I'd better be making a move; you never know—' he jerked his head '—there might be more damsels in distress.'

When he was seated behind the wheel and had started up the car Elizabeth ran to the window and said, 'Thanks. Thank you again.'

'Any time.' Again he jerked his head, and she laughed now and stood back, while he drove away.

When she rejoined her father and walked up the steps he did not commiserate with her in any way. Instead he asked rather stiffly, 'How did you manage to get into a scrape like that?'

She went before him into the hall and turned and looked at him, her face straight as she said, 'I didn't manage it, it just happened. I was outside taking the air.'

'On your own?'

'Yes, on my own, Dad. What's the matter with you?'

He closed his eyes for a moment and turned his head to the side. 'What I mean to say is, why couldn't you take one of the girls with you?'

'I didn't want to take one of the girls with me.'

'What is it? What is it?' Maggie came from the drawing-room and looked from one to the other. Then, her eyes coming to rest on Elizabeth, she said, 'You're back early, what's happened?'

'Oh.' Elizabeth made an impatient movement, then pushed past her mother into the room; and Rodney following her said, 'Some fellow got fresh with her and a taxi driver apparently knocked him down and brought her home.'

Pausing a moment, Maggie looked down the room to where Elizabeth was now standing tapping her finger on the edge of a small table; then she hurried towards her, put her arm around her shoulder and said, 'You all right, honey?'

'Yes, yes, I'm all right, Mam.' There was an impatient note in her voice.

'Sure?'

'Yes, only—' She turned and looked past her mother to where her father was picking up the evening paper and she said, '—only Dad seems to think it's my fault.'

Rodney crumpled the paper angrily and dashed it against his knee. 'That's a nice thing to say.'

'Well, it was your attitude, Dad.'

'My attitude? What did you expect my attitude to be, gay? I said you shouldn't have let yourself in for that kind of thing, and I mean it, especially you in your position. And what, may I ask, were Father Monaghan and Father Armstrong doing when this was happening?'

'They were in the hall seeing to things.'

'While louts were crawling around outside! And you like a lamb took a walk among them.'

Elizabeth now bent her head and screwed up her eyes to hold in the tears; then turning, she dashed down the room and through the door.

Maggie didn't follow her but remained where she was, looking towards Rodney. Then in a voice which she tried not to raise, she demanded, 'There's something I want to ask you, an' it's just this, what's eating you? There's something up with you and I've got a right to know, so spit it out.'

When he didn't answer her or look towards her, her voice suddenly spiralled to a shout and she cried at him, 'I'm not putting up with any more of your mute protests; whatever you're protesting about, I want to know what's wrong. If you don't tell me I'll damn well make it my business to find out.'

She was to remember afterwards the quick turn of his head, the look he gave her, then the deep intake of breath as he said, 'Aw, it's one thing after another. Things are going wrong on the Morley Estate. That underground crack is spreading; four walls got it yesterday. And there's bloody union agitators at it on the Rollingdon site.'

Her anger was swept away, she was all contrition. She came and sat before him, her knees touching his, her hands gripped on her lap. 'Is it bad?' she asked, her voice just above a whisper.

'It isn't good.'

'I mean is it dangerous? Will the houses sink?'

'Oh no.' He shook his head. 'Not as bad as that. It's a minute settling really but it's enough to crack the walls and the windows in its path.'

'How are they reacting to it, the people?'

'Oh, need you ask? You know people.' He rose and went to a table, opened a cigarette box and took one out. Then went on, 'Yelling their heads off, demanding compensation. I'm going to see my solicitor, one tells the other, and it becomes like a parrot cry.'

'How long has this been going on?' she asked.

He glanced in her direction still without looking at her; then after a pause he said, 'Oh, some time.'

'Why couldn't you tell me?' She too had got to her feet now, but she didn't go towards him. 'At one time if a fellow put a brick out of place, or the cement wasn't running well, you told me. Why not now?'

He inhaled the smoke of the cigarette, then strained his

neck out of his collar before saying, 'It's big business now, nothing like the early days. Anyway, I have Sam and Willie to unburden to; that's what they're paid for.'

He moved from the table and walked slowly down the room, and when he reached the door he paused a moment and said, 'I'm away up.'

When she was left alone, it came to her that he hadn't looked at her once since he had entered the room. She sat down, telling herself to wait a moment before going up to Elizabeth. She wasn't satisfied with his explanation; there was something wrong between her and Rod. Was it because she had insisted on accepting the Duke's invitation? No, it had blown in well before that, this last chill wind. When then? How many weeks ago? How many months? How many years?

Deep within her she was aware that she had always loved him more than he had loved her; all she needed in life was him; but his needs were greater, more varied. One night a while back as she lay wide-eyed and thinking it had come to her that he was in love with his business, he had always been in love with his business. He had courted success like a man courts a mistress, but she had never been jealous of the attention he gave to his work. A man had to have something outside the house and what better or safer thing than work. No, she had never been jealous of his work; but now she was jealous of something. She didn't know what, she only knew she was jealous. She got heavily to her feet. She was tired, weary, life wasn't running right; and now this latest business concerning Elizabeth. She must go and find out all about it.

Part Three

CHAPTER ONE

THE DUKE

'Oh, Arlette, I can't believe it, I can't.' Maggie surveyed the reflection in the mirror. There was nothing about it she recognised, not even the face. 'Eeh!' She shook her head. 'It's just as you said. Mind you—' she turned towards Arlette '—although you kept tellin' me what she could do I didn't believe it, I really didn't. She's a miracle worker if ever there was one.' She flapped her hand towards Arlette, her mouth full of laughter. 'I bet the Pope could do with her because she's achieved more on a hundred and seventy-five pounds than all me forty years of praying.'

'Oh, Mam!' Arlette's eyes were bright, partly with pleasure, and partly because of a film of tears oozing up out of the sadness that was weighing on her.

Her time of waiting was almost up, the time she had given to this woman to keep her trouble-free until this great event, the event of her life, was over. She would also let the week-end pass, because on Sunday they would all be here basking in reflected glory, and she mustn't spoil that. But on Monday morning early, as soon as he had gone out, she would leave. She had everything arranged, at least about where she was going. She would take with her only a couple of cases, a few necessary things, for the slightest hint of packing would put him on his guard. He was quick was Sam. She looked at Maggie, who was looking at her. She was going to miss her so much, the comfort of her, the common-sense of her, the reality of her. She'd miss all the others too. But there was one other she would miss especially. A month ago he had just been one of the rest. Yet that wasn't true; he had never been just one of the rest; but now he was one apart. He had become the materialised essence of a dream, a dream that had grown with her adolescence and had not ceased to grow after she had married Sam. In fact the dream had expanded as the days of her marriage mounted; its vagueness hardening into longing and the longing threaded with regret, and the regret in turn full of recrimination for standards lowered, for being so weak as to be led by the desire of the flesh alone. And she had paid for her weakness, only God and herself knew how she had paid. Ask and ye shall receive. Her body had demanded that its needs be fulfilled, and it got what it had asked for, with a measure running over. Dear, dear God, and how it had run over.

'You look as mesmerised as me, dear.' Maggie put out her hand and touched Arlette's cheek, and Arlette said with a catch in her voice, 'I'm so happy for you, Maggie. Oh!' She put her hand to her mouth and closed her eyes; and then they both fell together and laughed and Maggie said, 'Aw, that was good to hear; you called me Maggie. I prefer it to Mam. You call me that in future, lass.'

'And have the rest of them after me?' Arlette pulled a face, then added, 'I'm in Frances's bad books already but I hope she'll forgive me when she sees you.' She held Maggie at arm's length, saying now, 'When Madam Hevell suggested midnight blue velvet I thought, I'm not sure, but she was right because it brings out the depths in your eyes. And the cut; it's beautiful, isn't it?'

Maggie turned to the mirror again and after staring at herself she said, 'I tell you, lass, I just can't believe it.' She gazed at her face made up as it had never been before, and she thought in surprise, I could be good looking at that. She looked from the square neck of the dress that showed the upper part of her breasts lying like moulds of smooth deep cream, down the fitted bodice to where the velvet dropped in two folds from the right side of her waist to the top of her left hip, then flowed away loosely down the side of the wide skirt, which almost touched the top of her pale pink shoes. It was on these her eyes rested as she said, 'I hope me feet don't swell; there's no room for expansion.' She laughed. 'And me corn's giving me gyp already.'

'Didn't you have it attended to? I thought you were going to the chiropodist last week?'

'Oh.' Maggie made a guilty movement. 'I . . . I couldn't fit it in so I just pared the top off.' She wagged her foot around. 'They're just a bit tight but they'll ease off. I should have worn them afore to get used to them . . . But that's not the only place I'm tight.' She patted her flat stomach. 'Yet it's worth it. You wouldn't believe it; I only lost ten pounds, but I don't look much over twelve stone, do I?'

'You don't look even that. There now, here's your bag.' Arlette handed her an embroidered bag, of the same tone as her shoes, then looking into her face she said softly, 'Now make up your mind you're going to enjoy it all. There's nothing to worry about, just do as I said and remember that after all the Duke is only a man, and . . . and rather a nice man into the bargain.'

'It should be you who's going in place of me.' Maggie's face was unsmiling now. 'You could carry it off, especially since you've met him.' And now she bit on her lip and said, 'And fancy that, fancy keeping it to yourself, even if it did happen afore you were married. If I'd met a duke the whole damn town would know, an' they will an' all after this.' She gurgled deep in her throat. Then striking a pose, she walked across the room towards the long mirror again, her head held high, her back straight, and she extended her hand and said to her reflection,

'How . . . do . . . you . . . do?' and turning swiftly to Arlette, she said, 'Are you sure that's all?'

'Yes, your names will be announced; you'll go in together, but you'll be introduced to the Duke first. He will shake hands with you and say "How-do-you-do?" and all you answer is "How-do-you-do?" '

'I don't say Your Grace?'

'No, there will be no need; you'll just walk on into the room and be given a drink. You'll stand chatting . . . '

'Oh my goodness . . . stand chatting.' She put her hand to her head. 'With them lot!'

'Half of them lot are dim . . . you'll chat. Of course you will, you're the biggest chatterer in Felburn.'

'Aw lass, I'll be so tongue-tied they'll think I'm a deaf mute.'

'Not you. Come on now, let's go down.'

'What's the time?'

'Six o'clock.'

'SIX O'CLOCK!' Maggie's face screwed up in surprise. 'And he's not in yet? He's got to get shaved and changed, and we're supposed to leave at half-past.'

'He may be downstairs.'

'He shouldn't be downstairs, he should be up here, and ready.' She laughed now and said, 'Aw, that voice doesn't go with this rig-out. I'll never get rid of Maggie Gallacher.'

'Don't try,' said Arlette, 'and stop worrying, it won't take him long once he's in.'

'It'll take him more than a half-hour. Oh, my God! if he's late and we don't arrive . . . '

'Now don't get agitated,' Arlette said soothingly. 'It's all right. Come on downstairs. I'll bring your coat.' She lifted the matching blue velvet, collarless cape-sleeved coat from the bed, then followed Maggie out on to the landing.

When they reached the top of the stairs Maggie cast a glance over her shoulder towards Arlette; then, as if going into battle, she lifted her chin and sailed down the stairs, to be brought to a halt on the last stair by Annie entering the hall from the kitchen to stop dead in her tracks and exclaiming, 'Good God!'

Maggie felt the colour flowing over her face. Annie, naturally, had seen the dress before and her verdict had been, 'It's a plain piece; you've been done if you ask me.'

'Well?' The syllable was a demand for approval, and Annie, walking slowly across the hall, stopped before the woman who was not only her mistress but her life-long friend and now she smiled generously at her and said, 'If it keeps dark you'll pass.'

'Aw, you!' Maggie thrust her aside but grinned at her as she did so, then went into the drawing-room where, waiting for her were Nancy, Paul, Frances, Helen and Elizabeth. Sam and Willy, Dave Walton and Trevor Gillespie weren't expected until later; they had all arranged to be here for the return. But now the eyes of her female family were on her, and also those of her daughter-in-law, Nancy, and her best loved son and she knew that she had astounded each and every one of them. In a way this was disturbing knowledge, for it emphasised the fact that she had been letting herself go these last few years. But that was all over. These past weeks had taught her something; she had learnt that people like Madam Hevell could make an old bag of hay look like a million dollars. Not that she had been an old bag of hay, and her million dollars' look had cost a hundred and seventy-five pounds. But it was money well spent, and she was going to spend more of it in the future, yes she was. She realised now she'd never had a decent rag on her back in her life worth bragging about. If Rod could pay over two thousand pounds for a new Rover then she was entitled to a few hundred a year to keep up with him. She had been too soft, too easygoing; you could be sat on. By! you could that.

'Well I never!'

'Oh! Mam. Mam.'

'You look wonderful. Wonderful. I can't believe it's you.'

'It's me all right.' Maggie put her hand out and slapped Elizabeth's cheek playfully. 'I have only to open me mouth. Now don't, don't rumple me. Me hair's all set and everything; it's so stiff with lacquer that if I fell on me head I'd bounce.' Maggie now turned and looked from Frances to Paul. They hadn't spoken and again she uttered the demanding 'Well?' commanding their approbation, and Frances, her head wagging, said grudgingly, 'Yes, yes, it's very nice. Bit full on the hips I think, but very nice.'

'Thank you.'

Paul came to her now, and taking her hands, he bent forward and kissed her and, his eyes bright and laughing into hers, he broke into song, 'There's nothing like a dame,' he sang; and now they were all laughing, their heads bobbing, their mouths wide.

'Aw, you, our Paul!' Maggie pushed him on the shoulder, and he stopped in the middle of a line and said, 'It's true, there isn't anything like a dame, and I've never seen a better looking one than you, Mam . . . Mame, that's who you're like, Mame.' Again he kissed her and she grabbed at him and held him to her for a moment before pushing him roughly away, saying, 'What's up with you? Look, you've crushed me frock. What's up with you all anyway? You'd think you'd never seen me without me pinny on in me life.'

'Dad's in for a shock.'

'Oh, thank you!' Maggie nodded at Frances, who had the grace to blush and say, 'Well what I mean is . . .' but Maggie interrupted her. 'I know what you mean, lass. Anyway, speaking of your Dad, where is he? Turned five past six and not a sign of him.'

'Yes, he should be here now; he won't have much time to change.' This was said in different ways by them all.

Nancy and Frances went to the window and looked out, Lizzie ran into the hall and to the front door. Arlette said, 'Shall I phone the office?' and Maggie replied, 'Aye, yes. But I hope he's left the office afore now, or we're going to be in the cart.' Then turning and catching Paul's eyes still on her, she moved over to him and hissed in mock menace. 'Don't you stand there looking at me as if you'd never seen me afore else I'll box your ears for you'; and he, smiling tenderly back at her, said, 'It's a lovely evening, Mrs Gallacher, and it's a full moon, everything's set fair.'

'Aye.' She still kept her voice low. 'Except your Dad isn't here . . .'

It was turned ten past and Maggie was standing with hands gripped tightly before her. A sick agitation was adding to the deep nervousness that was already filling her when Elizabeth shouted from the hall, 'Here he is! And Sam's with him.'

Maggie tried to compose herself as she watched the door, to force a smile to her lips to ease the tension that had stiffened her jaws. She heard Rodney answer Elizabeth, saying, 'There's plenty of time, there's plenty of time.' Then he was standing within the open doorway with Sam just behind him, and he was staring at her. His look held surprise and a sort of alarm.

There was a silence in the room while they waited for his reaction, and he must have felt this for his eyes flickered round them before coming to rest on Maggie again. Then he moved forward, not right up to her, just to the other end of the couch and on an embarrassed laugh said, 'It just shows you what money can do, doesn't it?'

At one time she would have taken this remark as a compliment. She would have laughed and pushed him and said, 'Aye, lad, it does, doesn't it? And I'm going to keep on showing you what it can do.' But although he was surprised, even a bit flabbergasted by her changed appearance, she knew he wasn't pleased; for some reason or other he wasn't pleased. Perhaps his attitude was like this because he was still worried about the business. But on a night like this, surely to God he could have put it aside, for although she hadn't talked much about the do to him, she had talked enough to let him know it was going to be the night of her life.

In reply to his words she said, unsmiling, 'Isn't it about time you made a move?' He looked into her eyes made a deeper blue by the reflection of the velvet and larger by the effect of her eye shadow, and in this moment altogether beautiful, and then dropped his gaze from hers and turned and went out of the room.

They all looked after him in silence. Then Frances, turning to Sam, who was now standing behind Arlette with his hand on her shoulder, asked, 'What's up with him?' In answer Sam raised his eyebrows, gave a shrug and said, 'Nothing more than usual, why?'

'He seems worried.'

'Perhaps he has things to worry over. Don't we all?' He looked across to Paul now, and Paul returned the look, straight and unblinking; then Elizabeth, who was standing by Maggie's side, said, 'Well, you haven't said what you think of her?'

'Oh.' Sam took his hand from Arlette's shoulder and walked slowly across the room towards his mother. He stopped within an arm's length from her and, like a farmer surveying the points of a heifer which he might or might not purchase, he looked her over, before giving his verdict with a smile on his face. 'A rose by any other name,' he said.

Paul had said there's nothing like a dame, and he had spoken from his heart. Her man had said it just shows you what money can do, and she hadn't known whether it was meant as a compliment or not. But now her eldest son, smiling at her, his mouth wide, his eyes cold – she hadn't noticed how cold Sam's eyes were until recently – meant her no compliment with his quotation. In this moment, and for the first time in her life, she became really aware of this son, aware of him as he really was; someone frightening. He wasn't the man he appeared to be on the surface, and it came to her with sickening realisation as she looked back into the eyes of her firstborn, that he didn't like her. 'Our Sam doesn't like me.' 'Don't be barmy, woman.' A private conversation was going on in her head. 'I'm not barmy; I know what he meant by a rose by any other name. He was telling me that fine clothes won't make much difference to me, that I'll still be the same old two pennorth of copper in his eyes. He's got on and he's got too big for his boots; he's like his dad in a way. What's the matter with you? Stop it. Smile. Give him as much as he sends.' But, if she were to behave like that she'd have to raise her voice and shout; she always shouted when she was angry or annoyed.

She made herself smile broadly, and she looked past him to Arlette as she said, 'That's the one I've got to thank for the transformation.'

'Nonsense!' Arlette went towards the couch and sat down. 'All I did was to give you the name of a shop.'

'Oh no. Oh no.' It was Sam speaking again, and leaning over the couch, over Arlette's shoulder, his face close to hers, he said, 'Give honour where it's due; you're the girl that can cause transformations. I should know.' When, with a swift movement, he went to kiss her cheek she was swifter still in moving away from him down the couch, and her repulse was like a slap across the mouth. Straightening up and for the moment unable to bring his smile back to his face, he looked about him, from Frances to Helen, from Helen to Nancy, from Nancy to Elizabeth, from Elizabeth to Paul. Elizabeth and Paul were standing near his mother. They seemed linked, bound together in their affection, mother love and child love. But as he stared at them a swift surge of power rose in him and helped to placate his ego. He knew things about them that would blow their little complacent worlds sky high, and he intended to do just that, with each of them.

His mother's face was made up like he had never seen it before, but one sentence from him could wipe the make-up and the grin off it, and leave it stark, and not only for the night, but for ever. But the time wasn't ripe for that yet, she wasn't at her peak. Let her come back with the pollen of the Duke dripping from her, then he would tell her. 'It's a bloody shame,' he would say, 'but you've got a right to know. Dad's got another woman. Not some flossie either but one of the nobs; he's flown high.'

His attitude towards Paul would be different. Aye, by God it would. He'd take him by the throat and say, 'You white livered pup you! So that's why you jumped the church, lusting after your brother's wife.' And there was another thing he had found out about his brother. When he went through his room yesterday his search had not only disclosed a picture of Arlette on her wedding day, cut off from him, oh yes cut off so that no part of him remained in the picture, just her, in her virginal white looking like the Madonna, blast her, it had also disclosed the identity of Lacker. All those writings and potty little poems locked away in the bureau, hundreds and hundreds of them. By God, when he'd finished with his brother he'd wish he'd never been born. And there he was standing smiling at their mam; her blue-eyed boy, whom, although he nearly broke her heart when he became a spoilt priest, she still loved better than either himself or Willie, or any of them, except of course her youngest, whom she was now betting on to restore holy glory to the family. But, that was another thing, wasn't she in for a shock with her dear innocent little Liz? Damned little sneaking hypocrite.

Well, Liz was one bomb he needn't wait to explode; he would drop it gently into his mother's hands now before she went out, and that would stop her being so bloody pleased with herself. Should he start the ball rolling by chipping Liz? Or should he take his mam aside and tip her off?

Elizabeth deprived him of the first outlet for his venom when Maggie said to her, 'Go and tell your Dad to get a move on, he'll be less likely to bawl at you than at the rest of us.' She pushed Elizabeth gently away from her and Elizabeth went from the room, saying, 'I don't know so much.'

Sam looked towards the door through which Elizabeth had just disappeared, then he turned to Maggie and said, 'What's she up to, do you know?'

'What do you mean? Liz?'

'Yes.'

'What do you mean, what's she up to?'

'Are you in the dark about it?'

Maggie narrowed her eyes at Sam, and when Frances repeated, 'In the dark, our Sam? What do you mean?' Sam turned to her. Then he cast his glance round the others, and when his eyes met those of Paul again he shrugged his shoulders, looked down and turned away, saying, 'Oh well, it doesn't matter. Sorry I spoke.'

'Look here.' Maggie had taken three rapid steps towards him and caught him by the arm. 'You're getting at something; spit it out.'

'Oh, later, later, not now and you about to go out.'

'Never mind about me and going out; if you know something that I should know then let me have it, and quick.'

Again Sam cast a swift glance at the rest of them. They were all looking intently at him now, Arlette too, and he said, 'Well, it's this fellow! I've seen her with a fellow, the same one, a few times lately.'

'Our Liz with a fellow? Who?'

'Oh, well now, from the looks of him and the car I think he's the taxi driver that brought her home that night Dad told me about.'

'And you've seen them together since?'

'Aye. The first time was when I was passing the school just at the bottom of the road, and I saw her standing on the pavement with him, near the car. She was pointing along the street and naturally I thought he was a taxi driver and had been asking her some address or other, I didn't think until after that it could be the same fellow. And then it came to me that there's no houses along there except the school and the convent house.' When he shrugged and said no more, Maggie put in quickly, 'Well, that's all it could have been, she could have been showing him the way.'

'Well, yes, as I said that's what I thought, until I saw them in the car together.'

'When was this?'

'The first time you mean?'

'Yes, yes.'

'Oh about three days after that.'

'You've seen them since?'

'Aye.'

'My God!' Maggie put her hands to her mouth and began to tap her lips; then her voice rising, she demanded, 'Why didn't you tell me?'

He stepped back from her. 'Well, it's evident, isn't it? Look at the way you're taking it now. And anyway, I didn't think anything of it until yesterday. Even then I thought she would have told you; she tells you everything, doesn't she?'

She tells her everything. Yes, yes, Liz told her everything, at least she used to; but she hadn't told her about meeting this man. By God no, because she would have put a stop to her gallop. But wait; she had said she had seen him once since that night. It was on the Saturday morning and she had met him in the Market. He was shopping and she said she had felt sorry for him. She said his wife had died after they were married only three months, she'd had leukemia. But she had said nothing about seeing him after that. Yet she remembered now that she had been very quiet these past three weeks, and she herself had been so occupied with transforming herself that she hadn't taken much notice of it. In her daft blindness she had thought her quietness was a form of meditation. Meditation, be damned! My God! If there was anything in this and she renegaded like Paul had done she wouldn't be able to bear it, she would die.

But Liz wasn't underhand, Liz was as open as the day, like a child. Yet the child had been meeting this man on the quiet. If Sam had seen them four times how many times hadn't he seen them? Oh dear, dear God, there was always something to rub the shine off her happiness. Now she would have this at the back of her mind all the night, and not so far back either.

She moved towards a chair and sat down, for her corn was already beginning to sting and her legs felt weak. Then her eyes were drawn towards Arlette who had made a strange sound, like a growl. She was looking at Sam and her face was tight, hard in fact; she had never seen Arlette look hard before.

The room held a chilled silence; no-one spoke until Sam ground out, 'I should have kept me bloody mouth shut.' Then all of them were startled by Arlette's response to this. 'Yes, you should have but you didn't, did you?'

Not one of them had heard Arlette speak to Sam in this way, ever. They watched him stare at her and she at him. There was bare hatred gleaming from her eyes. They were amazed, even shocked. She looked as if she loathed the sight of him. The look disturbed Maggie so much that she forgot about Liz and the man for a moment, and said quickly and placatingly, 'There, there now, there'll be an explanation for this, quite a simple one; I'll get it in the morning. Say no more the night. Shut up all of you; here they come.'

When Rodney and Elizabeth entered the room, they all looked at them but none of them remarked on their father's appearance. The novelty of seeing him in a dinner jacket had worn off years ago.

Helen attempted to lighten the atmosphere when, looking at her father, she exclaimed, 'Quick change artist; I've never known anybody able to get ready as quick as you. Trevor takes longer than me, I can never get into the bathroom.'

Her father made no remark in reply to this pleasantry but, glancing at Maggie, he said, 'Well, are you ready?' and her reply was, 'Well, if I'm not now I never will be, I've only been waiting down here half-an-hour.'

Turning quickly about, he went into the hall, and Arlette came towards Maggie, holding up her coat for her to put on, and as Maggie went to get into it she noticed that Arlette's hands were trembling. This was a new side to Arlette. She had never seen her like this; she was always composed and controlled. She had always envied her these qualities, but now she could see she was in a temper, no, more of a rage. Dear, dear. Liz on her mind, and now Arlette; well, let her get outside before anything else happened.

They all came to the door, and they laughed as they called to her while Paul helped her into the car.

'Mind your manners, Mam.' This from Frances.

'Ask him if he's looking for a saucy secretary, or a receptive receptionist.' This from Helen.

'Keep your eyes and ears open for all the scandal, Mam.' This from Nancy.

'You'll outshine them all, Mam.' From Elizabeth.

And Paul, just before he closed the door, bent towards her and said, 'Enjoy it, Mam; make it the night of your life,' and she put her hand up and patted his cheek.

There were two who had made no comment; one was Sam who was standing on the top step looking over the heads of the others, the expression on his face unguarded for the moment because no-one was looking at him. The other was Annie. Annie had made no parting comment because she was too full, for behind her hard-bitten exterior, her snappy, crabby front, which was the only defence against the emptiness in her life, she was repeating over and over again to herself, 'Like a fairy-tale it is. Like a fairy-tale.'

And some similar thought was passing through Maggie's mind as they drove away. Here she was, Maggie Gallacher, sitting in a most luxurious car, dressed up to the nines in velvet and silk going to meet a duke. It was really unbelievable. Yet in a way the event was stripped of its happy phantasy because the man beside her, this man with the short cropped hair, this handsome man, for her Rod was handsome in a peculiar sort of way, was silent, sitting like a stuffed dummy. There was something wrong, something radically wrong with him and she didn't believe now it was wholly the business. No, no, he'd had tough times before but they had never caused him to be like this.

As the car left the town and made for the open country her nervousness increased. She had told herself that if he wasn't going to open his mouth, then she wouldn't, but now she thought they couldn't go on like this because she would arrive there all het up, more than she was already. She looked at his profile and asked, 'You nervous?'

' . . . What?'

'I said are you nervous?'

'No . . . well, perhaps just a trifle.'

Was he nervous? Yes, he'd say he was nervous, but not for the reasons she thought. God, if only this night was over. But why was he so bothered? Rosamund would carry things off; that was her line, carrying things off. Maggie here, she wouldn't notice anything. How could she? Then what was the matter with him? This kind of thing happened almost every day of the week to most men, their wives and their mistresses meeting, and the end of the world didn't come about because of it. Yet it was just this, the thought of seeing Maggie and her together that made him sick to the depths of his innards.

Was it, he asked himself, that he didn't consider himself competent enough to play this kind of game? No! No! He was as competent as the next. He had kept it going for eighteen months, hadn't he, and not a flicker had appeared on the surface. It was just that there was something in him that couldn't bear the contrast between the two of them. That was it. Rosamund showing all she was, and Maggie showing all she wasn't, in spite of her rig-out. Yet that had been a surprise he had never expected, her being turned out like this, even at the cost of a hundred and seventy-five pounds. But still it wasn't clothes that made the woman; clothes might make a man but not a woman. She had only to open her mouth and start jabbering about her family; her Paul, a school teacher; Sam and Willie in the business; her two elder daughters very comfortably married; and then there was Elizabeth, Elizabeth who was going to be a nun. And this, no matter whom she talked to, would be the extent of her conversation. Oh, if only a man had his wits about him when he was young, if he could have seen where the right values lay. Aye, and if he weren't a bloody ass and allowed himself to get trapped . . . Aye, trapped . . .

'How long do you think it will last?'

'About three hours I suppose . . . Maggie?'

'Aye, Rod?'

'Don't you drink much, mind.'

'What do you mean, don't drink much? I never drink much; what do you mean?'

'No, I know that, but on the other hand it doesn't take much to get you going, does it?'

'Oh my God! That's a good start to the evening.'

'Well, I'm just warning you.'

'Well, you've no need. And there's something else I'll say while I'm on. You needn't worry your head, I can pass meself. I won't start doing cart-wheels up and down the baronial hall, nor knees-up-Mother-Brown either. I'll talk their language if that's what's needed, from Bach to Liszt, Beethoven to Berlioz, so . . . '

His head turned towards her so swiftly in astonishment that he swung the car over the middle line of the road. If she had come out with a verse in Greek it wouldn't have astounded him more.

And he wasn't the only one who was astounded; Maggie had astounded herself. She didn't think she would remember what Arlette said the other night about the music that might be played, but now she was glad she had remembered for it had put her stock up. She'd let him see.

When the car turned off the main road and into the drive they became one of a number going in the same direction. The car in front of them was a low, red open sports car in which were a young man and woman. It didn't seem quite right to Maggie that people should arrive for a function like this in a sports car. The car in front of the sports car was a battered looking Wolseley. But when Rodney was directed by an attendant to the side of the drive Maggie found they were lined up between two posh cars. She didn't recognise them as a Rolls and a Bentley, but she thought, with cars like people, there were all types.

Rodney opened the door for her but he didn't help her out and her emergence was a little clumsy to say the least; but there was no-one looking, so she smoothed her gloved hands over her coat and stretched her neck upwards. This was a trick Arlette had shown her and it worked like magic. You hadn't to pull your tummy in one way and your buttocks in the other, you just had to stretch your neck as far as it would go, keeping your chin in, until, like Val Doonican, you walked tall.

She walked tall across the gravel drive and up the stone steps, green at the sides, she was quick to notice, with moss; then through a wide high door into a hall. She hadn't time to take in the hall before a manservant, bowing his head slightly towards Rodney, said, 'This way, Sir,' and a maid, using the same action to Maggie, only adding a smile to the proceedings, said, 'The powder room is this way, Madam.'

And Maggie thought, as she followed the girl across the bare marquetry-patterned floor, a guide would be needed in this place. They'd traversed two corridors before the maid, standing aside and still smiling, opened the door for her, and she, smiling at her in return, said, 'Thanks,' then went into the room.

Inside were a couch, some chairs and two dressing tables, and a long mirror standing in a corner between them. At the dressing tables were seated two women in animated conversation. They turned their heads expectantly towards her; then not recognising her, they smiled weakly and continued attending to their faces and talking to each other.

'The Duchess won't be here then?'

'No; they went up on Friday. I understand it's his brother. Archer said he'll be back in time for this evening but the Duchess won't be returning with him.'

'That's a pity; she always sets the tone I think.'

'Yes, yes; but she doesn't follow the arts like he does. Quite candidly I think she gets a bit bored with the musical dos. You weren't at the last one?'

'No; we were in Switzerland.' The speaker rose from her seat now and, turning to Maggie, where she was standing in front of the long mirror nervously patting her hair, said pleasantly, 'Lovely evening, isn't it?'

'Yes; yes, it is.'

The woman turned to her companion again, waited for her to close her vanity bag, then went on, 'There will be a full moon later; it should be very pleasant in the gardens. The walk in the gardens always finishes it off so nicely, I think.' Her voice trailed away as she went out.

Left alone Maggie took off her coat and again surveyed herself in the mirror. Well, there was one thing, she was better dressed than either of them. You'd think that fair one had slept in her frock, and the other one was dressed in a three-quarter length dress and she looked odd and old-fashioned somehow. She touched her cheek with her hand. She was going to do nothing to herself. She'd better get back; Rodney would be waiting for her.

As she walked towards the door she stopped. She felt a little sick, and her blooming corn was playing up. She looked down at the pink shoes peeping from below the blue velvet hem. The leather was soft; it shouldn't be hurting like this, but they were a bit too narrow. She had told her she couldn't wear narrow shoes.

She went out, found her way along the corridors and so into the hall. There were two men standing waiting, but Rodney wasn't there. She looked about her. The hall, she considered, was very disappointing; it was ugly. The floor, that at first she thought was stone, she recognised now was marble. Opposite the door was a big fireplace and huge black dogs holding fire-irons but, incongruously, the fireplace itself was blocked up and in front of it now stood an imitation fire basket holding imitation electric logs. At each side of the fireplace were white pedestals on which stood white marble busts. All the wall space was covered with pictures. Very dingy they looked to her, and she couldn't even see what the higher ones were supposed to depict. There was a deep long sofa against one wall and a few leather chairs. She thought to herself that it looked like a club room, and a dingy one at that. She had expected something different, something like she had seen in the stately homes on the telly.

Where was Rod? What was keeping him? People were coming and going all about her now, and the women, she noticed, were in various kinds of get-up. She had even seen two in mini skirts, and they weren't young lasses either, well into their thirties she would say. She felt a little piqued when she realised it was only the really old women who were wearing long dresses.

Where was Rod? She had been standing here over ten minutes; it was after seven and the thing was supposed to start at seven. What was he up to?

Her temper was rising to meet her nervousness when he appeared out of a corridor walking between two men, deep in conversation, serious conversation by the looks on their faces. He didn't come immediately towards her but went on talking, and she stared at him, willing him to break away and come to her because she was beginning to feel all fingers and thumbs. She saw him nod to the men now, then look around before making his way towards her. He didn't speak when he reached her side, and she said under her breath, 'Fine thing, leaving me here standing on me own all this time.'

He cast a glance at her and, equally low, he replied, 'Now don't start, don't start. They're important men, I had to have a word with them.'

'Important!' She choked back the word as they went towards a door at the far end of the hall, because, she warned herself, she mustn't get het up. NOW. NOW was the moment. Just put out your hand and say 'How-do-you-do?' That's it, just say 'How-do-you-do?' You can smile but not too broadly; be dignified, keep your neck up.

There were two couples in front of them. She couldn't see the Duke.

Then there was only one couple in front of them, and there he was, tall, fair, young, smooth-faced . . . but surely!

Her thoughts were cut off. She was standing in front of the man and he was shaking her by the hand while at the same time saying, 'How-do-you-do? I'm so sorry, the Duke hasn't arrived yet, he has been detained, but I'm sure he'll be here soon. I'm his secretary.'

'How-do-you-do?'

She was moving on with Rod by her side, weaving in and out of groups of people. She had a queer feeling as if she was suddenly very thin. She had never felt like this before. Deflated; that was the word, deflated. For a full month working up to this, and then . . . nothing, her hand shaken by his secretary.

'Hello there.' They had stopped before a couple. The man was short and thick-set; his wife, taller than him, had a palish face and was dressed in a very ordinary fashion, in a sort of dress-cum-suit affair, as Maggie put it. But Rod was introducing her.

'This is my wife, Councillor Redfern, Mrs Redfern.'

'How-do-you-do?'

'How-do-you-do?'

So this was Redfern. She had heard a lot about Redfern. He had power on the Council. As Rodney said, he could open or close doors but you had to supply the oil for the key whichever way it went.

'The Duke has been held up then.' Mrs Redfern was speaking to her, and Maggie was comforted to hear she sound no better than herself.

'Yes. Yes, so I understand.'

'It's his brother, he's ill.' The councillor nodded knowingly. 'The one next to him you know, very close, very close. But if he can possibly get back he will; he loves his music, ah yes, ah yes. He's got a scheme in mind, did you hear?'

'No.' Rodney's voice was casual sounding.

'Quartets in the villages and running competitions, you know on the lines of the brass bands. I think it's an excellent idea, don't you?'

'Yes, indeed, yes; the very thing. Get people culture-minded again.'

Maggie looked at her man. Rodney talking about culture, and he knew as much about music as she did herself, and that was damned all. In fact, if it came to the push she could give him a few points, for she did listen in to Mantovani and Eric Robinson, and she liked to watch the ballet an' all.

'Ah, excuse us a minute; there's the Beddinghams. I want a word with him.'

As they moved away a waiter came up with a tray and, holding it out to her, said, 'Sweet or dry, Madam?'

She paused before saying, 'Sweet,' and he took a glass from one side of the tray and handed it to her, then looking at Rodney, he said, 'Dry, Sir?'

'Please.'

They took their drinks and stood near an open window that led on to a terrace and steps down to the gardens below. She guessed this was the side of the house for, beyond the terrace, she could see the drive where the cars were parked. She sipped at the wine and kept her eyes focused outside. Although she was feeling deflated it had done nothing to ease her nervousness and tension. She wished she could sit down; this corn was giving her absolute gyp now.

'Ah; hello, Gallacher. Didn't think you were a musical man.'

'Oh, hello there.'

She turned to see a thin man and woman so alike that they could be twins. The woman was well dressed, a bit over-dressed Maggie considered, for she was weighed down with jewellery, four rings on one hand, a heavy necklace, matching earrings and an ornament in her hair. Flashy, she would say. Arlette would have condemned her out of hand for bad taste. She felt slightly comforted and smiled pleasantly as they were introduced.

'How-do-you-do?'

'How-do-you-do?'

Pearce. Another big pot. Pearce was rotten with money, he had his finger in every pie in the town, so Rodney said.

'Your daughter attends the convent, doesn't she?'

'Yes.' She nodded pleasantly at the woman, proud in this moment to have a daughter at the convent, proud even to be able to send a daughter to the convent, because the convent fees were the stiffest in the town.

'My niece goes there. She has mentioned her name, Elizabeth, isn't it?'

'Yes, yes, Elizabeth.'

'I understand she's going into the Church.'

'We're hoping so.' She sounded, she thought, quietly proud, dignified.

'Wonderful vocation; but then it must be a vocation, mustn't it, especially these days?'

'Oh yes, yes.' But now her mind had jumped back to Liz going out with that fellow. She'd have to get this cleared up tomorrow morning; there was more in this than met the eye, for the simple reason that Liz had kept it to herself. Wait till she got her tongue around her . . . Aw, but no; she must take a gentle hand with her. My God! If anything happened to stop her going in . . .

'Yes, yes, it is a beautiful evening, delightful.'

'Quite a number here; more than usual I should say.'

Mrs Pearce, whose gaze had swept round the room while she had been speaking, suddenly cried, 'Ah! there's Rosamund. We must have a word with Rosamund, Charles, before we go in. Will you excuse us?' They both made a motion with their heads, then moved away.

The room was packed now and buzzing with conversation, everybody chatting to everybody else. They seemed to be the only two people standing alone. No, there were two others along at the other end of the second window. She recognised them as the young couple she had seen in the sports car. They seemed much too young for this occasion, sort of out of place. She looked at Rod and was about to speak to him but he was moving his head slowly from side to side as if looking for someone; then when there was a general movement she saw he was looking at the Pearce couple and the people they were talking to. She noticed, too, that he was sweating round the mouth and that his face was red, like when he was angry or upset, or nervous about something. But he couldn't be nervous; he was used to these dos. Still, he didn't meet a duke every day, but he did get out and about. Anybody, she considered, who was a member of Ransome's couldn't be nervous.

The woman whom Mrs Pearce had called Rosamund now turned and looked towards them. She looked at Rodney first; then Maggie found that her eyes were covering her, going down as far as they could. It was like someone playing a torch over her. Then she watched her leave the group and make her way towards them.

'How-do-you-do, Mr Gallacher?'

There seemed to be a very long pause before Rodney said, 'How-do-you-do, Mrs de Ferrier?' Then, his head bent slightly, his left hand extended forward, his elbow tight to his side, he indicated Maggie and said, 'My wife.'

'Oh.' The thin hand was held out to Maggie, and she took it.

'How-do-you-do?'

'How-do-you-do?'

Maggie looked back into the wide grey eyes. They were looking directly into hers, yet at the same time seemed to be taking in every aspect of her from her feet to her hair.

'Delightful evening isn't it?'

'Yes, very nice.'

'Who do you think we're going to hear tonight, Mr Gallacher?' Mrs de Ferrier was looking at Rodney now.

'Your guess is as good as mine.' He sounded nervous, ill at ease. Maggie couldn't understand it.

'Well, we won't have to wait long, shall we?' Mrs de Ferrier turned her eyes again on Maggie. 'His Grace always supplies programmes; they're on the seats awaiting you, just like church you know.' She laughed here, a high, soft laugh, and turning to Rodney said, 'He's got a new man at the piano tonight, a young protégé, Flynn. Have you heard him before?'

There was a pause again before Rodney said briefly, 'No.'

'Bernstein's playing the cello and, of course, Dorothea Craig is singing.' She made a slight face; then, her voice dropping, she added, 'And I wish she wasn't. Whom do you favour?' She had turned abruptly to Maggie, and Maggie, nonplussed, said, 'Who . . . what . . . I don't understand?'

'Oh! What I mean is are you a Bach or a Beethoven fan?'

'I think I prefer Mozart or Liszt.' Thank God for Arlette.

'Ah, you're a romantic.'

Maggie stared at this woman. She didn't like her; there was something about her that made her uneasy. She seemed to be laughing at her, at them both. But that was her imagination; she was likely used to talking about music and asking people what they liked, it was her own ignorance that was at fault.

'Ah, there you are, Gallacher.' Apparently, this was Mr de Ferrier, for he had put his hand through the woman's arm. She had never seen a man with such a white pasty face, it was so smooth as to be almost sickly. He was well into his fifties, she thought, but he hadn't a line or a wrinkle on his face, which made him look odd, characterless.

'Nice to see you. Nice to see you.' He was now shaking her hand. 'How-do-you-do? How-do-you-do?' He repeated everything. 'The troubadour hasn't turned up yet.' He was speaking to Rodney, and she deduced that by the troubadour he meant the Duke.

'I understand,' said Rodney, 'that his brother is ill and that he had to go to him?'

Mr de Ferrier leant his full white face forward and, his eyes darting from Rodney to Maggie and back again, he muttered on a smothered laugh, 'He's back all right, saw him in Newcastle early this afternoon. Enthusiasm waning; bet your life that's what it is. He starts these things on the top of a wave, gets everybody going then leaves it to them and wonders why the tide recedes. Ha! Ha! Oh, but I'm not saying he won't turn up; he'll turn up, but when all the palaver's over and he can just sit down and enjoy it. I've never known him miss anything he's organised yet, but I've never known him to be there at the start either.' He nodded knowingly, then laughed before exclaiming, 'Ah look. Ah look; they're making their way in.' He turned back to Rodney again, saying, 'We all have our allotted seats, I suppose. Be seeing you then. Be seeing you.'

'Yes, yes.' Rodney nodded to him, then towards Mrs de Ferrier, who in turn inclined her head deeply towards him.

As they, too, made to move towards the music room door there was a stir at the far end of the room, a hush, then a murmur, and everybody stopped and turned and looked in the direction of the man who was threading his way between the groups, shaking a hand here, having a word there.

Here he was then . . . the Duke.

Maggie's heart began to race; the feeling of excitement returned. She watched him coming nearer and nearer. He wasn't very tall, in fact he was short and nothing to look at, sandy hair, a small thin face, and weak looking eyes, but he was the Duke of Moorshire and he was coming to greet them. He was talking to the couple in front of them, he was even patting the man's arm; he had just to come round them to the right and then it would happen.

But the Duke didn't come round to the right, he went to the left and stretched out his hand towards a man who gripped it and smiled broadly and said something to him; then he was going ahead of them into the music room.

Again her body seemed to sink inwards. Rod had hold of her arm, pressing her forward. They were in a sort of disorderly queue now; then they were in the music room and being directed to their seats. The room was large and bare, nothing in it but chairs and, on a dais at the end, a grand piano.

Maggie found herself sitting to the extreme right of the dais with one side of her chair against the wall. Below the dais, sitting apart, were two men and a woman and she saw the Duke shaking each by the hand. Then he sat down and was lost to her sight and the two men and the woman went up on to the platform.

She looked at her programme. The man, Flynn, was to start. He was playing . . . what! Suite fü Klavier Op. 25 – Schoenberg. And the woman? Lieder! What the devil was Lieder? Anecreon's Grab – Hugo Wolf. Lord! Knees up Mother Brown.

Her attention was again drawn towards the dais.

The cellist and Miss Dorothea Craig had taken seats to the side of the piano and the pianist had seated himself; then the Duke's secretary, standing just below the dais, said, 'Ladies and Gentlemen, Mr Flynn.' He extended his arm backwards, then walked to the end of the first row and sat down.

A hushed waiting silence fell on the room; then Mr Flynn fell upon the piano. That's how Maggie put it to herself. He bent low over it and the sounds he brought forth appeared to her like a lot of bairns banging away for fun.

She sat still, watching him, fascinated for a moment by his antics. She could only see part of the keyboard and one of his hands, but that was enough. Before he'd been playing two minutes she wished to God he'd stop. She'd never heard anything so untuneful in her life. If this is what they called real music they could keep it. Why, when she thought of Mantovani and those lovely violins!

She was hot; it was airless in here. Her corn was going mad and she couldn't keep her neck stretched up like this, yet she couldn't slump altogether, her foundation wouldn't let her. How long was this bloke going on? If this was a sample of the things they were going to hear all evening she didn't know how she was going to sit through it.

When finally the pianist finished what she now thought of as his contortionist act, the applause was loud and prolonged, in which she herself joined, all the while calling herself a bloomin' hypocrite.

Mr Flynn bowed and bowed; then wiping his hands and brow, he walked to a seat at the side of the piano, and Miss Dorothea Craig took the centre of the dais and her accompanist took Mr Flynn's place.

Dorothea Craig began. Her mouth wide, her breast swelling, she went into Anecreon's Grab . . . So this was . . . what did the programme say? Lieder. Well! Well!

Maggie had no knowledge of this kind of singing, nor had any groping taste towards it. If she saw such work billed in the *Radio Times* she passed it over, thinking, Oh, that stuff! Yet she told herself, she liked Moira Anderson and that nice woman who died, Kathleen Ferrier, but she couldn't stand this.

Oh! her corn. If she could only ease her shoe off. She moved her left big toe towards her right heel and slowly began to lever the shoe off. This action caused her right knee to move up and down, but ever so gently, but gently as it was, it attracted Rodney's attention. She saw him turn his head slightly towards her, then slant his eye towards her knees. The next second she almost jumped out of her chair for his cautionary pressure with the heel of his shoe found its target on the very spot she was trying to ease. She only just stopped herself from yelling out, and she covered up her reaction to the assault by crossing her legs.

She was breathing as heavily as the singer now. Oh God! Wait till she got him home. What a bloody silly thing to do. He knew that that corn was as tender as a boil; he knew that it had troubled her all her life. She had gone to a chiropodist with it once but he had poked and poked it so much that the cure became worse than the disease. He had advised her to go to the hospital and get the root out, but she hadn't gone to the hospital and she hadn't seen him again. She had tended to it herself with a safety razor blade. She'd had a go at it only last night, but as the man had said, it was the root that caused the trouble not the hard skin on top.

Oh! Would that woman never stop bawling.

Didn't they have any windows open in this place? She was running with sweat, she would ruin her dress. That was another thing; nobody had taken any notice of her get-up, the biggest sensation she had caused was when she came down into the drawing-room. She'd like to bet she was better dressed than anybody in the room, and that went for that Mrs de Ferrier an' all, although she too got her clothes at Madam Hevell's. But she had no figure, she was as flat as a pancake.

Lord! How long was this going on? The man now was sawing away at the cello and attacking it as the previous one had the piano.

Maggie was experiencing real boredom for the first time in her life. She had never, up till now, had time to be bored. If there appeared nothing further for her to do in the house she made it her business to find something. She would go into the kitchen and knock up a cake or two; she would take up a piece of embroidery – she had been a dab hand at it once; it was her only talent, she considered, besides running a home. Then she knitted for them all; she couldn't sit looking at the television, her hands idle. And when she got her nose in a book, a real good book with a story, she became lost in it. No, she had never experienced boredom until this present minute and the forty-three minutes preceding it.

When at last the cellist ceased battling with the blown-up fiddle – that's all it was, and she couldn't help it if the Prince of Wales did favour it, every man to his taste – she let out a long drawn breath, just as, had she but known it, did more than half the company. When the clapping had died down there was no immediate rising; no-one left his seat until the Duke, accompanied by Dorothea Craig, Mr Flynn, and Mr Bernstein walked towards the ante-room, then the secretary indicated it was in order to follow him.

There was now a slow dignified concerted movement. Rodney, glancing at her, rose to his feet and when she, with a smothered sigh, stood on hers, she wished for a moment she hadn't, for although she considered anything better than sitting there, she found to her consternation that not only was her corn playing her up, but that the heel of her other foot now was feeling the pressure of the back of the shoe. She was subject to skinned heels with ordinary shoes, but these were very soft – and so they should be she thought, they had cost enough. It must be the seam of her stocking directly over the pressure point. Once out of here she'd go to the ladies' room and fix it.

This intention was baulked as soon as she entered the ante-room again for it seemed more packed than ever, and Rodney, after glancing quickly around, took her by the arm and led her along the wall to a corner. There they stood side by side, not uttering a word. Three minutes of this and it began to seem like three hours. She glanced at him. What was up with him anyway? He couldn't fault her; she had done nothing, she wasn't letting him down.

A waiter, threading his way between the groups, offered them their choice from the tray and again she had a sweet sherry, but when she was about to sip it Rodney muttered under his breath, 'Don't drink that unless you have something with it. Stay here and I'll get something to eat . . . Hold that.' He handed her his glass, then he left her. And she watched him, not without indignation, winding his way between the groups towards a long table set against the far wall.

Well! She looked nice didn't she holding two glasses! What would people think? She drank half her sherry, but when she was about to empty the glass she hesitated. He had said wait until she had something to eat with it. He was frightened it would affect her.

Another three minutes passed and she was demanding

of herself, where had he got to? Surely it didn't take this long to get a sandwich.

At this point a man moving from one group to another nudged her with his elbow, and as he turned to excuse himself his gaze dropped to the two glasses she was holding away from her dress now, and he said on a laugh, 'I'm sorry.' Then he added, 'But that's what I always say, be prepared, keep one in stock,' and before she had time to get out the words 'It's my husband's,' he had joined another group.

Everyone was laughing and talking; they all seemed to know each other. She was the only woman standing alone. No; there was one along there. She looked to her extreme right. The woman was standing near the window but she managed to catch her eye and half smile at her as much as to say 'We're both in the same boat.' But they weren't in the same boat for long, for the woman's husband came up with a plate in each hand, and once more she felt alone.

Where on earth was he? She'd have to get to the ladies' and see to her feet. If she could only sit down again.

Then she saw him. She couldn't mistake his head; he was making his way back across the room excusing himself as he circled round the couples. She was letting out a long breath of relief when it was checked, for he had stopped. He was talking to somebody. Oh, no! No! It was a woman, it was that Mrs de Ferrier. 'Come on. Come on,' she willed him, but he remained talking.

Her irritation, touching on anger, was suddenly soothed when she caught sight of the Duke. He had moved from behind a group and was not more than four yards from her . . . And here she was standing with two glasses in her hand! Oh, Rod Gallacher! Rod Gallacher! Wait till I get you home.

Well, she wasn't going to meet the Duke like this with no free hand to shake. With an unladylike gulp she finished her sherry; then almost in the manner of a curtsy she bent her knee and put the glass down on the floor near the wall. Upright again, she stretched her neck and brought a smile to her face, ignoring in this moment the pain of her corn and heel, as she watched him walk to the next group.

Her stomach churned when he moved to the right to join another couple; his next move would be the left and to the four people standing at arm's length from her; then there would be only her.

Her heart seemed to move upwards towards her throat when she saw her host make his last move. At the same time she thought she saw Rodney leave Mrs de Ferrier then turn to her again, but she took her eyes from him for here was the Duke not a yard from her. She heard him greeting a plain looking, dowdy woman, calling her by her christian name, Ida. 'Ah, Ida,' he said, 'it's so nice to see you again.' He was shaking hands all round now. She stopped herself from thinking again that he was ordinary looking, not a bit like she imagined a duke to be, not like the Duke of Edinburgh for instance. But he WAS a duke, and in a few minutes, even seconds, he'd be shaking her by the hand. They were all talking about the performers. The plain woman was enthusing about the singer. 'Wasn't she magnificent!' she was saying. Magnificent! Well, everybody to their taste, like the woman who kissed the cow, as her grannie used to say.

'Your Grace.' The secretary seemed to have materialised out of thin air; he was standing to the side of the Duke, bending towards him, and the Duke, turning and looking up at him, said, 'Oh, yes, yes, mustn't hold things up.' He laughed from one to the other, then turned about and walked away with his secretary.

Her body wasn't deflating this time, but every part of it was pouring out its disappointment in perspiration. What was the matter with her the night? Was there a jinx on her or something? And to add seeming insult to injury she now saw the de Ferrier woman put her hand out towards the Duke, and he stopped in front of her and Rodney. She could see, too, there was laughter because Rodney hadn't a free hand to proffer the Duke until Mrs de Ferrier took one of the plates from him, and there he was shaking hands with the Duke, smiling and, she thought grimly, putting on his best manner.

Now her body did begin to deflate and, strange for her, she had a desire to cry.

The stir in the room changed; like an ebb tide on shingle she saw the groups breaking up and moving back towards the music room again, and as Rodney now made his way directly towards her there arose against him an anger that would have found vent in a bellow if she had been in any other place. Instead, she lifted his glass of sherry to her lips and drained it, and she was just finishing it when he came to her side.

When he was foolish enough not to start with an apology but with a reprimand, saying under his breath, 'I told you not to . . . ' she hissed at him, 'Don't you talk to me!' Then to his consternation she was pushing past him and walking on her own into the music room.

He stood for a moment nonplussed with two plates of food in his hands; then sighting a waiter with a tray of empty glasses he pushed the plates on top of one another on to the tray before joining the slowly moving throng.

When he took his seat beside her there was no-one as yet seated near them, and he muttered, 'I was held up, it wasn't my fault.'

She turned and looked at him, her blue eyes the colour of a stormy sea now, and her voice cold but controlled, she said, 'I've been out there twenty minutes if a minute. You left me standing like a nobody; I was the only woman in that room by meself.'

His eyes were as hard as hers as he retorted in a thick whisper, 'I told you in the beginning you shouldn't have come.'

Oo . . . h God! If only she was at home; in more senses than one, if only she was at home. But if she had been there at this moment he would have got more than the length of her tongue, for she wouldn't have been able to keep her hands off him.

There was a rustle of gowns behind her. She sat straight as a ramrod watching the entertainers once more mounting the platform. The movement and chatter in the room subsided. Mr Flynn again went to battle stations at the piano, and then the whole boring business was repeated.

By the time the cellist gave his second recital she was so hot and tired, so bored to extinction, she could have fallen asleep; at one point she did feel her eyelids drooping. It was the same feeling that at times she experienced at Mass.

. . . Then it was over, and this very fact brought her wide awake. If that was a musical concert they could keep them; the only thing that she was going to get that was worth while out of all the money that had been spent on her, not counting the worry and anxiety of the past four weeks, was meeting His Grace.

When she made to rise the pressure from Rodney's knee warned her not to. She looked past him to where in front of the dais the Duke was standing with Mr Flynn, Dorothea Craig, and Mr Bernstein, and people were coming up to congratulate them. For what, she thought? This went on for four or five minutes; then gradually, the Duke and the performers leading the way, everyone once more returned to the ante-room.

As if it was a place that had been reserved for them Rodney went to lead her along the wall to the same corner that she had occupied earlier. But no; she wasn't having that. When she caught at his sleeve and brought him to a stop, he looked at her and asked, 'What is it?'

'This'll do, thank you very much.'

He seemed puzzled for a moment; then staring back into her eyes he let out a long, slow breath.

Again a waiter came up with a tray of drinks, and again she took one, just pipping Rodney from saying, 'No, thanks, we won't bother.' With the drink in her hand she stared at him and he himself was forced to pick one up from the tray, and as he lifted it to his lips he muttered, 'I warned you.'

'What did you say?'

He sipped at the wine, gulped in his throat, glanced round him, then bending his head he muttered, 'Give over.'

She bent towards him now, a tight smile on her lips, and again she asked, tantalisingly, 'Pardon. What's that you say?'

He looked at her apprehensively now; this attitude was part of her battle tactics, the prelude to a blow-up. He glanced about him almost furiously for some aid with which to damp down the fire. He found it as a man passed him, and he said in an overloud voice, 'Oh, hello there.'

'Oh, hello!' The man turned. It was evident he was making his way to join another group but he stopped and smiled at Maggie as Rodney said, 'My wife . . . Mr Bailey.'

'How-do-you-do?'

'How-do-you-do?'

'Have you enjoyed the concert?'

She stared at this man; she stared into his long thin face, the deep set eyes under the bushy brows, and in the seconds it took her to bring the lie on to her tongue, he read her thoughts, and glancing like a conspirator from side to side, he bent towards her and whispered, 'I agree with you,' then laughed, and added, 'Nearly went to sleep. Not my cup of tea at all.'

Maggie smiled now, her mouth wide. She liked this man; he appeared at this moment to be the only human being in the room.

He now nodded at her, then at Rodney, and said in his terse style, 'Seeing you. Must have a word with Jamieson. Goodbye.'

'Goodbye,' she said. She was laughing, until she looked at Rodney. His face was dark with temper. She took a sip from her glass, then airily she said, 'Glad to know I'm not the only one. If you'd had any spunk you would have agreed an' all, then that would have made a trio . . . we'd have had our own trio.' She laughed at her own wit. And her laugh startled him. He knew that laugh of old. She was always about to get jolly when she laughed like that.

His lips scarcely moving, he said now, 'I thought you wanted to go to the ladies' room?'

'Oh yes, I did; but that was a long time ago. I've stuck it out so far I can stick it out to the end.'

Go to the ladies' room, he said. Yes, and it would be just her luck that the Duke would make a round while she was away. She wasn't moving from this room until they said their goodbyes. Arlette said the Duke might stand at the door and they would shake hands when they were leaving. It would be hail and farewell for her, but at least she would have shaken hands with him. Go to the ladies' room indeed! She took another sip from her glass, then said, 'There's that Mrs de Ferrier over there. Why don't you go and have another natter to her?' She wasn't looking at him as she spoke, but she felt his body jerk round towards her.

In the old days when he jerked round like that it meant the flat of his hand across her ear-hole and a bloody great row to follow; but it was funny, after every row the making up was better. They hadn't had a real big row for over two years now. Things had changed in the last two years. She felt a sudden sadness swamp her as she again asked herself the question, What was it? What had happened? Were they getting like the married people she read about in the weekly magazines, them that wrote asking for advice? Aw, what was she thinking, and in a place like this an' all?

She turned her eyes over the heads of the crowds and high up through the open french windows. The moon was shining, it was a lovely night. Some people were walking on the terrace. She would like to walk outside. She wished she could go out now for a breath of air, but she had gauged from those women in the ladies' room that the procedure was to say goodbye to the Duke then wander down the garden before going off, and the procedure, she saw, had already begun, for some people near the french windows were already saying their goodbyes.

This fact hadn't escaped Rodney and so, clasping her almost roughly by the arm, he led her forward, twisting and turning in and out of groups until they came within a few yards of the open french windows and the Duke, who was shaking hands with a couple.

They could be next. At least Rodney surmised this, but it was she who noticed the concerted gaze on them from a line of couples that stretched back into the room. With an embarrassed laugh she nudged him and, motioning towards the row of faces with her gloved hand, she said, 'We'll have to take our turn, there's a queue.'

'Oh, I'm sorry. I'm sorry.' Rodney's best manner was again to the fore; and the faces were laughing with them now, and one man murmured, 'You're not the only ones, we did it too.' They were both smiling when they took up their positions at the end of the queue.

The procession towards the door was slow, the Duke seemed to be holding a long conversation with each couple. Well, she didn't mind that; they would get the same measure when their turn came. She ignored the pressure of the corn and her skinned heel, these would soon be eased.

There was more laughter when another couple was directed to the end of the queue. There were only five couples in
front of them now, then four. He spent quite a long time
talking to this couple, but at last they moved on to the
terrace; then there were only three couples, then two.

Between the heads of the couple in front of her she
could see the Duke's face and it was no longer smiling.
He was talking very seriously, and he went on talking
and talking and talking . . . And then it happened. Before
her widening eyes and drooping mouth he took the arm
of the woman and turning his back on the company,
he walked between her and the man across the terrace
and towards the sunken garden.

Maggie was dimly aware that the couple in front of her
were looking at each other. They stood uncertain what
to do, wondering perhaps if he meant to return. The
woman rocked slightly as if she were balancing herself.
They turned and looked at Maggie and Rodney, then along
the faces behind them, after which they walked stiffly over
the step and on to the terrace. And Maggie followed them,
her eyes not on them but on the slight figure still walking
between the two people and close to the stone steps now
that led to the sunken garden, and the only thing she could
say at this moment was, 'Well! What do you make of that?'
And it came out on a loud wave of indignation. It startled
the couple in front of her, and the woman, turning quickly,
said in a polite hiss, 'Ssh! The Duke will hear you.'

Maggie glared from the woman to where she saw her
host's head bobbing as it went down the first two steps into
the garden and no power she possessed, no power on earth
could have stopped her at the moment from expressing her
feelings:

'BUGGER THE DUKE!'

The head of His Grace stopped bobbing. His face was
turned towards her. All faces were turned towards her. If

the announcement had just been made of a great national tragedy the hush that precedes the expression of deep emotion could not have been more full; for a long second it hung over the assembly, and when it broke into indignation from some quarters and smothered laughter from others, and amused astonishment from the main party concerned, she knew nothing of it, for she was being whipped along the terrace as if in the hands of a giant.

Not even when he reached the car and found he had left his keys in his overcoat pocket did he immediately loosen his steel hold on her. Still gripping her he glared at her in an almost maniacal way. His face in the moonlight looked like a devil's. His eyes bloodshot, his teeth grinding, he looked in this instant as if he were about to murder her, and she didn't care. When, with a rejecting thrust of his hand, he threw her against the car bonnet she fell on to her elbow and remained there for a moment watching him now running to the front of the house.

She didn't care, she didn't give a damn. She'd had enough, more than enough. She'd been ignored all night, put down by her own in the first place. Aye, no-one had ignored her like he had, her own man. And then that bloody little Duke. Who did he think he was anyway? Christ Almighty! To turn at the last minute and walk away like that!

It would have been no comfort to her to know that she wasn't the only one who had suffered from the Duke's bad manners which went under the name of absent-mindedness. Nor was it any comfort to know that he hadn't walked away deliberately from her but from the couple in front of her. She only knew that she wasn't sorry for what she had said, not yet anyway; tomorrow morning was a long way off.

At the present moment she could comfort herself that she was in the right; but also she realised that tonight was the end of something, that things would never be the same again. Well, it didn't matter, it didn't matter, it was about time they changed. She had stood on the sideline long enough, waving on the one-man team. But she had shown him; yes, begod she had shown him. She now straightened her body. She had shown him all right . . . she had shown him up as no man had been shown up before.

He came back at something between a walk and a run and rammed the key into the car door, and after flinging himself into the seat he did not lean across and open the door for her but, reaching to the back door he rammed down the lock and banged the door back.

She stood looking into the back of the car for a moment. So that was it, he couldn't bear her anywhere near him. Well, it suited her; they were both of a like mind.

She had hardly seated herself when the car bounded away. At another time she would have cried out at him because of the speed he was going, but not tonight. She had said enough, enough to last a lifetime . . .

Almost before the car had stopped the front door opened and there they all were. But she remained seated, she remained seated until she saw Rod going in among them, pushing his way like a bulldozer through them, their startled glances following him. Lifting one leg heavily after the other she pulled herself out of the car and walked slowly towards them, and they surrounded her, all saying the same thing in different ways, 'What is it? What's happened? Where's your coat?'

She, too, pushed her way silently between them. And then they were in the hall, and there he was standing, waiting for her, glaring at her, and the hate in his eyes pierced the armour of her defiance and hurt her like no hurt she had yet received in her life.

'Will you tell us what's happened?' Paul was standing in front of her. Without answering him she pressed him gently to one side and walked towards the stairs, but when she was on the second step she turned and looked at him and said, 'You'd better ask your dad.'

As if a valve had been opened to allow boiling steam to erupt, Rodney took a step towards her. His shoulders hunched up round his ears, his chin thrust out, he looked like a gorilla about to spring as he cried at her, 'You big, fat, ignorant slob you! Talk of trying to make a silk purse out of a sow's ear . . .'

'Dad! Dad! What's this? Let up!' It was Willie shouting now, and Rodney turned on him and cried, 'Let up, you say! Do you know what she's done the night? She's ruined me. She's ruined us all, our business. You Sam, you Willie and you Dave, you'll soon be out of work because of that ignorant numskull. Tomorrow we won't be able to lift up our heads in the town, not even in Bog's End never mind in Ransome's or such places.'

They were all staring at Maggie now, a woman dressed in blue velvet and pink slippers, and they said almost in a whisper to her, 'What happened?' But it was Rodney who replied, 'She buggered the Duke, that's what happened. Your dear mother buggered the Duke of Moorshire because he didn't shake hands with her; because he dared to walk away from her with two of his friends she buggered him, an' for everybody to hear. A bomb couldn't have caused a bigger sensation.' His voice a deep bellowing roar, he finished, 'Can you believe it, she buggered the Duke!'

They all gaped at her, speechless, and they knew, each one of them, that their mother had in some strange way this night altered their lives.

Part Four

THE DISINTEGRATION

Rodney paced the long narrow lounge of the flat. 'It's the finish, I'm leaving her.'

'No!'

He stopped in his stride. 'What do you mean, no?'

'Just that, no. You're taking the whole matter too seriously. It's a joke; everyone's laughing at it. There's never been so much laughter on the phones as there has been today . . .'

'Stop it! Stop it!' He bent his head deeply and thrust his hand out towards her; then looking at her again he said, 'I'm a laughing stock, all right I'm a laughing stock.'

'I wouldn't say that at all; it wasn't you who buggered him.'

He stared at her. It was odd, she could say the word and it even sounded musical, but coming from Maggie it sounded coarse and low, depicting what she was. The word was bandied like 'God bless you' the whole length and breadth of the Tyne, but in the main by men; women who used it were considered common, and she was that, by God! She was that.

He said now bitterly, 'No, but I'm her husband, and do you think all the toadies and suckers in this town are going to let me off with this? There are those who voted me on to committees only because they thought I was well in with Pearce and Bailey and their like.'

'You may be surprised.' She reached out and brought a brandy glass to her lips and sipped at the neat spirit before she said, 'I wouldn't mind having a pound for all those in this town who themselves would like to bugger His Grace. I really think your wife has done something.'

'By God she has!' He dropped down beside her on the narrow couch and, his voice quiet now, he said, 'Stop trying to smooth things over; I know the reactions of the town, I've experienced them already. I purposely went into the Club this lunch time and two men actually walked past me and didn't see me.'

She raised her brows. 'Friends?'

He tossed his head. 'Not exactly, but I've spoken to them.'

'You could be imagining it.'

'Look, Rosamund, this is serious, something's got to be done. I'll never live this down, not unless I do something definite, cut adrift from her. It would at least show what I think about the whole business.'

With a swift, easy movement she rose to her feet and looked down at him. 'You know what I think, Rodney . . . ? You're an upstart of the first water. To put it as your wife might have done, you're a bloody upstart.' She pronounced it bleedy, and she laughed at him as she said it and he didn't take it as an offence.

When, holding out her hand, she said, 'Are you coming?' like a child he allowed himself to be drawn up from the couch and into the bedroom.

As she stood lazily taking off her clothes she looked at him through the mirror and said, 'If ever you wanted soothing that time is now, don't you think?'

He didn't answer. Continuing to look at him through the mirror she picked up the conversation where it had been dropped some moments before. 'Whatever you do you mustn't leave her; that would do you much more harm than good.'

His fingers became still on the last button of his shirt

and, returning her gaze, he said, 'You know, I can't really understand you. I thought you would have wanted me to break . . . get a divorce, and you to do the same. Wouldn't . . . wouldn't you want that?' He waited while her eyes looked into his, the cynical playful expression no longer in them. Then turning from the mirror and wriggling out of her last garment she stared unsmiling into his face and said, 'Don't be childish, Rodney. Really!'

He watched her go to the bed and lower herself on to it, lie down and stretch her legs, then raise her arms and put them behind her head, and he looked at her like a small boy might look at his teacher who had slapped him for saying something silly.

As he stared at her lying there stark naked waiting for him to take her the anger in his body was replaced by fear, the fear turned itself into a thought, and the thought was unbearable. If she ever left him, went out of his life. The thought was sapping him; he was undressing like an aged man, not like a man in his prime, and an ardent lover at that. With a sudden spurt he ripped off the remainder of his clothes and flung himself down beside her.

Willie, Paul, Dave Walton and Helen were in the drawing-room. Paul had just come in, and Willie who was pacing up and down, very much like his father had done last night in the lounge of the flat said, 'Something will have to be done with her. She can't stay up there for ever, and she's got to eat some time.'

'Has she not been out at all?' asked Paul.

'No, not that we know of. You go on up again,' he nodded at Paul, 'and have another try.'

'Where's Elizabeth?' asked Paul now.

'At Mass.'

Paul went out and up the stairs and, knocking on his mother's bedroom door, he said softly, as he had done numbers of times yesterday, 'Mam, it's me, Paul.'

There was no reply. Again he knocked, and speaking louder this time he called, 'Mam! Look, if you don't open this door I'll burst it open. Come on now. This has gone on long enough.'

There was silence for a moment, then he heard the soft padding of her feet across the carpet and her voice, strange sounding to him, said, 'I'm all right, Paul; just leave me alone. I'll be down presently. I'm all right.'

He stood looking helplessly about him before turning slowly and going down the stairs. Just as he reached the hall Arlette came in through the front door and made straight towards him. 'Is she down?' she asked.

He shook his head.

'Is Dad in?' she whispered softly now.

'No; I understand he came back late last night, slept in Willie's room and went out again early this morning.'

Arlette now looked about her, then said quickly, 'Come here a minute,' and hurried towards the breakfast-room at the end of a short corridor, and he followed her.

She closed the door behind him, then stood with her back to it looking at him, and he at her, while he asked, 'What's the matter? Something else?'

She blinked her eyes and gulped deeply in her throat before saying, 'It's Sam. I . . . I think he's going mad, really mad; he's hardly stopped laughing since he started on Friday night. All day yesterday it went on, and he keeps saying things like—' she bit on her lip '—B— the Duke. My mam said B— the Duke. Clever woman my mam . . . Paul—' she stepped nearer to him— 'He's . . . he's revelling in it. He hates her . . . Why?'

Paul shook his head, then looked down towards the floor; but after a moment he was looking at her again and he stared hard into her eyes for some time before he asked, 'What about you?'

She lifted one shoulder, then turned her head towards it as if wanting to hide her face in its hunched hollow. 'It doesn't matter, it won't be long now.'

'You're going tomorrow then?' The question was soft.

'Yes.'

'Arlette.' He caught her hand and gripped it but seemed unable to speak. 'Will . . . will you let me know where you are when . . . when you're settled?'

She still did not look at him as she made an almost imperceptible consenting movement, and at this he drew her hand tight against his breast and whispered, 'Arlette! Oh Arlette!' But now she tugged it gently from his hold and, shaking her head as if throwing off her own worries, she said, 'There's something else. Do you know anything about Dad? I mean, has he been up to anything that Mam wouldn't know of?'

'In what way?' he asked.

'I . . . I don't really know.' She bit on her lip. 'Don't mind me saying this, but he . . . he wouldn't have another woman, would he?'

'Dad!' His face screwed up in disbelief. 'Dad! No, no. However much they go for each other they're close, they always have been; they've fought all their married life but they've made it up immediately. Laughter and tears was my childhood. I cried when they were fighting and joyed with them when it was over. Another woman? No. What makes you ask that?'

'Well.' She moved from him and walked towards the window and looked out for a moment before turning to him again and saying, 'He, Sam, he keeps hinting that he can blow her sky high, and . . . and, Paul.'

'Yes?'

'You too . . . He . . . he knows about you . . . and . . . ' She dropped her head.

He didn't move from where he was when he said grimly,

'He can't; nobody knows that, only Father Armstrong, you and me.'

'He does, Paul.'

'Is it because he knew you came to the flat that Saturday morning?'

'No, no, something else . . . photographs that you've kept. I don't really know, but something in that line.'

'My God!' He drew his chin into his neck and gritted his teeth; then raising his eyes to hers, he said, 'He's been through my room. Well—' his chin came up '—let him do his worst. If he confronts me with it I'll tell him. And, you know—' he smiled sadly at her now '—it'll be wonderful to bring it into the open, to say . . . '

'No, no! Please, Paul, don't.' She came towards him. 'He's quite capable of . . . ' She stopped, then went on, 'Please don't say anything. Whatever he says or does please, please don't say anything.'

After a moment he replied, 'Very well.' Then his voice thick and low he added, 'I won't see you after today, not for some time then?'

'Not for some time, Paul; it'll be best that way.'

'Arlette.'

'Yes, Paul?'

'I'm used to waiting. I've been waiting all my life. I'll wait, no matter how long.'

She pressed the tears back into her eyes with her tightly closed lids, then she walked past him – close to him and he didn't touch her.

Frances had just entered the hall accompanied by her two children, and her greeting was typical. Almost glaring at Arlette she hissed under her breath, 'It's all round the town. They all know at church, there were giggles as I came out. We're getting out of this as quick as possible; we've had enough. This is the end.'

Arlette said nothing. What could she say? But Helen,

standing in the drawing-room doorway cried angrily, 'You'd better take Trevor with you, our Frances, for all I've heard since yesterday is "What will Mr Pattenden say?" What I say is, "Damn, Mr Pattenden!" Lord, you'd think it was the end of the world.'

Frances slowly turned towards Helen. Her voice flat and ominous, she said, 'You've said it, the end of the world. And it's the end of our world in this town, you mark my words. God! If only one could pick one's parents.'

CHAPTER TWO

THE WHIP

Maggie didn't feel hungry. It was strange; she hadn't eaten since Friday tea-time and now here it was Monday morning, and she didn't feel hungry. She had let Annie in last night with a tray of tea. There were some sandwiches and things on the plate but she hadn't eaten them; she felt she never wanted to eat again. She guessed she had enough fat on her to keep her alive for a week or so without eating, but she knew if she were to keep alive, then she must face up to life and leave this room.

Monday morning and they were all at work. There was nobody in the house only Annie, and Annie, strangely enough, had said no word of censure to her. Then, neither had any of the others; none of them had said anything. No, but their thoughts had been plain to read in their eyes on Friday night as she had looked down on them from the stairs. And they were right, they were all right to censure her, condemn her. She had done a terrible thing. She no longer defended her action. She no longer recalled, as she had done all day long on Saturday, a whole month of worrying, fittings, trying on clothes, repeating over and over the right procedure, sick with excitement and anticipation every hour of every day of that month, then at the last minute waiting for him coming in, and him late, and hearing about Lizzie, and finally, those two long sessions of boredom, and the heat, and her corn and her skinned heel, and nobody bothering with her, not even him. No, he could stand and talk to another woman for over ten minutes while she stood in a corner lost and alone . . . And then the Duke. Within an arm's length of her, and her thinking the moment had come to shake him by the hand, and him being called off. But that was nothing, no, nothing, nothing, until that very last moment and the slight, unintentional perhaps, but nevertheless a slight. Still, she might have covered it up if her tongue hadn't been loosened by the four sherries.

But since yesterday she hadn't used this way of thinking in her defence, for she had seen herself as Rod had seen her, an ignorant, fat, big-mouthed slob. A pig in a drawing-room! That's what he had shouted up the stairs after her. And that was how she now saw herself, a pig in a drawing-room. And what could you expect from a pig in a drawing-room, he had said, but grunts and muck.

He had said she had ruined him, ruined them all, and she knew she had. In different ways that one night out in her life had ruined them all; an invitation from a duke had changed all their lives. What was going to happen from now on? She wouldn't blame him if he wanted to leave her. No, she wouldn't blame him, but deep in the soul of her she prayed that he wouldn't go to that length, for, with him she didn't amount to much but, without him she'd be nothing, muck indeed.

But she must get herself out of this room, she must go downstairs. And tonight she must talk to Liz. She had been thinking a lot about Liz these past few hours, but whatever she said she must say it quietly. Anyway she couldn't ever see herself raising her voice in her life again.

She walked out of the bedroom and crossed the landing as if she was in a strange house, and when she reached the foot of the stairs she stood looking about her. When the telephone bell rang it startled her, and as Annie came out of the kitchen to answer it she saw her, and they looked

at each other. Then Maggie turned and went to the side
table and picked up the phone.

'This is Arlette.'

'Yes, Arlette?'

'Oh! Oh, hello, Mam. Oh, how are you dear?'

'Well, lass—' Maggie let out a quiet sigh '—just as you
would expect, repentant, flat, wanting to die.'

'Oh, Mam, don't . . . Mam.'

'Yes, dear?'

'I want to see you. I . . . I'm going away.'

'What did you say?'

'I said I'm going away, Mam.'

'That's what I thought you said, lass. Where are you
going?'

'I . . . I can't tell you but . . . but I want to see you
before I go.'

'What is this?'

'I'm . . . I know it will come as a shock to you but I
wanted to tell you some time ago, but I didn't want to
trouble you until—' There was a pause. 'Anyway, Mam,
I'm telling you now. I'm getting a divorce from Sam; it's
all arranged.'

Maggie held the phone from her face and stared at it
and she heard Arlette's voice saying, 'Are you there? Are
you there, Mam?'

'Yes, I'm here, lass. When . . . when did you decide on
this?'

'Oh . . . oh a long time ago, Mam. May . . . may I
come round and have a word with you? I don't want to
go without seeing you.'

'Yes, lass; yes, of course.'

'I'll be there within fifteen minutes.'

'All right, lass, all right.' Maggie slowly put the phone
down. What was happening to everybody? Arlette going to
get a divorce from Sam. He'd go mad, he thought the world

166

of her. Well, there was only one consolation in all this, they couldn't blame her for it, could they? Yet, coming as it did at this time, they would in a way link it with her.

But if Arlette went away that would mean . . . it would mean she wouldn't see her any more. Her body seemed to be coming into life again, there was pain in it, pain in her mind, protest. No, no, this shouldn't be, not Arlette and Sam. But, face up to it, she had known that there was something amiss for a long time, and Friday night in the room when she had turned on him, she'd never seen her look like that before. Dear, dear, God. A divorce . . . Father Armstrong! But worse still, Father Stillwell.

She went into the kitchen, and like a stranger she said, 'Have you got any tea in the pot, Annie?' and Annie said, 'Sit yourself down and I'll get you some breakfast.'

'No, no, I don't want anything to eat, just a cup of tea.'

'You've got to eat; if you don't want to land up in that room permanently you've got to have something in your stomach. Now I've just made that toast fresh. There—' she slapped the plate on to the table '—sit yourself down and eat it. Now go on, do as you're bid for once in your life.'

It was comforting to be ordered about. You belonged when you were ordered about. She sat down and took a bite from the toast but she had difficulty in swallowing it. Nevertheless she ate a slice and she drank two cups of tea.

She looked at Annie flitting back and forth about the kitchen for some time before she said, 'Arlette's coming round, she'll be here any minute. She's going away . . . she's going to get a divorce from Sam.'

Annie stopped in her bustling and looked at Maggie. Then raising her eyebrows and drawing in a sharp breath she said, 'Well, that doesn't surprise me; in a way it doesn't, for that lass has never been happy. She was too good for him. If you remember rightly I said that afore they were married. And if I also remember rightly you said something very like it yourself. But a divorce! We've never had one of those in the family. But there's always a first time. I wonder what will happen next?' She took a jug from the cupboard, poured a bottle of milk into it and ended, 'Everything goes in threes. Let it come soon whatever it is and we'll get it over with.'

It came soon, soon in Annie's reckoning, but long in Maggie's.

Arlette didn't come within fifteen minutes, she didn't come within an hour or two, or three. Maggie got on the phone to the house but couldn't get a reply. At twelve o'clock, only because she was extremely worried, she phoned the office to find out if Sam had been in. Miss Whitaker answered and said no, he had phoned from the house early that morning to say he was going straight into Newcastle and not to expect him.

She felt uneasy. She said so to Annie, and when Annie suggested her going round to Arlette's to see if she was still there she said, 'Oh, no, no, I couldn't do that.'

But when Annie said, 'It's fishy to me. Arlette isn't one to break her word; perhaps there's been an accident and she's landed up in hospital,' Maggie said, 'If she had we would have known before now. But all right, I'll go round.'

'Will you phone for a taxi?'

'No, I'll walk down to the hill and get the bus from there, it stops just beyond the bye-road.'

'Do that,' said Annie soothingly; 'it'll do you good to get out.' She didn't say '. . . take your mind off your own trouble,' but that's what she meant . . .

It was a quarter to one when the bus put her down on the main road, and she walked the few yards to where a lane turned off leading to the bungalow.

The bungalow was situated in a good position, being set well back from the main road and surrounded on two sides by open fields, and on the third side by a riding stable. The next bungalow was beyond the riding stable, a hundred yards away. She went up the lane and let herself in by the main gate, walked up the path between the rose beds – all in full bloom now – and to the front door, and there she rang the bell.

When there was no answer to her ringing the first, second or third time, she went and looked in the sitting-room window. But the blinds were drawn. The blinds were drawn too in the dining section. She walked all around the house. All the blinds were drawn. Why had Arlette drawn the blinds before she left knowing Sam would be coming home?

When she passed the bedroom window she thought she heard a noise and she walked back to it and put her ear to the glass and listened. The curtains were lined and padded. Cost the earth those curtains, and they muffled the sound. She stared at the blank window for a moment, then walked to the kitchen door. It was locked. She went to the front door again and she stood there, not ringing now, just waiting and listening. Then she heard a sound inside that she recognised. It was a door being quietly opened, and a moment later she knew there was something standing within an arm's length from her.

She felt herself sweating with an unknown dread. Sam was in there. Their Sam was in the house and all the curtains were drawn. And Arlette was in there, Arlette was in there an' all. Of that she was sure now.

She moved her feet on the stones of the porch, then purposely pushed the foot scraper into place near the step before walking away down the path. She let herself out of the gate and clicked it shut, then went down the lane again, but only a little way beyond the back gate.

169

The back gate led between a wall and a high privet hedge to the side of the house and the loggia, at the end of which were the outhouses and the garage. Inside the garage was a private door leading into the house, and a spare key for the garage, she knew, was kept on the flange near the top of the drainpipe – that's if her son, in his planning, hadn't already removed it.

She went noiselessly up the path, tip-toed across the loggia, reached up and felt for the key. And there it was. Gently she unlocked the garage door but opened it only wide enough to allow herself to squeeze through. Then she was walking between the two cars, Arlette's and his. She paused and looked in the back of Arlette's car. Two suitcases were lying on the seat.

Gently now she turned the knob of the door and went through into the narrow hallway, which led to the kitchen and bathroom. She had to cross here and go through the dining end of the lounge before she could reach the bedroom. She was walking stealthily towards the bedroom door when she heard Sam's voice, low, thick, laughter-filled as if he was drunk, saying, 'She's gone. Your dear, dear friend's gone. The ignorant old sow's gone, your last hope. Now what you going to do about it, eh? Are you ready for another dose or are we coming to some arrangement? You've only got to nod your head.' There followed a silence, then the voice changed. 'You stinking, scheming bitch you! A divorce is it? You would have gone and left me without a word, not giving a damn, leaving me in hell, leaving me to my own devices.' His voice was rising; it seemed to be screaming, yelling, yet it was eerily low.

When she heard the unmistakable crack of a whip and a smothered yelp and moan, her own body jerked and cringed. It came again, and yet again, before she sprang forward and burst open the door, only to come to a petrified stop when she saw her son, a whip in his hand, flaying his wife, who was tied naked to the bed, a gag in her mouth. For a full moment she thought she must be dreaming or she had gone mad, that the business of Friday night had turned her brain. Only when Arlette's head lifted towards her and her eyes beseeched her for help did she know that this was no dream bordering on madness. But she wished to God it was, for that maniac was her son, her own flesh and blood with a whip in his hand!

Now they were gaping at each other and both standing as if looking for an opening to the other's throat.

'You devil in hell!' The words were wrenched up from her stomach, deep, ominous. She cast a quick glance to each side of her for something to grasp, to throw. To the right of her on the window sill was a pair of vases, but they were too far away. But on the dressing table to her side was a tall glass candlestick. She thrust out her hand and grabbed it and the next second it was hurtling across the room.

It wasn't the first time she had thrown things at a man and with practice her aim had become good. The bottom of the candlestick caught Sam on the temple, and when he staggered back, stunned for the moment, his hands to his head, she was on him. Tearing the whip from him she slashed at him, beating him about the head and face and uttering sounds that could not be translated. But the very blows themselves brought him alert again, and she found herself flung backwards on to a chair, with his hands on her throat and his wide hate-filled face hanging over hers.

'YOU! YOU!' This was the only word he seemed capable of uttering through his tightly clenched teeth and he went on repeating it while his fingers tightened on her throat. With a strength born of desperation she brought her knee up and caught him hard in the groin, and he sprang back from her like a stone from a catapult. His body doubling up, he held himself as he groaned.

Slowly now she dragged herself to her feet, and rubbed at her neck while she stumbled towards the bed. Her eyes hard on him, she tugged at the knots in the pieces of torn sheeting that bound Arlette. When she had freed her she stared down in horror at the blue and red wealed body of her daughter-in-law; then gently she drew the eiderdown round her and brought her upwards on to the side of the bed, still keeping her eyes on her son who was standing upright now, or almost so. As they glared at each other she knew she was looking into the face of a maniac, not a maniac whom the law could pin down, say was mad and so lock up, but a clever, sly, scheming maniac, and she knew that she'd always been aware of this.

'Get out! Get out before I do for you.'

He moved sideways towards the door, his eyes un-blinking, but there he stopped. The knob gripped in his hand, he licked at the froth round his lips before saying, 'There's more ways of killing a cat than drowning it. You're finished, you're as good as dead, Mother Gallacher, and I knew I'd see this day with you. Do you hear? I've been waiting for this day . . .'

'Get out, you dirty, filthy scum. Get out!'

For a moment she thought that he was going to spring across the room at her again; and so did Arlette, for her body shrank against Maggie's. But he only bent forwards, almost double now as he cried at her, 'You to call anybody dirty, you, you who begot me in a cupboard! You were determined to have me dad, weren't you? And that was the only way you could hook him. But he nearly slipped through your fingers even then. A shotgun wedding at the last with a priest on either side of him so that I wouldn't be a bastard. YOU, to talk about anybody being dirty! I was seven when I learned what you were, you fat loose piece, and I've hated you ever since.'

She stared at him, her face lengthening with her surprise. Like looking through old snaps she picked up in her mind the very night she and Rod had gone for each other, and the one and only time he had thrown it up at her that he'd had to marry her. And that lad had been listening, and all these years it had been fomenting in his mind. It didn't seem possible. But it was possible. You read about these things but you never thought they happened to you or yours. But dear God, all these years! How many? He was almost twenty-seven; twenty years he had been holding that against her. Dear, dear God! For the moment she felt a spasm of pity for him and an overwhelming sense of guilt against herself. The sins of the fathers. Aw yes, indeed, the sins of the fathers shall be visited on the children.

But what was he saying now? His words seemed to make her face contract, her eyes narrow, screwed up against their meaning.

'So Dad got his own back; he's played you for a sucker. These last two years he's played you for a sucker. He's got another woman. D'you hear? And not just any woman. No, a lady, by the name of . . . Mrs de Ferrier. And they've got a love nest in the flat behind the office. A Mrs Morland lives there. Eight pounds a week she's supposed to pay. It's cheap at that. She's a friend of Mrs de Ferrier; one good turn deserves another. Mrs Morland leaves every Friday night and Dad and his lady take up residence. Now what d'you think of that . . .? Even before you made yourself the big-mouthed scab of the town you were a laughing stock, for everybody's known that you were being duped. Friday night Rod goes to Ransomes.' Now he was mimicking. 'Saturday night Rod goes to a club in Newcastle, or a dinner or some such doesn't he?' He waited while he glared at her; then his tone changing and his face taking on an even deeper hatred, he spat at her, 'You're finished, finished. You've got nothing. They're all leaving you, all

173

except perhaps your dear son, Paul. And here's something else I'll tell you afore I go. Do you know why he didn't become your blue-eyed priest? . . . Because of her.' He stretched out his arm, his finger stabbing towards Arlette. 'He fell for her, and they've been having a go together ever since. Now what do you think about that, Mam? And another thing. Did you know he was a poet, eh? It's him who writes that piffle for the paper. God help him when I tell our Willie. Fell off a lorry! He'll look as if the lorry had gone over him when Willie's finished with him . . . Well now.' He went to straighten himself, then put his hand to his groin again and it was evident that he was still in pain. 'There's a nice little lot for you to go on with, eh? . . . And as for you, Mrs Gallacher Junior. Give you a divorce? I will that, over my dead body. You try to get one and they'll hear my side of it. What I've done to you is because I found out you were carrying on with my brother; after egging him on to leave the priesthood. That's my case. Go on, try an' see who'll get sympathy in court. Go on.'

They stared at him now as if they were stupefied, and both saw him as something less than human, something epitomising evil.

Even after he was gone they didn't move. They heard him go into the garage, but the car didn't start up right away. It wasn't until it did that Maggie sat down on the bed beside Arlette, and they both looked at each other, with wells of pity in their eyes for the other's plight.

Maggie's brain was in a whirl. Mrs de Ferrier. That Mrs de Ferrier. She didn't question the truth of Sam's words; she seemed to have known it for a long time. There had been just a thin curtain in her mind that had hidden the knowledge from her. This then was the difference in Rod; all these months, all these week-ends he had been going with another woman, and all this time she had been sitting at home . . . like a fool; a great, fat slob with no brains to work things out, a trusting, great fat slob; a blind, ignorant, great, fat slob. But no! No! Her mind was protesting now. Rod wouldn't do that to her. He couldn't, not to her. She had borne him six children; she had worked like a slave for years. She had worked almost up to the last minutes before Sam, Willie and Paul were born. She had kept her job on in the factory so that they'd get a home together; and even when they started to get on and make money hand over fist, she had still continued to work and do for him and all of them, saving on this and that, not spending a penny on herself. What was more, she had been content to sit at home at nights with Annie and mend and sew and see to the bairns while he gallivanted – making contacts he called it. My God! And he had made contacts, hadn't he? De Ferrier; the woman who had looked her up and down as if she was something the cat had brought in, and all the while he had stood there knowing; and he had left her standing against that wall while he talked and talked . . . to his mistress. As if he didn't get enough of her, he had to stand in the middle of that room, a plate in each hand looking at her, while she had stood alone. It was an act of scorn, rejection. All his acts lately had been acts of scorn and rejection. All the while he must have been comparing her with that woman, that society piece, that flat shapeless piece, but a piece who had class written all over her. Aye, there was the answer.

She felt her size diminishing; the feeling on her now was not only one of deflation but also of extinction. She was nothing, nobody, not even fit to be treated as a pet rabbit, fit only for breeding. He had finished with his breeding spell and had moved on to higher things.

She stared before her dry-eyed, but she was crying with every pore of her body. There was no fight left in her; she had nothing more to fight with, nothing more to fight for.

When Arlette shivered in her arms she forgot her own misery for the moment. This lass, this lass. She looked into Arlette's face. It was like a piece of alabaster. Her eyes were half closed and, strangely, there were no signs of tears on her cheeks. How had she suffered this without crying, how? She bent down and muttered, 'Sit still, lass. Now don't move; I'll phone for a taxi.'

When she came back it was obvious Arlette hadn't moved. Everything about her was the same; she looked like a mummy.

'Do you think you can get into your clothes?' she asked her softly. She glanced round the room, at the scattered garments lying on the floor and the chairs; then she went and picked up a blue dress and, bringing it to the bed, said, 'If you could just slip into this, that would be enough.'

Still Arlette didn't move, and when she went to take the eiderdown from around her she had to force her fingers open. As she slipped the dress over her head she felt the shudder of her body and she closed her own eyes tight for a moment as if her skin too had been seared. She put on her shoes and helped her to her feet, then led her gently to a chair, saying, 'Sit there, and I'll get your things from the car.'

When she entered the garage again she stood aghast. The whole place was littered with the contents of the cases from the back seat of the car. There were petticoats, brassières, suits all scattered about as if a hurricane had whirled them into the air. He was mad, mad, but in his madness he still remained petty and small. She gathered up what she could and pushed them back into the cases, then re-entered the hall and as she did so the front door bell rang.

When she went into the bedroom again Arlette was sitting just as she had left her, and she put her arms about her, saying, 'It's all right, lass. It's all right. We'll soon be home.'

The taxi driver looked enquiringly but asked no questions. But when he put his hand on Arlette's shoulder to help her into the back of the car and she winced audibly he glanced at Maggie, and she, looking at him, said, 'Savile House on The Rise.'

Ten minutes later she helped Arlette gently into the house, calling as she opened the door, 'Annie! You there, Annie?'

Annie appeared at the head of the stairs, and after staring at them for a moment she ran down, saying, 'Good God! What's happened to her?' and Maggie said, 'Let's get her to bed; then ring for the doctor, her own doctor. I think it's Bentley. You'll find his number . . .' Her voice trailed away in the effort she had to exert to get Arlette to lift one foot after the other up the stairs . . .

It was an hour and a half later before the doctor arrived, and when Maggie drew down the sheet the man stared for a number of seconds at the criss-cross pattern of blue and red weals, some showing dots of dried blood now. Then, without lifting his head, he lifted his eyes upwards and looked at Maggie, and she could not return the look because shame was weighing her down. That flesh of her flesh could have perpetrated a deed like this! She could have understood a killing; she could have forgiven him in a way if he had shot or strangled her; but to do this!

Ten minutes later, out on the landing, the doctor walked slowly to the head of the stairs, Maggie by his side, and said quietly, 'The state of trauma, shock—' he inclined his head towards her '—may last. Keep her quiet, let no-one see her; but don't leave her, for when this passes off the reaction . . . well, it could be anything.'

He was half-way down the stairs when he said, 'If she had taken my advice and that of her solicitor she could have avoided this. I warned her.'

She waited until they reached the hall, then, standing in front of him, she asked quietly, 'You . . . you knew? About it going on?'

'Yes.' He nodded at her. 'For some time now. But not to this severity . . .'

'Then . . . then why did she put up with it?'

He shrugged his shoulders and moved his head. 'She's a very thoughtful, considerate person, she . . . she didn't want to cause trouble. She was to leave him five weeks ago and then because of some happening, some occasion in the family—' he paused for a second, his look questioning '—which she didn't want to disrupt by starting a divorce, she put it off.'

'Dear God!' Maggie hung her head and the doctor said, 'Well, it's no use worrying, it's done. But . . . but I'd better warn you that your son could be in trouble over this. This is not a case of mere flagellation which he demanded that she should practise on him and he on her, but an attack, a criminal assault and we have yet to see what the result will be. I think that you should get in touch with her solicitor. He's a relation of hers I understand, and it will be up to him to advise what steps should be taken.'

She nodded dumbly and he left her; and slowly she mounted the stairs again. Flagellation, assault, divorce, mistresses; her world was indeed exploding about her ears.

In the afternoon John Fenton called and Maggie told him that Arlette was asleep under the sedation the doctor had prescribed and no-one could see her.

She had heard about Arlette's cousin but had never before met him. He was a young-looking fellow, like one of her own lads, too young, she felt, to fight people's tragedies in law courts, that was until he started to talk. Had she any inkling, he asked, of what her daughter-in-law had been going through these past few years?

No, she hadn't.

Had Arlette mentioned nothing to her at all?

No, she hadn't.

Then he thought it was better she should know the facts of the case before it went into court, because he doubted if Arlette would give her the details, seeing that the man concerned was her son, and remembering, as he said, that Arlette had a deep esteem for herself.

As Maggie listened to the brief, short sentences which showed her son as a sexual pervert she wanted to be sick, to vomit out the knowledge which was being forced into her. You read about these people in the *News of the World*, but they were the kind of people you yourself would never have any truck with. They didn't live in your world.

When he left she went into the bathroom and stood over the basin for a time; she even put her fingers down her throat but she could get no release, the feeling of abhorrence was too deep.

In the bedroom, she took over from Annie and sat down by the bed, and while she sat she wondered at her own feelings. There was a strange calmness on her now. It wasn't like the old feeling, that calmness before the storm when she would remain speechless for a time before bursting into battle with Rod. This calmness was the calmness of despair, weighed heavily with guilt. But guilt for what? She didn't know, she hadn't done anything really bad in her life. Was what she had manoeuvred at her party all those years ago bad? Was that the reason why she was suffering now? One thing was sure, it was that act that had turned Sam against her, twisted his mind; in that moment of joy when she had started his being she had also fermented the seeds of hate. And had she lost Rod then, at that moment when she had trapped him? Or was it just because she was loud-mouthed at times, given to bawling her head off that she was sitting here now under this dragging, damning pressure of guilt?

If she hadn't bawled at Rod that night all those years ago he would have never thrown the truth up in her face and Sam would never have heard, but would that have made any difference to Sam's nature? Was the knowledge that he'd been got on the side enough to turn him into a queer? Because that's what he was, and not just an ordinary queer, a man who went after men; that was a quirk of nature and she pitied all such, but a queer that was so twisted in his mind that only the unnatural was natural to him, that only the unspeakable could bring him pleasure. Was she responsible for such a man? No! No! She denied it loudly in her head, for then she would be responsible for the lass there, lying in this state.

But she was responsible for Rod's defection. Deep, deep down in herself she shouldered the blame for this, for she realised now that as he had moved upwards she hadn't had the sense to follow him. But this admission did not stop her from hating him for doing the dirty on her; she would hate him until the day she died. She was consumed with the pain of her hate. She moved her buttocks back and forwards on the chair as if the pain were physical and she knew that if she let her mind escape this outer case of calmness and dwell on him she would throw herself on the floor this minute and beat her fists against it as an opiate to the agony. But there were other things she must deal with before she allowed herself to come to the main issue.

First there was Paul. Sam had said that he had been carrying on with Arlette, that she was the reason why he hadn't gone into the church. Was this true? She'd have to know.

And Liz? She had been so stunned over the week-end by her own actions that she had forgotten about Liz; but now she must see to her, and quick. She herself hadn't pressed her to go into the church. It had come as a surprise when Liz had first voiced her intention; but once she had known she had hugged the idea to herself and wallowed in the aroma of sanctity that the vocation presented for her daughter. It seemed then, in her naïvety, that God was making up to her for the disappointment she had experienced over Paul.

But she told herself she'd settle one thing at a time, she couldn't tackle them otherwise, and by this time tomorrow it would all be over.

Annie came up at half-past four. Tip-toeing into the room, she said, 'Liz is in; she's asking for you. I didn't tell her anything about—' she nodded towards the bed '—I thought I'd leave it to you.'

Maggie nodded back at her, then rose from the chair, and automatically Annie took her place.

When she entered the kitchen Elizabeth was sitting at the corner of the table drinking a glass of lemonade. She got to her feet immediately and, coming towards Maggie, put her arms around her and asked, 'Are you feeling better, Mam?'

Maggie answered, 'Aye, lass, aye. I'm all right.' Then looking straight into her daughter's face, she said, 'I want to talk to you.' When she saw a look like a dark veil pass over Liz's eyes and her head droop slightly, she said flatly, 'Come into the drawing-room, it's cooler there.'

In the drawing-room Maggie seated herself by the window, and when Elizabeth went and stood near the head of the couch she said to her gently, 'Come here and sit down . . . Bring that chair.'

Elizabeth obeyed her and sat down. She still had her head bowed and Maggie said to her, 'Before I get on to you I'd better tell you something, you'll have to know it sooner or later. Arlette's upstairs, she's pretty bad.

Sam—' she wet her lips and swallowed '—Sam's beaten her up . . .'

'O . . . ur S-Sam?'

'Our Sam.'

'Arlette?'

'Arlette. And—' Maggie pushed her lips outwards '—you're a bairn no longer, you've likely read about these things and now you'd better hear them. He . . . he did it with a whip. And not only the day, it's been going on for a long time.' As she watched Elizabeth put her hand across her mouth and grip her face she said, 'There'll be a divorce.' And now when Elizabeth's eyes stretched on the word divorce she thought, Aye, lass, you can open your eyes but there's no priest on God's earth, counting Father Stillwell, that'll be able to stop it in this case. She squared her shoulders and stretched her neck upwards, as if she were practising Arlette's trick of pulling her stomach in, as she went on, 'And now we come to you . . . Are you going to tell me, lass, or have I to ask you questions?'

When she saw the pitiful look in the young girl's eyes she wanted to thrust out her arms and pull her into the shelter of them, saying, 'There now, there now. Go whichever way you want.' But no, no, she warned herself, her road was already mapped out for her, there mustn't be a second farce.

When Elizabeth didn't speak she asked, 'This fellow, this taxi driver, you've been seeing him?'

Elizabeth shook her head, gulped, then pressed her fingers tightly across her mouth before taking her hand away and muttering low, 'Not really. Not really, Mam.'

'What do you mean, not really? Either you've been seeing him or you've not been seeing him.'

'It wasn't . . . it wasn't intentional, not planned, not planned or anything like that.'

'No?'

'No.'

'That's the truth?'

'Yes. Yes, Mam.'

'Go on then, tell me how it happened. Remember, you don't know what I know so be careful of your words.'

Elizabeth shook her head from side to side, then began haltingly, 'It was . . . it was after that night he brought me home. I . . . I was coming from school. I was just at the end of the grounds; his car was drawn up at the kerb; he was asking a woman how . . . how to get to the Convent House. She didn't know, she was a stranger, and I stopped and told him. I told him to gò round the block into Woodward Road and down the lane. He told me he was to pick up someone to take to the station, it was Sister Anna Maria; the jallopy, I mean the road car, had broken down.' She stared at her mother, gulped again, then went on more slowly now, 'The second time was in the Market. You had left me to go into Grimes's and I went to the chemist. He . . . he was in there. We just said hello, and had a word. That was all . . . I told you about it. But, but . . .'

'Yes, all right, go on.' Maggie's voice was quiet.

'The next Tuesday I was crossing over by the lights in Fulham Road to get the bus and he saw me and pulled up and . . . and asked if I was going home. I said yes, and he said he had to pick up a fare on The Rise, and to jump in . . . and—' she moved her head in a wide sweep now '—it seemed silly not to, and so he brought me home.'

They stared at each other, the silence like a wall between them until Maggie asked the question, 'Is that all?'

Elizabeth's eyes were wide now, unblinking. She said very slowly, 'The next time I saw him he was talking to Father Armstrong outside the Club. He was going to show the boys judo. We all stood talking and Father Armstrong, well, he joked and said if Peter—' she screwed her eyes up tightly and bowed her head, and Maggie's voice cut in on her. 'Peter? He's Peter, is he?'

'Well—' the head was still bowed but there was a note of defiance in the voice '—Father Armstrong calls him Peter.'

'And you call him Peter?'

'No, I don't.' Her head came up; her chin was bobbing. 'But that's his name.'

'Go on.'

Some seconds passed before Elizabeth muttered, 'Father Armstrong said that . . . that God worked in strange ways, that I had to be rescued before he could get anyone to teach the boys judo.'

Father Armstrong! That simple-minded, big nit of a man, he would say things like that. But she must keep calm. She was calm; yes, she was calmer than she'd ever been in her life before. She said, 'Tell me the rest.'

'There's nothing more to tell only that he gave me a ride twice more from school. It wasn't planned or anything because, well, one night we were doing the rehearsal for the play and I didn't come back till six, remember? And last Wednesday afternoon; well, it was games day and I was home early, before four.'

Maggie looked at the crumpled face, the dry, bright eyes. It was all so innocent sounding. And perhaps it was innocent, but nevertheless she had been with that man five times in the car and she wasn't unaffected by it. No, she wasn't unaffected by it. She asked her quietly now, 'Did you tell him what you intended doing with your life?'

The answer was some time in coming. 'No.'

'Why?'

'It . . . I . . . it . . . I didn't think it concerned him.'

Again they were staring at each other, and Maggie wanted to ask the one question that mattered now, 'Are you in love with this fellow?' But no, no, that was taking things too far. What she said was, 'I think you had better tell him, don't you?'

Again there was a pause before Elizabeth answered, and then she said softly, 'Yes, Mam.'

'When will you be seeing him again?' It was a trick question but Elizabeth did not fall into it. She said, 'I don't . . . I don't know, Mam. I told you, they just happen, the meetings.'

'Well promise me something, promise me something now girl, will you?'

'I'll . . . I'll try, Mam.' Elizabeth's voice was breaking.

'When next you see him you'll tell him of the decision you made at the beginning of the year, promise me?'

'I promise, Mam.'

Maggie got to her feet and went and stood by Elizabeth's side; then taking her head in her two hands she pressed it against her waist for a moment before going out.

Elizabeth sat staring in front of her. She was trembling from head to foot, weighed down with the enormity of her guilt. Within her mind's eye she gazed upwards, looking for the face of the Blessed Virgin, and when she found it the head was bent in sorrow, bowed low with grief, and near her stood Joseph with the infant child in his arms and their faces were turned from her. She looked from them down a long, long corridor. It was lined on each side with nuns. At the far end stood the Mother Superior, and next to her Father Armstrong, and behind them and above, overshadowing them all, stood Jesus, the bridegroom, who in her mind she knew she was betraying. His face was not turned from her but was full of pain and sadness for the rejection he read in her thoughts.

She dropped her head forward and cried into her hands.

*   *   *

Maggie phoned Paul at five o'clock. He said, 'Oh, is that you, Mam? How are you?' and she answered, 'I'll never feel any worse than I do at this moment. You'd better come round, there's things I have to see to.'

There was a pause before he said, 'Right, Mam.' And she put the phone down . . .

Twenty-five minutes later he came hurrying through the front door, and she was waiting for him. He went straight to her and kissed her and held her at arm's length, and as he looked into her face he thought, It's done something to her, she'll never be the same again.

They walked into the drawing-room, his arm around her shoulders, but there she disengaged herself from him and said in a voice that was strange to him, 'Sit down, Paul.' He did as she bade him as if he were a small boy again.

Sitting opposite to him, as she had to Elizabeth, she came straight to the point. 'Things have happened, Paul,' she said, 'and I'm not referring now to Friday night's business. Arlette's upstairs in bed; she's pretty bad.'

His body jerked to the edge of the chair. Then he became still. 'What's happened?'

'I'll tell you after you tell me something. Have you and her been carrying on?'

'NO! NO!'

Her head began to nod now as if it were on wires, and then she asked, 'Was it because of her you didn't go into the Church?'

He was still sitting taut on the edge of the chair and he held her eyes for a moment before he said, 'Yes; yes, it was.'

'Did she know?'

'NO! *No!* Well—' his cheek jerked with a movement like a tick '—not till recently. A few weeks ago she told me something, what she intended to do. It was then she knew, although I . . . I didn't say anything.'

186

'She told you she was going to get a divorce, didn't she?'

There was a short period of silence before he moved his head once.

She said now below her breath, 'Sam found out she was leaving him this morning. Perhaps he heard her phoning me to say she was coming to see me before she left. I don't know, she hasn't spoken. But anyway, he tied her to the bed and then—' she bit tight on her lip before she ended, 'he took a whip to her. Three hours of it she must have had before I got there.'

From under lowered lids she saw him rise from the chair and when she lifted her head and looked at him she looked quickly away again. She said now softly, as if stating an ordinary fact, 'Sam's a sex maniac. I had her cousin here this afternoon. He told me what she's had to put up with for a long time now.'

When Paul still made no comment she straightened her shoulders, lifted her head and looked at him again. His face was drained of every vestige of colour, making his red hair look like a flame on top of a wax candle; his eyes were black and staring, wild looking. The anger and the rage that should have been tearing through her she saw in him, and she wished in this moment that she could feel some of it instead of this deadness that had taken possession of her.

She watched him turn away and walk out of the room. It wasn't until he was in the hall that she realised he was making for upstairs, and she hurried after him. She caught him on the bottom step and held his arms and said, 'It's no use, she won't speak; she's in shock, the doctor said.'

He looked at her until she released the hold on his arm; then he turned and mounted the stairs. When he reached the landing her voice came after him, saying quietly, 'Willie's room.'

When he opened the bedroom door Annie turned in her seat and looked at him in surprise. Then she rose, and when he reached the foot of the bed she whispered, 'Nice state of affairs, isn't it?'

Slowly he took his eyes from her and gazed at the form lying under the sheet, the face above it looking like that of a corpse; and when Annie said, 'If you'll stay a minute I'll go down and make you a cup of tea, I'm sure nobody else'll think of it with the state of things,' he moved past her and took the seat she had vacated.

When he heard the door close he bent forward and lifted the hand that was lying limply on the sheet. Bringing it up to his cheek he pressed it there as he uttered deep thick unintelligible sounds. As they made way for his thoughts he wanted to get his brother by the throat and choke the last vestige of life out of him. Pray God they didn't meet up for some time.

A whip! He had used a whip on her? That was what she wouldn't tell him. Cruelty, she had said. 'Oh Arlette, my love, my love.' He laid her hand back on the bed and his fingers wavered over the edge of the sheet, which was all that covered his brother's handiwork for her shoulders were bare of straps, indicating no night attire. He held the sheet gently, lifted it from her breasts upwards but couldn't pull it back. He brought his hands together so that his nails dug into the backs of each, and oblivious of the pain his mind raced into the future. He'd give in his notice; he'd get a job elsewhere; he'd take her away. When the divorce was through they'd be married. They had everything in common. She liked him, he knew that she liked him. Did she love him? He didn't know. But the love he had, and could give to her, couldn't help but find its echo in her.

He heard the door opening behind him. He didn't turn round but he knew it was his mother standing near him. When he got to his feet, she said in an odd tone, 'Come back in the morning, an' by that time I'll have something else to tell you.'

He looked into her face and the change he saw in her hurt him; he had never seen her like this, she was quiet, controlled. Yet controlled wasn't the word, sort of lost. He whispered now, 'What is it?' and she said, 'I can't tell you till later. Come in the morning, as I said . . . And Paul—' she had half-turned from him and now she glanced at him over her shoulder '—Don't tell the others, not till the morning, not anything. Then—' she sighed '—and then you can give them all the news together.'

When she sat down it was like a dismissal, and he stared at her averted face for a moment, then looked again at Arlette before slowly turning and going out of the room.

It was quarter to twelve when Rodney came in. It had been quarter past eleven the other two nights. Although she had been locked away in her room she had known the exact minute that he entered the house, and she had followed his movements. He had locked the front door, then gone into the cloakroom, taken off his hat and coat, after which he had made straight for the stairs and the spare room. Tonight the procedure tended to be the same.

She had been waiting in the darkened drawing-room and when she heard his key in the lock she got to her feet and stood within the doorway while he locked up, then went into the cloakroom. At this point she switched on the drawing-room lights and when, a minute or so later, he crossed the hall he was brought to a standstill by seeing her standing in the framework of the doorway.

Stopping, he looked at her, then, dropping his head, he made to go towards the stairs but her voice checked him, and in a strange way, for it was flat and quiet. The words too were strange, coming from her, for she said, 'Don't go up there just yet, please. Come in here a minute, will you?'

When he looked at her again she had her back to him walking slowly into the room, and he paused before following her. Just within the doorway he stopped and stood watching her still walking towards the far end of the big chesterfield couch, where she turned and faced him. And again when she spoke her words were strange, not in keeping with the situation, for there was nothing repentant about her, no spate of words coming from her trying to explain her mad act, no abject apology, no calling herself a bloody fool. What she said was, 'Have you anything to tell me?'

'Tell you?' There was a slight sneer on his lips now. 'I thought I told you enough on Friday night.'

'We're not talking about the same thing.'

His face straightened out, stretched a little. 'What do you mean? What are you getting at?'

'The trifling matter of another woman called . . . Mrs de Ferrier?'

His mouth was dropping into a gape when he brought it shut with a snap. So it had come, had it? Well, it was time for it; nevertheless it was going to be damned awkward, bloody awkward, and noisy if he knew anything. He glanced swiftly round the room. She would likely pelt everything movable at him. There was the heavy cut glass ash tray on the side table within arm's reach of her; there was that set of vases on the mantelpiece, not to mention the alabaster figure in the middle. It was well he was standing with his back to the open door.

'It's true isn't it that you've been living with her over the past year in the flat behind the office?'

She waited, but he just stared at her.

'I want an answer.'

He squared his shoulders, moved his neck up out of his collar, then said, 'If you know it all why bother to ask?'

'Yes or no?'

Her voice should have sounded like the crack of a whip but it still held that strange off-putting flat sound.

He breathed in deeply; then as he let the breath out the words floated on it. 'Yes. Aye.'

The clock in the hall became audible, the seconds ticking away. What she said next was, 'You called me a big, fat, ignorant slob the other night, didn't you? You took me to that do and compared me with your fancy wife and found me wanting, badly wanting, didn't you? And you said you couldn't make a silk purse out of a sow's ear, didn't you? Well, perhaps you're right about that, but neither can you make one out of a hog's ear. I can see now why you've been breaking your neck this while back to play the gentleman. Naturally you wanted to match up to her style. Huh! I'm sorry for you, Rodney Gallacher, for that's one thing you'll never be, either in looks or manners. The fifty guinea suit you're wearing at this minute doesn't cover what you are, what you were, what you sprung from. You're built like a navvy, you come from a line of dockers at best; it's in your face, and you only have to open your mouth to give yourself away. Nobody's ever pointed this out to you afore, have they? No, it's me that's been the gobskite. You've never let me forget I've got a big mouth; but there were at least some times when I opened it when something else came out besides wind . . . What do you talk about, you and your fancy wife, music, painting, science?'

'Have you finished?'

'No, not quite.'

'Well, whatever you've got to say make it slippy, because I'm tired, and if you want to bring this up again I'll go into it the morrow.'

'OH NO YOU WON'T.'

For the first time her tone was one he recognised, but when she went on her voice was level again. 'This business is going to be finished the night . . . now. You're going upstairs, and you're going to pack your things and you're going out of this house and you're . . . NEVER COMING BACK.' Again her natural self had broken through.

He was stretching upwards now, his chest out, his voice coming from his bull neck. 'I'll go out of this house when I damn well please. This is my house and I . . .'

Her voice, although controlled again, was belied by the expression on her face. Her lower jaw worked from one side to the other as she broke in, 'You'll go out of this house now. If you don't I'll get on the phone . . . Look at the clock.' She pointed. 'It's near twelve. Well, twelve or no twelve, I'll get on the phone, first to her man – I've got all the numbers here.' She pulled from her pocket a sheet of paper and read, 'Mr Roger de Ferrier, Brixton Manor, Felburn 27789 . . .' She held his staring gaze. 'And after him there's Mr Norman Pearce, and Mr Arthur Redfern . . . Councillor Mr Redfern. Then there's Mr Talbot on the Housing Committee and Mr Grey. They might all think I've gone mad after last Friday night's do, but if you're not out of this house within half-an-hour I'll phone every one of them an' chance it.' Her tone changing completely now, she cried at him, 'Every bloody one of them, Mr Gallacher! And I'll do a bit of twisting on me own; I'll tell them that the exhibition I made of meself the other night was due to me learning about you and her, and for the moment I lost control . . . An' it could be true at that, couldn't it?'

He was glaring at her now, very like Sam had done earlier in the day, and she thought for a moment he was coming at her, as he had done so many times before, to let out with the flat of his hand, if not his fist. But he didn't; he stood swaying slightly backwards and forwards as if he were drunk, and after a silence filled with their mutual hate she went on, 'You know this town even better than me, and you know that the aforementioned gentlemen are all very good-living citizens. You remember what happened to that Mr Price some years ago, him that had the business on the corner of the market and was going to expand to the next shop? The leases were up along Talbot Place; and then it came out. He was carrying on on the side, and him a Chapel man. And remember what happened? You told me the story yourself. They wouldn't renew the lease, not even on his own shop; they gave it to Woolworths after having refused it to them in the first place . . . and all because he was keeping a woman on the side. And it wasn't all that long ago, only four or five years. They're still the same men, those who are running this town, now.'

He wetted his lips, then dug his teeth tight into the flesh of the lower one, and the action seemed to drag his head down and his shoulders with it. Then he said in a tone that made her sick because it held a fawning quality, 'Look, Maggie; let's . . . let's be sensible about this. I . . . I know I haven't played it straight but I can explain, an' I'll promise . . .'

'You'll promise me nothing, so you can save your trousers and get yourself off your knees. For twenty-seven years I've been a doormat, a big, fat slob of a doormat, and a dim-witted bugger into the bargain, but no more, no more. As for you turning your coat at the last minute, even if I wanted to believe you I wouldn't. An' I'll tell you another thing. I wouldn't let you within a mile of me ever again. Do you hear? The very thought of you touching me makes me bowels rive . . . Now, as I said, you've got your choice, get packed and get out, back to your nice little nest, or listen to me phoning your pals.'

Again there was the silence, and when she broke it her voice held a tremor. 'Two more things I've got to say to you and then that'll be the end. First, I'm going to a solicitor the morrow about a legal separation. I'll see that you provide for me; I've worked for that at least. The other thing is, I would say to you, go and collect your eldest son and take him with you because it's a shame to waste two houses between you. His wife's lying upstairs. She's been beaten up, not in a natural way, but with a whip. He's flayed her nearly to death, and it isn't the first time. He found out she was leaving him and that's what he did.'

She watched his face stretch as he muttered, 'Sam! our Sam?'

'You can call him your Sam if you like, but he's not my Sam, he's a maniac, a sexual maniac. Like father like son, I would say.'

'Well don't!' he bawled at her now, his shoulders hunched. 'Don't you say that to me. Anyway you know it isn't true; I've . . . I've had one woman on the side, that's all, one woman.'

'Oh! Just one?' She nodded at him. 'Well, you should have known that just one would be one too many for me.'

He was glaring at her again, anger turning his face to a turkey red. His lips moved; he mouthed words that were soundless; and then he swung round and went out. From where she stood she saw his hand gripping the banister as he ascended the stairs.

Slowly she sat down on the couch. It was over. Her life was split in two. Why hadn't she battled with him? Why hadn't she thrown the things? She looked to the side of her, at the glass ash tray, then at the ornaments on the mantelpiece, at the two wine tables flanking the fireplace. She had thought when she came into the room earlier on that she would move all these small things in case she were tempted; then she had said to herself, 'No, leave them as they are; get through this last with a bit of dignity; take the wind out of his sails. He'll expect you to fly at him, swear, and throw things about. Don't let him see how deep the cut is, don't give him that satisfaction.'

Well, she had got it over with a certain amount of

dignity; but what satisfaction had she? God in heaven! What did satisfaction matter? She would have felt better if she had bawled him down, thrown every movable object in the room at him, marked him so that he'd have something to remember her by; but it was done now, done . . . quite done.

In less than half-an-hour he came downstairs again. She heard him slam the cases down outside the cloakroom door. When the front door banged the noise reverberated through the house. A few minutes later she heard the car start up and the revving was like that of a roaring motor cycle. She followed it round the drive, and down to the gate, then down the lane and on to the main road.

She was about to bow her head into her hands when she saw Elizabeth standing in the doorway in her dressing-gown looking piteously towards her. And now, a yell spiralling up from the depths of her, she screamed at her daughter, 'Get yourself away, out of me sight!' And Elizabeth, after one startled glance, turned and ran across the hall and up the stairs, whilst Maggie, her head and shoulders slowly drooping, fell forward on to the couch, and pressing her face into a cushion, let her pain flow from her like a torrent from a burst dam. All her past life, now in wreckage, was tossed and flung here and there, right back down the years to that day when she had come alive the day she had first set eyes on Rodney Gallacher.

CHAPTER THREE

THE CHASE

The following morning Elizabeth didn't go to school. Her eyes were red and she couldn't hide the fact that she had been crying; she had cried most of the night for her world, too, was shattered into fragments. The main catastrophe at the moment was the fact that her father had left her mother for another woman. She had stood on the stairs and heard all that had passed between them. She had known she shouldn't have been listening, but she had been unable to turn and fly to her room and bang the door on reality.

She couldn't believe that her dad had done this thing, because he was a lovely man, kind and generous. She loved her dad; she thought she loved her dad more than she did her mother. But no, no; at this moment her love for her mother was so deep, and the pain of it so awful as to be unbearable. Yet she knew that her pain was but a reflection of what her mother was suffering; she also knew she mustn't add to her sufferings, and so she must carry out her promise, she must see Peter today. She knew where he would be at a quarter-past six this evening, he would be going into the old school, where the boys' club was held.

She had passed the gates of the school twice and was on the point of retracing her steps for the third time when his car turned the corner and drew up to the kerb. Pushing his head out of the window, Peter called, 'Hello there.'

'Oh, hello.' She forced herself to smile at him, and she looked back into the eyes that were covering her face, her swollen lids, her puffed cheeks, and naïvely she said, 'I've got a cold.'

'Oh, that's bad; the summer ones are hard to get rid of. Been doing your rehearsal?'

'No, not today.'

'I'm just on me way to throwing me weight about again.' He laughed and nodded in the direction of the school, and she smiled and said, 'Oh yes, yes.' Then the smile slipping from her face, she bent down to him and asked softly, 'Can . . . can I come in for a minute?'

'Yes, yes, of course.' He leant over and opened the side door, then watched her walk round the bonnet of the car. His eyes were still on her when she took the seat beside him, but now her head was bowed and he asked, 'Is anything wrong?'

She raised her head slowly and looked at him. It was strange. She had known him for only a few weeks but she could talk to him freely, more than she could to anyone in the family, including her mother and Paul. 'Yes,' she said, 'things are very wrong at home. Everything . . . everything has happened at once.'

'I'm sorry to hear that.' He sounded sorry too.

And now for her piece. 'It . . . it appears.' She seemed to be searching for words. 'Well, the fact is my mother is going to be left alone. My dad, he's, he's gone . . . and it's worrying me because . . . well, you see I'm—' her head moved twice backwards and forwards '—I'm going into the convent . . . the Church, at the beginning of the year. I'm . . . I'm to be a nun, and she'll . . . she'll be left—' the last words trailed away '—alone, quite alone.'

She waited for him to say something: then her head still bowed she said, 'I should have told you before.'

'Oh.' His tone sounded airy, startlingly airy. 'I knew that's where you were for. Father Armstrong told me the first time I met him after that night.'

She was looking into his face, into his round kind face, into his round brown eyes, the eyes that she had looked into night and day for weeks past now, not being able to get their kindness out of her mind, and her chin wobbled slightly before she whispered, 'You knew?'

'Aye. Yes.'

She watched his adam's apple move up and down as he swallowed. His eyes held the same kindly expression, only deeper and more warm now. She wanted to hold her face in her hands, rock her body from side to side and cry and cry in an effort to erase not only the pain now, but the feeling of shame. He hadn't been thinking of her like that, it had all been in her own mind. He had just been acting kindly, you could say honourably, and she hadn't recognised it. After all, she didn't know many honourable men. Her father, Sam, they weren't honourable men; and Willie, with his pilfering, he wasn't an honourable man; perhaps Paul . . . she even had her doubts about Paul. But this man here, he had acted decently towards her, and all the while she had been reading something else into it, what her heart wanted her to read. She forced herself to mutter now, 'That's . . . that's all right then,' and he bent towards her and took her hand and asked quietly, 'It's what you want, isn't it?'

As she stared back into those eyes she couldn't bring herself to say 'Yes,' but she inclined her head, and at this he patted her hand gently and said, 'Fair enough.' Then he leant across her and opened the door and she swung slowly round on the seat and stepped out on to the road, and as she did so a car passed her. But she didn't notice the driver until it stopped a few yards ahead and the door burst open, and there stood Sam, looking as she had never seen him before, because their Sam always dressed smartly. But now he was wearing neither collar nor tie, his shirt neck was open, his black smooth hair was all tousled, his face was flushed like when he had been drinking a lot. However, it was his eyes that held the greatest difference; they were staring out of his head, thrusting forward, as were his head and shoulders.

As he made towards her, she sprang back into the car, shouting, 'Start up! Start up! Back it . . . back!'

'What!' Peter was answering her command automatically, at the same time repeating, 'What! What's up? Who's he?'

'Back quickly. It's my brother; he's, he's out of his mind.'

The car was moving swiftly backwards now towards the end of the road, and Sam was at the window running beside it, banging on it, shouting, 'Come out! Do you hear, Liz? Come out, you dirty young slut. Come out of that!'

When the car gathered speed he stopped, watched it for a moment, then raced back to his own car, by which time the taxi had turned about and was speeding down the main road.

'What's caused it?' Peter sounded as agitated as she was for from the glimpse he'd had of the fellow he could see he was wrong in the head, and though he wasn't afraid of any man, no matter how big he might be, maniacs were a different kettle of fish. What was more, she was scared to death.

He said now, 'Do you want to go home?'

'No! No!' She did not want to add fuel to the fires that were raging in the house by having him drive her up to the door, that was the last thing she wanted tonight, so she muttered as she looked through the back window, 'Drop me somewhere, a side road.'

They came to the traffic lights and, glancing through his mirror, he said, 'I don't think I'll be able to drop you without him coming up, he's only about four cars behind. What do you think I should do?'

So afraid was she now, she almost said, 'Go to a police station.' What she did say was 'Can you drive round by the docks? There are side streets there; you'll know your way better than him, you could dodge him.'

Yes, that was an idea. The lights changed and he spurted forward, overtook two cars, took a side turning to the High Street and went through the Market. Not being market day, there was little or no traffic in it at this time of night. Then he was making for the waterfront and the maze of small streets running off it. He knew what he would do; he'd turn down D'Arcy Street and on to the jetty that fronted Cowell's Warehouse – there'd be no boats unloading now and he'd have a straight run along the waterfront – and come up Ferry Street.

When he turned sharply into D'Arcy Street she cried out in alarm, 'Where are you going, the river's down there?' and he said, 'We can turn along the quay. I've been this way before.'

But when he came to the end of the street there, barring the entrance to the landing stage, was a great iron chain. It was attached at one end to a staple in the end wall of the warehouse and at the river edge was hooked to one of the timbers supporting the jetty. There were two boys sitting on the middle of it swinging back and forward and he wound down the window and yelled to them, 'Unhook the chain, lad, will you? I want to get along.'

'What do you say, mister?' They came to the window.

'Will you unhook that chain? I want to drive along there.'

'Along the quay, mister?'

'Aye. Yes.'

'The warehouses are all shut.'

'I know that. Here, do as you're bid.' He thrust his hand into his pocket, pulled out a shilling and handed it to the taller boy who was about twelve years old. 'Get going, quick.'

'Ta, mister. Ta.' They scampered across the jetty, but as they did so Sam turned the corner of the street.

Since the taxi was half slewed round it was Elizabeth who saw him first and she cried in deep agitation, 'Oh! Hurry, hurry; here's our Sam. Oh dear Lord! Oh dear Lord!'

Peter glanced to the side and saw the car bearing down on him and thought, if it's a show-down, it's a show-down. He had turned swiftly round again and had opened the car door when Elizabeth screamed, and his own loud cry joined with hers only a second later as he saw the bonnet of his car taking a nose dive over the end of the quay. Then he was falling forward with her clinging to him and her screams tearing through his head. As they plunged into the oily waters of the dock he thought, Why in God's name, why?

CHAPTER FOUR

REACTIONS

'It's as if we've been struck by lightning, everything's happened at once. I can't believe it, I can't take it in.' Helen looked around at them all gathered in the drawing-room, Willie and Nancy, Frances and Dave Walton, and her own husband, whom at this moment she was disliking wholeheartedly, and she finished, 'Where's it all going to end? That's what I'm asking meself, where's it all going to end?'

'I know where it's going to end for us.' Frances got to her feet; her face looked pinched and white. 'We're moving, we're getting out as soon as is humanly possible; I'm not going to go through this town with my head down to my knees for the rest of my life.'

'Well, if we all do that the boat will sink, won't it?' It was Nancy speaking, Nancy who was not supposed to have much up top.

Frances turned on her, her voice harsh. 'It's all right for you, Nancy, you're not of the family.'

'Well, I'll be damned!' Willie now reared upwards, pushing his hand through his hair. 'She's only me wife and she's not of the family!'

'You know what I mean, our Willie.'

'No, I don't. We're all in this, all concerned, every damned one of us.'

'I'll thank you not to say that I'm concerned with our Sam's goings on, nor with me dad's either, for that matter.'

'Sit down, sit down, and shut your mouth.' Dave Walton

tugged at his wife's arm, and Frances flopped down into a chair. But she would not be silenced and muttered now, 'And it caps all, our Paul and Arlette.'

'Now look.' Willie was pointing his finger at her. 'That was Sam's story. I know our Sam. He'll say anything at the best of times to put the onus on somebody else, but you're not going to tell me that our Paul didn't go into the Church because of Arlette. I tell you Sam was mad. He talked like a madman. And the night's business has proved it, hasn't it?'

'What about him writing the poetry then?'

'Oh that! Aye, well. By God! I'll have that out with him, see if I don't. "Fell off a lorry". The bloody nerve of him, spying. That's what it was, spying. And on his own folk at that. Aye by God! I don't know how I'll keep me hands off him . . . But the other business. No, I won't believe that. Why, he was all but a priest . . . An' don't tell me that priests are now campaigning to get married. I know all that. But they wouldn't be priests if they did, not to my mind they wouldn't.'

They were all silent now until Frances, her thoughts bursting from her again, cried, 'What was she doing in the taxi with that fellow anyway? She must have been up to something for Sam to chase them like that. Our Liz! I tell you it makes me mind boggle. If she doesn't go into the Church me mam will go mad.'

'If she dies she'll go madder.' They looked at Helen.

'Well, she's got a chance.' Willie's voice was quiet now. 'And it's thanks to that fellow, because if he hadn't dragged her out and held her up, an' that must have taken some doing in the condition he was in with her dead to the world, she'd have been a gonner in no time. And if those kids hadn't been there they'd both have been gonners.'

Helen began to walk about the floor now, shaking her head as she said, 'I wonder where he is?'

'We'll know soon enough; the police'll nab him.' Dave Walton stared towards the ceiling. 'Those kids were cute to take the number of the car.'

'What do you think they'll do to him?'

Dave Walton glanced at Helen who had stopped near the table, her joined hands pressed together between her breasts; then he lifted one shoulder and said, 'What do you think? Likely charge him with attempted murder?'

'My God!' Frances got up from her seat, and looking down on her husband she said, 'Come on, we'd better get back; I can't expect Mrs Denton to sit up all night with the children. Are you staying?' She turned to her sister, but before Helen had time to answer, Trevor Gillespie, his features more pinched, his manner more pedantic, his voice thinner than ever, said, 'We really must be making our way back too; I have to be at business tomorrow morning . . .'

Helen's voice now cut into his as she cried at him, 'Oh, for God's sake, Trevor!' She stared at him; then cried, 'Damn your business and Mr Pattenden! Tell him to go and stick it.'

'Hel-en!' The small thin body was straining upwards as he rose to his feet, and Helen cried back at him, 'Don't Hel-en me, not at this time. Go on home if you like, but I'm staying until Mam gets back from the hospital, if it's two o'clock in the morning, so there!'

'Very well, please yourself.' He walked out of the room, trying to keep his step steady. He would talk to her when he got her home. Yes, indeed he would talk to her. Damn Mr Pattenden she had said; and how he, in the depths of his being, damned him too! But Mr Pattenden had him trapped like a wild rabbit. The shop had been like a torture chamber yesterday and today. Helen's mother's affair – he didn't think of her now as Mam – was a joke being enjoyed by everyone in the town, and particularly by

Mr Pattenden. That piece in the *Saturday Evening Herald* headed 'Pygmalion Episode at Duke's Musical Evening' had set everyone in the town asking why and what, for the reporter hadn't gone into details such as names or described with any accuracy what had taken place, he had merely referred to a certain lady becoming disgruntled with His Grace and voicing her displeasure.

Who was she? and, what had she said? were the questions everybody was asking. And they soon got the answer. Gallacher, the contractor; it was his wife and she hadn't only bloodied the Duke, she had buggered him.

'No!'

'Yes!'

'What a lark!'

And those were the words Mr Pattenden had said to him. 'What a lark, Gillespie! So much for your folks consorting with the gentry, eh?'

He, like Frances, wouldn't be able to stand it, he'd have to get away from this town. He had had similar thoughts before, but Helen wouldn't leave the proximity of her family. That was the trouble with families like this one; when a bomb exploded under the parents everybody got splinters.

He was pleased with his simile. He shrugged himself into his coat and went out into the wet night thinking, I'll get away. We'll get away. I'll put my foot down, she'll have to come . . .

Frances said almost the same thing to her husband when she got into the car five minutes later; iterating her earlier statement, she said, 'We're getting out of this.'

'I've got a business don't forget,' he answered flatly; and to this she replied, 'You can travel to your business; we're getting out of this if it's only into Newcastle.'

He said spitefully now, 'I thought you had plans for taking over Savile House some time; and by the looks of things it'll soon be to let.'

'Don't be bitchy, Dave Walton,' she said.

He let out a deep sarcastic laugh. 'Bitchy, she says.' Then he set the car going . . .

Back in the room, Willie said to Helen, 'Look, I'll just slip Nancy home to see to the bairns, then I'll be back, I won't be twenty minutes.'

'All right,' she said dully. 'All right.'

So, ten minutes later when Maggie and Paul returned from the hospital, there was only Helen of all the family to greet them, and as she helped her mother off with her coat, she asked quietly, 'How is she?'

Maggie let out a long slow breath before she said, 'She'll survive.'

'And him?'

'He'll pull through an' all, with a bit of help.' As she went across the hall she asked, 'Where's Annie?' and Helen replied, 'She's in the kitchen, she was asleep. She's dead beat, she's never been off her feet.'

Maggie nodded, but when she entered the drawing-room she stopped and looked around her, then looked at Paul, for he too was surveying the empty room.

Sensing their feelings, particularly her mother's, Helen said apologetically, 'They had to go because of the bairns . . . and things, but Willie'll be back, he's just dropping Nancy. And . . . and I sent Trevor off because he's got to get up in the morning.'

Maggie moved her head twice up and down, then went heavily towards a chair and sat down.

'Can I get you something? A strong coffee?'

'No, a cup of tea, lass.'

When Helen had gone Maggie looked at Paul, who was standing now, his elbow on the mantelpiece, looking down on the bowl of flowers that filled the empty fireplace, and she said, 'What's hit us, lad?'

He turned his head slowly towards her. 'These things

happen, Mam. You can go on for years plain sailing, and then you run into a storm. These things happen.'

She shook her head slowly, took a handkerchief from her pocket and, wiping her mouth with it, said sadly, 'It's funny, but it all seemed to start with that invitation, and the climax came on the night, Friday night, and it's still going on. Arlette—' she paused '—your . . . your dad, and now Liz. And it isn't finished yet; when they catch him there'll be worse to come.' As quietly he replied, 'These things haven't just happened over the past days, or months. You know yourself, in . . . in all cases they've been brewing for a long time.'

'Aye, aye, you're right,' she said. 'We've all been blind, at least I have, as blind as a bat, stupid, gullible and blind.' Bitterness was in her voice now.

'This fellow,' said Paul, 'the taxi driver. Why was he with Liz? Or why was she with him?'

Maggie spread her handkerchief across her knees, pulling the edges straight, smoothing it as if it was important that all the creases should be levelled out, and then she said, 'She had promised me to tell him that she was going into the Church. He . . . Sam, he had seen them together. You heard him the other night, Friday night, afore I went out. I tackled her last night. She was upset, so upset that I thought there was more in it than she made out, and the irony of it is—' she closed her eyes and shook her head before ending – 'Father Armstrong told me the night that the young fellow knew all along she was for the Church, and that he was a good fellow and he had no intentions that way towards her. "Honoured her", was the term Father Armstrong used. But she, she had her own ideas about him, I'm sure of that.'

The door bell ringing startled them and Paul said, 'That'll be Willie back,' and she answered him, 'Willie wouldn't ring.'

'No, no, he wouldn't.'

She was on her feet now walking towards the hall and he followed her. Annie was coming from the kitchen, heavy-eyed as if she had just woken up, with Helen behind her, a tray of tea things in her hands.

It was Paul who opened the door and stared at the policeman and the plain-clothed man with him.

'Mr Gallacher?'

Paul inclined his head, then said, 'One of them. This is my mother.' He extended his hand towards Maggie, then said, 'Come in.'

When they entered the hall he did not ask what had happened, he left that to his mother, who, looking from the policeman to the plain-clothed man, said, 'Yes?' and the policeman moved his hat round between his hands before he spoke. 'We've bad news for you, Mrs Gallacher,' he said. 'We've found the car . . . and your son.'

She made two small assenting movements with her head then waited, and the policeman went on, 'We had been to the house, to the garage. It was empty. Then just half-an-hour ago a patrol car looked in. The garage was then locked where before it had been open; the car was inside, the engine still running, and . . . and I'm afraid your son is dead, Mrs Gallacher.'

For years afterwards, she denied to herself that the feeling she felt at that exact moment was one of deep pleasure, almost joy. As time went on she made herself look upon it as relief, but here and now there was this feeling that was telling her that the badness had gone out of her life, the wickedness, the perversion, the evil. When she trembled it was with remorse and fear of the feeling itself.

When Helen and Annie, one on each side of her, turned her about and helped her into the drawing-room, she really needed help for her legs were giving way beneath her. The feeling was still on her and her mind was gabbling, there

208

would be no trial, her Elizabeth wouldn't have to go into court and face all that, and the business of her going to be a nun in the headlines . . . Then there was Arlette. She knew nothing about what had happened this night; she had slept most of the time since yesterday. Now she was free, no divorce court, no reporters, no muck spreading.

The feeling of release was so great that she felt it lifting her from the floor, and she heard Helen's voice from a distance saying, 'Look out! She's going to faint.' She had never fainted in her life before but she understood that when you did you were enveloped in an awful blackness. But this wasn't blackness, this was a peculiar kind of light, and gratefully she went into it.

CHAPTER FIVE

THE BRUSH OFF

Rodney sat facing Willie across the desk in his office, facing him but not looking at him. He had always been fond of Willie, more so than of Sam, perhaps because Willie's coming hadn't held a pistol to his head. But now his son's eyes were cold, condemning.

During the past two weeks or so when they had met Willie had hardly opened his mouth to him, and he had longed to explain and tell him how things were, that he hadn't wanted this to happen, that it just had and he couldn't do anything about it. He wanted to say to him that he was sorry for Maggie, deeply sorry, and that she had a case, oh yes, she had a case. He wanted to say that he knew he should have been back in the house shouldering the responsibilities for all that had happened. But he could say nothing of this because Willie's face wouldn't let him.

But he wanted to talk. Oh God! How he wanted to talk to someone, for not only was his home life shattered, but also there was something happening in his other life, the life in which his love was, that he couldn't understand, or, more to the point, didn't want to understand. And there was another thing, the firm. It seemed to be sliding away like quicksands beneath his feet.

He had imagined that, after that Friday night's business at the Duke's, his reaction in leaving home – they weren't to know he was ordered out – would have met with sympathy in some quarters, those that mattered anyway. But without anyone speaking about the affair openly to him he gauged that, instead of the episode being taken seriously, it was being treated as a huge joke; and there was even sly admiration for the perpetrator. Apparently Mrs Gallacher had voiced the opinion of many with regards to His Grace, and even His Grace himself, Rosamund had informed him, had laughed heartily over the matter. He had, she said, a rare sense of humour.

Public opinion might, he knew now, have kept to the level set by the Duke if it hadn't been for him giving Mrs Morland her notice from the flat.

After an uncomfortable night on the office floor and four lonely ones in an hotel he didn't see why this state of affairs should continue when there was the flat attached to his office.

But he reckoned without Mrs Morland's reactions. She was a dear friend of Rosamund de Ferrier and therefore, he thought, she would understand. But Mrs Morland didn't understand anything except the fact that because of the inconvenience she put up with in being turfed out every week-end she felt she more than earned her rent-free residence.

He hadn't realised the seriousness of his action until Rosamund had stormed in on him. And that was the word, for he had never seen her anything but calm before. On this occasion, however, she had gone for him in a way not far removed from that which Maggie would have used under the circumstances. Did he, she asked him, not know that Adelaide Morland was a spiteful bitch! Now their association would be passed on from one to another – as a deep secret of course. He was a fool! Did he not realise what a free flat meant to a widow with no means and expensive tastes?

There had been no sporting on the bed during that visit, and Friday night and Saturday night had both passed and she hadn't come. That was ten days ago. It felt like ten years. And the knowledge that the world of his business was being sucked away from under his feet seemed linked with her absence.

Willie was saying in a clipped, cold way, 'The Ratepayers Association have taken it up. There's another twenty-three houses affected on the Morley Estate, and they're in Bewlar Avenue now, not going straight across, but branching off. That could mean all that section, more than a third of the estate. The Chairman of the Association tells me that Redfern's coming out the day with the committee.'

His cheeks pushed up, bringing deep lines to the corners of his eyes. 'Redfern?'

Redfern was his friend, or had been. Redfern had pushed a lot of things through for him on the Council; if Redfern turned against him he could say goodbye to the Marina contract.

'There's something else you should know, you'll find it out sooner or later.'

'Well?'

'Sam had been fiddling on his own.'

'Sam!'

When, at the funeral, he had knelt in the chapel and watched the coffin disappearing through those curtains to meet total extinction he still couldn't believe that his son was capable of all the things that had finally brought him to his death. Sam who was always for a laugh. Sam who had always acted the goat and who, as Annie would say, was full of antrimartans. He himself didn't laugh easily, but at times Sam had caused him to double up with mirth; and all the time Sam had been odd, queer. It made you squirm deep inside to know you'd given birth to something like that.

'Well, go on,' he said.

'Riley came to me yesterday and asked if it would be the same arrangement as he had with Sam. I asked what that was, and he told me. For every ten lorry loads of sand and cement that were booked in only nine were delivered and they split the difference.'

On this Rodney bounced to his feet. 'What! Sam and Riley. You mean that they'd been doing me for . . . ?' His mind boggled as it groped at the amount that his son and the subcontractor had made out of him over the past years. He stood gripping the edge of the table. Sam, his own flesh and blood, who received twenty-five per cent of the profits of the whole concern, as did Willie. Most of his own profits were ploughed back, except the money needed to keep the house going and what was necessary for himself to keep up his position.

'Sam? The swine! But wait a minute.' He looked at Willie; then said slowly, 'But he'd be cutting his own throat in the end.'

'Aye, you might think so on the surface, but if you work it out you'll see different. He was getting his cut from the firm, yes, but you take the price of the load of one lorry in every ten and count that up for a week, just one week, and remember Riley was contracted for both sites, then divide it in half.' He paused. He was laughing. 'Talk about falling off a lorry!'

'What?'

'I said talk about falling off a lorry.'

Falling off a lorry? It went on all the time, high and low. He knew it went on among the sub-contractors; you had to keep your eyes on them, and that had been Sam's job. He had delegated more and more of that side of the work to him over the past years while he himself had supervised from the top level, thinking his main job now was to go out and mix, meet the men who would stand you in good stead when the votes were running thin on a wavering contract.

'Another thing.' Willie's tone was still chill. 'Just a small thing, but it might be the thin edge of the wedge. I passed

Bailey on my way here. He's always been very pleasant. We were on waving terms a fortnight ago, but the day he pretended he didn't see me . . . That's enough to be going on with I think.' He rose from his chair, looked hard at his father for a moment longer, then walked out without a so-long, a ta-rah, or a goodbye.

Rodney stood gripping the end of the desk. Bailey was a friend of Pearce, and they were both thick with de Ferrier, in fact they were the trio who, from behind cover, ran the town. He hadn't seen de Ferrier since the night of the Duke's party. Prior to this he had never minded meeting him, in fact inwardly he had enjoyed it, laughing to himself about making a monkey out of the white-faced, superior-acting nowt, as he termed him in his own mind. But now, although he hardly admitted it to himself, he was afraid of meeting him. De Ferrier, he knew, could break him; they, Bailey, Pearce and he together could break him into small pieces, strip him clean. If he didn't get the Marina contract, and if the Council stuck its heels in about the subsidence on the Morley Estate, and it became front page news – up till now the trouble had been given only brief notices near the back page – it would mean that the rest of the houses on the new estate adjoining Morley would stick. People weren't fools, they weren't going to buy houses where the walls were apt to split and the door joists come apart within weeks.

He sat down and groaned, and again he thought, God! If I had only someone to talk to, someone to go to; if only she would come . . . He couldn't go on like this, he couldn't, he'd have to phone her; if anybody could straighten things out she could. But he couldn't phone from here; there were those two back in the outer office who had ears like cuddies' lugs; he'd have to go into the flat.

He let himself out by a side door, went down the court-yard and unlocked the door of the flat. It was odd about the flat. Since he had lived in it he had come to dislike it heartily, even the sight of the bed did something to him. He sat down and picked up the phone and when he got through a polite voice with practised ease repeated the number, and he said, 'I would like to speak to Mrs de Ferrier.'

'Who's speaking please?'

'Oh.' His pause was accompanied by a jerk of his head. 'It's just a friend. I . . . I just want a word with her.'

'A moment, please.'

The minute sped to three minutes and then the same voice said, 'I'm sorry, Sir, Mrs de Ferrier is not at home.'

Again his chin jerked upwards. 'When will she be at home?'

'I . . . I couldn't say, Sir.'

He felt a blind anger rising in him. He could see her standing within arm's length of the phone, he could feel her, almost smell her; that scent she wore, that was like nobody else's. His voice was high when he answered, 'Tell Mrs de Ferrier that I will ring back in ten minutes' time,' and on this he banged down the phone, then sat punching one hand hard into the palm of the other.

Was she brushing him off? Was she telling him something? No, no; he would not, he could not allow himself to believe that. She was a bit scared about all the talk, that was all. Her scared! The thought brought him to his feet and he moved his body from side to side against the suggestion. The devil in hell couldn't scare her; she was the type that could freeze an opponent with a look. He stopped in his pacing. Was she freezing him? NO! NO! He brought out the words loud and definite. She was just angry with him for phoning the house. But didn't she realise that he would phone if she didn't come to him? Didn't she realise that he'd have to see her? It was ten days now since he had looked on her face, spoken to her, touched her, and although he told himself that he would want her all his life, he would never want her more than he had done during these past days.

Ten minutes later almost to the second he rang the house again, and her voice came immediately to him, 'Yes?'

'Oh, there you are.' He aimed to appear cool. 'I thought you'd taken a holiday.' He did not realise he was using the same tactics with her as Maggie had done with him.

'What is it you want?'

What did he want? He looked into the mouthpiece of the phone. What did he want? Then he said softly but grimly, 'That's a daft question isn't it, what do I want? I want to see you of course. Do you know it's over a week?'

She made no reply to this. Then her voice came to him just above a whisper, saying, 'I think it would be better for the time being if we leave things as they are.'

Again he was looking into the mouthpiece of the phone; and then he was bellowing. 'Now look here!' He gulped and his voice changed as if some of his vocal chords had been cut. Slowly and quietly now he said, 'Rosamund, look. I've got to see you, I'm . . . '

'I'm, I'm sorry but we are going away.'

'We are what!'

'It's . . . it's holiday time you know.'

He detected a lightness in her tone now as if she were discussing the weather.

'People do go away at this time of the year. We're going . . . '

'Look! Do you hear? Stop it, and listen to me! You're not going away, at least not before I see you. I'm coming over there.'

'Rodney!' The lightness was gone. 'I forbid you to come near the house.'

'You can forbid me nowt, nothing; I intend to see you.'

There was a blankness on the line and for a moment he thought she had cut him off; then her voice, as if it was coming through a thin reed pipe, said, 'I'll be there at seven o'clock.'

'You'd better.'

Just before he heard the phone click he thought he heard her say, 'How dare you!' but he wasn't sure. Yet, 'You'd better' must have sounded like a threat to her. He had forgotten he wasn't dealing with Maggie.

She arrived at seven. He opened the door of the flat as she stepped out of her car, and he held it wide as she passed him and went into the sitting-room. Then they were facing each other, three arms' length apart. No grabbing her to him now, no sudden pressure of her body against his, exciting him to a point of delicious delirium. Her face was whiter than usual, the grey of her eyes almost blue.

'Well? You wanted to see me?'

He remained quiet, staring at her. Some section of his mind was registering an odd thought; she was speaking to him like an upstart mistress would to a servant. She reminded him for a moment of that woman on Brampton Hill years ago. They were building an extension to her garage and she came and looked up at him and said, 'Kindly stop that whistling, it's irritating.' And he remembered he had stood with the trowel in his hand and watched her walk across the garden and into an arbour, and it was all he could do to restrain himself from sending a full-blooded mouthful after her.

There was a sickening sensation churning in his bowels now. He said slowly, 'Yes, I wanted to see you; we've met before, remember me?'

'Oh Rodney!' She turned her head to the side but remained standing where she was. 'Don't be childish. Must one spell things out for you?'

'Spell things out?'

'Yes, spell things out.' She was looking at him again, her eyelids blinking rapidly now, some of her coolness gone, her thin chin wobbling slightly. 'We've . . . we've been very happy, but all good things must come to an end. That's a platitude, but it's true. And when all's said and done you've only got yourself to blame for the abrupt termination of our friendship. You should never have turfed Adelaide Morland out of here the way you did; she can be a very good friend but an equally bad enemy.'

The sick feeling in his stomach was increasing; added to this he suddenly felt gauche, as if the veneer he had laid on himself over the past few years was rapidly slipping off him, as if his body had been covered with an extra strong paint remover, and he was back where he was at the beginning of things, a big brash young fellow who talked loudly, acted quickly, pushed, and greased palms, but a big young fellow who never grovelled. He had never grovelled in his life to man or woman, and what he should be saying to himself now was he wasn't going to start at his age. But this woman was in his blood as Maggie had never been. Maggie had been forced on him, but this woman here had burst into his life like a meteor and he had reached out and caught her and held her, and lost himself in her dazzling brightness. And she had loved him, she still loved him . . . Loved him? Could he remember her ever saying she loved him? That was beside the point. Her every reaction to him had translated her love. You could say in a way that she had translated it through many different languages; she had even taught him things he didn't know, and he'd thought he was wide in that way. But you lived and learned. Aye, you lived and learned.

But there was one thing he didn't want to learn at this moment, in fact he refused to recognise what was staring him in the face.

He went towards her, holding out his hands as if in supplication, and said, 'Rosamund, look I'm free, we're separated. I . . . I've fixed her up. She's all right. I've got nothing on me conscience, she'll give me a divorce presently, I know she will. You can have it any way you like.'

'Oh, please! Please!' She was stepping back from him, her head bowed but swinging from shoulder to shoulder. If he had been a strange man and was exposing himself to her she couldn't have shown more distaste, and this got through to him and he yelled, 'Look! Stop playing games with me. We've been at it for the last eighteen months, remember? You've been my mistress. And when I took you up I wasn't just some second-rate citizen, I was Rodney Gallacher, the contractor, the big contractor, working over two counties. True, you fiddled for me and I was grateful.' He paused before saying, 'In more ways than one.' But he didn't add 'You saw you had it in cash and not in cheques.' A lightning thought at this moment sweeping through his tormented brain yelled in an aside, 'Aye, a hundred pounds at a time for her nicknacks, and if you managed to remember a card on Maggie's birthday you thought that was enough.'

The look on her face cut off his tirade. He watched her hitch her handbag further up on her arm before she said, 'We're leaving tomorrow for France. After that we're going on to Spain and Portugal. We may be away six weeks to two months. When . . . when we return you'll likely be in a different frame of mind, and by that time also you'll no doubt have seen that what I am doing now is the most sensible thing for both of us.'

When she went to walk past him he thrust his arm out and grabbed her wrist and she became still; and once again he was pleading, 'You can't drop me like this, I need you; I need you in all ways, in all ways. Don't you understand?'

She was looking at him almost pityingly now and for the first time her voice held a tender note as she said, 'I'm doing everything for the best, Rodney, believe me. Taking Roger out of the way you'll have one less to contend with. He's a power behind the scenes is Roger, you know that. He's already seen to it that you won't get the Marina contract. I would suggest that you go quietly for a time, put the houses right on the Morley Estate, and keep your eyes open for Redfern, Pearce and Bailey.' She now looked down at his hand that had become limp on her wrist, and when it dropped away she said quietly, 'Goodbye, Rodney.'

He made no reply, he just stood there with an agony in him as if he had been disembowelled.

CHAPTER SIX

THE GIVING OF A DAUGHTER

She sold the house as it stood for twenty-two thousand pounds because, she said to Annie, she was taking nothing out of this old life into the new.

She had more money now than she had ever had in her life before, or ever thought to have. When Rodney had made money her share of it had been new carpets, curtains and furniture, but he had never given her any money for herself besides the housekeeping. He hadn't been stingy with that, but she wasn't one to skimp here and there in order to line her own pockets. When she needed clothes she would tell him so, and he would say, 'Well, go and get what you want,' which she did, but it was always third-rate stuff, at least compared with the other wives of big business men in the town. But now she hadn't only the twenty-two thousand pounds for the house, she had the rent from the flats in the two houses in Milden Place, and the rents came to close on thirty pounds a week.

He had been generous at the last, giving her the three houses. She supposed she had Paul to thank for that, for he had done the bargaining: for an empty life – payment, three houses.

The day after tomorrow they'd all be gone, separated for good. Arlette, Paul and Lizzie were going out of her life as irrevocably as Rod and Sam had gone. Aye, and Frances and Dave, because her snooty daughter had moved into Newcastle only last week, Helen and Trevor had been gone this past month to Hexham. It had all been too much for that little upstart, Trevor. Now there were only Willie and Nancy left, and in the bungalow where she was going to live she would be at one end of the town and they at the other.

But these last separations had all been quiet, without heartbreak, unlike the one this afternoon when Liz went in. But in a way she'd be glad when Liz was safely tucked away, locked away, for she weighed heavy on her conscience. If she hadn't made her promise to tell that young fellow her intentions none of this would have happened, at least they wouldn't have been thrown into the river and Sam wouldn't have died . . . But there, God's ways were strange.

Elizabeth's presence had tormented her since she had come out of hospital for she neither smiled nor laughed any more. Of course one didn't expect her to laugh under the circumstances, though a smile now and again would have been in order, but her face was set like a marble statue in a church. Indeed sometimes she put her in mind of such an effigy for she looked like someone already dead.

She had said to Father Armstrong, 'Ask her if she is sure, if her mind's still that way,' and he replied, 'She's sure.'

She shouldn't have been going in until the beginning of next year but she had asked to be taken in earlier. She had not returned to school after the holidays and her days were spent in helping Annie, or sitting in her room reading, reading the lives of the saints, the gospels, the tortures that the martyrs underwent. When Maggie looked at these books she shook her head and said to herself, Oh my God! But didn't know exactly why she was saying it, only that she thought, She's so young for all this.

Then tomorrow, Arlette was leaving. She was going off with Paul, and it didn't seem right. It was right that she should marry again, but she wasn't going to marry Paul, at least not yet she said; the very thought of marriage terrified her. At first she was going off on her own just as she had intended doing on that fateful Monday morning, but Paul had apparently worn her down. He was persistent was Paul; if he had been as persistent in his vocation he would have been a priest by now. That's what she thought was wrong about it, about them, for in her mind he was a priest, he simply hadn't taken the vows that's all. She had said as much to him just the other day, and he had come back with arguments that baffled her. He had wanted her to believe that his leanings towards the Church had come about because he was fascinated by the paraphernalia of the services, drugged by the incense, the Latin, and the holiness he attributed to all priests. He had said that if he'd had a real vocation the love of a woman would have appeared as merely a temptation set by the devil, and he would have had the strength to conquer it.

She looked round the room at the open cases and the blue velvet dress and coat lying on top of the largest one. She had never thought to see the coat again, and she had never wanted to see it again, but it had arrived the morning following the night when Rod had left the house, or, as she reminded herself when her ego was at its lowest, the night she had thrown him out. Anyway, the coat had arrived neatly packed, addressed to Mrs Gallacher, Savile House, The Rise, Felburn, nothing else. She had thought, I'll give it away. But who would she give it to? It would fit no-one in her family and she knew no-one outside that it would be of any use to either. Who did she know who would wear a thing like that unless they were going to a fancy dress ball or . . . a duke's musical evening?

She went out of the room and was crossing the landing to the bathroom when she saw Arlette and Paul in the hall below. They had just come in and they looked up towards her and Paul said, 'We're back.'

She nodded at them, then went on to the bathroom.

In the hall Arlette looked at Paul, then bowed her head and walked down the short passage to the morning-room, and there she turned swiftly to him and said under her breath, 'Paul, she's upset. I think you should stay with her, at least for a time. I've told you I'll be all right.'

Gently now he took her by the shoulders and he stared into her face for some seconds before he spoke. Then, his tone low and urgent, he said, 'Arlette, Arlette, we've been over this. I'm not staying with her. Anyway, there are only two bedrooms in the bungalow.' He closed his eyes and shook his head. 'I know I could get a flat, but I'm not going to. It's arranged, isn't it? It's arranged the way we want it. Anyway, darling, darling, don't you realise that nothing or no-one can keep us apart now? If—' he just prevented himself from saying, 'If I gave up God for you then I can give up my mother' '—if you never marry me,' he went on, 'it won't matter as long as I can be with you. And—' he moved his head slowly – 'you don't want anyone else.'

She stared lovingly back into his face. Then she said, 'She's shocked in so many ways. She's shocked because . . . because you love me, but more so I think because I . . . we're going to live together. She can't understand why, if I care for you, I can't marry you, at least, not . . . not yet.' This fact also shocked some part of herself and once more she asked the question why, if she loved him, she wouldn't agree to marry him. And although the answer was in her mind she would not let it have voice, she would not say, 'In him runs the same blood as in Sam.' Sam was loving and tender once, but marriage, like the breaking of a spell, had ripped the outer skin off him and showed the wild beast. She couldn't risk that again. If, she reasoned, she found after living with Paul they weren't suited – she used this term to replace the one that spelled out 'unnatural traits' – then he had no power to hold her, she would not have to endure torture a second time. She knew now her brain would never withstand another Sam, she'd become demented. She had thought amid the long silence following that terrible morning that she was going into madness and the horror of it was still on her. No, she could not risk a second Sam and only time would prove what her heart kept telling her, that Paul was no Sam.

Anyway, living with Paul or marrying him, staying in Felburn or leaving it, the family was no more, for from Willie down to Lizzie they were condemning her. At first, each of them had had difficulty in accepting the fact that Sam had been abnormal. Even when he had tried to kill Lizzie and Mr Portman, not one of them would totally accept that anyone in their family could be capable of behaviour that stemmed from madness.

But as she had struggled back from that terrible border-land over which Sam had tried to thrust her, their concern for her seemed to prove that they did believe what their brother had done, and had been doing for years before their mother had witnessed it. But this attitude lasted only until they knew for a certainty that Paul, their reserved brother, their aloof brother, their brother who wouldn't soil his hands accepting nicked goods, was proposing to go off with her, live with her. The very fact that he had always been in love with her seemed to them to be something more dirty than any act Sam had ever per- petrated. In fact their sympathy swung back to Sam, and she knew they were now saying among themselves that perhaps Sam had had cause after all for the way he had acted. Lesser things than that had turned a man's brain.

Of them all, she knew that Willie was the most bitter against Paul, and she guessed it wasn't simply because Paul was going away with her but because, as Willie had said, Paul had downed his own, he had gone behind their backs and shown them up in the paper.

The lines, 'They fell off a lorry', had stung him and the fact that Paul was the writer, Lacker, had roused his hatred and he wouldn't come near the house if he thought Paul was in.

Truly the family had broken up, but what hurt her most was the break between herself and Maggie.

She leant her head against Paul and relaxed in the gentle pressure of his arms. The die was cast; she was about to start a new life; as Paul was . . . as Lizzie was . . . as Mam was.

And Dad? No-one mentioned Dad; it was as if he too had died and was buried.

Two o'clock that afternoon Maggie went with Elizabeth to the convent. She had been in the convent a number of times before, at least in the school side of it. She had laughed with the nuns, even joked with them, but had always sat mute before the Mother Superior.

Today she went across a courtyard, down a long stone corridor to a part that she had never seen. A smiling nun opened a door to them and welcomed them, then led the way to a sparsely furnished room and asked them to wait, and they were left sitting looking at each other.

There was an indescribable pain in Maggie's heart. She had experienced all kinds of pain during the last three months but this was like nothing she had experienced before. She put her hand out and gripped her child's, because that's all she was, this tall, thin wisp of a girl, she was a child, but seventeen, she mightn't know her own mind. She said in a low rush, 'Liz, listen to me. There's still time. I . . . I won't mind, honest to God I won't mind if you don't want to go through with it. I'm telling you . . . '

Elizabeth looked back at her mother with dry eyes. That was another strange thing about her, since the accident she hadn't cried, she who was given to tears; any hurt, any sadness penetrated the thin skin to the sensitiveness below, and the tear ducts responded. That was until she awakened in hospital to find herself still alive. It was in the middle of the night when a nurse came to her and she had asked her, 'Is he dead?' and the nurse had tucked the sheet around her chin and answered, 'No, dear, he's all right.' And she had gone to sleep knowing that there was nothing more to cry for.

She said now to Maggie, 'It's all right, Mam, don't worry, this is what I've got to do.' Her face was straight, unsmiling, not sad, not happy, a neutral look, an unreal look.

Maggie sat back in her seat and said, 'Oh, lass! Oh lass!'

The nun came back into the room and led them down another corridor and into another room, and there was the Mother Superior, who took Elizabeth's hand and smiled at her and drew her to her side, drew her into another world, leaving Maggie in this one, staring dumbly at her daughter and regretting with every fibre in her that she had let the last comfort in her life go, for she knew that if she had pressed her earlier Elizabeth would have stayed with her. She could have convinced her that her own need at this time was greater than God's.

She was never to remember what the Mother Superior said to her, she only knew that Elizabeth kissed her and clung to her. Then she was walking blindly back down the corridor, out of the grey stone house, across the courtyard, through the school and into the street; and she was alone as she had never been in her life before.

Part Five

CHAPTER ONE

THE NEW LIFE

She had been in the bungalow six weeks. After the house it appeared to her like a little box, but this she didn't mind, she wanted to be enclosed. She wished a dozen times a day, and most of the long nights, that she were enclosed for ever in a box, not feeling, not thinking, not remembering.

Willie and Nancy came to see her, as they had always done, on a Friday night, but things weren't the same because she wasn't the same. And they weren't the same, at least Willie wasn't. Willie was solemn now, quiet, different.

Frances had been over from Newcastle to see her twice. Dave hadn't come with her. Frances had made her uneasy, especially on her last visit ten days ago, for then she had hinted at more trouble to come. But what more trouble could befall them? They could die, each and every one of them, but at this time she didn't look upon dying as trouble, only as release.

Helen had written every week from Hexham. Both Trevor and she had got work, but Trevor wasn't happy . . . Trevor would never be happy, Maggie thought, unless he won the pools. Then he would go headlong to hell.

She'd had one letter from Paul and one from Arlette. They had obtained a flat in Kingston and Paul had started teaching in a secondary modern school, and Arlette was taking languages at a college of further education. Both the letters said they were thinking about her and would like to see her; would she consider coming down to see them for a holiday, there was a spare room?

Such was her make-up that she would as soon have thought of taking a holiday in a brothel as she would of staying in a house where her son was living with a woman he wasn't married to. She told herself she wasn't narrow, but she couldn't face that. Yet, at the same time, she asked herself, would she have thought it so wrong if Willie, Dave Walton, or Trevor Gillespie were in a similar situation? Her answer to this was that her Paul was none of the others, he had been and still was somebody different, special – he had almost been a priest.

She had dreaded New Year's Eve because New Year's Eve was a time when they had all been together. There had never been a New Year since she was married when she had been separated from one of her children . . . or her man. Even during the war. He could have been called up in '43 when he was eighteen, but he had been working in munitions. And then he had got out of his National Service too.

No, they had never been separated until now, and she didn't know how she was going to get over this day, particularly the night. But yes she did. That's why she had got the hard stuff in. Two or three glasses of hard stuff, a bottle of beer or so, a glass of wine, she'd be out like a light, the mixture would see to that. Tomorrow she'd have a head like nobody's business; but tomorrow would take care of itself, she had to take care of tonight.

She was expecting Willie, Nancy and the children this afternoon. They were coming for tea after they had done their shopping. There had been no mention of their staying to see the New Year in.

But it was around eleven in the morning when Willie came in the back door. She was standing in the little kitchen with Annie, and Annie was saying for the hundredth time since they had come to the bungalow, 'Talk about swinging a cat! Take a deep breath and you'll bounce off the walls.' They both turned and looked at Willie, and after a moment's pause Maggie said quickly, 'What's the matter, you under the weather?'

'Aye, I suppose you could say that.'

'I've just made some tea,' said Annie; 'it's bitter out. Or would you rather have coffee?'

'Anything, anything,' he said walking past her and into the eighteen by twelve foot room, which served as both dining- and sitting-room.

When Willie stood with his back to the fire, his hands on his buttocks, his palms outwards to the flames, his eyes cast down looking at the hearth-rug, she said, 'What is it now?'

'You might ask!' He raised his eyes to hers. His face looked drawn, old, like that of a man over forty and he'd only had his twenty-sixth birthday last week. He said now slowly, 'I should have told you afore. If I'd had my way I would have, but he said no. Well, now he can hide it no longer.' He paused. 'We're going bankrupt.'

She lowered her chin downwards and to the side while still keeping her eyes tight on his. She didn't repeat, 'Bankrupt? Is that what you said, bankrupt?' She had heard aright, he was going bankrupt. She didn't think either of Willie standing there miserable or of Dave Walton – who, although not a partner, had his livelihood tied up with theirs – but at this particular moment she thought of Rodney, and being Maggie, Mam, the mother, no matter what her previous attitude had been, she should have become overwhelmed by compassion for this terrible misfortune. That it was a terrible misfortune, she was fully aware, if not totally for Willie, then for his father, the man who had put that long ladder up against the towering battlements of Felburn society and, rung after rung, had grappled his way up it, until when he reached the top he had picked from that society a woman . . . a lady, and kicked aside the one still holding the bottom of the ladder steady for him.

'MAM!'

When her head went back and there issued from her lips a rumbling chuckle like an echo coming up from a deep well and, her mouth wide, her tongue wagging, she laughed, Willie again exclaimed, as if in horror, 'Mam!' But she continued to laugh, and the sound closed her ears to something Annie was saying as she stood within the doorway, the tea tray in her hand. She laughed until Willie's voice penetrated her unholy joy as he bawled, 'FOR GOD'S SAKE, MAM!'

As her laughter subsided she passed her hand over each cheek and wiped the tears away, and Willie said in a trembling voice, ' 'Tisn't like you; you were never the one to hold spite, or be vindictive.'

'No.' She was still shaking with her mirth as she sat down by the side of the table and supported her head in the palm of her hand, and she repeated, 'No, I was never the one to be vindictive, but times have changed, lad, times have changed.' She took out her handkerchief and wiped her face, then said, 'Well, go on; I'm listening.'

'If this is going to be your attitude I want no more of it.'

'Don't worry, I've had me fun. When did it happen?'

He took the cup of tea from Annie's hand and helped himself to four teaspoonfuls of sugar before he said, 'These things don't just happen, they cover time, a long time. It was the Morley Estate that was the final blow. But we've been having trouble on the Rollingdon one for the past year or more, slacking, thieving, stuff being nicked. It was the ganger there who was the trouble, but the men were for him and we couldn't do much about it. But . . . but we

234

would have weathered the lot if Dad could have extended his loan. He went to three banks; they all said no.'

He now banged the cup down on to the corner of the table and the tea splashed upwards and into the saucer and on to the fancy cloth. He did not apologise but turned away and marched to the window and back again, his fist clenched and wagging before his face as if threatening himself. Then he ground out between his teeth, 'That bloody woman! That bloody bitch!'

On this Annie turned and walked into the kitchen, and Maggie waited for him to go on. When he didn't, she forced herself to ask, 'What's she got to do with this?'

'What's she got to do with it?' He looked at her over his shoulder. 'What hasn't she got to do with it! Everything, every damn thing; or at least her man has. There's different ways of killing a cat besides drowning it. You can choke it for instance, and that's what he's done to us; he's choked every avenue that would have been of help. And the others are like a lot of sheep. No—' he made a spitting movement with his mouth '—rats! When she showed she wasn't having anything more to do with Dad now that things had come into the open they scuttled from him just like rats from a sinking ship.'

She was staring at the back of his head as he stood looking down into the fire and she made herself ask, 'When did she leave him?'

He turned and looked at her, then said quietly, 'Almost straight after he left home; she was one of those who didn't mind an affair on the side, but nothing must sully the name of de Ferrier. I know Dad's acted like a swine, and I was for killin' him meself, but she was a clever woman. She's been clever for years along that line. One of the things he's had to suffer is the knowledge that Pearce and Bailey were his predecessors; the difference was, they were sensible, they didn't want to make an honest woman of her, so to speak,

235

and so everything was cushy and comfortable, and they got positions where they could call the tune. Second fiddles to her man perhaps, but nevertheless they were kept in the orchestra . . . and what they play this town dances to. My God! the things I've learned recently . . . And then our Paul. That bloody snot writing to the papers about falling off a lorry. A few pairs of stockings, socks, a jumper, he would have exposed me and all of us for that, while at the same time there were things going on in this town on the council and in every blooming tin-pot industry you could mention, trickery and wangling, thousands changing hands, and them getting medals pinned on them for it . . . God Almighty! And they say the tax men are cute. Blind, bloody blind the lot of them.'

She now made another laughing sound but kept it in her throat. It was funny how her mind was working these days. She was thinking that here was their Willie yelling about the tricksters yet it wasn't only the day or yesterday that he had been aware of this, for he and his Dad and the firm had done their share of it, thrived on it in fact. She remembered the presents, the money presents. Fifty pounds. One time it was a hundred that Rod had forked out, and you didn't give presents like that if you didn't expect something in return, and not little things at that . . . And then that bit he had said earlier on about the men thieving on the Rollingdon Estate. When he did it himself it was fiddling, when other people did it it was stealing.

She, too, had learned a lot lately, perhaps because she'd had time to think. And now she had something to think about, he had gone bust. Well, well! The big fellow had gone bust, and here was she with more money than she knew what to do with. After she had paid for the bungalow she had put eighteen thousand into building societies at five per cent, and this was to bring her in nine hundred pounds a year. Just think of it!

As if Willie had gauged her thoughts, he said, 'You must give him credit for one thing, he saw you all right first.'

'So he should.' She was on the defensive now.

'I'm not saying he shouldn't, but I'll tell you this. He hung on until the two houses were fixed for you. I mean the deeds through and everything settled because if he hadn't they would have been swallowed up an' all.' He could have added, ' . . . but they'd have cut down his losses.'

She asked now, 'What's he down?'

'A hundred thousand or so.'

'My God! A hundred thousand.'

'It's nothing, it's not much, taking everything into consideration. If we'd had a break he'd have weathered it. There's forty houses almost completed on the Rollingdon end, and they would have been done if it hadn't been for those blasted lazy swine. Yet they're not the stumbling block, it's de Ferrier, the pasty-faced bastard!' He was marching up and down again. 'Can't keep his wife so he . . . ' He stopped suddenly and swung his head downwards. Then, after remaining silent for a moment or so, he looked at her again and said, 'Some New Year.'

She wet her lips, one over the other, before she asked, 'What are you going to do?'

'Oh.' His body slumped, and he answered, 'Start again, I suppose.'

She went up to him now and said softly, 'There's eighteen thousand in the building societies, you could get going on that.'

'What!' He drew his head away from her as if she was aiming to strike him. 'Ah, Mam.' He gave a shaky laugh. 'Do you know what you're saying? Do you want him to lay me out? Because that is what would happen if I touched a penny of it. But . . . but thanks all the same.' He put his hand out and took hers, and said again, 'Thanks. I won't forget that you offered it, but knowing the struggle he's had to keep them at bay until the deeds of those flats came back, aw my! And you know something else? I think the fact of you knowing about this has affected him more than the town's reaction.'

'It would, wouldn't it?' she said with bitterness in her voice now. 'The big fella. The big head gone bust. He wouldn't want me to know that. He wouldn't want to give me the chance to gloat.'

'You're not gloating, are you, Mam?' It was a soft enquiry and she lowered her eyes and stared at the floor before saying, 'I don't know.' Then, 'Yes, I do,' she said. 'I'll tell no damned lie about it. I'm shoutin' inside meself, "Serve him damned well right, it's justice." One doesn't often live to see justice done, but in this case I have.'

He took his hand from hers now and, walking from her, said, 'Aye, I suppose so; but if we all got our deserts I wonder where we'd land up?'

'Willie.' He turned to her again.

'I . . . I can't help being bitter. He . . . he brought me low; he made me feel like nothing; scum; he said I was a big fat ignorant slob. I never felt a big fat ignorant slob until then, and since . . . well, I haven't seen meself as anything else.'

He came swiftly back to her and, putting his arm around her, kissed her, and his voice was thick as he said, 'You're my mother, and I've always thought you one of the best. Happy New Year, Mam.' He kissed her again, then turned quickly away and left her with the tears pouring down her face.

The church bells were ringing in the New Year, the hooters were blowing; in the town there would be people dancing round the old Memorial all singing and cheering, but here, in the living-room of the end bungalow, in The Crest, Balham Road, there was no sound except when

238

they put their glasses back on the table. As the last echo of the church bells died away they looked at each other but didn't wish a Happy New Year.

When Maggie began to cry she pushed the tears from her cheeks with the side of her thumb, and the whimpering sound in the back of her throat changed to laughter and she said, 'Drink up, Annie. Drink up.'

They had been drinking more or less steadily since eleven o'clock. Maggie had had two glasses of whisky, a pint bottle of Guinness and two glasses of wine, and now as she sipped at her third glass of whisky her laughter mounted. Swaying forward, she leant across the little table towards Annie to where, glassy-eyed, she sat lost in the armchair, and said, 'You know what I'm thinkin', Annie? You know what I'm thinkin' about at this minute? . . . The party, the musical soirée.'

'No! Maggie.'

'Aye. Aye, I am, Annie. I'm right back there, an' I can even feel me damn corn givin' me gyp.' She sagged downwards and pressed the top of her slipper. 'And remember the way I was got up, Annie? Did you ever see anybody got up like me?'

'Never, Maggie, never.'

'And think what I spent, think of that money. A hundred and seventy-five pounds!' She drained her glass, then half filled it again from the bottle to her hand. 'And those creeps on the platform. He played like this, Annie. Look; look, this is how he played.' She pushed some of the bottles aside, almost upsetting them; then using the table as an imitation piano she bent her body over it and waved her hands wildly up and down. 'Tha's . . . tha's how he played, Annie . . . just like that.' Again she gave a demonstration. Then leaning back in her chair, she now cried, 'And the fellow with the cello, the blown up fiddle. Squawk, squawk, squawk.' Her knees wide apart, she was

239

now imitating the cellist. Then staggering to her feet, she struck a pose and on a high and full throated note she burst into song. But what she sang in imitation of Madam Craig was O Salutaris.

'O Salutaris Hostia, quae coeli panis ostium; Bella premunt hostilia. Da robur, fer auxilium.'

Her Latin was pronounced as she had learnt it at school. It would have made a Latin master cringe, and the fact that she was caricaturing the singer yet using the hymn that opens the Benediction, would, at any other time, have appeared as sacrilege to them both. But now Annie was rolling in her chair.

Following this, she started a perilous parade up and down the room. Strutting between the furniture, she demonstrated how different people she could remember from that evening had walked and talked. Then bending over Annie's chair, she laughed down at her as she cried, 'There was one snotty-nosed piece – you know the type, you see them in the magazines – when she opened her mouth you'd think she had a lump of paste in it. Honest, honest to God. And him, him the Duke, weak-kneed little squirt, he talked to her an' called her Ida.' She now did a jig, singing, 'Ida, Ida, aren't you a little snider.' Then stopping abruptly, the laughter leaving her she said, 'You know what, Annie? The mornin', I'm goin' to sit down an' I'm goin' to write to him. Duke or no Duke . . . I am, I am.'

Annie flapped her hand at her and spluttered, 'You'll have to learn to spell, Maggie.'

'I can spell when I want. Don't you forget it. Oh—' she backed away and flopped into her seat, '—if ever there was a snobby snot, he was one. But I told him, didn't I, Annie? I told him. I told him what he was. By God! I did.' She now became quiet and, her head moving slowly from side to side and her voice changing, she muttered thickly, 'But . . . but I should never have done it, Annie, should I?

I should never have done it. I let meself down a ton. An' not only me, but Rod. He's no good is Rod, he's a nowt, a nowt; but I let him down, an' I let meself down. Aye . . . ' She pulled herself forward on to the edge of the chair and, putting her elbows on her knees, she dropped her face into her hands and now her whole body gave one great heave before the tears burst from her eyes and an agonised sound was wrenched up from the tormented depths of her being, and came out through her mouth in a prolonged wail, which finally broke itself up in disjointed words. 'Liz. Our Liz. In there, for life. Loved that bloke, she did, she did. Liz. Aw Liz.'

'Don't, Maggie.' Annie was standing wavering in front of her. 'Come on to bed, lass. Come on to bed. Forget about it. Come on an' sleep it off. You can't better none of it. Come on, come on, lass.'

It was a good five minutes later when Annie got her up out of the chair, and erratically they made their way to their rooms, Annie to fall into a dead sleep almost straightaway, Maggie to lie fully dressed on the bed alternately crying and dozing until the early morning.

The drinking bout on New Year's Eve began a pattern for Maggie. The hangover Annie had on New Year's Day deterred her from further indulgence; she might have a glass of gin or a bottle of beer in the evening but that was as far as she would go. Not so Maggie; each evening now she would sit late by herself drinking, drinking and thinking. But she no longer cried. Sometimes she would not rise in the morning until eleven o'clock, and as the weeks went on she was no sooner out of bed than she was longing for the night to come when she could have a drink.

She did not drink during the early evening in case anybody should drop in, though few dropped in now. Willie and Nancy brought the children every Saturday.

They were now living in Gateshead where Willie had been fortunate enough to get a start as a costing clerk with a building firm. Some weeks he would drive over of an evening by himself. It could be any evening, and so she never started to indulge until about nine o'clock. But one evening he came at half-past nine, by which time she was starting on her third whisky. She hadn't time to hide the evidence before he was in the room, and he looked hard at her for a moment. She made an effort to pull herself together and talk about the things they usually talked about, the bairns, their school, Nancy coping in a small flat, and the awful weather. But this night the whisky had brought down her guard and all of a sudden she said, 'Where is he?'

'Dad?'

She didn't answer but continued to stare at him; and then he said, 'I don't know. After the business of the Official Receiver was over he said he was moving out. He wouldn't tell me where he was making for. They would likely know, he'd have to leave an address, but I didn't pry. He . . . he wants to be left alone . . . Why do you ask?'

'Why do I ask?' Her voice was thick. 'Well, you'd ask after a mangy dog wouldn't you, if you'd once fed that mangy dog? Stands to reason.'

'Would you have him back?'

She almost sprang out of her chair and her voice was loud. 'No, begod! No, not if he was dying. Have him back after having her on the side for years! What do you think I am? I might be a big fat ignorant slob but somewhere in all this bulk—' she thumped her stomach '—is a little bit of pride, just a little bit, and I'm going to hang on to it. Have him back you say!'

He had left almost immediately after this but before leaving the room he had looked at the bottle and said,

'I'd go careful on that if I were you, it leads nowhere but downwards.'

Two days later Frances had come to see her. She had not remarked upon her changed appearance but her look had been plain enough. It said, 'You have let yourself go, haven't you?' She didn't like their Frances, that was another thing she had learnt . . .

It was a bitter snowy night towards the end of February. She was sitting before a blazing fire that could not warm her, for she was shivering inside, waiting for the moment when Annie would go to bed and she could take a drop. Not that Annie didn't know that she was indulging, but somehow she didn't like drinking in front of her.

Annie was sitting at the opposite side of the hearth reading the paper. Suddenly she said, 'Well I never! Here's that Madam Hevell that you went to, advertising.'

'Oh yes?'

'She wants a model.'

'A model?'

'Aye, it says here: Wanted, a person of smart appearance, to model outsize exclusive gowns.' Annie laughed now and looking over the paper, said in a tone that was slightly derisive, 'If you hadn't put on so much lately you could have had a shot at it.'

'Aye, I could, couldn't I?'

Maggie looked straight back at Annie and their eyes held. She saw that Annie was looking at her with the same expression as had been on Frances's face, pity and scorn mixed, though in Annie's look there was more of the former.

Shortly after Annie went to bed, she got up and brought the bottle from the sideboard and poured herself out a good measure. She shuddered as it burnt its way down into her stomach. With her hand on the bottle about to pour a second measure she stopped, then looked down at herself. Her breasts were hanging slack, her stomach was bulging, she was wearing an old pair of corselettes. She must have put on a stone during the last few weeks. She went to the mirror over the mantelpiece and peered at her face. She'd always had a good skin, clear and cream-tinted; now it was blotchy and there were bags under her eyes. She stuck out her tongue. It was coated white to the tip, and the sight made her feel sick.

Helplessly, she sat down again and, resting her elbow on the table, laid her head on her hand. As she sat thus, she looked down on the paper that Annie had left there. On the front page was a picture of the Mayor and Mayoress and their guests at the Annual Ball. Standing next to the Mayor was Mrs de Ferrier, slim, elegant, smiling with a thin superior smile. The eyes seemed to come out of the page and appraise her with a combination of the expressions she had seen on the faces of Willie, Frances and Annie, only intensified a thousandfold. She took her fist and banged it down on to the paper; then as if she had been prodded out of the chair she got up swiftly and went into her room.

Standing before the long mirror, she looked at herself. She was a big, fat hulk. She was forty-four and she had a body on her like some old trollop from Bog's End. Swiftly now she tore off her clothes and, going to the bottom drawer, she took out the foundation that had been made for her eight months ago. With an effort she got into it, but struggle as she might she couldn't get the zip to fasten over her stomach. Her flesh sticking out through the gap was an embarrassment to her; it looked indecent. She tore off the garment, then got into her nightdress and into bed and lay with her face half buried in the pillow. But she did not cry; nor, when she could not sleep, did she get up and help herself to the bottle . . .

During the following week she hardly ate anything, so little in fact that she began to worry Annie, but each night

244

she helped herself to one glass of whisky. She had to have that she told herself, no more, no less. The second week she endeavoured to make the measure less each night.

It was on the Friday night of this week when Annie was once again reading the weekly paper that she exclaimed, 'It's still in! That Madam Hevell's still got her advert in for a model. She must be finding it a job to get suited. You would have thought with all the fat lasses around the Tyne she'd have had somebody by now.' She stopped and looked half apologetically at Maggie, who said, 'It's all right, me skin's thick.'

'I wasn't meaning anything.'

'I know, I know; don't be so touchy.'

'Well, don't you think it's funny she hasn't been suited?'

'No, because I reckon you want more than a big figure to be a model, outsize or otherwise.'

'Yes, I suppose you're right.'

Later the same evening she tried the foundation on again and for the first time in weeks she smiled at herself in the mirror as the zip slipped over her stomach, perhaps not with the same ease it did when she had first worn it, but it fastened. Well, that was a start, she told herself; she was coming up out of the bog.

On the following Monday morning, when the wild idea came into her head, she looked at the Friday night's paper and for the first time read Madam Hevell's advertisement and knew that the idea was no spontaneous thing bred of the moment, the seed had been set a fortnight ago when Annie first read it out to her. But she was saying nothing to nobody, she wasn't going to make a fool of herself again, she would just see what came of it.

She didn't really expect anything to come of it but the fact that she was willing to have a shot at it meant something. She looked at her face in the mirror. If she could only get a start in a line like that, wouldn't it show them, the lot of them, every damned one of her family . . . but most of all, aw yes, most of all, HIM. Wherever he was at this moment, she wanted to give the lie back to him, to ram his words back down his throat, not in the old way by bawling and shouting but in a kind of refined way that would in itself prove that she was no big, fat ignorant slob.

'Where you off to?' Annie asked, when she saw her dressed for outdoors, and in her best coat and hat at that.

'I thought—' She turned her back and swallowed. 'I thought I would look in on Frances; I feel I want a trip of some sort. I haven't been out of the house for ages.'

'Aye.' Annie nodded at her. 'That's what you should do, go and see Frances. Take a trip, that's right. Will you be back for dinner?'

'I shouldn't think so.' She smiled. 'If she doesn't offer me any I'll go to a café.'

'Do that. Enjoy yourself, go on. Ta-rah then.'

'Ta-rah, Annie.'

Her legs trembled as she went down the path and into the road for she knew Annie was watching her. They trembled when she got on the bus; they trembled when she got on the train to Newcastle. They trembled all the way up Northumberland Street and down various side streets and the trembling had taken possession of her whole body when she stopped outside the small window of Madam Hevell's that showed one suit, a pair of shoes, a handbag and a hat. She gulped deeply, put her shoulders back, then opened the door and stepped on to the deep pile carpet.

A slim, elegant young assistant came towards her smiling. 'Good morning, Madam; can I help you?'

'I . . . I'd like to see Madam Hevell.'

'Oh yes. What name will I say?'

'Mrs Gallacher.'

The girl was new to her, she hadn't been here when she was in the shop before. She waited, looking nervously around the rose and gilt room. Then through the curtains at the far end Madam Hevell came towards her, her plump hand extended. 'Ah, Mrs Gallacher. How nice to see you. Come this way. Come this way.'

She wanted to say, 'Now look I'm not going to buy anything.' She wanted to explain why she was here, but Madam Hevell was talking rapidly. 'I have thought a lot about you, Mrs Gallacher; you did not return to tell me how you enjoyed the soirée.' As if she would. Madam Hevell knew all about the soirée and at this moment she was really amazed to see Mrs Gallacher for she also knew, through her ladies in Felburn, that Mrs de Ferrier had played the dirty on this woman's husband, shooting off like an astronaut for the moon when things on the Felburn planet got too hot for her. She thrived on intrigue did Mrs Rosamund de Ferrier. She wondered what kind of wear Mrs Gallacher had come for. From the look of her, outdoor, she thought, for her coat had peg written all over it. She must have money, but from where? She had heard they were separated and that he was in difficulties. She said now, 'A cup of coffee? I am sure you could do with a cup of coffee. Have you come straight from Felburn?'

'Yes; and thank you, a cup of coffee would be very acceptable.'

'Justine, ask Marianne to bring coffee for two.'

The girl bent her head almost obsequiously, saying, 'Yes, Madam.'

'Ah now!' Madam Hevell sat her short body down on the edge of a gilt chair. 'You are well?'

'Yes, yes, thank you.' Maggie smiled nervously. She had liked this woman; during the fittings she had found her very amusing. She liked to hear her talk; although she spoke English well, her French-Belgian extraction gave

247

a quaintness to her speech. But she thought, I shouldn't have accepted her coffee, she thinks I've come to buy; I'd better get it over.

'Madam Hevell.'

'Yes, Mrs Gallacher?'

'I feel I'd better tell you right away. I . . . I haven't come to buy anything.'

'No? Perhaps then just to look? Very well, very well, we don't charge for looking. We like that you should look. Look all you want . . . '

'Nor to look, Madam Hevell. You see, I'm . . . well, it's this way. You had an advert in the paper, you wanted . . . ' She stopped when she saw the smile slip from Madam Hevell's face and the black eyebrows move upwards and the lips form themselves into a silent whistle.

'Ah! Ah! The model for the outsize. Ah yes! Ah yes! Well, well.' The smile was creeping back to her face. 'No harm done, no harm done, Mrs Gallacher.'

'Have . . . have you been suited?'

Madam Hevell rose from her chair, joined her hands together, wagged them in front of her and looked about her sumptuous fitting-room as if someone else were going to supply the answer to this. Then her small body became still. Her face solemn now, she looked down at Maggie and said, 'No, no, I have not become satisfied because, you see, there are special requirements for such as this.'

'Yes, yes, I understand.' Maggie nodded apologetically and made to rise, and at this moment Justine came through the curtain bearing a tray on which were a silver coffee jug, matching milk jug and sugar basin, together with two cups. Madam turned to her as if with relief and said, 'Ah. Ah, this is nice. Just there, Justine, just there.' Then, going to the tray, she cocked her head on one side and asked of Maggie, 'You have it black or white?'

'White . . . er white, please.'

After she had poured the coffee Madam Hevell sat down again and asked, 'You're in need of employment?'

'Well . . . well no, not really.' Maggie put her head first to one side, then to the other. 'I have plenty of money . . . what I mean is—' she closed her eyes for a moment '—I've got more than enough for my needs.'

'Oh, that is good, good.' Madam Hevell smiled widely.

'It's only . . . well, I need a job . . . occupation, and I haven't been trained for anything. Oh—' she put out her hand apologetically '—I know you need training to be a model, but I thought, well perhaps I could go in for it. I wouldn't mind paying to be shown . . . ' She broke off lamely here and they looked at each other.

Madam Hevell's mind was wont to work rapidly; it was doing so at the moment, even perhaps working overtime. She was badly in need of a model, and one of about this woman's size, for unhappily she had come to know that by the time the men made money, real money, their wives seemed to have expanded. There seemed to be a majority of careless ones, and they would pay the earth to appear a stone lighter without sacrificing their cakes and sweets and titbits. But there, you needed more than bulk to fashion clothes. Yet this woman here had herself suggested that she would pay to be trained; none of the applicants who had so far applied had made such a suggestion. Moreover, she couldn't start her Flout Street branch until she had a suitable person, who, besides modelling, could act as a representative for the . . . she would not even think the term, second-hand garments . . . off-models.

'Stand up.'

'Wha . . . Oh!' Maggie put the cup down so quickly that it rattled in the saucer; then she stood up.

'Walk to the curtain.'

Maggie walked to the curtain.

'Relax. Walk up and down the room.'

She willed herself to relax and move her arms as she had seen the models doing on the telly, but at one point her two arms went forward simultaneously and she stopped. Madam Hevell laughed and said, 'It's all right, it's all right, don't worry. Sit down.'

Maggie sat down.

'Stand up.'

Maggie stood up.

'You're light on your feet, that is something, exceptionally light.'

Maggie smiled.

'If I consented to train you myself personally, would you work for six months inclusive, I mean with the training, without a salary?'

'Oh yes, yes.' Maggie beamed as if Madam Hevell was bestowing some great favour on her, as indeed she was, though to no-one else would she have dared to suggest six months without pay.

'Well now, I think we may come to some arrangement.'

'Oh! Madam Hevell.' Maggie's body folded up, only to be brought stiff and upright again by Madam Hevell saying sharply, 'Now, now, no matter what the emotions, do not become a concertina. You know . . . ' She now demonstrated with her hands going in and out and up and down, and Maggie laughed nervously as she said, 'Yes, Madam. No, Madam.' She felt like a young girl going after a first job. It was strange but she had never been interviewed for a job in her life; her mother had gone to see about her being set on at the factory.

Madam Hevell was talking rapidly now. 'I am opening another business in Flout Street. It is not in the form of a shop, but an apartment, and it is for, well slightly used garments . . . we refer to them as off-models, you understand?'

Maggie nodded at this. It was a definite motion.

'The entire stock are garments from the upper . . . very wealthy people . . . you know. And not from this part of the country . . . no, no. But they're all models; quite a number of them are on the large size. What will be required of you will be to wear these models, interest my clients in them; these are the ones who cannot pay the price asked here.' She hunched her shoulders and spread her hands wide and looked about her. 'But they are clients with taste and who want to look well dressed and yet have no fear that the garments will be recognised in this part of the country. You understand?'

All Maggie did was to nod again.

'I may say that some of these garments originally cost . . . oh—' again she shrugged her shoulders '—twice as much as anything I have in my establishment. But my agent buys them reasonable, very reasonable, and I sell them reasonable, reasonable for the quality they are. But Flout Street will not only be a model agency it will also be a service; the stock sizes will sell themselves but the outsizes are best demonstrated. The model may sometimes have to be taken to the house of a client. In this way many sales can be effected and a personal relationship brought about between the client and me . . . us. You understand?'

'Yes! Yes! It sounds very interesting.'

'Stand up.'

Maggie was already an employee, she stood up smartly.

'Turn round. Ah yes!' Madam Hevell now placed her hands on both Maggie's hips and pressed them tightly, then said, 'You could do with at least seven pounds off here, and more off the stomach. Your legs, your legs are perfect. If you will learn to use them right then there'll be nothing to worry about there.' She now placed her hands under Maggie's breasts, saying, 'These will do; they're very fashionable at the moment. Make up your mind to lose at least half a stone in the next two weeks, then gradually get it down to a stone. I should say then you will be just right . . . Now, Mrs Gallacher, when can you begin?'

Maggie drew in a long breath and let it out again before she said, 'Oh, anytime, Madam Hevell; my time's me own.'

'Well then.' Madam Hevell was all business now. 'Well then, I think you should come here and stay in the background. Those are work-rooms and cutting-rooms.' She pointed to the wall to the right of her. 'There is also another large fitting room. There I can put you through . . . well, through your paces as they say; that is in between times when I'm not busy with a client. Other times you can watch Annette. You remember Annette? Ah yes; she helped to dress you. Well then, you can watch her at work with a client. You will pick up a great deal from Annette. It may take a month, two, or even longer before you are ready in any way. It all depends on your adaptability, you understand?'

'Yes, Madam, and . . . and I'll try my very best.'

Now Madam Hevell smiled. 'I am sure you will, Mrs Gallacher.' Then abruptly the smile went and she said, 'Be here tomorrow at nine-thirty.'

'Oh!' Maggie gathered her bag and her gloves into her hand, then said, 'I . . . I don't know about trains. I live on the far side of Felburn now; if I'm a little late . . . '

'You haven't a car?'

'No.'

'Do you drive?'

'No; I'm sorry, I don't.'

Madam Hevell now brought her small hands to her waist and poked her chin forward as she asked, 'Could you afford a car, Mrs Gallacher?'

Maggie hesitated a moment before saying with a shaky laugh, 'Oh yes; two for that matter.'

'Indeed! Indeed. Then I should suggest that you buy a car and take lessons. In the meantime we'll say that you'll be here . . . what? Ten o'clock?'

'Yes.' Maggie was slightly dumbfounded now, and as she went towards the curtain Madam Hevell said, 'Why I suggest the car is, it will be an asset when you go to visit your clients.' Again she smiled. She was bending towards Maggie from the waist and she patted her on the shoulder as she would a child as she ended, 'Go along; you could have a very interesting time before you.'

Maggie went out into the street, but she had nearly reached the station before she came to herself. She was breathing heavily as if she had been running. She knew she was smiling. She wanted a drink, oh she did want a drink. But no, that was finished. Tea or coffee. She'd just had coffee. There was a café opposite the station; she went in and ordered a pot of tea.

She, Maggie Gallacher, the big, fat, ignorant slob, was going to be a model. Not one of them would believe it; no-one on God's earth would believe it. She couldn't believe it herself. How would she break it to them? How would she tell Annie, and Willie, and Frances? Eeh! What would their Frances say? She was nodding to herself now. What would their Frances say? Frances who had always looked down her nose at her. She would write and tell Paul and Arlette. They wouldn't believe it either, but Arlette would understand. She had a longing to see Arlette. If Arlette were here she would put her arms around her and say, 'Oh, Mam, you're just cut out for it.' That was Arlette. And Paul, too; he would be glad for her. There's nothing like a dame! That had warmed her heart. There's nothing like a dame. If only they weren't living together, if only they'd get married. And Liz. What would Liz think? She shut her mind as to what Liz would think and asked herself how she was going to break it to Annie.

253

What would be her response? Would she laugh her head off . . . ?

Annie didn't laugh her head off. She just sat down on the kitchen chair and stared up at her. What she said was, 'You're kiddin', aren't you?' and Maggie replied, 'No, I'm not kiddin'; I'm going to model for Madam Hevell. What's more, I'm going out tomorrow to buy a car, and I'm taking lessons, as many as I can get in in a week. You see, as Madam Hevell said, in a position like mine I'll need a car.'

'God Almighty!' said Annie, but there was no disparagement in her tone, only sheer unadulterated amazement.

Part Six

CHAPTER ONE

THE MODEL

It was the first Monday in March. The morning was bright; there was a nip in the air that made you bustle and step out just that little bit faster. It was the kind of day that portended good for everyone.

Margaret Gallacher looked up into the clear blue sky as she finished her grapefruit and started on her toast, and she remarked to Annie, 'This is just the morning for it; this is the kind of light Arthur likes.'

'Have another piece of toast,' said Annie; 'you can't go out on that.'

'All right, just one . . . No, no, I'd better not.' She wagged her head, then added, 'Why do you keep pressing me when you know that I mustn't have it?'

'You're getting like a lath.'

'I'd better not—' Maggie laughed up at Annie now '—or I'll lose my clients. And that would never do, would it?' She poked her face mischievously towards Annie.

'Where are you going this mornin'?'

'Along the quay in Newcastle first, to take in the bridges, and then the Scotswood Road end of all places, where they're pulling down the houses.'

Annie stopped with the teapot in her hand. 'Along there?' Her face screwed up. 'What do they want to photograph models along there for?'

'Don't ask me,' Maggie shook her head, wiped her mouth, then got to her feet. 'But he hopes to take me just at the moment one of the houses is coming down . . .

It's artistic.' She pushed Annie, and Annie laughed and said, 'We live and learn.'

'Aye, we do that.'

Maggie hurried out of the little kitchen, through the living-room and into her bedroom, and having taken off her dressing-gown she made up her face, then sat back and examined her reflection before going to a rack that stood along one wall and took up about a quarter of the room. From it she selected a russet coloured two-piece suit, and from a tray standing on top of a low chest of drawers she chose a pair of tan leather court shoes, and a bag and gloves to match.

Having dressed, she draped over her shining lacquered hair a scarf of the colour termed seared leaf yellow, then she went back into the living-room, and Annie, coming from the kitchen, stopped and said, 'Oh aye! That looks grand, but that's not an off is it?'

'An off! No, this is a Hevell, sixty-five guineas.' She walked in an exaggeratedly sedate manner down the room, then looking over her shoulder she grinned and said, 'No patter with a Hevell; now if it was an off—' She assumed a higher tone and strutting slightly, said, 'Twenty-five guineas, Madam, and very reasonable, very reasonable. It's a model by . . . Spifflico. The original price was a hundred guineas. Yes, indeed, Madam, a hundred, and it's as new, Madam, as you can see.'

'Go on with you! What time will you be back?'

'Oh, let me see.' Maggie lifted her head and thought. 'He'll take a couple of hours over the quay shooting; then we'll go to the Station Hotel for lunch . . . '

'He'll take you to the Station?'

'Oh yes, he's generous is Arthur. Anyway, he should be. He doesn't pay half here what he does in London, I understand, and he gets better pictures. Still, I'm not grumbling. Oh.' She paused. 'What time will I be back?

If things go smoothly, say four o'clock. No, half-past.'

'Frances and Dave should be coming over the night don't forget.'

'No, I won't forget. Ta-rah.' As she went out she thought, And I wish they weren't.

She always chided herself for feeling cynical when she thought of Frances but she couldn't help it, for the fact was that since her status had changed Frances had hardly been off the doorstep. Yet it was she who had laughed loudest when she had been told that her mother was going to model for Madam Hevell, and her reply had been, 'When I see pigs fly I'll believe that.' She hadn't said it to her face. She had said it to Annie, who had given her the news in the kitchen. Frances had forgotten that they weren't in Savile House any more but in a little bungalow where her voice carried.

Willie and Nancy, too, had taken a lot of convincing. Not so Helen. But then Helen had had time to get over the shock before she phoned her from Hexham. She said, 'Good for you.' And now Trevor condescended to visit her, at least once a month. Of them all, it was Trevor, she felt, who thought her changed status a flash in the pan. She always detected in his eyes the awaiting of midnight, when she would change back into Mam, and Maggie Gallacher.

If any of them had joyed with her, it had been Paul and Arlette. But then she would have expected them to, though not to make a journey from London just to congratulate her. She had loved seeing them that time. She had been less embarrassed and condemning within herself towards them than she had expected, but their happiness in each other had made her sad, for it had emphasised her own aloneness.

Now, eighteen months later, she still couldn't understand why, loving each other as they did, Arlette wouldn't consent to be married; surely she knew Paul by now. Still it was their affair and she left it at that.

And Liz. She was the one now for whom she was concerned, and only her. Although it was three months since she had last seen her, her face still haunted her. This was at the time when she was about to take her second step towards her vows. When she had asked her, 'Are you happy, lass?' she had answered, 'Yes, thank you, Mother,' like a child repeating a phrase, but her eyes had seemed steeped in sadness. And there was an expression on her daughter's face that she didn't see on the faces of the other nuns; most of them looked smiling and happy. Some of the older ones had that look of settled serenity as if they had already been given a glimpse into their future home, the home for which they had spent a lifetime preparing to enter. She had said to Father Armstrong, 'I'm worried about her,' but his reply had been in the form of a reprimand. 'Then you should come to Mass and pray for her,' he said.

She was on the pathway to the garage when the phone rang, and she went back and saw Annie at the side table with the phone in her hand. 'It's Arlette,' she said.

She took the phone from Annie and said, 'Hello there, dear.'

'Hello, Mam.'

'Hello, lass.'

'Mam.'

'Yes?'

'I've got news for you. I'm going to have a baby.'

Maggie's mouth opened, then closed. She nipped at her lip, then said, 'Oh, that's fine, lass.'

'And Mam.'

'Yes?'

'We're . . . we're going to be married.'

Maggie was now smiling down at the phone and the

smile came over in her voice as she said, 'That's even
better news, lass. Oh, I'm glad.' She swallowed deeply,
then asked, 'When?'

'Thursday.'

There was a long pause now before she asked, 'Where's
it to be?'

'In church.'

'Thank God!'

She was Margaret Gallacher, the model. She was known
all over Felburn now. She was a big fish in a little pool,
yet not such a little pool. No; it was a pool big enough to
drown people in. Yet under her new skin, under her poise,
she was still Maggie Gallacher, narrow in her views where
they touched on morality. She told herself she couldn't
help it, she was made that way. If she hadn't been, Rod
might still be with her now, but if he had been – and she
reminded herself often of this fact – she certainly wouldn't
be Margaret Gallacher the model going out at this minute
dressed as she was, to be photographed for a magazine.

'Are you there, Mam?'

'Yes, yes, lass, I'm here.'

'I never asked how you are?'

'I'm fine, on top of the world. I'm on me way to be photographed on the quay in Newcastle. It's for a magazine.'

'You're not!'

'Yes, I am.'

'Oh, Mam, it's wonderful.'

'Yes, isn't it? Funny the things that can happen in two
years. You remember when you told me how I should
walk and stretch me neck?' Arlette's laugh came to her
now, and she went on, 'Well, Madam endorses all that.
But she adds to it. Lift your rib cage, she keeps saying;
lift your rib cage. And you know, she's right. See to your
neck and your rib cage and the rest of your carcass takes
care of itself. Aye, the things you learn.'

'I wish I were near you, Mam.'

'I wish you were at that.'

'Would you like us to come that way again, Mam?' Her voice was soft, enquiring.

'Would I? Aw, lass, I would love it.'

'We were talking about it last night. Paul wants to be near you, and it goes without saying I do. We'll slip down next week and talk about it, eh?'

'Do that. Oh, that would be lovely. Wait a minute, wait a minute, I must look at my diary . . . Margaret Gallacher must consult her diary.' She laughed derisively at herself, then said, 'Tuesday and Friday I could finish early, around three; the rest of the week I'll be full up.'

'All right, dear, we'll make it Tuesday or Friday. Bye-bye, Mam. Bye-bye.'

'Bye-bye, lass. And tell Paul I'm happy for you, happy for you both. Bye-bye.'

'Annie!' She turned around. 'They're going to have a baby.'

Annie stood at the kitchen door nodding her head. 'I gathered as much. Well, you can't say they've rushed into it. And they're going to be married an' all?'

'Yes, they're going to be married.'

'Well, that'll be another weight off your mind.'

'You've said something there. But now I must fly. Ta-rah!'

'Ta-rah,' said Annie.

She felt happy, happy as she hadn't been for a long, long time. Her new job had brought into her life a feeling of excitement and pride that she had never experienced before. It hadn't brought her happiness, not as she thought of happiness, but a certain contentment, yes, and a strange fulfilment. There were times when she felt there was nothing of the old Maggie Gallacher left in her until, as a while ago, the issue had arisen of her son marrying in a church or in a registry office. It was at these times she knew that there were large remnants of herself still left, old-fashioned, environmental remnants.

Because of the parking problem in Newcastle she had arranged to meet Arthur Leonard on the quay itself, and as she turned down a side street towards the river she saw his car, and him standing beside it already waiting.

When she drew up alongside him he came and greeted her effusively in his quick-fire way. 'Ah, Margaret, had a time getting through, did you? But you're only five minutes out. Let me have a look.' He held her away with one arm. 'Ah! Yes. That's it, that's it. And it's the light for it.' He looked up into the sky, then across the river. 'There's a boat at the quay discharging into a warehouse. We're lucky, I'll get you at the warehouse doors with one or two of the fellows looking at you. Then I'll see the skipper; might get you on the gangway. Come on.'

He took her arm and led her on to the quay. As he approached the opening to the warehouse through which the men were trundling trolleys piled high with boxes, he called to a distant man, 'All right, mate?' and the man turned and looked from him to Maggie, and smiling broadly said, 'I don't see why not.' Looking back at him, Maggie returned his smile and said, 'Good morning.'

'Morning, Miss.'

Miss! On forty-six and being called Miss! The man could give her twenty years, but still to be called Miss. Her eyes twinkled at him and she said, 'Your eyesight's bad,' at which he let out a loud guffaw, then answered gallantly, 'Don't you believe it.'

The session on the quay went well and as they were leaving one bright spark called out to her, 'Doing anything the night, lass?' and she called back, 'Yes, washing the bairns,' and at this there was a great howl of laughter.

Arthur Leonard, leading her along the quay now over

the uneven planks, squeezed her arm and said, 'Margaret, my love, you know if you would come up to town you'd go like a bomb. Still, you do all right here, don't you?' She gave him a sidelong glance and with mock seriousness answered, 'And it's cheaper, Arthur, isn't it?'

He laughed and chided, 'Naughty. Naughty.'

They now did some takes outside the civic centre and in front of the gates of the college, and it was turned one o'clock when they went into the Royal Station Hotel for lunch.

After lunch she went back to Flout Street and changed into another model, not an off, but a three-piece she had brought from Madam's yesterday. The coat and skirt were autumn yellow, not unlike the colour of her head scarf. With the suit went a fine wool sweater in chocolate brown and a large matching hat with a floppy brim. She wore the same shoes, but her gloves and bag were of a darker tan. She looked back in the mirror and surveyed herself. She liked this rig-out; she had thought of buying it herself, all except the hat. You couldn't go round Felburn in a thing like this. Madam might let her have it near cost; she wasn't bad that way.

When the door bell rang she opened it to Arthur Leonard. He had been along to see Madam Hevell, and in high approval he now exclaimed, 'Aw yes, yes. This is it, glamorous autumn. Ah yes, now there's a title, glamorous autumn, what do you think?'

'Very good.'

'And you're very good, dear.' He patted her. 'Except the hat. Just a little more to the side.' He adjusted it. 'That's it. By the way, do you know you're high up on her list, Madam's? Do you know that? She calls you her swan. Not that you were ever an ugly duckling, dear, never could have been—' he touched her cheek '—not with that skin, and those eyes.' He jerked his head at her, then bent closer and whispered, 'You could go places with Madam, you know. She's no family, no ties. Anyway, dear, you keep your eye on the main chance and you could work towards a partnership, at least at this end. Very nice little business here, ve-ry nice. Do you know what she makes on these?' He touched the lapel of a coat hanging on a rail.

She said somewhat stiffly now, 'No, I don't, but I know she gives me a generous bonus on the sales, and that's all that matters.'

'Well!' He shrugged his shoulders and his tone became light. 'If you're satisfied, dear, we're all satisfied. Come on. Come on.' He looked at his watch and cried, 'What are we standing here for when those houses are coming down like nine pins? I want to get you just as that great ball hits a wall, you know, the second before it disintegrates and the dust starts. Come on.' He almost hustled her from the room now and she had to pull him to a stop outside, saying, 'Wait a minute! Wait a minute; I must lock up . . .'

The demolition squad looked as if it had almost finished its work, at least on this section, for only two warehouses, at the end of a long open rubble-strewn space, were still to be disposed of. Grabs were biting into the rubble and filling lorries, while a crane with a great iron ball swinging from its cable stood to the side of the building. In front of it, the dust was settling on the rubble of a side wall against which the ball had just crashed. Most of the front wall of the building, too, had gone, exposing the inner sections like the combs of a beehive.

Maggie drew her car up on the opposite side of the road. Getting out, she stared for a moment in amazement at the men clambering about on the battered walls, and she said to Arthur Leonard, 'Surely that thing doesn't work with them inside there?' He laughed, saying, 'They're all right, they know when to jump.'

'They'll need to,' she said; then pausing in the middle of

the road, she added quickly, 'Now, Arthur, I'm not going too near that lot, no matter what you say.'

'I don't want you to, dear; you're much too precious.' He put his arm around her shoulder and as she pushed him off he laughed again and, leading her tentatively forward, said, 'Just here, near the edge of the pavement on the corner, so I can get the interior in.' He pointed upwards to the honeycomb shell. 'And a bit of the crane.'

As she posed herself on the edge of the gutter she slanted her eyes at him and said, 'This get-up and that!' She jerked her head backwards. 'I can't see it meself.'

'Art, love, art. Circular staircases, marble halls and woodland glades are out; reality, reality, that's what they want. And—' he moved back from her, talking all the time, '—if I get this as I want it, it will be reality.'

He put his eye to the camera, then came hurriedly towards her again and took her by the arm and led her further towards the corner of the building. They had now attracted the attention of some of the men who were knocking the loose interior walls down by hand, but it was the crane man himself who shouted, 'I hope you know what you're doing, mate. You'd better look out, there'll be a hell of a dust in a minute.'

'All right, pal.' Arthur Leonard shouted up at him, a wide grin on his face. 'Fire away, that's what I want.'

'Look,' said Maggie, posed with one foot in the gutter, one foot on the kerb, her head well back and looking in the direction of the crane; 'I don't like this. What happens when it hits that wall?'

'Nothing will happen, dear, nothing.' He was backing from her. 'If you're uneasy, as soon as you see it contact give yourself one, two, three, and then dash back. But it won't fall your way . . . can't.'

'That's what you think.' She saw the great ball swing backwards, then forwards, and she didn't hear the click of the camera but as soon as the iron weight came in contact with the brickwork she dived back across the road, then clung to Arthur, laughing all the while.

Most of the wall settled into a great pile of rubble, and when the dust subsided he said, 'I'd like one or two more of those. All right, all right, dear—' he placed his fingers across his lips '—I'll settle for you in the front.'

'I should say so.'

He was walking away from her now, still talking. 'Yes, that's it, dear. Yes, all right, love. Put your head to the side this time. Look upwards to the men swarming about.' He dashed back to her and tilted her hat. 'Like that. Lovely. Lovely. You know,' he grinned at her as he said under his breath, 'you're a good looking lass, as they say around here, Margaret. But as I said to Madam, Maggie would have been much better on the bills. Maggie Gallacher, much more character than Margaret Gallacher.'

She suppressed a grin but said nothing. She liked Arthur Leonard, he had a way with him. Anyway, he could make her laugh and make her forget everything but the job in hand. She looked upwards and into the eyes of three men who were standing perilously balanced on a narrow ledge of wall. Their only support seemed to be the huge iron hammers in their hands. Then her gaze became focused on one, and although he was covered in dust there was no mistaking Ralphy Holland. She held her pose, a half smile on her face now, staring up at him and he down at her. During the time she waited for Arthur's voice to say 'Right!' she watched Ralphy's mouth drop into a great gape. She saw his tongue curl over his lower lip, licking at the grey dust that covered his face. She noted that his tongue looked grey, too, not pink. Before Arthur shouted, 'Right!' she saw Ralphy drop from the wall as though he had fallen. But when Arthur's voice came to her saying 'Good enough,' and she straightened up and moved towards him, Ralphy Holland came running from the floor of the building towards her. About a yard away he stopped and stared at her.

'Hello, Ralphy.' Her voice was quiet, ordinary, and at the sound of it he let out a high whoop like a cowboy, riding a broncho, and the next minute he was holding her immaculately gloved hand between his grime-covered ones. 'Why! Maggie. Maggie, I thought it was you, but I wasn't sure, I couldn't be sure. Even a second ago I couldn't be sure.' He was shaking his head. 'But I said to meself there couldn't be two of her, there couldn't be two Maggies. Aye, lass. What you up to? What's come over you? God above!' He stood back from her, still holding on to her hand. 'Like a million dollars. Who would believe it?' He turned for confirmation to the man at her side, and Arthur Leonard, his face prim now, said, 'She should add to that million dollars by claiming a new pair of gloves.'

'It's all right, Arthur, it's all right. This is, this is . . . Mr Holland, an old friend of mine.'

'Oh yes?' Arthur Leonard didn't show any enthusiasm, but he couldn't quench Ralphy's pleasure and excitement.

'Known her since she was that big.' He relinquished her hands and measured a distance three feet from the ground. Then looking at his hands and dusting them quickly, he said, 'Sorry, Maggie, sorry; I should have known.'

'That's all right, Ralphy. How are you?'

'Oh, I'm all right, Maggie. You know me; beer and a bed and I'm satisfied.'

'Oh, Ralphy!' She shook her head at him sadly, and on this he became quiet and the expression on his face changed. The excitement went out of it and he looked about him as if he had just remembered something. He looked towards the crane behind them, then to the far side of the warehouses where one wall was still intact; then his gaze became still and she followed it.

A bulky figure was standing half hidden by the side of a naked chimney breast on the second floor. He was, like the rest of the men, covered from head to foot in grey dust, and like them he was holding an iron hammer. She could see only half his face and half his body, but it was more than enough. Across the road and over the space of the bottomless floor their eyes met, the eyes of the elegantly dressed woman and those of the demolition labourer.

The weakness attacked her first in the throat, flowed down her arms, then to her legs. She turned away, then half turned towards Ralphy again, saying, 'Goodbye, Ralphy.'

'Ta-rah, Maggie, ta-rah. Nice seeing you.' His voice was quiet, apologetic now.

As she went towards the car Arthur muttered, 'Look, come on. He won't trouble you any more. Just another few.'

'No, Arthur, not here.'

'Oh! Look, Margaret.' He spread out one arm with the elbow bent, the fingers stretched in his characteristic manner, saying, 'Have a heart, have a heart; I won't get another chance like this, it's a marvellous set-up.'

'NO!'

'What is it?' His voice was quiet, enquiring now.

She kept her back to the buildings and speaking down to the car door she said, 'I want to get away from here . . . now.'

He glanced slowly over his shoulder, then said, 'OK, Margaret. OK. There are other places.'

When she took her seat in the car he said, 'Drive to the church, just beyond the station; we should get parked there.'

Ten minutes later he was looking at her again, and he asked quietly, 'That fellow upset you?'

'No.' She shook her head.

'What then?'

It was some time before she answered, 'I saw my husband.'

'Oh.' He nodded twice, then said, 'Oh, I get it.' And after a moment he exclaimed, 'That's life, that's life, Margaret. At least that's what they said to me when they put me along the line for bigamy.'

She wanted to laugh, but there was no laughter in her. Yet there should be, for was she not Margaret Gallacher, the model? Model for the larger woman, photographed for magazines, in demand for store lunch parades, not only because she modelled well but because she drew the customers. She was a character, for was she not also the woman who had buggered the Duke of Moorshire?

Oh, she knew what they said, and thought. She knew that her mercurial rise in this cut-throat profession owed as much to her raw outspokenness on that particular Friday night as to her ability to wear clothes and suggest to the onlooker that they only had to possess them for their fat to fade.

But there was one other thing to which she owed her success and this was the urge, the desire in the early days that had almost become an obsession with her, the desire to show him, and the hope that some time or other they would meet and her very appearance would ram his words down his throat: 'You big, fat, ignorant slob, you!' But she had never dreamed it would be like this. There was that old saying in the Bible, 'How are the mighty fallen,' and begod! it was true in this case. If ever justice had been done it had been done today, for now, not only were their places reversed, but he was lower than she ever imagined he could be, a labourer in a demolition squad.

She should be crowing, but she felt sick.

She said, 'I'm going to change and go home, Arthur.' And he said, 'Yes Margaret. Yes Margaret . . . '

When she reached home she put the car in the garage and

entered the house by the kitchen door. Annie was mashing a pot of tea at the stove and she turned quickly and said, 'Oh, hello there. You're before your time . . . You've got a visitor.' Then putting the lid quickly on the pot and bringing it to the tray on the table, she narrowed her eyes at Maggie and said, 'What's up, something happened?'

For answer Maggie said, 'Who is it?'

'Father Armstrong.' Her voice dropped low. 'But what's the matter? You look like death; you feeling under the weather?'

'I'm all right, I'll tell you later. What does he want?'

'I don't know, he didn't tell me, but he asked when you'd be in. He said he'd wait.'

They were still whispering when Annie, lifting the tray from the table, said, 'How did the quay session go?' and Maggie stared at her for a moment before saying, 'Oh, that went all right.' Then she opened the door and walked ahead of Annie into the sitting-room.

Father Armstrong rose from his seat by the window. 'Ah! There you are, Maggie. My! You are looking well.'

'How are you, Father? I suppose you could do with a cup of tea?'

'I wouldn't refuse one, I never refuse tea.' His words were light, but his manner wasn't jocular, and she knew instinctively that this visit wasn't one of his parishional calls.

When the kitchen door had closed on Annie and she had poured out the tea they both sat drinking it for a moment before he said, 'I'm coming straight to the point, Maggie; I'm the bearer of bad news.'

Her eyes tight on him, she put out her hand and placed the cup back on the table, feeling against the edge so that it wouldn't drop off.

'Bad news you say . . . Elizabeth?'

'Elizabeth.'

She waited, and the waiting she knew wasn't something born of the moment, a silence created in her by his shock tactics, but went back weeks, months, back in fact to the day she had left Liz in that grey room. Part of its substance had been a dim apprehension, an alertness whenever Father Armstrong called and brought up her name; and now the waiting was over.

'Now you must not take this too badly, Maggie, for she has tried, we all know she has tried. There's no-one to blame. She thought she had the vocation . . . so did we all.'

She brought her joined hands up to her mouth and bit hard on her thumb nail. 'It's that fellow, isn't it?'

There was a pause before Father Armstrong said, 'It may have been in the beginning, but it isn't so now. She isn't coming out to go to him, I can assure you of that. And you mustn't blame him. Peter Portman is a good man, a really good man. I only wish some of my own flock were as good . . . Ah yes, you can look like that, Maggie, but I happen to know him. He has done some very good work for the boys over the past two years. He doesn't believe in God but he believes in his fellow men, and that is something to start on.'

Maggie got up and walked to the fireplace and leant her elbow on the mantelpiece. There was another saying. It never rains but it pours. It was odd but everything seemed to happen to her in dollops. She could go on for years as she had done, with life mundane, uneventful, and then the explosion had taken place under her home and had blown it sky high. She had picked herself up and made another life for herself, a different life, an exciting, rewarding life, a life that she never imagined she could live, not a big, fat, ignorant slob like her. Her life over the past eighteen months had acted like a salve on the pain of her heart, at least during the daytime hours, and lately it had promised her, some time in the future, total freedom, forgetfulness. This morning its promise had been great. The morning had been bright, it was a day on which no bad thing could happen, and it had been given a good start with that telephone call from Arlette . . . And then she had to see him. In the most unlikely place in the world, she had to see him.

It was over a year now since she had heard of him. Willie had said he understood he was working for a firm in Doncaster, and she had imagined him in a managerial position. Never for a moment did she think he would go for anything less, nothing less than assistant works manager to a contractor. But there he was, not only back where he had started, working with Ralphy on the buildings, but knocking old ones down. Yet somehow, in a way, it seemed symbolical that he should be tearing things down.

'What did you say, Father?'

'I said, Maggie, that she doesn't want to come home.'

She turned about sharply now, her voice high. 'Why?'

'Well, I've been trying to explain, Maggie. As I said, she doesn't think she could bear to witness your pain in this. This is the second time you've been hurt in this way; she knows it only too well and it's worrying her. I . . . I think she would have made the break in the first year of her noviciate if it hadn't been for the thought of letting you down. She has tried, God knows she has tried, but it's not to be.'

'Well—' Maggie's voice was high and rough sounding now '—if she's not coming home, where does she think she's going? To that fel—?'

The priest closed his eyes and lifted his hand in protest. 'Maggie, she is not going to that fellow. Nor would that fellow want her to. Get that into your head: that man had no designs on her. What might have happened if she hadn't been going into the Church I don't know, but he respected the fact that she was. He doesn't know she's coming out, no-one outside knows this, until this moment.'

Her voice was low now as she asked, 'Well, what is she going to do, Father? Go into a home of sorts, or what?'

'No.' He stood up, placed his cup on the table, and said briefly, 'She wants to go to Paul.'

'Paul!'

'Yes, Paul.'

'Huh! Well, birds of a feather.'

'Now, Maggie, you mustn't take it like that, that's bitter.'

'Bitter? Huh! How do you expect me to take it? Does Paul know of this?'

'I've told you nobody but yourself outside the convent knows of this.'

'Would you consent to her going to Paul and him living with another woman?'

'Well, the fact is, Maggie, once she leaves the convent she can please herself. For myself, I think it's a very wise decision.'

'You mean I wouldn't be good for her?'

'I'm not meaning anything of the sort. I only mean that if I were in her place I wouldn't like to live with you and see the disappointment in your eyes every minute of the day.'

'Oh, Father, Father.' She sat down suddenly in the chair and her head drooped on to her chest, and he came and put his hand on her shoulder and said, 'There now. There now. This is life.'

Again she said, 'Huh!' This was the second time she had heard that within an hour.

'I must be off now, Maggie.' He patted her shoulder twice. 'I'll look in again at the end of the week; things should be finally settled by then.'

'By the end of the week?' She looked up at him.

'Yes, she could be leaving by Friday.'

She moved her head slowly from side to side, then bit hard down on her lip, and when she felt him walking from her she turned her head to the side, but didn't look at him, as she said, 'You might as well know that they are to be married, Paul and Arlette. She phoned me this morning.'

. . . 'In church?'

'In church.'

'Thanks be to God for that. Goodbye, Maggie.'

'Goodbye, Father.'

She didn't rise to let him out.

What had life against her? What had she done that every wish of hers should be bogged? She wouldn't care if they were selfish wishes. She had never wanted anything for herself.

When Annie came in their eyes held. 'You heard?'

'Yes,' said Annie, 'I heard. And . . . well, it's not news to me, I'm sure you must have been expecting it yourself. Anyway, it's nature.' She went to the table and picked up the tray, and as she walked towards the kitchen with it she ended, 'She's pleasing herself now and her instincts, not God or you.'

'What did you say?'

Annie disappeared into the kitchen, then came back to answer the question, and she stood with her hands joined at the front of her waist and said flatly, 'You heard what I said, an' you know as well as I do she only went in there to please you, at the end I mean.'

'She did nothing of the sort.' Maggie was on her feet now, her voice loud. 'Don't put the blame for that on me an' all.'

'It isn't blame, it's just the plain fact. It was the case of Paul all over again, only in her case, poor lass, she hadn't a chance, not right from the beginning, because she was partly brought up within the walls of the convent, being there from when she was seven, the nuns hovering around her all day like plastic angels, though some of them were far from angels. That Sister Martha had a tongue on her like a navvy's ganger. Remember that day we went to see them playing hockey? I was never more shocked in me life, running with her gown tucked up to her knees and bawling her head off. It wouldn't have surprised me if she had come out with a mouthful an' all. But there was Liz, in that atmosphere, Holy Marys two a penny; she hadn't a chance. Then she was just at an impressionable age when Paul did his bunk, and she saw how it affected you, so sacrifice, sacrifice, she offered herself, and you let her. I'm going to say this, though I shouldn't at this time, but if you had faced up to Paul's desertion and not gone on as if he'd just missed being made Pope that lass would have got over her fancy, and it's two to one she'd have been married by now. So there! That's flat.'

'Shut up! What's come over you, what you getting at? You out to get me mad or something?' Maggie was leaning over the table. 'I'm warning you, Annie Fawcett, be careful of that tongue of yours else you'll be sorry.'

'I'm never sorry for telling the truth.' Annie flounced round and went into the kitchen, and Maggie remained bent over the table, her hands gripping the edge now. The truth, the truth. What was the truth? Had she pressed Liz into the convent? Had she in some unspoken way let her see that's what she wanted for her, a life between four walls, a life of restriction, of denial of natural desire? . . . Oh, my God! What was the matter with her now thinking like this? She began to pace the floor. Yes, yes she had wanted her to go in, because nuns were happy. You had only to look at their faces, you had only to hear them talking; did you ever hear them grumbling? And what's more, inside there they escaped most of the torments of life, and deep down that's what she had wanted for Elizabeth, a life free from emotional torments, of battles and reconciliation, and aye, even of the joys the questionable joys of love, the rending of the body in a moment's ecstasy. And for what? Pregnancy after pregnancy. The distortion of the body wasn't beautiful. When she had carried Sam she had carried him high, seemingly under her breasts – Sam. Oh my God! Sam. – But her grannie had looked at her on her weekly visits and explained the position by saying, 'Young cows carry high, old cows carry low.'

Cows, yes; that's what she had tried to shelter Elizabeth from, the indignity of being a cow.

Looking back on her life at this moment she recognised with some surprise that for years there had been a private war raging inside her. Buried in her bulk, there had been another and quite separate individual who had been striving for life, a life of its own, but it had been smothered by her early environment, then by routine . . . and love, blind, adoring, unquestioning love for a big young fellow with short cropped hair, deep set eyes, puggish nose and bull neck, and everything had become subordinate to that love, principally the struggling self.

And now Lizzie wanted to go to Paul, and if Paul agreed it would mean they wouldn't come this way to live. How could they, Liz feeling like that? She couldn't win, not with her family she couldn't.

Annie had come into the room again, with another tray in her hand. She put it down on the table, picked up a cup of tea and handed it to her, saying, 'I've made a fresh one.' It was the usual form of apology.

Maggie didn't want more tea but she took it and sat down by the side of the fireplace, and Annie sat opposite to her and as she stirred the spoon round in her cup she said, 'You'll get over it; it's a small mountain to the others you've climbed.' Then having put the spoon in her mouth and licked it, she placed it on the saucer before asking, 'What upset you outside?'

277

There was a long pause. The words were there but she couldn't get them out, not until Annie, impatient now, said, 'Well?'

'I've seen him,' she said.

'Rod? Where?' Annie bent quickly forward and put her cup down on the tiled hearth. 'Did he speak to you?'

Maggie shook her head.

'You didn't pass him?'

Again Maggie shook her head. 'It . . . it wasn't like that. I . . . I was down the Scotswood Road. Arthur was taking me against some buildings they were pulling down, big warehouses. I was looking up and . . . and I saw Ralphy.' She stopped for a moment and they stared at each other, and then she went on, 'He . . . he came dashing down and spoke to me, and . . . and then I happened to look up and there he was, on one of the walls with the gang.'

'Labouring?'

'Labouring.'

Again they were staring at each other.

'And you were all rigged out special like?' Annie's voice was low.

'Very special like. The yellow rig-out I was telling you about, and the big floppy hat, very special like.' She shook her head.

'Poor Rod.'

Maggie blinked her eyes as if coming out of a dream and demanded, 'Poor Rod? Whose side are you on anyway?' She was on her feet now staring down at Annie. 'Blaming me for Liz, and now taking his side.'

'I'm not taking his side, you know I'm not, but . . . but did you get any satisfaction out of seeing him labouring? I ask you, did you?'

She walked to the window and stood looking out. The little garden showed faint signs of spring. There were yellow crocuses in the border and the buds of the daffodils

278

were fattening. She began to wonder where he was living, in lodgings somewhere, perhaps with a landlady. Aye, her thoughts hardened, very little doubt about it, there'd be a landlady.

'He'll feel like hell the night.'

Again she turned swiftly on Annie. 'You're sorry for him, aren't you? Would you still be sorry for him if he was with her and in a white collar job?'

'No, I wouldn't; but he's not with her an' in a white collar job.' Annie too was on her feet. 'He's, as you say, labouring, and if he's with Ralphy Holland, it's a poor kind of labouring he's at.' There was a personal bitterness in her voice now. Against this Maggie bowed her head, and under her lowered lids she watched Annie grab up the two cups and march into the kitchen.

Later that night, having had her bath, creamed her face, set her hair in preparation for the activities of the following day, Maggie came into the living-room to say good night to Annie.

Annie was sitting staring into the fire. Usually she had her nose in a book at this time, some love story she'd got from the library, or following a serial in any one of the three women's magazines she took each week.

'Good night,' said Maggie quietly.

Annie turned sharply round and said, 'Oh, good night.' Then, as Maggie was going into her bedroom, she said, 'Maggie.'

'Yes?'

'Would you have him back?'

It was like the old days when some incident caused the cork to fly and, her voice seeming to spiral out of the top of her head, she would bawl her opponent down whether it be one of the lads, one of the girls, Rod, or Annie herself. 'What! Have him back? You've lived with me all these years and you're stupid enough to ask me that!

Have him back, did you say? I wouldn't let that man come near me if he was to crawl on his hands and knees. If I was dead and he came and looked at me I would know an' spit in his eye. HAVE HIM BACK!'

The bedroom door banged and Annie stood looking at it for a moment, then raised her eyebrows, sat down and continued to stare into the fire.

CHAPTER TWO

THE LEOPARD'S SPOTS

During the summer months the picture of Margaret Gallacher appeared on the front pages of the *Messenger* at least three times.

On two occasions the demonstrations had taken place in private restaurants. The third had been in the dining room of an ultra-modern hotel on the outskirts of the town and had been given star billing.

Naturally Maggie didn't appear alone at these dress parades, but nearly always it was her picture which appeared in the papers. There had been good models in Felburn before, but if once during her career one of them had had her photograph in the paper she had felt flattered, and very lucky. Madam Hevell attributed the generosity of the press first to the quality of her models and secondly to the ability of a big woman like Maggie to carry them, and to this she added unself-effacingly the fact that Maggie owed her present success entirely to her coaching.

What Madam didn't realise was that reporters were very observant people; also there were those among them who were patient and given to hunches, although the hunch they had with regards to Margaret Gallacher relied more on fact than feeling. A leopard didn't change its spots; under her finery Margaret Gallacher was the woman who had buggered a duke; wait long enough and anything could happen.

Maggie was not insensible to all that was going on around her. She realised that she was lucky to get her billings in the paper. She realised that she was very lucky to know a photographer like Arthur Leonard; she realised that she had fallen on her feet, so to speak, the day she went to Madam Hevell's, and she was now interested, and not a little excited, at the prospect of a partnership in the Flout Street business.

Her salary was double what it had been this time last year and her bank balance was rising rapidly. She was financially on top of the world. She was envied, not only by others in the profession, but also by the members of her own family, and not by Frances alone now, but by Nancy, pregnant once more, and struggling on housekeeping one third of what she had been used to. Indeed, she was not the easygoing, laughing girl of three years ago but a peevish woman who questioned the right, and not always in private, of a mother-in-law who had all the breaks.

Helen was pretty much the same, except when Trevor came visiting with her. Trevor's innuendoes, like his face, were sharp and Maggie gauged that he thought it highly unfair that she, who, to his mind, had been the instigator of all their troubles, should not only benefit from them but come away out on top.

Elizabeth's reactions to her were puzzling. She had seen her only twice in the six months since she had left the convent, and on each occasion she had been filled with embarrassment and not a little guilt.

It was six weeks after Elizabeth had gone to live with Paul and Arlette that she journeyed to London to see her. She had expected to be confronted by a subdued, pale, reticent creature, someone nulled; what she found was a highly excitable, rakishly-dressed, loud talking girl. She made Maggie think of an animal that had been trapped and suddenly let out, dashing here and there, and it was this that engendered the guilt in her. She felt responsible for robbing her of two years of life. Her daughter had greeted her as if she had just left her yesterday, and she had talked and talked, she had never stopped talking. She had wanted to yell at her, 'Stop it, girl!' But this wasn't Liz, not the Liz she remembered, this was the girl who had been hidden under the surface of Liz, Liz of the vocation.

Three months later, when they met again, Liz had a post as secretary in a firm in the City. She had been learning typing since she was sixteen while at the convent, and apparently she was very good at shorthand. Her conversation on this visit had, in itself, been embarrassing for she had talked of her boss and the men in the office with cheap familiarity.

She had asked Arlette, 'Is this just put on for me?' and Arlette had shaken her head and said, 'No, Mam; she's like this all the time.'

Maggie looked at her daughter-in-law and said, 'It must be wearing for you.'

Arlette had smiled at her but made no comment except to say, 'I think she'll get married soon. There's a boy in the office; they're seeing a lot of each other.'

She had turned her gaze away from Arlette as she muttered, 'I seem to have a lot to answer for.' And Arlette had put her arms about her and kissed her and said, 'You mustn't blame yourself for anything.' Arlette was still a comfort.

Last week Paul had phoned to say that they had had a daughter. She was happy for him, happy for them. He had also said he thought he had better tell her that Elizabeth had moved out; she was sharing a flat with another girl. But she hadn't to worry, he was keeping an eye on her. Anyway, he thought she would be married soon; she was going strong with a young fellow.

Was he a Catholic?

283

No.

Well, it didn't matter, did it?

No, he said; it didn't matter, not these days.

'It's October again,' Annie said as she brought the post in. 'If you were blind you could tell by the mornings, the air hits you. You've got a nice lot this morning, eight. And look.' She sorted one out. 'There's one from the television people. Tyne-Tees, it's got on it.'

Maggie pulled a face and took the envelope from Annie's hand. When she opened it and read the contents she gave a little laugh, looked at Annie, then handed her the letter.

After reading it Annie said, 'My! My! You've hit it now, haven't you? Them asking you to go on a programme and paying you for it . . . Television! What'll it be next I wonder? Eeh! Wait till this gets about.'

'They're not asking me to do a series.' Maggie slanted her gaze up at her. 'Nor giving me a half-hour to myself, they're just asking me to demonstrate while one of them is talking.'

'Oh yes.' Annie looked at the letter again. 'You won't have to open your mouth?'

'No, I won't have to open me mouth . . . Isn't that a good thing?'

'Aw you!' Annie threw the letter on the table; then seating herself, she said, 'Nevertheless, it's a start; it could lead to anything.'

'Yes, anything.'

'What's the matter with you, you sound as flat as a pancake this morning.'

'I've got a headache, didn't sleep much.'

'Well, you went to bed early enough.'

'Yes, I know I did, but as I said I didn't sleep.'

'Eat your breakfast.'

'I've had all I want.' She rose from the table now, taking her letters with her, and Annie said, 'You sickenin' for something?'

Maggie bowed her head, then turned round and looked at Annie, and in a childish voice she simpered, 'Yes, Ma, mumps.'

'Aw you! Go on with you,' said Annie, and they both laughed.

That morning, she had to visit a Mrs Penrose on the outskirts of Felburn and take half-a-dozen off-models. She had met the lady before and classed her as the huntin', fishin' and shootin' type, of which she now had a number on her books. But she wasn't prepared for Compton Place, and she was made to wonder as she drove her car up the long drive to the Tudor-style house why anyone living in this style should need to buy second-hand rig-outs. But inside the house, where there was an absence of staff, except for one indifferent looking maid, and a great deal of unpolished furniture and dust, she thought she had the reason. The off-models were one of the reasons for keeping up appearances like the two horses she had seen coming out of the stable yard. The Colonel, too, must keep up appearances. Well, she told herself, as she was shown upstairs, it was their life; but she wouldn't like to live it.

She came away from Compton Place quite satisfied with her own way of life, and her case lighter by an evening gown, two suits and a coat.

She had another call about two miles away in Burlington Terrace. This was breaking new ground. The Burlington Terrace district was an upper working class part of the town adjacent to Bog's End. One wag had said that the social aspirants jumped like fleas out of Bog's End into Burlington Terrace, then crawled like snails to the foot of Brampton Hill. The appointment was for twelve-thirty, an odd time she thought; perhaps the woman went out to work and was dashing back at dinner time. Muriel had thought this, too, when she had made the appointment, but she realised she was a new customer, so didn't haggle about the time being awkward.

Muriel was an acquisition of six months' standing in Flout Street. She took in the calls, made the appointments, pressed the gowns and did alterations. She was a find, was Muriel, because she was a widow who needed the money and never quibbled about staying half-an-hour late. Moreover, she was Maggie's size and they got on well together.

About a mile from Burlington Terrace the road was up for repairs, and joining a slow stream of cars she made the detour that wound into Bog's End. At the traffic lights she turned down Farley Road. Farley Road was a narrow road, always congested; it ran for about a quarter of a mile and was made up of odd shops, factories and small houses. Towards the end of the road, as if it had been stuck on by mistake, was a row of four-storey terraced houses which, in better days, had housed in grand isolation captains and their like, but which now from the top of their ornamental blackened chimneys to the rusted iron railings at their feet appeared like genteel ladies who, through no fault of their own, had been reduced to penury.

When she was almost half-way along the row she had to pull to a sharp stop; there was a hold-up in front of her. She leant back in her seat and relaxed; she had plenty of time, twenty minutes, and she was only five minutes away from Burlington Terrace. She turned her head casually and looked out of the window across the pavement to where a man was leaning against the stanchion of a door. He had his hands in his pockets, his eyes looked blank, he appeared a picture of dejection. Her shoulders came up sharply from the back of the seat and she brought her face to the open window, and perhaps it was this quick movement that drew the man's attention, for within a second his whole manner had changed, and with three strides he was at the car window.

'Why, hello, Maggie.'

'Hello, Ralphy. How are you?'

'Oh, you know.'

Yes, she knew. Twelve o'clock on a weekday leaning against a wall meant out of work. She stared up into his face. It was sad, as always when he was sober.

The traffic was beginning to move. She looked quickly through the windscreen, then back at him. She couldn't leave him like this, he was on his uppers; she'd have to give him something but she couldn't stop. She said quickly, 'I'll have to be moving; get in a minute.'

'What!'

She leant over and opened the back door of the car, and like a shot he was in.

She took the first turning up a side street, then drew the car to a stop. When she turned round and looked at him he was leaning forwards with his forearms resting on the top of the seat. She began in the usual way, 'Well, how are you, Ralphy?'

'Oh, alive and kickin', Maggie.'

'Are . . . are you living back here now?'

'Yes.' He jerked his head upwards. 'Along there, number seventeen. I've got a room.'

They stared at each other, and she waited for him to go on, but he just sat looking at her wide-eyed, a half smile on his face that gave it an expression of wonder.

'Are . . . are you working?'

'Well, not at the moment, not at the moment, Maggie; things are black. You wouldn't believe it, all this talk of new industries comin' in, and when you go they're full up . . . but—' he put his head on one side and grinned at her '—if you're a young lass you can get a job anywhere.'

They were silent again, and again she waited; then she asked, 'Haven't you tried the buildings?'

'Oh, they've got their regular chaps, you know how it is . . . You're looking bonny, Maggie. Aye, I can't believe it. Not that I didn't always know you had a fine figure.' He jerked his head to one side. 'By! Aye! You always had a fine figure; but I've never seen you dressed up to the eyes like this afore, I mean until I saw you that day havin' your picture took. Eeh! and it was a picture. You were a sight for sore eyes, an' I said that to Rod . . . '.

His chin dropped and his eyes followed suit, and she asked, her voice tight, 'And what did he say to that?'

He raised his eyes to hers. 'Nowt much, Maggie.'

'Nowt much!' She repeated his words.

'Oh,' he was quick to assure her, 'he wasn't nasty or owt like; he was just, well, taken aback, floored like. An' I'd never seen him floored like that afore, the wind was taken completely out of his sails. I might as well tell you, Maggie, I thought at the time, it serves him bloody well right, but I still couldn't help feelin' sorry for him. You know what I mean?'

'What did he say?' Her tone conveyed her persistence.

He looked down again; then said quietly, 'Well, it was nothin' really, just what you make out of it. What he said was, if you spit against the wind you always get your own back.'

It's what you make out of it. She stared at Ralphy, at his unshaven face and his bleary eyes. She wanted to say to him, 'Where is he now? Has he got a room in number seventeen an' all?' But she couldn't bring herself to ask such a question because there was always the possibility that Ralphy would go straight back and tell him. The next minute, however, Ralphy gave her the answer without her asking.

'The job in Newcastle finished just after that, but the firm had a contract for here, lower Bog's End, Fenwick Street an' thereabouts, an' one way an' another he could have had another three weeks' work, but he went off, said he was goin' south.'

Her body was deflating again. It was a long time now since she had experienced this feeling; it was a strange sensation. Underneath her smart make-up and elegant clothes she was falling inwards to the core of herself, where the truth lay.

She stemmed the shrinkage by opening her bag and looking in her wallet. Her fingers were on a five-pound note when she thought, If I give him this much he'll blow the lot. The thing to do with Ralphy was to dole it out in small amounts. But then she might not see him again for months, if ever. She crumpled the note up and pushed it into his hand, saying, 'Now get yourself some food in.'

He did not look at what she had given him but attempted to push it back at her, saying, 'No, no, Maggie. Now look; now there's no call for that. And I wasn't after anythin'. Look, I get me dole the day after the morrow, I'm all right. But,' his fingers now closing over the note, he ended, 'thanks, lass. You've got a big heart, Maggie.' He moved his head slowly. 'Although it's been broken you've still got enough left for two.'

She half turned from him, her throat tight; then looking at her watch she said quickly, 'Ralphy, I'll have to be putting a move on, I've got an appointment with a client.'

'Oh aye. Yes, Maggie. OK.' He opened the door and got out. Then putting his head through the window, he said, 'It's been grand seeing you, lass. Things were lookin' black this mornin', but there's always a silver lining, isn't there? Always a silver lining.'

As she stared at him the smile went from his face and it became serious, as did his tone as he ended, softly, 'If it's any consolation to you, Maggie, he . . . he never bothers with women. I've worked alongside of him for nearly a year now, on and off like, one place and another. He's had a chance; but no, he wouldn't look the side they were on.'

She cleared her throat, took in a long breath and, her face tight now, she said, 'It's no consolation, Ralphy . . . Bye-bye.'

'Bye-bye, Maggie. Ta-rah, lass.' He straightened up, and she started the car and moved off.

If it's any consolation to you, he never bothers with women. No; perhaps he was still pining for his lost lady-love. She wondered what Mrs Rosamund de Ferrier would have thought if she had seen him, as she herself had seen him a few months ago; or how he would have re-acted if he had come face to face with the lady. Well, to hell! It made no odds, it didn't matter a damn to her how he reacted; as he had said, he had spat against the wind and had got his own back.

She left Burlington Terrace at quarter past one, after having sold a dress and a suit, knowing she had made another good contact. She went into a restaurant and had a hasty lunch. There was one more call to make at four o'clock, but before that she must get back to Flout Street and collect the appropriate models for the customer, and if time allowed she intended to drop in to Madam's and give her the details of the two sales she had already made and put a suggestion to her that they should add shoes to their list. Twice within the past week, she had been asked if they dealt in these. And last but not least, she must tell her about the television invitation . . .

It was just on three when she entered the shop and she noted at once that business was brisk. It was rarely that Madam had more than three customers in at a time, but now Annette was busy with a client at one end of the room, and Marianne was trying to interest another in a lamb's wool twin-set, while a third sat in one of the gold brocade chairs and waited, with seeming patience.

Leaving her client, Annette came swiftly to Maggie and said under her breath, 'Madam's in the dressing room with Lady Shaw.' She pulled a face. 'And there's another one waiting in the Blue Room.' She thumbed genteelly to where the blue velvet curtain hung down over the archway. 'Have you any time to spare . . . ?'

It was at this point that Madam opened the door of the fitting room. Evidently she had been going to give Annette a message, but seeing Maggie she exclaimed brightly, 'Ah! Margaret. You have come at an opportune time. You have a few minutes to spare? Come.' She took her by the arm, then whispered, 'Have a word with Madam, will you? I'll be with her shortly.' She led the way to the blue velvet curtain, pulled it aside and stepped beyond into the room, and Maggie followed her, at least as far as the archway for there she stopped and looked to where the client was sitting reading a magazine. The client looked up at her, and recognition was mutual.

At this moment Maggie was solid and sober. She had been solid and sober for two years now, so her reaction to the sight of the client could not be said to have been aided by drink. The only difference between her reactions now and on the night she swore at the Duke was that now there was nothing spontaneous about it, she took her time over it. Drawing herself up to her full height, her eyes cold, her tone icy, she proclaimed in a voice that carried, not only into the shop but into the fitting room, 'I don't wait on whores.'

291

She could have counted ten in the silence before she turned away from the white, shocked face of Rosamund de Ferrier, and she had walked down the shop and was going through the door before the indignation, coming solely from Madam, burst behind her.

CHAPTER THREE

POWER

Maggie did not see Madam Hevell until forty-eight hours later.

When she had arrived home after the incident, Annie, looking at her and noting that the barometer was down, asked quietly, 'What's happened now?' and Maggie, in a few precise words told her, after which Annie stared at her, then cupped her face with her hands, rocked herself gently and said, 'Woman! you're going to land yourself in trouble one of these days.'

'Doubtless,' said Maggie, and went into one of her long silences, which meant that she was either very angry or full of remorse; but Annie knew it wasn't the latter in this case.

The following day she kept to the house and there was no word from Madam, but at noon the next day the phone rang and Madam's voice giving nothing away said, 'Margaret?' and Maggie said briefly, 'Yes.' She didn't add Madam.

'What is the matter with you, why haven't you been in to your work?'

Is she joking? Maggie looked about her as if in search of eyes to answer the question. When she made no reply, Madam's voice came again, saying, 'You are ill, are you?'

'No, I'm not ill.'

'Then perhaps you'll oblige us by calling this afternoon?'

'Very well.'

At three o'clock Madam and Maggie faced each other across the table in the fitting room. At this time yesterday

Madam would have cried at her, 'Get out! I never want to see you again; you have ruined my business. You are a disgrace. Why did I ever think of taking on a person such as you.'

But since then she had gone over the whole scene yet again, with Annette, Marianne and Justine and, not least, Muriel from The Rooms, and all dropping their deferential manner for once, had said that although Margaret had laid it on a bit thick she was nevertheless right, for Mrs de Ferrier had had more men on the side than there were fingers on their hands.

Ah but, Madam had countered, her morals were of no concern of theirs but her custom was, she was a very good client.

'Well,' Annette had said, 'you'll lose her, so what! But I bet when this gets around you'll have more customers than ever; if they only come to see Margaret, someone who had the nerve to tell that piece what she was. She has a lot of enemies, has Mrs de Ferrier, and Lady Shaw is one of them. I bet her phone's been hot since she left here.'

And then there was Arthur.

'What!' he had cried. 'Sack Margaret?' All right, she had called a client a whore. A scene like that was good for business these days. Better still if Mrs de Ferrier sued her. Sack Margaret! She must be mad.

And lastly there was Muriel. Muriel had been very upset when she heard what had taken place because, she ended, 'This would put paid to the television do.'

'What television do?' Madam had demanded, and Muriel had told Madam of the letter Margaret had received from the Tyne-Tees people.

So Madam now looked at Maggie in great sorrow, and with her head on one side and her hands clasped together at the top of her bony breast she said, 'Ah, Margaret, Margaret, you are very naughty, very naughty indeed. I should be very angry with you, but there.' She now sprung her hands apart and held them out palm upwards as if in supplication to Maggie herself. 'What have you to say?'

'What can I say?'

'You called her a very bad name.'

'To my mind she's a very bad woman.'

'Ah yes. Ah yes.' Madam nodded her head sympathetically now. To give her her due, when she had ushered Maggie into the Blue Room she had forgotten completely that it was Mrs de Ferrier who had stolen Maggie's husband. But she wondered now that the two hadn't met before, for at certain times in the year Mrs de Ferrier would come at least twice a week for fittings. Again she shook her head at Maggie.

Far from finding Madam's attitude reassuring Maggie was finding it irritating. If she was going to fire her she didn't want it buttered up like this; anyway she had already fired herself, it didn't matter. She would get another job, her name was good . . . Good for what? Aye, good for what? This was the second time she had blotted her copy book in this town. It would seem that Rodney Gallacher was right, she was at rock bottom nothing but a big, fat ignorant slob. But she wasn't sorry for what she had said to that one. No, by God! She had often thought of how she would react if ever they met, and when it happened she'd had very little time to think. Nevertheless, her thinking had been straight and to the point. No, she wasn't sorry.

Her eyebrows moved slowly upwards as Madam, rising to her feet, said, 'Well now, it is over, done with, finished. I will, what you say, cut my losses. And—' she wagged her finger down into Maggie's face '—there will be losses. Ah, yes. Ah, yes. Her cheques were big and regular. But there, there; that is life.' Again she spread her hands; then when they were joined once more at her breast, she said, 'And now, have you replied to the Tyne-Tees people?'

Maggie stared at her, and after a moment she had the desire to burst out laughing. She wasn't being given the push; she must be more important than she realised, indeed, yes. Have you answered the Tyne-Tees people? She smiled at Madam. She was cute, was this little French-cum-Belgian woman; she wasn't keeping her on because she loved her, but because in her own way she had assumed some sort of power. Funny that, her, Maggie Gallacher, having power of any kind. She thought secretly to herself in an aside, 'I could start off on my own in this business now, and if I was to let that drop to Annette or Marianne, I'd like to bet a partnership in here would be forthcoming the morrow. Huh! Wheels within wheels. Rod used to call it legal blackmail.'

Rod? He had gone South then. She might never see him . . . Funny how things seemed to happen to her in batches.

'Well, I haven't answered it yet but I'll get it off tonight.'

'That's right. Margaret, that's right. Now along you go.' Madam patted her on the shoulder as if she were a child, and as if she were addressing a child she ended, 'And behave yourself. Do you hear, Margaret, behave yourself. And be grateful that I am so fond of you.'

On her way out she winked at the girls, and in the street she paused a moment to look up at the sky. Life was funny, and not always heartbreakingly funny, sometimes ha-ha-funny!

CHAPTER FOUR

RALPHY

Life went on, day after day, week after week, getting busier and busier; more clients, more bonuses, pictures in the local paper, her name, Margaret Gallacher, in heavy black print below. At one time it would have read: Margaret Gallacher modelling gowns for Madam Hevell. Now it merely said: Margaret Gallacher, the model. People noticed her when she walked through the town. Strange women stopped her and spoke to her. It was all very exciting, very gratifying; that is when she could give her whole mind to the job in hand, but as time went on she was finding this more difficult.

She could say that for perhaps two-thirds of the day and part of every night her mind was on other things, and not least the futility of her life. It was very strange, even disturbing when she recognised she was less fulfilled now than she had been during those long years when she was tied to the house, first with the bairns, and then as a waiting wife, waiting for her man coming in – the big, fat, ignorant slob sitting waiting for her man coming in.

She found that for long stretches at a time, mostly in the early part of the night, she would think of individual members of her family, taking them as it were from a box in her mind and standing them before her on the palm of her hand, very like the trick photography you saw on the television. And from the vantage point of distance, she would search for reasons for their behaviour; Paul's, Liz's, Frances's; but not Willie's or

Helen's, theirs seemed ordinary and predictable. Lastly, it would be Sam she would examine. She could do this unemotionally now, and she had come to think that Sam's trouble was that he had suffered a kind of rejection, too, by knowing that he was an accident in the first place and hadn't been wanted, at least not by his dad. Yet it was on her he had vented his spleen.

The more she thought the more she delved, and the more she found out about the members of her family the more she realised that they were mostly strangers to her, that they always had been. There was only one person who had been no stranger, and if she'd had him alone and had never conceived one of her six children she would still have felt satisfied, still have been fulfilled.

But strangely Rodney was the only one she didn't put on her hand and look at. She had no need, she knew all about him . . .

'Surely,' said Annie, 'you're not going photographing the day?'

'Surely, we are,' Maggie mimicked her as she shrugged herself into a Kolinsky coat which was to be sold as a mink.

'You'll freeze.'

'What! In this?' She did a few professional steps across the narrow hall, then turned and said, 'Original price, fifteen hundred, Madam; it's an utter bargain at three fifty.

'Yes, of course, Madam, I can leave it; I only have my vest and knickers on underneath, but anything for you . . . and business.'

'You're daft.' Annie had her head down trying to suppress her laughter. Then, her face straightening suddenly, she said, 'It's going to snow or come down in ice cubes by the feel of it. I bet you a shilling we'll be up to the eyes in it afore Christmas. It's bad enough when it starts in the New Year. Do you think you'll get home for a bite of dinner?'

Maggie considered for a moment, then said, 'Well, I might and I mightn't. I've got three calls to make this morning then I'm going back to Flout Street this afternoon to pick up Muriel. I'm taking her out with me. It's to an old customer; she wants fitting.' She considered again, then said, 'I'll try, but if I'm not in by one-thirty don't wait, have your own.'

'It's a casserole, it won't hurt. Get back if you can, no matter what time. You want something inside you, weather like this, not restaurant ket.'

'Ta-rah,' said Maggie; and Annie, coming to the door, called after her as she walked carefully down the frost-glistening path to the garage, 'Mind how you drive. If the roads are like this you'll be up a lamppost afore you know where you are.'

Maggie was still smiling when she brought the car out of the garage, and she waved her hand out of the window to Annie, not in farewell but to indicate that she should get inside out of the cold. As she drove into the road she thought, as she had often done of late, that life would indeed be stark if it wasn't for Annie. It was odd how God, the designer of fates, or whoever it was who traced out the map of your life, managed to leave you a little comfort. She never went to church now but her lack of religion didn't trouble her. She was fortunate in this way that she could question without fear.

She arrived in Newcastle about ten o'clock. Her first client's address was in the residential part of Gateshead. This was breaking new ground, and she wasn't quite sure how to get there. As she drove over the bridge across the river she decided that once she got clear of the main stream of traffic she would ask her way; and this she did a few minutes later.

'Oh, Steinbeck Crescent,' said the man on the pavement. 'Oh, no, missis, you're some way from that, you've come in at the wrong end. But look I tell you what.' And now, like all northerners when directing a stranger, he drew a map with his hands, his head, and his tongue. 'You go up there, you see, and you take the first turning on your left, what I mean, the big turning, not that little one, that leads to a cul-de-sac, the turning after the third lamppost, you see? Well now, that's Bourne Road. Now you go down there.' He paused and considered and stared slantwise up into the grey sky before he continued. 'Then you come to a crossroad. There's no traffic lights, just a sort of halt. Now you turn right there and you're in Delia Road. Now that's a long road; keep straight on.' He paused again. Then his arm extended to its fullest length, his finger pointing as if directing her destiny, as, unknown to them both, it was, he went on, 'At the end you come into a huddle of shops, some new, some old. They've built a supermarket there recently, that's 'cos of the new estate. But that's on your left. Now you cut through there until you come to a library. It's a branch library, you can't miss it; it's an old greystone building like a miniature town hall. Now you turn sharp left there and once you do that you're all right. Just keep on, and if I'm not mistaken you come plumb into Steinbeck Crescent. All right?'

She laughed up at him. 'All right, and thank you very much.'

'Now you've got it? First turning on your left, turning after the third lamppost, down Bourne Road till you come to a crossroad, turn right into Delia Road and then straight along and there you are.'

'Thanks,' said Maggie again.

'Ta-rah,' said the man.

'Ta-rah,' said Maggie. She was laughing as she repeated to herself: Left, right, then straight along. And he was right in his directing, for eventually she came to the huddle of shops, a baker's, a grocer's, a fish shop, newsagent's, a post office. It looked as if it had all once been part of a village. Then further on she spied the library. It was just as he said, like a miniature town hall, with an ornate façade and a flight of steps going up to double doors. She was actually passing the steps when she recognised the figure walking down them. It was Ralphy Holland, but what was more strange than the sight of Ralphy in this unexpected place was that he was carrying an armful of books.

She pulled to a stop at the side of the kerb and looked back. He was coming her way. When he was abreast of her she put her hand out of the window and said, 'Hello there.'

'Why, Maggie!' His face lighted up. 'Fancy seeing you.' He bent down to her and stared at her. 'By! You're looking well . . . bonny.'

'How's yourself?'

'Aw.' He moved his head stiffly. 'Not so bad, not so bad.'

As she stared up at him icy drops of rain began to fall and he said, 'Here it comes!' At the same time he pushed the books under his coat, saying, 'They go for you if you get them wet.'

'Far to go, Ralphy?'

'St Frances Road, Maggie; a step or two it is.'

She opened the door and, hopping in, he said, 'Oh ta, Maggie. Thanks. By!' He shivered. 'It's lovely in here, warm.'

She didn't start up the car but sat looking at him, willing herself to ask the question but unable to come straight to the point.

'You studying something, Ralphy?' She nodded at the books now stacked on his knees.

'Me?' He dug his thumb into his chest. 'Me studying, Maggie? Now you know me better than that. I've got nowt in me head to study with, lass.' His tone was self-deprecating. 'No.' He paused while looking straight into her face. 'These are for Rod.'

'Oh!' She pursed her lips and moved her eyebrows, and Ralphy went on, 'He reads all the time, can't keep him supplied. Studying electricity now he is, electronics or some such, I don't know. Anyway, it gives him something to do 'cos you can't just lie in bed and think. 'Tisn't good for you thinking too much, is it, Maggie?'

'No, Ralphy. He's in bed then is he?'

'Oh aye; of course, you wouldn't know, but he's been bad, right bad, bit of bronchial trouble he had. Got wet; you know how it is. And you know what he's like, don't you? Won't change his shirt when he should an' dry off, and it turned to pneumonia. The doctor's warned him to stay put for another three weeks, but you might as well talk to yourself.'

Ralphy was staring at her now, not speaking, and she turned from him and started the car.

Bronchial; he had never had bronchial trouble, he was as strong as a horse. But then he had never gone out in wet things, she had seen to that. Oh yes, she had seen to that. He'd hardly got in the door before she had his things off him, even if his shoulders were just damp. She had even whipped off his socks in the winter when she had suspected his feet were wet, knowing he wouldn't go to the trouble to take them off himself. Knelt on the floor before him, she had, and unlaced his shoes and pulled off his socks and rubbed his feet between her hands. The things she had done! And now he was having bronchitis . . . Well, that wasn't going to make her fall on her face and weep.

Her eyes were fixed straight ahead when she asked casually, 'You living together then, Ralphy?'

'Aye Maggie, I brought him to my place. 'Tisn't much, God knows, but it's better than where he was. But you know of old, Maggie, you can't satisfy Rod; he hates kipping in with anybody. But he didn't know much about it the time I fetched him. Thought he was a gonner; so did the doctor; and they couldn't get him to the hospital, it was full. There was a flu do a few weeks back, spread like wild fire it did . . . You turn off here, Maggie.'

She braked sharply and turned the car into a side road, and he said, 'One-two-five, near the middle; it's a Mrs Bradshaw's place. She lives upstairs and she lets the bottom two rooms; we've got the front one.'

A few seconds later when he said, 'This is it, Maggie,' she drew the car up outside a dingy house that seemed to be but one of hundreds in the dingy road. She added dirty to the dingy, for as far as her eyes could see there was peeling paint everywhere, and on the window right opposite to her a piece of brown paper had been stuck over a crack.

'Maggie.' His voice brought her eyes to him. 'You wouldn't . . . ? What I mean is, you wouldn't come and . . . ?'

'No, Ralphy, I wouldn't.' She thrust her hand into her bag and, opening her purse, again took out a five pound note and pushed it towards him. This time he made no protest but muttered gratefully, 'Ta. Thanks; it'll come in handy, Maggie. Ta, lass.'

'It's for food, not the hard stuff, mind.'

'Aw, I know, Maggie, I know.' His eyes became suspiciously bright and he turned quickly from her and fumbled at the door handle. She had to lean across him to open it, and as he stepped on to the pavement her eyes passed him and went to the window, not more than four feet away, and to the face looking out through the dirty pane. Her gaze became riveted for a second. It was his face, yet not his face, only the eyes seemed recognisable; they had always been deep set, but now they looked like round black blobs lying in sickly white hollows. The face was unshaven and seemingly without flesh . . . Oh, Holy Mother!

When Ralphy turned and glanced at the window the head disappeared and he looked at Maggie again and said, 'I . . . I put his bed against the window so he could look out.' He stared down at her, waiting for her to say something. Then he watched her pull herself upright and take the wheel. Bending down again, he said, 'Thanks, Maggie, it's been grand seeing you. Take care of yourself.'

Still she didn't speak, just nodded her head once, then started up the car.

Annie said, 'Why didn't you then? Why didn't you go and have a word with him?'

'WHAT!'

'Never mind what; it would have been an act of charity, if nothing else. And I'll tell you something.' She stabbed her forefinger at Maggie. 'It wouldn't be, because you didn't want to. And don't bawl at me 'cos I know what I'm talking about.'

'You know damn all if you're such a numskull as to think I'd move a step out of me way even if he was pegging out.'

'You're hard, Maggie Gallacher.'

'Yes, I'm hard, Annie Fawcett; and I'm going to remain hard.'

'The way you go on you'd think you were the only woman who had been let down in her life. And I'd like to remind you that if you hadn't been let down you wouldn't be where you are the day, an' in the position you're in.'

Damn the position! She only prevented herself from saying it aloud, but of late she had kept damning it, yet she didn't really know why, for she liked the work and she didn't know what she would do without it. It not only filled her life but it was like a snowball growing larger with every move she made, for now she had connections that took her miles out of Felburn.

She went to bed early on this particular night . . .

During the following two weeks she had no need to go through Gateshead or to pass the library that looked like a town hall, nor was she likely to have a client in St Frances Road, but she drove down it, at speed, at least once.

But it was not in St Frances Road that she met him, it was in the street market in Newcastle. She had some business to do in Northumberland Street and had left the car at the nearest point of parking, which was a good five minutes' walk away. She liked the Market arranged as it was along the pavement. In the early days she and Rod had come here all the way from Felburn to do the week's shopping. They could have got the stuff as cheaply in Felburn Market but they looked on it as a trip, a day out. There was a particular stall that used to sell scallions, and he would make her laugh her loudest by buying a bunch, nipping the tops off and eating them as they were, and he always smelt like a poke of garlic devils afterwards.

She was side-stepping to let a woman with a pram pass, and there he was opposite her, as if he had been conjured up out of the past, or she had stepped back all those years. It was him, and yet it wasn't him.

They stared at each other, eyes unblinking, mouths closed. When she was pushed aside by two laughing couples larking on, his hand came out to steady her, but stopped before it touched her and dropped to his side again. They still stared, neither of them speaking. She had always told herself, mostly at night time when she lay thinking, that if ever she did meet up with him, if ever this moment did happen, she wouldn't be the first to speak. But now she was forced to. 'Well!' she said. 'How are you, then?' She kept her eyes on his lips in case they should stray over his suit, a cheap summer suit, shiny and worn.

'Oh, all right, Maggie.' His voice had a hoarse, hesitant sound; it seemed not only a chesty voice, but one not often used. 'You busy these days?'

'Yes.' She looked into his eyes now. 'Pretty busy. And you?'

'Oh.' He jerked his chin. 'I keep going.'

They were silent again. She watched his neck straining up out of his collar, a remembered sign of agitation, and then he said, 'Well, I mustn't be keeping you.'

She heard herself saying, 'That's all right; I don't work on a Saturday, although—' she gave a short laugh '—that's not their fault, they'd keep me at it all the time. You know how it is.'

He made a small movement with his head and said, 'Yes, yes.'

When someone dunched into him now she said, 'I think we're holding up the traffic, I'm—' She tried to prevent herself uttering her next words but they came out in spite of it. 'I'm making my way down Pilgrim Street. There's a little place off where I go for lunch.'

'Oh yes. Yes.' It seemed as if this was all he was capable of saying, and it came to her with pitying knowledge that it was about the sum total of what he would ever say to her, placid as they both were now.

When she turned, he turned with her. But when they had cleared the crowd he stopped; and he looked into her face, from one feature to another, before he said, 'It's been nice seeing you, Maggie.'

She swallowed but was unable to say anything.

'I'd just like to say I'm glad about . . . about all that's happened to you.'

306

He was glad about all that had happened to her. Dear God.

'Goodbye, Maggie.'

'Goodbye, Rod.'

He turned from her, and she turned too – she wasn't going to be left standing – and they went their separate ways.

'Why didn't you ask him to have a bite?'

'How could I . . . ?'

'Because he wasn't got up?'

'No, no. Use your head, woman. Could you imagine him sitting through a meal and me paying the bill at the end? Talk about coals of fire on his head.'

'You know what you are? You're a fool. Look inside yourself. Who are you hurting? You're a fool.'

'Then there are two of us, aren't there?' Maggie's voice was flat sounding.

And on this Annie turned away, saying, 'Our cases are different. Ralphy was a soak, he was born with the taste for liquor, and he'll die of it. I was sensible, an' you know I was. Look where I'd be the day if I'd taken him. And don't say—' she flung round and stretched out her arm, her finger pointing '—don't say that I would have made a man of him; Ralphy Holland's not the kind of man any woman could alter. There are some made like that.'

'He's got his good points.'

'But they aren't good enough.' Annie's voice was flat too now, and she turned away and went into the kitchen, but reappeared in a moment and, standing with her hands on the stanchion of the door, she said, 'Have you made up your mind about Christmas yet? I want to know what to do. Here it is, only a fortnight off, and neither a puddin' nor a cake made.'

Maggie looked at her, then into the fire. Paul and Arlette were anxious for her to go to London. Willie wanted her to spend Christmas with them. Even her daughter Frances had extended a warm welcome to her. She shook her head. Frances was cunning. A sprat to catch a mackerel, that was Frances. And Helen; she'd had no word from Helen for the last few weeks. Helen hadn't asked to come here, or her to go there. Helen was having trouble with Trevor; she'd always have trouble with Trevor. She wouldn't be at all surprised, or upset for that matter, if one day she walked in and said she had left him, or indeed said she wanted a divorce. No, nothing would surprise her any more.

And Liz? Liz, of all of them, had seemed to drop away beyond her horizon. Liz was leading a life of her own, having a good time, she called it, still not married. It was strange, but Liz was as dead to her as was Sam. Sam in a way had succeeded in killing her.

She looked up at Annie and said quietly, 'I think we'll stay put.'

At this Annie jerked her head once, then turned about and went into the kitchen.

CHAPTER FIVE

CHRISTMAS EVE

It snowed on Christmas Eve, as it had done on the four days previously. The main roads were being kept clear but the drifts at each side were four feet high, and more against the doors of the houses. The town was hushed as if under siege.

Willie had made his way over early in the day and brought her and Annie their Christmas boxes, and she had piled him high with parcels for the children. To him and Nancy her present had been a substantial cheque, which he had received gratefully with a muttered, 'Thanks, Mam.'

She had sent a cheque, too, to Frances, and one to Helen.

With one exception they had all sent her presents, mostly household things of more use to Annie than to her now. The only present that would be of any use to her had come from Arlette and Paul; this was a gold wristlet watch. The exception was Liz; Liz had sent her a Christmas card, a cheap, gaudy Christmas card, nothing else. Liz was indeed an enigma. Paul had said on the phone earlier in the day she hadn't to worry about Liz, she was finding herself, and one of these days, he said, she would open the door and there Liz would be standing, a new Liz, even better than the old one. But in the meantime she was to have patience. Liz was now attending an art school and her work was surprisingly good; this might be the answer.

So, on Christmas Eve she was alone. She did not count Annie. Although there was hardly a day went by now that she didn't thank God for her, Annie wasn't her family. She had six children and a husband; yes, she still had a husband, legally, and she was alone.

It was turned seven o'clock and they were sitting looking at the television when the phone rang. Annie went to answer it. A moment later she was back in the room. Standing looking down at Maggie, she said, 'It's Ralphy; he . . . he says . . . he says Rod's in a bad way, very bad way. Thinks his number's up. He thought you should know.'

Her head was back, her mouth was hanging open. There was a feeling between her breast bones as if an icicle had pierced her ribs.

'What'll I tell him, he's waiting?'

She got to her feet and stared at Annie. Then like a child seeking advice, yet knowing what she had to do, she said, 'I'd better go, hadn't I?'

'Yes, you had. I'll tell him.'

When Annie came back from the phone, Maggie was pulling on her high-legged boots, and she said, 'I wonder if I'll get through.'

'They'll have kept the main roads clear. You'd better wrap up well . . . Do you want me to come with you?'

'No.'

'Well, let me know how things are.'

'Yes.'

A few minutes later she eased the car on to the icy side road, and cautiously drove to the main road. Twice the car skidded, and as she hadn't experienced this before it scared her.

It was an hour-and-a-half later when she reached St Frances Road, and when she knocked on the door Ralphy opened it to her.

'Hello, Maggie.' His voice was a whisper.

She stepped into the hallway, and she not only saw the dirt, even in the dim light, but smelt it.

Silently now Ralphy led the way down a short passage and opened a door, and she went past him and into the room. And there he was lying on the bed fighting for his breath. He had changed so much, even from the time she had last seen him in the market, that he was almost unrecognisable.

When she stood by the bed his eyes met hers, no look of stubbornness in them now, no remnants of pride, just the knowledge that he was dying . . . and something else, something standing out from the sorrow. A plea.

His lips moved, but only a breath-heaving croak came from them. She sat down on the wooden chair that Ralphy had pushed forward and she lifted the sweaty hand from the dirty rumpled candlewick bedspread. Rod! Rod! The name was filling her, swilling clean her body with pity and remorse. He had been lying in this stinking, dirty room for God knows how long, and she could have prevented it. She could even have prevented his condition at this moment if on that Saturday in the market just those few weeks ago she had said, 'Rod, let's talk; let's go somewhere and talk.' For only she could have made the first move. Their positions were so reversed. He was lying flat at the bottom of his ladder and had no hope of climbing back to where she was, not even to where he had left her three years ago. All he'd possessed on that day in the market was a fragment of his self-respect, and he had hung on to that – it had been up to her.

She turned to Ralphy and whispered, 'The doctor. Has he had the doctor the day?'

'No, Maggie; I . . . I phoned him yesterday. He said he was full up, he'd be in the day. An' we've waited, an' he hasn't come . . . it being Christmas like.'

She released the hand that was holding hers with a weak grip and got to her feet; and now said to Ralphy, 'Does he live far?'

'Oh aye, quite a way, Maggie.'

'Do you know his number?'

He went to a table in the corner on which stood a gas ring and some old cooking utensils; above it was a shelf with a row of hooks holding a few cups and a jug. From one hook he took a piece of paper and, coming back, he handed it to her.

'Where's the nearest telephone box?'

'Oh, just at the top of the street. Will I go, Maggie?'

'No, I will.'

When she reached the telephone box she was sweating although the air was cutting at her throat.

A female voice answered her ring and to her enquiry said immediately, 'Oh, I'm sorry, Doctor Fine is out.'

'This is Doctor Fine's private address, isn't it? Well, you tell him to come to the phone.'

'I've told you—' the voice took on a haughty tone '—the doctor has been called out.'

'And I'm telling you, whoever you are, I don't believe you. Now look; the doctor had a message to come to this patient two days ago. He's got bronchial pneumonia and he's dying. Do you hear? Dying!' She was bawling in to the phone now. 'He won't last the night. If your man isn't at number one-two-five St Frances Road within the next hour or so you can tell him from me somebody's going to hear about this.'

'Who's speaking?' The voice was quiet but stiff now.

She was for saying Mrs Gallacher, and then she said, 'Margaret Gallacher,' and repeated, 'Margaret Gallacher. And it's my husband I'm talking about.' She didn't know whether her small fame had spread as far as this, but it just might have, and names counted for something with some people. 'If a doctor, and I don't care which doctor it is, but if a doctor isn't here as I said within an hour then I'm phoning a hospital, and if they won't take him in without a doctor's note then I'm phoning the police. If this man dies through lack of attention, by God! I'll make somebody pay.'

She rammed the phone down, then leant against the partition and closed her eyes. Maggie Gallacher was back, blaring, shouting, bludgeoning her way through. She only hoped it worked. But she had meant what she said. If he didn't come within the hour or so she would phone the hospital.

When she opened the door of the room again Rodney's eyes were waiting for her. She went quietly up to the bed and, once more taking his hand, she bent over him and said, 'It's all right. You're going to be all right, the doctor's on his way.'

He moved his head slightly, tried to say something, then was racked with a fit of coughing.

When her arm went under his shoulders and supported him it was as natural as if she had done it yesterday, as if they had never been separated. When she withdrew her hand it was wringing with sweat; his whole body was bathed in sweat, the bed was wet with it, the sheets were wet. She walked from the bed and beckoned to Ralphy. 'Have you any other bedding, sheets?'

He shook his head, then said, 'She only supplies three altogether and they're not much cop. That one there.' He pointed to where a worn grey flannelette sheet was lying over a chair in front of the gas fire. It was sopping. 'I keep drying them and puttin' them back.'

She bit on her lip, then asked, 'Has he had anything, I mean a drink, milk, or brandy?'

His lips moved into a quirk. 'No, Maggie. Anyway, he couldn't take it, he couldn't swallow.'

'Have you any milk?'

'There's half a bottle in the cupboard.'

'I don't suppose—' she moved her head as she whispered '—you have any brandy?'

Again his mouth went into a quirk.

'Here.' She went to her bag and, taking from it a pound note, said, 'Get a miniature brandy, a double, and have a glass of hard stuff yourself. Just one mind, because I want the change.'

'Yes, Maggie, yes.'

'Go on then, quick!'

'Yes, Maggie.'

She now took an old towel from a line hung up over the shallow sink next to the table, and went to the bed and began to wipe his face and hands with it. All the while his eyes stayed on her, but she could not meet them in case she broke down. Now and again she spoke, saying, 'You're going to be all right. Once the doctor gets here you're going to be all right . . .'

It was almost two hours later when she heard the car draw up outside and Ralphy whispered, 'That'll be him.' And she said, 'Leave it to me, I'll open the door.'

She was still wearing her coat because it was cold in the room, but she hadn't a hat on, and when the doctor stepped into the passage he recognised her as someone alien to these surroundings. He stared at her coldly as he said, 'Are you the person who threatened my wife?'

'No, I am not the person who threatened your wife, doctor, I'm the person who threatened you, or any other doctor, who would leave a man in the state my husband is in.' She jerked her head towards the door. 'You were phoned two days ago.'

'I'm a busy man.'

She stopped herself from saying, 'Not too busy to get bottled,' for his breath wafted of spirits. Christmas Eve; he had likely been having a party or some such. And why not? Why not? But then, he hadn't been at a party for two days.

They stared at each other, hostility between them, and he said now, 'I left a prescription for your husband, and if he had followed my instructions over the past two weeks he wouldn't have needed even that.'

He marched from her and into the room and put his bag down on the table with a thump, then went to the bed. Bending over Rodney, he stared down at him. He had no need to examine this man's chest; he put his hand down under the bedclothes and over his heart. Then he held his wrist, and as he stood with it in his hand he looked across at Maggie at the other side of the bed. His eyes met hers for only a moment before travelling upwards, downwards, then around the room, and she knew that he was concerned.

When he put the hand back on the bed he went to his bag and took out a syringe, knocked the end off a glass tube and sucked up its contents into the valve, then he pushed up the loose shirt sleeve on Rodney's arm. When the needle went in Rodney made no sign.

He was at the bag again when he looked at Ralphy and said, 'The pills I gave you for him?'

'Aye, doctor.' Ralphy went to the iron mantelpiece and took down a bottle, which he handed to the doctor. It was three-quarters full and the doctor, shaking it, said, 'I told you he had to take them every four hours; it was imperative he took them every four hours.'

'He's stubborn, doctor. And then his throat got so sore he didn't want to swallow.'

The bottle on the palm of his hand, the doctor turned to Maggie and said grimly, 'If he had taken these he would have never reached this state.'

She was silent for a moment; then she said, 'But he has, and what's got to be done about it?'

He stared at her as if he hated her with a personal hate; then he looked towards the bed again and, his eyes on her once more, he said, 'He's allergic to drugs, heavy drugs. These are mild; they would have taken time but they would have been effective. Well now I will have to put him on something that will act more quickly. It will be drastic, and there might be side effects. There undoubtedly will in his case, but we'll have to deal with them as they come. There's an all-night chemist open somewhere.' He now fumbled in his pocket and brought out a diary. Flicking over the pages he passed his fingers down a list of names and said, 'Crowley's, Fowler Street; they're open for service. Ring the bell.' As he ended he turned and looked at Ralphy, but Maggie put in, 'I'll go; my car's outside.'

He was looking her up and down now, from her high black leather boots to the green open coat, with the fur collar showing the red quilted lining and the dress beneath that matched the coat. Then his eyes slid from her to the bed. She saw that he was trying to work it out.

He said to her now as he wrote out the prescription, 'One every three hours for the next twelve hours, then one every four hours for the next forty-eight hours.' After a moment, as he snapped his bag closed, he added, 'I'll look in in the morning.'

She wanted to thank him, but she didn't. She'd wait till the morning when they'd both be in a better frame of mind.

As he went towards the door he said over his shoulder, 'I've put down a linctus and a rub. He should be changed frequently. Keep him dry if you can.' Now he turned his head right round and looked fully at her. 'But I can leave that to you, I suppose?'

'Yes.' She inclined her head stiffly towards him. 'You can leave that to me.'

When she let him out a church clock struck twelve, but neither of them remarked it was midnight on Christmas Eve; they didn't even exchange a goodnight . . .

By six o'clock the next morning she had changed the bed completely four times.

Annie had come in a taxi with a stock of sheets, pillow cases, blankets and towels and between them they had changed him and sponged his fevered body, and got a trickle of warm milk down his throat. Now at six o'clock on Christmas morning they were both weary and tired, but wide-eyed, because whatever was going to happen they knew would happen within the next two hours. He had seemed, for most of the night, to be only partly conscious but now his breathing was so painful that Maggie's shoulders were permanently hunched against the sound of it, and against the sound of Ralphy's snores, too, from where he was lying in the corner of the room. At three o'clock she had persuaded him to go to bed, telling him that he would be needed later on and that he must get some rest.

As she sat now watching the bedclothes rise and fall, as if they were being pumped by automatic bellows, she wished she were alone with him, for she wanted to put her face down to his and answer the question that had been in his eyes and say that she forgave him, even say that the blame was hers because she had been a stupid woman, a fat, easygoing – no, not a slob; no, never a slob – just a fat, easygoing stupid woman. To tell him that it was her fault in letting him climb up the ladder by himself; she should have known that there were all kinds of dangers on the way. But she hadn't been worldly enough, smart enough. You read your weekly magazines and the philosophy they put over, all about people like her and Rod, but you didn't take it in; it was never going to happen to you, it was just fiction.

She was startled when she heard him croak, 'Maggie!' His eyes were open and she bent above him and looked into them and said softly, 'Yes, Rod?'

'Maggie.'

'Yes, I'm here.'

He made an effort to say something, but when his heaving chest blocked the words she said, 'There now, don't try.' He was sweating again. The water was actually standing in blobs on his short hair before running down his brow and the sides of his face, and they changed him yet again and into, of all things, one of her own soft brushed nylon nightdresses, for she had long since got rid of any clothes he had left behind.

When he was settled again, Annie gathered up the wet sheets and, standing with them in her arms, she looked at Maggie and said under her breath, 'It would be easier, wouldn't it, if he was back home.'

Maggie's eyes did not flinch from hers and she answered, 'I know that; I'm going to put it to the doctor when he comes . . .'

The doctor came as he had promised. His face still looked grim. He gave Maggie no greeting, he did not even knock when he came in, but after looking down at Rodney for some minutes, then taking his pulse, he turned to her and said, 'Well, you're lucky . . . he's lucky; it's done the trick, but he's not out of the wood yet not by a long way. One of the off-shoots now will be diarrhoea. He's in a very weak state; that'll need a fight all on its own.'

She drew in a long breath. She would deal with whatever had to come. She said, 'It's difficult nursing him here, how . . . how soon could he be moved?'

'Oh.' He made a sound in his throat and looked at her as if she was an idiot and, his voice filled with sarcasm, he said, 'If you want to bury him, move him any time within the next week.'

She stiffened. 'I was thinking about an ambulance,' she said.

He lifted his bag. 'I wasn't thinking about a push bike.'

How was it, she thought, that you could hate a man you'd only seen twice?

He went out of the door and into the passage; then he turned and looked at her standing in the middle of the room. She was a fine looking woman, even tired as she was, and a battler. With a quick drooping movement of his head, he said, 'I'm sorry. I'm sorry.'

As she looked back at him she wondered now how it was that two words of apology could sweep away all bitterness. Her own voice was quiet as she replied, 'Me, too, doctor.'

He turned from her and went to the front door and, without looking at her again, he said, 'I'll be along later.' And now she said, 'Thanks. Thank you.'

When she had closed the door she stood for a moment staring along the grimy passage, and all of a sudden she felt weak, slightly sick, and had a great desire to cry. It was Christmas morning; the bairns were all playing with their toys, the mothers were getting the dinners ready, the dads were seeing to the drinks. Christmas day, Christ was born.

She had prayed intermittently all night; she had promised to go to Mass and her duties, if only he was spared. Well, she would keep her promise, and not only that, she would try to be better. She wasn't, she considered, a good woman, she was too big-mouthed, too quick with her tongue, saying things first and thinking after, but from now on she'd be different, not only outwardly like Miss Margaret Gallacher, but inwardly where a change was needed most.

CHAPTER SIX

THE CHOICE

After weeks of a repeated pattern of snow-storms and thaws the streets were now clear of sludge and the sun was shining; but as people prophesied, that wouldn't last long as it was only the beginning of February.

Maggie had made a point of not visiting clients on a Saturday; Saturday she took as a day off, except on the occasions when she was asked to join in a dress show at one of the leading restaurants, and on this particular day she had just finished one in Newcastle. She had shown three garments, one consisting of a two-piece ensemble, a woollen dress in turquoise, and a three-quarter length coat with a collar of turquoise that could be manipulated into a hood. This brought a great deal of applause, and Madam Hevell, who was sitting at a reserved table, patted her hand and gave her the smile of approval.

The business of the day over for her, Maggie didn't bother changing but went home as she was. She'd be modelling this again on Monday in any case. She was pretty sure she had a customer for it.

She drove the car to its limit and was home within half an hour. Annie was in the kitchen making some coffee, and she turned and looked at her and said spontaneously, 'Oh! I like that.'

'Yes, so did they.'

'Everything go off all right?'

'Fine, fine . . . How is he?'

'Oh, just as you left him.' Annie's voice was light and airy.

'Did he eat all his dinner?'

'No, but he got through a good bit.'

She went across the sitting room and into the bedroom, her bedroom, and started talking as she opened the door. 'Well, that's over. It's lovely out, lovely to see the sun.' She looked at him propped up in the bed, a little more flesh on his bones than there had been a few weeks ago, but he still remained a shadow of the man she knew, the big fella.

Unlike other times, he did not speak and say, 'Hello, Maggie.' He never just said, 'Hello', or 'Hello there,' as one would to someone close, but 'Hello, Maggie,' and the use of her name indicated a courteous diffidence, a polite barrier. Not that he wasn't grateful for all that had been done for him; the gratitude was in his eyes, but even so his look was always veiled. But now she watched his eyes covering her from head to foot; then she laughed with embarrassment, saying, 'Oh, this! I didn't change; the dressing rooms are always crammed in those places, and it's warm. The collar's a hood, look.' She twisted the collar up and the blue hood framed her face, and when he closed his eyes she let it drop back on to her shoulders and, standing at the foot of the bed, she stared at him until he opened his eyes again, then she turned from him and went out and into the room she shared with Annie.

Sitting on the edge of the bed, she looked at herself in the wardrobe mirror opposite. The blue velvet get-up the night of the do; it must have reminded him, for this too was all blue . . . and dressy. She was too dressy altogether. Everything she had in her wardrobe was dressy, everything.

All the years she had been married to him he had never seen her look like she did now. He likely could have if he had spent money on her, and that's what he must be thinking. Her success was a reproach to him, everything he saw in her must be like a thorn in his flesh, that's why he couldn't talk to her. She was nobody he recognised. He had been in this house a month now and they had never talked. It had been 'Yes, Maggie,' and 'No, Maggie,' and 'Thanks, Maggie.' The politeness was wearing. Oh dear God, she never thought she'd know the day again when she would welcome a crack across her lug. But never again as long as they lived, and if they should live together, would he raise his hand to her, she knew this.

If they should live together? As soon as he was well he would go. She knew this too in her heart, because he could never be the husband of Margaret Gallacher.

There was only one way to stop him, to hold him.

She stared at her reflection until her face seemed to take up the whole space of the mirror and when it spoke to her and voiced her thoughts she cried at it 'No!' in loud protest. But when she uttered it for the third time the protest was much weaker, and her reflection said, 'Well, it's either one thing or the other, it's up to you to choose, you can't have it both ways. That's life, you can't have it both ways.'

CHAPTER SEVEN

MAGGIE GALLACHER

From the Monday of the following week she went out early in the mornings and returned home late each night, and on the Thursday night Annie said, 'Look, what's up? Have you taken to working overtime?' and her answer to this was, 'Something like that.'

'There's something up with you, what is it?'

'I'll tell you tomorrow,' said Maggie.

'That Madam Hevell been on at you?'

Madam Hevell been on at her? And how! Yes, and how.

On the Thursday night too Rodney said, 'I'm getting up the morrow, Maggie,' and she answered, 'I wouldn't hurry, there's plenty of time. You know what the doctor said, go careful.'

'I've gone careful for weeks,' he said quietly; 'I've got to make a start.'

'Well, just as you wish,' she said, and he looked at her, puzzled by a certain sadness that was in her manner, but a sadness that didn't seem connected with himself.

And then came Saturday. She was working this Saturday she said, but she should be home around five.

She wasn't home at seven, she wasn't home at eight. At half-past eight Annie said to Rodney, 'Something's up, something's been up all the week. Has she said anything to you?'

'No, Annie.' He shook his head. 'But then she wouldn't, would she?'

She looked at him where he was sitting by the side of the bed in pyjamas and dressing gown and she said, 'Maggie's changed you know, Rod,' and he answered, 'Yes. Yes, I know that, Annie.'

'Nobody ever realised what she was capable of.'

'No, they never did.' His head was bowed.

'I'm not blaming you, Rod.'

He raised his eyes to hers. 'Then you should.'

Yes, Annie should blame him, everybody should blame him, but even then their combined censure would not match the blame he took upon himself. Why had a man to go through hell before he could see things clearly, see himself for what he was? But then he always thought he had known himself. He was Rod Gallacher, the big fellow, knowing where he was bound for, and what road he was going to take, and the more short cuts he made the quicker he would arrive. Maggie had been an obstacle laid across that road. The day he had stood at the altar rails with her he had cursed her and the whole bang shoot of them, Father Stillwell and Father Armstrong included for saddling him with a big-mouthed, brainless, laughing lump. Still, the outcome had been better than he had expected. She was a worker both inside and outside the house, and she had satisfied his needs more than a little because she was crazy about him. Then as the years went by he had been pleasantly surprised when she became a sort of comfort to him. After going at it hell for leather all day she was there for him to go back to, to coddle him like a mother, feed him like a wife, and love him like a mistress. Things were all right, he had told himself as time went on, he hadn't made such a bad bargain after all; and what was more she didn't want much, not for herself. She wasn't demanding in that way, what she wanted was a home and the bairns. He could leave her at night and no questions asked, except perhaps a jibe when he got in late with a load on. But she never fought with him about this. He couldn't remember now what they had fought about, but they had fought, God, like tigers they had fought. That's one thing that had surprised him in the early days, her temper. Plump, easygoing people hadn't got tempers, at least that's what he had thought, but she had shown him differently, and it was odd but he had respected her more when she went for him. The times he had swiped her across the mouth! He bent his head against the memory.

Yet during all those years living with her he had never grown to love her; he hadn't loved anybody until he had met Rosamund de Ferrier. And the feeling he'd had for her? Was that love? He had asked himself this question countless times over the past few years. What was it anyway, love? Fascination? That had been the core of his feeling for Rosamund de Ferrier; he had been like a rabbit before a snake. But does a rabbit know the thing writhing before him is called a snake? A rabbit couldn't put any name to it, it could only feel powerless, drained of will, drained of the desire to turn and flee, capable of only one thing, waiting to be devoured. He had been devoured, then spewed up again. He saw her face now like the snake, her tongue licking away the taste of him. Could humiliation kill love, kill fascination? If that was possible then his love for her had died quickly, drowned in the well of self-denigration.

In those early days of agony he had not let himself think of Maggie, because when his thoughts touched on her it showed him up as a fool, someone who had never been able to see farther than his own nose, his own desires. Yet the estrangement from the rest of his family had brought him no pain at this time; he felt no sense of loss with regard to them. When he was really alone and at bottom, there had been only one person he thought of, she who had been a trinity to him; and added to his self-knowledge was a picture of a man, an ignorant man, a nowt, a man who had been capable of achieving only one thing in his life, building up a business. And then not even capable of doing that properly. On the sideroads he had to take on the way to his objective there had been toll gates, and as he advanced farther up the road so the rates of entry had become higher. But you did not always have to pay in money, you paid in kind; scratched a back here and there, turned a Nelson eye, lifted your hand in a vote. One thing apparently wasn't allowed, setting your sights on the toll-keeper's wife.

It was hard now for him to believe that he had reached as far as he had in the big business world with such little sense, for real sense lay in judging people, judging their worth. He had judged Rosamund de Ferrier and found her a gift of the gods; he had judged Maggie and found her wanting. But let him be fair to himself on this point; any man would have reacted as he had done the night she buggered the Duke.

Nevertheless, he hadn't proved to himself how much he had changed until, having reached rock bottom, he knew he would rather come face to face with Rosamund de Ferrier than with Maggie. And then he had seen her. He had gazed down on her from that half-wrecked building, and his amazement couldn't have been greater had he witnessed the resurrection.

After that, he had flown from the north, swearing never to return, but in six months he was back, at least in the county. Why? He wasn't even big enough yet to give himself the answer.

He had seen her three times before the night when he thought he was finished, but he had never seen her as Maggie, the Maggie that had been familiar to him; not even since he had been in her house during all these weeks had he glimpsed her. There was just a faint memory of Christmas Eve when she came to him and she had held

326

him, and vaguely he remembered her arguing with the doctor. That had been Maggie.

He had told himself for days he'd have to pull himself together and get away. He couldn't go on much longer living on her charity, and seeing the pity in the eyes of his family. One thing he had to face up to and squarely: if he had changed, so had she. The irony of it was that the feeling he had for her now must, he thought, be something akin to what she'd felt for him in the early days. But also he felt that her feelings towards him were now as lukewarm as his had once been. She was still kind, compassionate. That was her nature, she couldn't be otherwise. And perhaps underneath there remained the old Maggie. If so, it was well coated with a veneer, a fashionable veneer. And it wasn't just a veneer, more like an armour, and he knew that he could never hope to penetrate it, not as he was now. Anyway, he wouldn't want to as he was now. If he could only get on his feet again . . .

'What's that you say now, Annie?'

'I said I'm going to phone The Rooms.'

'Won't they be closed?'

'Not if she's there.'

He sat waiting for her coming back. When she stood in the doorway and said, 'No reply . . . Do you think I should phone Willie?' he answered slowly, 'Give her another few minutes.'

It was a quarter of an hour later when, pulling himself to his feet, he said, 'She could have had an accident.'

'They would have let us know, wouldn't they? She's . . . she's got papers on her.'

He bowed his head; there were some accidents that left no papers. He felt sick, frightened, weak, terribly weak. He sat down again. 'You'd better phone Willie.'

'You think so?'

He nodded at her.

'If she comes in, she'll go mad if she thinks I've made a fuss. I'll . . . I'll go down to the gate for one last look.'

It was as Annie reached the gate that the car came along the road, and she stood aside as it turned in at the driveway. But almost before it had stopped she was at the window demanding, 'Where do you think you've been?'

'Now don't start.'

'Start! You've had us nearly round the bend. Do you know what time it is, after ten.'

'I've been busy.' She went to push the door open, saying, 'Let me out.'

Annie let her out, then started again, 'Why didn't you phone?'

'I couldn't, I was held up.'

'Held up be damned! Surely you haven't been held up all that much that you couldn't pick up a phone.'

'I was at Muriel's place; she doesn't have a phone . . . not yet.'

'Then there are call boxes, aren't there?'

'Stop shouting, I'm tired.'

'You're tired, what about us? Him in there—' Annie thumbed back towards the house – 'he's nearly been round the bend.'

'Really!' Maggie's tone was cold and brought Annie's voice rasping at her low and angrily. 'Now don't start that again, time's past for make-believe. You know, and I know, and he knows there's got to be a showdown, or a clearing of the air, at least. He's got to know where he stands.'

'ANNIE!'

They were standing by the side of the car, their faces reflecting the light from within as Maggie hadn't yet closed the door. Her voice dropping, she said, 'I'm tired. I've been in a showdown all day, all week . . . And that's over now, it's ended.'

'What do you mean?'

'I'm finished with the business.'

'My God! No! Never!'

'Yes, that's what it's all about.'

'But why?'

'Aw, Annie.' Maggie made an unusual gesture by putting out her hand and gripping Annie's shoulder and, her voice soft and weary, she said, 'You know me, but you also know him. Would he settle for the set-up as it is?' She shook her head. 'Not Rod.'

Annie's lips were quivering now, her eyes were blinking. 'But . . . but to give it up after you've worked so hard and . . . and made a name.'

'What's a name, Annie?'

They stared at each other a moment longer; then Maggie said, 'I want a drink, something hot. Make me a coffee will you, put a dash of brandy in it?'

They walked side by side along the path, through the back door and into the kitchen, and Annie said, 'Go on in and relieve his mind; I'll bring it in to you.'

'Aye, Maggie.'

She took off her hat and coat as she crossed the sitting room, and when she opened the bedroom door he was standing at the foot of the bed. He looked thin and gaunt, his short black hair, greying in parts, accentuating the pallor of his skin. He was breathing heavily, as if he had trouble drawing the air down into his chest. He went to speak, but his lower jaw dropped, and his lips moved and he swallowed his spittle before he said, 'You were held up?'

She noticed that he didn't say Maggie. For the first time since their lives had come together again he hadn't used her name when speaking to her.

'You should be in bed,' she said. 'Go on, get back into bed.'

He shook his head with an impatient movement. 'I'm all right, I'm all right. What kept you?'

'Sit down,' she said. She went towards him but didn't touch him. He turned and walked unsteadily back towards the chair and she, looking round, went to bring a chair up to him but changed her mind and sat on the edge of the bed opposite to him.

She looked at his hands gripping each other on his knees, those big hands patterned like his face, square and bulky, but like his face now pale and washed-out looking. By the working of his fingers she could tell he was agitated.

She went to let her body slump but checked it. No, no more of that; that was one thing she wasn't going to let go. And she was going to keep dressed, and well dressed; she'd got a taste for dress and she'd promised Madam she'd always be a customer, at least at The Rooms.

'Something wrong?'

'No, nothing wrong, Rod; it's just that I've given up me job.'

'What!' The word was a muttered whisper.

'Yes, that's what's kept me busy all week, that and something else.'

'But why? You've made such a success of it.'

'Oh, I don't know, Rod.' Her head drooped and she shook it from side to side. 'It's tiring. And the people you've got to meet, they're not all that you would wish.' She gave a half laugh. 'Wanting the best clothes, but wanting them cheap and ashamed of buying them second-hand . . . Oh—' she closed her eyes and laughed softly '—you mustn't use that word, second-hand. God! The snobbery that you meet up with. Paying fifteen pounds for a sixty-guinea suit, then demanding to know which part of the country it came from, and are they likely to meet up with the previous owner? Then you waffle and give them the old talk: "I doubt it, Madam, unless you are going into

330

society." Oh, that always does it. They try to get names out of you then, and you have to stop yourself from letting your imagination run riot and start throwing titles about.'

She was smiling, but his face was straight, tense. 'Won't you miss it?' he asked.

'I suppose so, a bit; but then I need a rest. I'm not a girl any more.' She spread her hands and let her smile widen and watched his eyes move over her.

When he asked, 'What will you do with yourself?' she looked down on his joined hands, and when her answer came, 'I've got another job,' she watched them move slowly apart as he repeated, 'Another job?'

'Aye, a bit different though.' She pulled a face at him. 'And I'll need help, somebody in the know.'

As he waited for her to go on, Annie came in with the coffee on a tray. 'Get that down you,' she said, 'then come and have a bite, it's ready.'

'Thanks.' She took the cup of coffee and drank deeply from it, then she sighed and said, 'Ah, that's better.' And when she looked at him again, he asked, 'Where?'

'Oh well now, it's difficult to describe. It's past Denton. You know the estate on the right-hand side as you come out of Newcastle? Well, on the left there's the west road to Corbridge and Hexham. It's along there, it's a house.' She paused, and he screwed up his face and said, 'A house? You're going to work in a house?'

'Aye.' She nodded at him. 'You could say that, in a kind of way.'

'A big house?'

'Yes, biggish, fourteen rooms all told.'

' . . . What . . . what are you going to do there?'

'Well, for a start re-decorate I should say.'

He made a slight movement with his head.

'That's what I'm going in for, sort of re-decorating. I've been round some houses in the last few years and

331

I've always thought to meself if I had this I would do so-and-so. And now that's what I'm going to do. There's four acres of land attached.' Her face was straight now. She was looking into his eyes. 'There's building permission for two houses. They must have not less than half an acre each. It's that kind of district you know. I thought it would be sort of a good idea . . . When the big place is re-decorated it'll be worth two or three times what it's going for now. Well, then the other two houses could be built in easy stages, no hurry you know, and a nice little profit at the end. And in the meantime look round for other plots. You hear it said that all these places have been bought up, but that isn't so, I've been to three this week similar. But I picked on this because I, well, I thought the country air would do you good, and—' She could not go on to say, 'it's well away from Felburn,' but said softly, 'You could practically build them yourself with help from Ralphy . . . you always said you could build a house on your . . .'

'Maggie, for God's sake, don't!'

His head was deep on his chest, his shoulders were hunched, and she muttered, 'Rod, we've . . . we've got to talk.' She bent forward and put her hand on his and he groaned, 'You don't know what you're doing to me.'

'I do, Rod, I do. Believe me I do, but I was never very good at being subtle.'

'Oh, Maggie, Maggie.' Her name was wrenched up from the depths of him and his hands came away from hers and covered his face, and as the sobs racked his body she pleaded, 'Rod, don't, don't take on. Don't.' She went to put her arms about him but couldn't. This was one step she couldn't take, not on her own.

When he slipped from the chair and on to his knees and buried his head in her lap she closed her eyes tight before she gathered him to her, and like a mother now she held him and listened to him sobbing out his deprecation of himself.

'Maggie, Maggie, as long as I live I'll never forgive meself.'

'It's all right, it's all right. There, there, give over now.' Her own tears were washing her face, her own voice was broken.

'Maggie . . . Maggie, I want to say something to you.'

'Aye, yes, I'm listening, Rod.'

'I . . . I love you, Maggie. I love you, I do. Believe me, I do. Aw, Maggie, Maggie.'

She made no answer to this. She had been married to this man for almost thirty years and this was the very first time she had heard these words from his lips. Unbelievable when she came to think of it; she had borne him six children, and there had been times when they had frolicked and made love but never, never, had he said the words, 'I love you, Maggie.'

This was what it was all about. For this she had endured hell. For this she had thrown away the ladder that would have taken her to the heights, albeit the small heights where Margaret Gallacher would have reigned. She would be forgotten, except perhaps as that woman Maggie Gallacher who had buggered the Duke.

But it was to Maggie Gallacher he had said, 'I love you, Maggie.'

She pressed him fiercely to her.

THE END

JUSTICE IS A WOMAN
by Catherine Cookson

The day Joe Remington brought his new bride to Fell Rise, he had already sensed she might not settle easily into the big house just outside the Tyneside town of Fellburn. For Joe this had always been his home, but for Elaine it was virtually another country whose manners and customs she was by no means eager to accept.

Making plain her disapproval of Joe's familiarity with the servants, demanding to see accounts Joe had always trusted to their care, questioning the donation of food to striking miners' families – all these objections and more soon rubbed Joe and the local people up the wrong way, a problem he could easily have done without, for this was 1926, the year of the General Strike, the effects of which would nowhere be felt more acutely than in this heartland of the North-East.

Then when Elaine became pregnant, she saw it as a disaster and only the willingness of her unmarried sister Betty to come and see her through her confinement made it bearable. But in the long run, would Betty's presence only serve to widen the rift between husband and wife, or would she help to bring about a reconciliation?

0 552 13622 0

THE GOLDEN STRAW
by Catherine Cookson

The Golden Straw, as it would be named, was a large, broad-brimmed hat presented to Emily Pearson by her long-time friend and employer Mabel Arkwright, milliner and modiste. And before long it was to her employer that Emily owed the gift of the business itself, for Mabel was in poor health and had come to rely more and more on Emily before her untimely death in 1880.

While on holiday in France, Emily and the Golden Straw attracted the eye of Paul Steerman, a guest at the hotel, and throughout his stay he paid her unceasing attention. But Paul Steerman was not all he seemed to be and he was to bring nothing but disgrace and tragedy to Emily, precipitating a series of events that would influence the destiny of not only her children but her grandchildren too.

The Golden Straw, conceived on a panoramic scale, brilliantly portrays a whole rich vein of English life from the heyday of the Victorian era to the stormy middle years of the present century. It represents a fresh triumph for this great storyteller whose work is deservedly loved and enjoyed throughout the world.

0 552 13685 9

A SELECTION OF OTHER CATHERINE COOKSON TITLES AVAILABLE FROM CORGI BOOKS

THE PRICES SHOWN BELOW WERE CORRECT AT THE TIME OF GOING TO PRESS. HOWEVER TRANSWORLD PUBLISHERS RESERVE THE RIGHT TO SHOW NEW RETAIL PRICES ON COVERS WHICH MAY DIFFER FROM THOSE PREVIOUSLY ADVERTISED IN THE TEXT OR ELSEWHERE.

☐	13576 3 THE BLACK CANDLE	£5.99
☐	12473 7 THE BLACK VELVET GOWN	£5.99
☐	14063 5 COLOUR BLIND	£4.99
☐	12551 2 A DINNER OF HERBS	£5.99
☐	14066 x THE DWELLING PLACE	£5.99
☐	14068 6 FEATHERS IN THE FIRE	£5.99
☐	14089 9 THE FEN TIGER	£4.99
☐	14069 4 FENWICK HOUSES	£4.99
☐	10450 7 THE GAMBLING MAN	£4.99
☐	13716 2 THE GARMENT	£4.99
☐	13621 2 THE GILLYVORS	£5.99
☐	10916 9 THE GIRL	£4.99
☐	14071 6 THE GLASS VIRGIN	£4.99
☐	13685 9 THE GOLDEN STRAW	£5.99
☐	13300 0 THE HARROGATE SECRET	£4.99
☐	14087 2 HERITAGE OF FOLLY	£4.99
☐	13303 5 THE HOUSE OF WOMEN	£4.99
☐	10780 8 THE IRON FAÇADE	£4.99
☐	14091 0 JUSTICE IS A WOMAN	£4.99
☐	14091 0 KATE HANNIGAN	£4.99
☐	14092 9 KATIE MULHOLLAND	£5.99
☐	14081 3 MAGGIE ROWAN	£4.99
☐	13684 0 THE MALTESE ANGEL	£5.99
☐	10321 7 MISS MARTHA MARY CRAWFORD	£5.99
☐	12524 5 THE MOTH	£4.99
☐	13302 7 MY BELOVED SON	£5.99
☐	13088 5 THE PARSON'S DAUGHTER	£5.99
☐	14073 2 PURE AS THE LILY	£4.99
☐	13683 2 THE RAG NYMPH	£5.99
☐	14075 9 THE ROUND TOWER	£4.99
☐	13714 6 SLINKY JANE	£4.99
☐	10541 4 THE SLOW AWAKENING	£4.99
☐	10630 5 THE TIDE OF LIFE	£5.99
☐	12368 4 THE WHIP	£5.99
☐	13577 1 THE WINGLESS BIRD	£5.99
☐	13247 0 THE YEAR OF THE VIRGINS	£4.99

All Transworld titles are available by post from:

Book Service By Post, P.O. Box 29, Douglas, Isle of Man IM99 1BQ

Credit cards accepted. Please telephone 01624 675137, fax 01624 670923, Internet http://www.bookpost.co.uk or e-mail: bookshop@enterprise.net for details.

Free postage and packing in the UK. Overseas customers allow £1 per book (paperbacks) and £3 per book (hardbacks).